'*Mr Stoker and the Vampires of the L*[...]
A skilful blend of historical and fict[...]
it moves the reader through severa[...] [...]
and situations – from London to Danzig and beyond. The plot is
engrossing and full of unexpected twists and turns.

This is a fully realised Gothic world, a stimulating mix of
homely familiarity and lurking menace which will engage readers
of all ages.'

David Punter, author of *The Literature of Terror*

'Highly inventive... with a hint of the fantastic. A very immersive read.'

Neil Root, author of *Frenzy!* and *The Murder Gang*

'*Mr Stoker and the Vampires of the Lyceum* is a seamless blend
of historical fact and narrative fiction, sparking the reader's
imagination even as it chills the blood.'

Daniel Stashower, author of *American Demon*

'It is the late 1880s, and London is being terrorised by reports of the
Whitechapel murders in the newspapers. Meanwhile, at the Lyceum
Theatre, a no less gruesome outbreak of vampirism has occurred.
Could the two events be linked? Bram Stoker, the theatre's manager
and future author of *Dracula*, is called on to investigate.

This is no ordinary first novel. Over the last two decades,
Matthew Gibson has established himself as a global authority
on the history of vampirism, Bram Stoker's life and career (he is
currently compiling the first collection of the writer's letters), and
Victorian esotericism generally.

Not the least of the pleasures of this tautly plotted thriller is the
author's delicately nuanced depiction of the sometimes fractious

relations which existed between Stoker and his boss, Henry Irving – the greatest actor of his era.

In short, whether tackling an infestation of vampires at the Lyceum, dealing with the internal power dynamics of the theatre, or leading us across northern Europe to the main vampire's lair, the reader is in Gibson's very capable hands.'

Terry Hale, editor and translator of the Penguin edition of J-K Huysmans' *The Damned (Là-Bas)* and *The Dedalus Book of French Horror*, and a Chevalier de l'Ordre des Arts et des Lettres

MR STOKER

AND THE VAMPIRES OF THE LYCEUM

Matthew Gibson

The Book Guild Ltd

First published in Great Britain in 2023 by
The Book Guild Ltd
Unit E2 Airfield Business Park,
Harrison Road, Market Harborough,
Leicestershire LE16 7UL
Tel: 0116 2792299
www.bookguild.co.uk
Email: info@bookguild.co.uk
Twitter: @bookguild

This novel is, in part, based on real people, events and circumstance,
but does not claim to personal or historical accuracy. It is a work of fiction.

Typeset in 11pt Minion Pro

Printed and bound in the UK by TJ Books Ltd, Padstow, Cornwall

ISBN 978 1915603 869

British Library Cataloguing in Publication Data.
A catalogue record for this book is available from the British Library.

This novel is dedicated to the memories of Delk Watson (a true Quincey Morris), my cousin Shelley Ward, and A.P.B.

ACKNOWLEDGEMENTS

This novel was inspired by my enduring scholarship on Bram Stoker and the Gothic, but would not be what it is today without the advice and support of the following people, to whom I would like to extend my heartfelt thanks.

My early readers – Lindsay Brown, Jane Clarke (and her fellow members of the Maida Vale Book Club), Oliver Cleaver, Sarah McMahon and Ginny Mills.

My colleague, Damian Shaw.

Chloe May, Chelsea Taylor, Liberty Woodward and the publishing team at The Book Guild.

In addition to these individuals, my thanks are also due to Ben Cameron for his work on publicity, Alison Chandler at Writing Room for her comments on 'the pitch', and Emily Randle for her work on rights.

Also, of course, to my partner, Barbra, Qianyi Shangguan, for her constant emotional support.

Above all, however, I would like to thank my agent and editorial consultant, Susannah Lear, for the unstinting commitment she has shown in managing the whole process, and for the many important suggestions she has made on the text over time.

CONTENTS

PROLOGUE

12 October 1896

A. Constable & Co.
London W.

Dear Mr Stoker,

Thank you for sending me the first draft of your latest novel, 'The Un-Dead', for which this missive is receipt.

I acknowledge your accompanying remarks that this piece is somewhat of a departure from your previous writings, and that, intriguingly, the original wellspring for its contents – or, as you say, prompt, for this is a work of fiction not a memoir! – was a series of events at the Lyceum and beyond, which occurred some years ago.

I know that your work at the theatre with Irving (now, of course, Sir Henry Irving) has been of immense importance to you, but that you aspire to be known as Bram Stoker 'author' rather than Bram Stoker 'acting manager'. I trust that, with my assistance as editor, and that of my esteemed colleagues at this house, you will one day achieve this ambition.

For now, I remain,
Very sincerely yours,
Otto Kyllmann

PART I

CHAPTER I

THE LYCEUM

'Are you ready? Is the scene set for my murdering?' boomed a voice out of nowhere.

'Almost, Mr Irving.'

'Have you inspected the floats as well? No leaks from the gas this time, I trust?'

'The footlights are all secure – I've checked, Guv'nor.'

'Good. We don't want the whole place going up in flames, now do we?'

The man to whom these questions were being addressed was standing on a wooden ladder near the front of a stage, facing the auditorium. Tall and broad, and sporting a trim but full russet beard, he was working methodically, his sleeves rolled up, his waistcoat pockets bulging with nuts and screws. Behind him stood a painted wintry backdrop, reminiscent of some mountainous continental scene, rendered on the canvas in sharp, spare lines. He and the Lyceum's stage manager, Harry Loveday (who had a reputation for sobriety – most necessary when charged with holding a ladder!), had been working for a quarter of an hour on these gas lights, set a yard back from the proscenium arch. Trailing a row of dim halos, the lights now stood ready to be boosted into brilliant illumination at the end of the play's first Act, revealing the gruesome murder which Mr Henry Irving's character would be committing every night until early October, in front of packed London houses.

Now turning his attention to a limelight, the bearded man checked it was correctly aligned to the sleigh behind him stage right and exchanged an old screw for a new one from out of a waistcoat pocket. This was the last of his many intricate tasks – tasks with which he alone was entrusted.

'I do not wish to trouble you,' called a woman's voice suddenly from the auditorium, 'but I was wondering how much longer you will be, as Edward and I need to meet my daughter and her... her new best friend tonight; most awkward!'

'Just finishing now, Miss Terry,' the bearded man replied. 'I'll be with you in a jiffy.' With this he lumbered down the rungs of the ladder, nodded briefly to Loveday – who immediately began collapsing the frame – and then turned to check that all the stagehands necessary for that evening's performance were in attendance. He counted three figures stage left, including fidgety young Edward Craig, Miss Terry's troublesome sixteen-year-old son – his collar and stud falling carelessly off his white shirt. Stage right, he counted two hands, as well as the Lyceum's lights manager (and fellow Dubliner), Aloysius Grafton, the man charged with releasing the multitude of taps on the pipes for the gas which fuelled the lights. Loveday now picked up the string of sleigh bells which would signal important cues for the hands backstage and moved to join Grafton.

'Ready now, Mr Irving,' announced the bearded man loudly, turning back towards the auditorium. And then, more quietly, turning back to the others, 'You do know all your cues, don't you?' The men nodded in unison and returned a low 'yes'.

'Good. Miss Terry seems somewhat out of sorts today... *again.*' He dimly caught the roll of Grafton's eyes from behind the lights manager's pince-nez and smirked before walking swiftly to the front of the stage, jumping over the footlights into the orchestra pit, and heading up the aisle towards Irving.

Irving was seated several rows back from the pit, in the stalls. Dressed in lightweight herringbone tweed with a silk cravat at his clean-shaven neck, his thin-lipped smile betrayed nothing but the imperious self-command which had always so inspired the bearded man's devotion. Miss Terry, however, was now coming down the aisle in a flurry of agitation. She was wearing a peacock blue dress with an elaborate bustle underneath a short blue cape – and looked as though dressed for some fine excursion.

She pressed the bearded man's hand into her own, then looked up at him imploringly through her heavy make-up.

'I'm so sorry to have waylaid you like that, Mr Stoker,' she began.

'I took not a whit of offence, I assure you,' replied Stoker, somewhat baffled by the fervour of her tone.

'It's just that I have to be home for dinner at nine – for Edith,' she continued exasperatedly. 'And I do not wish to be back late, what with news of a second woman being so brutally... murdered.' Stoker gave a reassuring smile: her concern made no sense to him.

'Belgravia is some way off from Whitechapel, Miss Terry. Decent folk, I'm sure, have nothing to fear.'

'I know, but a mother cannot help but be fearful, faced with such appalling headlines in the *Gazette* and elsewhere.'

'Come along, now, Ellen,' broke in Irving. 'We cannot delay matters. You will have plenty of time to get home.' Miss Terry smiled once more through her rouge and powders, then went to join Irving. She must no doubt be anxious at meeting yet another of her daughter's 'best friends', mused Stoker. He pitied her having two such difficult children.

Soon Stoker was sitting at the very front of the auditorium. He checked his silver fob watch – a rare and precious gift from his beautiful, but now sadly distant, wife: half past seven o'clock. Miss Terry would indeed have plenty of time to get home.

Now the slender gauze sheet that separated the painted wintry backdrop from the front of the stage – and which represented the thin veil restraining the conscience of the play's protagonist, Mathias – was let all the way down to the floor. The gauze created a vague, dream-like quality for the painful memories which continually haunted the character – memories which would be enacted by Mr Archer at the back of the stage as Irving, playing Mathias, fretted beneath a limelight towards the front. Now young Craig let down his canvas foredrop – a representation of the interior of an inn of Alsace, complete with painted-on windows, tables and chairs, and a large antlered stag's head over the door – before the gauze, entirely obscuring the back of the stage. Finally, the red velvet curtain was lowered, covering the whole of the front of the stage, except for the footlights.

Everything was set for the lights rehearsal for that season's production of *The Bells* – the terrifying melodrama detailing innkeeper Mathias's frantic attempts to conceal his feelings of guilt over a murder he had committed some fifteen years prior, Mathias being one of the Guv'nor's most renowned roles.

Stoker was beginning to feel excited, a little nervous even, and ran a freckled forefinger repeatedly across his top lip. It was always an honour to take part in these lights rehearsals, he reflected, as Irving would clear the theatre of everybody except his own imperious person, Miss Terry, Stoker himself, Grafton, Loveday and essential hands. No one else – not a flunky, musician, costumier, or any other member of the company – was allowed to be inside the theatre at such times, as Irving perfected the lighting for the phantasmagoria which, more than anything else, had made the Lyceum Theatre the most celebrated in London, and him the most famous actor in the world.

'Curtain up!' commanded Irving, the red velvet rising nobly to reveal the front of the stage newly lit, some half a dozen footlights all at perfect pitch, and a limelight directed to where Miss Terry – playing Mathias's wife – would be seated, spinning. 'Illuminate!'

he now intoned, calling into life two more limelights in sequence for the arrivals of the burly woodcutter and the young gendarme – the only character who harboured any suspicion of the innkeeper's dark past.

Although there were no players onstage (or indeed anyone else), Stoker could take easy delight in imagining the wide-eyed passion of Miss Terry as she spun at her wheel like Clotho the Fate, discussing the imminent marriage of her character's daughter.

Now came the call for Irving's own limelight as he would enter stage right. Already Stoker could conjure his boss's imposing frame, clad in a black cloak, scuffing off fake snow from his boots at the back of the stage; already hear the burst of applause that would erupt when the actor at last emerged to the audience's full, impatient view. Next, the first shake of the bells, accompanied by another half dozen footlights, just as discussions of the marriage were under way. Stoker could almost see the spasms that would contort Irving's face – a trick he had never been able to fathom.

'A little bit quicker on Mr Loveday's cue, Aloysius; I wouldn't want the audience to miss my expression. Shall we do it again?'

'Certainly, Mr Irving,' responded Grafton from the wings.

The footlights were turned down and now Grafton timed the flow of the gas perfectly to Loveday's shaking of the bells, easing off the pressure as the jangle slowed. This time Stoker imagined the actor's passing tremor in full, delivering yet another thrill of pleasure.

'Excellent! And now let us rehearse the final scene of the Act.' Again Loveday began to shake the bells as the lights dwindled to almost nothing in the foreground – leaving only the limelight intended for Irving's face. Now young Craig raised the foredrop to reveal the stark wintry backdrop behind the gauze. Stoker marvelled as the limelight cast the scene a spectral emerald. Already he could picture Mr Archer, miming the younger Mathias, attacking and killing the travelling seed merchant, Koveski, in his sleigh, Irving himself raving as the older Mathias in the foreground as the innkeeper's conscience broke loose. The crescendo of the bells, recalling the jingling from the seed merchant's sleigh, made the violence still more alive in Stoker's mind: he could see the terrifying axe being raised; the horrified expression of Koveski (to be played by Mr Alexander) as he turned to face his attacker; the splatter of blood as the blade sunk deep between his shoulders. He could almost hear Koveski's high-pitched, piercing scream.

'My God! What was that?' cried Miss Terry. The string of sleigh bells stuttered then clattered to the floor in the wings. Grafton and Loveday walked swiftly onto the stage, followed by Craig. A scream came again, shaking the plush red velvet and gold brocade of the auditorium. Stoker's reverie was broken. He turned to see Irving moving his lips inaudibly and Miss Terry standing alert, like a deer trapped by huntsmen. Stoker lurched into the orchestra pit and then onto the stage, moving towards Grafton and Loveday, whom he could discern at the back, cupping their ears.

'What was that, Aloysius?' he asked, lifting up the gauze and passing beneath it.

'Sounded like a girl screaming, Sir.'

'Where from, exactly?'

'I reckon from below stage, Mr Stoker,' replied Grafton. 'Beneath old Mr Fechter's trap.' Loveday nodded in agreement, the tassel of his Armenian smoking hat bobbing in sympathy, as both men now pointed towards a large trapdoor – a door which had been plastered over for some years and was now in disuse.

'Did you hear the same, Edward?' Young Craig, himself now installed behind the gauze, was vibrating with fear, his spectacles jerking down his nose, his teeth chattering uncontrollably.

'Yes. I think so… perhaps.' There was quiet for some few moments as the men seemingly waited to hear the scream again.

'Bram, what is the problem?' demanded Irving. Stoker stooped back under the gauze and faced his boss, who had moved towards the front of the auditorium.

'Did you not hear a girl screaming, Sir?' he asked.

'I heard nothing of the sort, Bram. Can we please all resume our rehearsal!' Stoker turned round to look at the others (now all assembled at the front of the stage), as if in search of support.

'Mr Irving,' ventured Loveday, 'I did in fact hear the same. There is someone down below, I'm sure of it – unless it's a ghost!' And, as if to confirm this statement, an eerie moan pierced the floorboards and consumed the whole of the stage.

'I must go down and investigate,' said Stoker suddenly. 'Will you come with me, Aloysius?'

'Of course.' Grafton rushed back into the wings to retrieve a lantern and then both men jumped into the orchestra pit, causing Grafton's prized pince-nez to go skew-whiff. Once through the pit, and past a disgruntled Irving, the two men moved up the aisle, then beneath the Royal Box (where that coming Tuesday the Prince of Wales himself would be seated) and through to a dimly lit corridor which led towards the foyer. After a few paces, Stoker stopped, removed a long brass key from a buttoned waistcoat pocket, then opened the door to the lights cellar. Grabbing the lantern from Grafton, he took in the maze of pipes extending beneath him in the dismal cavern. No lights – or indeed anything else – were stored there anymore, owing to the danger of leaking gas from this system of pipes which Irving had installed after taking over the theatre from Mrs Hezekiah Bateman some years prior.

Waving the lantern further into the gloom, Stoker made its dull glow reveal the depths. Now treading carefully down the few steps that led from the door, he advanced, trying his best to avoid the many pipes. Suddenly, after not more than a few yards, he made out what appeared to be the worn heels and holed soles of someone's boots from which, to his horror, extended stockinged legs. Stoker moved closer. Yes, slumped against a wall was a girl of about sixteen, her petticoats hitched over her skirt revealing her garters, her tightly bodiced upper body wrapped in a tatty red shawl. Slowly, and with fearful curiosity, Stoker nudged the lantern towards her face: the girl's eyes were closed, her lips quivering, her skin a deathly pale. She had long tousled blonde hair and was wearing a thin black band around her neck. Under the band were what appeared to be two small flesh wounds, like bites or punctures, from which were issuing two thin, ceaseless streams of blood. He must act quickly!

'Aloysius, will you come here?'

'I *am* here,' belted a voice from behind. Stoker almost dropped his lantern in fright: he had forgotten his lights manager would be following him.

'There's a young girl here, Aloysius, who's been attacked.'

'Oh my sweet Lord, I'm afraid you're right, Sir!' exclaimed Grafton.

'We must get her out of the cellar, quickly! Take the lantern, will you?' He handed the light to Grafton, who held it gingerly over the girl. Stoker then removed a cream handkerchief from his trouser pocket and started dabbing the girl's neck. She was quite silent now, having fallen into a complete lethargy. The wounds seemed most fresh and showed no sign of ebbing – like a lip nicked by a razor. He lifted the girl's head and tied the kerchief around her neck. Then, pulling her up in his powerful arms, he began to step crab-like through the cellar, guided by Grafton's light. All of a sudden, a large black rat with a terrifying shriek ran between his legs and into the brickwork, almost unbalancing him; he would have to speak to Grafton later about arranging some traps.

As the two men emerged from the cellar, and then out into the auditorium, they were met with a crowd of anxious but familiar faces.

'What the devil have we here?' cried Irving, his usual unflappability overcome with anger.

'Well, not a ghost, in any case. This young girl needs medical attention, straightaway!' replied Stoker.

'Who is she, and how on earth did she get down there?' asked Loveday, his face quite goblin-like in the half-light.

'Lord only knows,' sighed Stoker, shaking his head.

'Well, I think I may have an inkling,' said Miss Terry, extending a cold angry stare at her son, who was standing a little way back from the others.

'Let's take her up to the Beefsteak room,' announced Irving suddenly, his puckered brow relaxing to recall its usual self-command. 'We'll lay her down on the table and see if we can bring her round.' The cream handkerchief was now turning crimson and beginning to drip with blood, and before Irving had had a chance to say anything more, Grafton had picked up the girl's legs and he and Stoker were making their way towards some stairs at the back of the auditorium. 'Ellen and Edward, please come with us,' continued Irving gruffly. 'The rest of you may go home for the night; we'll finish the lights rehearsal in the morning.'

Up on the second floor, in the Beefsteak room, the girl now laid down on the long mahogany table and Grafton dismissed, Stoker checked her pulse: it was faint, but present. In the fuller light he could see that her face was marked as though with signs of the pox, and that her lips were now completely still and drained of life.

'We must get a physician immediately,' he declared.

'Enough of that,' retorted Irving, leaning over the girl to inspect her wounds. 'My word, what peculiar ruptures. I think it best if we give her physic ourselves.'

'But, Mr Irving,' protested Stoker, resting his hands on his hips, 'she is still bleeding. She may die!'

'Poppycock, Bram! These look more like cat scratches to me – or bites from an overzealous lover; they will soon be staunched. But I do wonder how she came to be down in the cellar.' And now he turned his imposing brow on the shivering Craig, who was standing by the half-opened door.

'Yes, Edward,' said Miss Terry with the haughty demeanour of a huntswoman over her prey, 'is this one of your trollops?'

The beaky, bespectacled Craig, in his loose-fitting shirt, falling collar and braces, looked an unlikely culprit. Nevertheless, his quivering frame intimated some sense of guilt.

'Well, no… no… I never,' he stuttered, backing his way through the doorway.

'Be honest, now,' his mother implored him, taking his hands in hers. 'We cannot help you if you lie.'

'Well, yes,' the youth said at last. 'Yes, I did take the girl into the theatre earlier today; early this afternoon, in fact – to show her the wings and the like. I met her while taking lunch in Piccadilly, after my morning's work here, at the Lyceum.'

'Edward, this woman is nothing but a common prostitute – a trollop, a wagtail; again!' shouted Irving, lunging furiously towards the youth as if to strike.

'No, no,' begged Craig, cowering. 'All right. Yes, we did do some fooling, near the props room, but not in the cellar. And I didn't attack her, not like that. How could I, I was—'

'Enough! Go home – and tell your sister I cannot meet her and her friend tonight,' declared Miss Terry suddenly.

'But I didn't attack her,' he protested. 'I didn't, honestly, Mater—'

'Go home *now*, Edward!' resumed his mother with added vehemence, her golden plaits beginning to unravel. 'And take my private carriage; I shall make enquiry as to the time of your arrival!'

Young Craig looked down at his feet but did not move, as Miss Terry shook her head in seeming disbelief at his inaction.

'Bram,' began Irving, now turning to Stoker, 'do you know of a druggist open at this time of a Saturday evening?'

'There's one at the top of Whitehall, just beyond the flower stall.'

'Good. Go quickly, then, and fetch some bandages, some smelling salts, some Turkey rhubarb and somewhat more of an elixir. Here,' Irving rummaged inside his trouser pocket and brought out a gold sovereign, 'go and fetch these items as quickly as possible. We'll stay here and look after the girl.'

'I still say we should ask a physician to come, Guv'nor,' said Stoker. Placing both hands firmly on his acting manager's shoulders, Irving bored into Stoker's eyes.

'Yes, Bram,' he said with quiet restrained violence in his voice, 'and a physician will notify the police, and then there will be questions for young Edward to answer, and for our whole company as well. The girl's not going to die from wounds as trifling as these. Now, please go and get the bandages and medicine.'

'What if I were to ask my brother, George, to come? He is only in Fitzroy Square.' Irving continued to bore into Stoker's eyes but said nothing. Finally, he spoke.

'I have only met your brother fleetingly, Bram, whereas you I know – and trust – completely.' Stoker considered this a moment: he himself admired his brother more than any other man and would certainly not wish him to be embroiled in events such as these. Sensing Stoker's hesitation, Irving relaxed his grip and spoke again.

'It really would be for the best, Bram.'

Stoker looked at the Guv'nor and breathed a heavy sigh. 'Very well, Mr Irving, I understand,' he said at last.

Marching out of the Beefsteak room and into his office down the corridor, Stoker took a box of matches from his trouser pocket and lit a lamp. His office was reassuringly familiar – if nothing else was that night: immediately in front of him, his teak bureau with its pile of unanswered correspondence; beside this his pens, his blue glass paperweight and stack of Lyceum-headed writing paper. Beside his bureau, a red leather armchair. Up on the wall, the familiar 'Spy' caricatures of famous actors such as Mathews and Kean, and the painting of the monstrous Metal Man statue, eternally washed by the tides out on his pedestal in the harbour at Rosses Point – Stoker's one concession to scenes from his youth, and a creature whose glowering presence he only tolerated as a memento mori: a constant and necessary spur to his ambition while in London. He walked over to the coat stand, rolled down and buttoned his sleeves, then retrieved his favourite brown bowler hat, his frock coat and brass-tipped cane. Thus equipped, he extinguished the lamp and locked up his office before making his way back along the corridor then down the narrow stairs which led to the stage door, then out onto Wellington Street and the Strand.

Once on the Strand, Stoker tried to hail a hansom. He struck lucky with the second cab to pass, whose horse pulled up with a skilful draw on its reins and a stamping of its hooves.

'Ah, Mr Stoker, it's you again, Sir!' announced the driver from his vantage at the back of the carriage. The cabbie was a wiry, clean-shaven Cockney of about thirty-five with a floppy cap and double-breasted navy frock coat. His manner was affable and assured, and Stoker was pleased to see him. 'Where is it I can take you to tonight, Sir?'

'Jonas, can you kindly drive me Mall-wards. I am somewhat pressed, so please don't spare dear Tinder.' Jonas pulled on a lever and released the cab door for Stoker to clamber in.

'Where *exactly* is it you want, Sir?' asked Jonas as soon as his passenger had settled himself on the leather-clad seating and closed the door.

'Down to the druggist at the top of Whitehall,' replied Stoker, arching his neck to talk through the little trapdoor-way at the back of the cab's roof then setting down his bowler and cane.

'Right you are, Sir.'

With a tug of Tinder's reins, the two men were soon crackling along the Strand, with its succession of theatres and music halls – newspaper boys screaming the headlines for *The Star* and *The Pall Mall Gazette* in the bright but uneven gaslight as they made their way. Here they passed the red-bricked Savoy – a sensation with its all-electric lighting, and the Guv'nor's most recent rival. Next, the understated elegance of his most bitter rival, the Adelphi, with its stock of lurid melodramas and painted villains.

Not that Stoker was taking much notice of all this: his thoughts were firmly on the troubling events he had just encountered in his own theatre. Why was it that this young girl seemed so ill with so trivial wounds? Stoker was sure she did really need a physician, despite what the Guv'nor had said.

It was clear that Craig had brought her into the theatre. This unlikely lothario, with his slight frame and anaemic complexion, had already caused several such upsets, involving overzealous horseplay, with a number of dubious young women, and were it not for the influence of his mother and the belief of Mr Telbin – the Lyceum's principal scene painter – in the youth's artistic talents, he would have been sent packing from the theatre months ago.

And yet, thought Stoker, as they made their way towards Trafalgar Square, there had surely been no possibility for Edward to get into the cellar. Only he himself, Grafton and Irving possessed keys to that cavern, with its maze of gas pipes that had made the Lyceum scintillate with lighting such as no other playhouse in the known world. Stoker himself had been eating a tedious lunch with Grafton up until they came to the theatre at four o'clock, enduring his lights manager's mock-Fenian jibes at his Protestantism. Stoker always took these slights in good part, not least because he knew only too well that English people took him and Grafton to be one and the same, despite what he considered to be his own more exalted faith – a faith in which, he had lately conceded, he had no real conviction. According to Miss Terry, Irving had come directly from the Garrick Club following an early supper with Wilson Barrett – a hugely popular actor whom Stoker knew Irving despised. Indeed, neither Loveday nor any of the hands had been in the theatre until late, and so the finger of suspicion must be pointed at Edward. But how did he get the girl into the cellar if he did not possess a key? And even if he had somehow managed to get hold of one, and attack in this quite outrageous manner, why were the girl's wounds so fresh – still in fact bleeding – as Edward had been under his own close supervision from late afternoon, without the slightest possibility of escaping his keen protecting eye? Indeed, Edward had been onstage when the girl's scream had rung out.

The hansom now entered Trafalgar Square, where crowds of demonstrators had gathered under braziers to listen to pronouncements on the evils of the Tsar and Albion's duty to stand by the Ottomans – an opinion with which Stoker heartily agreed, and one he had held ever since listening to his brother's tales of his beloved Turkey-land. Just in front of Nelson's Column, an old man with muttonchop sideburns and a battered top hat was launching into a tirade against Gladstone – denouncing his failure to protect his Ottoman ally – as a rag-tag of old soldiers and idle barrow-boys nearby started up chanting, 'By Jingo We'll Protect the Turk!' It was the very same chant, Stoker realised, as he had heard when he had first arrived in London, some ten years before – just after the Treaty of Berlin when, in a rebuff to Gladstone, Disraeli had managed to claw back some of the Ottoman lands from the predatory Russian bear.

The cab now slowed, Jonas continually having to rein in Tinder as careless demonstrators, many of them drunk, staggered towards the top-hatted ranter. It was always like this on a Saturday evening, reflected Stoker – a nuisance for a man in a hurry!

At last Jonas escaped the Square and drove around the corner into Whitehall, halting Tinder outside a backlit shop window with obscure bottles of potions and instruments on prominent display. Above the window was a wooden shop awning with the lettering, 'John Bartholomew and sons: Druggist', painted green on white. Stoker handed Jonas a half-crown through the cab's trapdoor before asking, 'Can you wait for me here, Jonas? I will not be long.'

'Certainly, Sir.'

'Good,' replied Stoker. 'Watch out for those dipsos, they might frighten Tinder!' he added with a laugh, before taking up his bowler and cane, and climbing out.

'Don't worry about Tinder, Sir,' replied Jonas. ''E's a strong old war 'orse wot's seen far worse in 'is time.'

Stoker entered the druggist's to the sharp 'ting' of the shop doorbell. Behind the counter was a rotund, red-faced man with a bushy beard, dressed in a grey waistcoat, a white collar-studded shirt with a square tie, and a white half-apron. He was smiling, as always.

'What can I do for you tonight, Mr Stoker?' he asked in a deep nasal voice.

'Good evening, Mr Bartholomew. I need some bandages, some smelling salts, a small phial of Turkey rhubarb and a somewhat larger phial of an elixir, if you can suggest one.'

'What is to be treated?' asked the druggist. Stoker hesitated: he had not wanted to be quizzed on this.

'Oh, it's just a young girl having difficulty waking,' he replied.

'I have just the things you need, then, Sir.' The druggist turned and took down two flasks from the packed iron shelves behind him and began pouring their contents into two phials, which he then stoppered.

'There, Mr Stoker,' he said, returning to his customer and placing the phials on the counter. 'This would get a banshee wailing over them peat bogs where you come from!'

Stoker grimaced.

Bartholomew now began cutting up lengths of bandaging and then, from a drawer beneath his counter, took out three small cubes, resembling billiard chalks. He proceeded to place these items, as well as the phials, into a large brown paper bag.

'There you are, Sir. That will be twelve shillings altogether.'

Stoker gave Bartholomew Irving's gold sovereign, and the druggist opened up another drawer, returning with some change.

'Thank you,' said Stoker, picking up the brown paper bag. He touched his cane to his bowler and afforded the druggist a rare crease of a smile.

'Watch out for them leprechauns as you go. A few too many slugs of gin in 'em!' exclaimed Bartholomew.

Stoker left without saying another word, or indeed revealing the contempt he felt for this man. He never rose to slights from the English, using his conversations with the likes of George Bernard Shaw and his defeated love rival, the brilliant Oscar Wilde, as necessary outlets for this particular source of steam.

Back on the street, a boy in short corduroy trousers was selling newspapers next to the flower stall. The body of a second woman had been found in Whitechapel early that morning. While this was no longer news as such, the boy was promising that his paper would reveal the victim's identity, should any passer-by wish to part with a tanner. But Stoker had no time to stop now, and hurriedly climbed back into Jonas's cab. It was odd, however, he reflected as the cab headed back into the Square, that a similar, although less grievous, event had just occurred in the bowels of his own theatre. All of a sudden, a terrifying thought flashed across his mind: what if Edward were in some way connected to these crimes? No, that was surely an impossibility – for while Edward was no doubt capable of horseplay, he was surely not capable of this! Still, Stoker did fear for the youth's future, given his overzealous passions.

The cab was soon rattling back along the Strand then turning left into the narrower Wellington Street, where it pulled up almost immediately before the grand, white-columned portico of the Lyceum. Stoker handed a further half-crown to the grateful Jonas through the cab's trapdoor, then grabbed the brown paper bag, his bowler and cane. As he was getting out, he felt the cab wobble violently and heard Jonas scream, 'Oi, you mind your way, you daft foozler!' Stoker turned round to see a black carriage with a peculiar many-petalled rose embossed in red on its back, hurtling down the street and into the Strand. The rose image was faintly familiar to him, but he could not recall why, or where he might have seen its like before. Stoker thanked Jonas and wished him good night before brushing down his frock coat and stepping smartly through the stage door.

Once up on the second floor, Stoker hurried to the Beefsteak room and knocked on the door – but there was no reply. He now tried the handle, to discover the door was in fact locked. He sighed, then turned and strode down the corridor to Irving's dressing room, where the door stood ajar. He knocked on it lightly, taking care not to push it any wider.

'Come in, Bram!' boomed his boss.

Stoker found Irving and Miss Terry perched on an ottoman at the back of this Aladdin's cave, with its wheeled wooden trellises stacked with hanging-up costumes, its chests crammed with props, and its dressing table groaning with brushes, pins and pots of make-up. Miss Terry's mouth seemed to be open in faltering astonishment, her golden hair now entirely tumbled out of its plaits and lying loose on her shoulders. Irving was sitting askance, his hands clasped on his lap. He appeared composed, almost regal, as he sat there in his herringbone tweed – although Stoker could not help noticing he was twiddling his thumbs wildly.

'I brought back the bandages and medicine for the girl.' Stoker held the brown paper bag aloft for them both to see.

'Thank you, Bram, but it will not be necessary,' replied Irving, dismissively waving his gnarled right hand towards him, the imposing silver ring featuring a square and compasses on his little finger glinting in the lamplight. 'After Edward left for home – which he did after some further encouragement from his mother – the girl came back to her senses and told us what had ensued between herself and the young man. A rather shameful affair, I must say.' Here Miss Terry began to cry, then opened up a little silk bag and withdrew a lace handkerchief.

'What am I to do about my son, Mr Stoker?' she sobbed. Irving shook his head.

'Well, anyway,' he resumed, 'we gave the girl some gold sovereigns, which seemed to end her complaints with immediate effect! She then upped and left.'

'But how did Edward get—?'

'Into the cellar?' broke in Irving. 'Well, before he left for home, Edward admitted to stealing Grafton's key to conduct this most unfortunate of trysts. He will not be taking part in any more productions for the foreseeable future. Indeed, Ellen and myself think it best if we immediately send him away to school, at Sedbergh, for a time – to keep him out of harm's way. Perhaps a good dose of the North will cool him down!'

'But how could Edward have attacked the girl,' pressed Stoker, 'when he was onstage when she screamed?'

'Some kind of delayed reaction or shock from the young trollop, no doubt.'

'And the blood, still streaming?'

'Well, we soon staunched that once you had left for the druggist.'

Irving got up and swept his hands through his impressively long, grizzled mane then went over to the bemused Stoker and patted him on the arm. 'Don't worry, Bram. We can do the final lights rehearsal on Monday morning, before the dress rehearsal in the afternoon.'

'But won't the theatre be full of all the other hands and players then, Sir?'

'Then kindly put a notice on both front and back of house to say that no hands or players – apart from those required for the rehearsal – can enter until midday.' Irving's tone was reassuring, and Stoker began to feel the high tide of excitement of the last few hours ebb away.

'Very good, Sir.' Stoker was about to wish Irving and Miss Terry adieu when Miss Terry suddenly spoke again.

'And please, Mr Stoker, not a word to anyone about what you have seen tonight!'

Stoker looked at the two of them, Irving seated once more next to his leading lady, both now noticeably calmer than they had been earlier that evening.

'I shall make sure that neither I nor anyone else breathes a word, Miss Terry. I promise.'

'Good night, then, Bram. Until Monday.'

'Good night, Miss Terry, Mr Irving. I shall be in early on Monday – eight o'clock sharp!' With that Stoker left the pair, the brown paper bag still clutched in his hand, and headed for his office further down the corridor, just beyond Miss Terry's dressing room. He unlocked then pushed open the door to hear its bottom scrape against some obstruction. Bending down, he immediately saw what it was: a sealed envelope. From the corridor light he could see the words 'Mr Stoker' penned in hurried looped writing across its front. He strode across to his bureau and sat down. Then, having set down the brown paper bag and lit a lamp, he slit open the missive with his letter knife to read the following.

8th September, 1888

Dear Mr Stoker,

I am truly sorry for bringing the young lady into the theatre earlier today. I know that I have done wrong, and that Mater is most upset with me. As I said before, I met the lady while taking lunch in Piccadilly, and wanted to impress her by showing her around the theatre when no one else was there – she is herself an actress, or so she told me. But please believe me when I say I never took her down to the cellar, and never attacked her. In any case, I do not possess a key to the cellar, and would not have taken her there, as you and Mr Grafton have always told me how dangerous any gas escaped from the pipes can be.

I do hope you will believe me, Sir, despite what Mater and Mr Irving might say – I am being honest.

Yours truly,

Edward G. Craig

Stoker considered the letter for a moment. The first part of Edward's hasty defence he knew was untrue: the girl was clearly an 'actress' of the more dubious kind – and Edward's predilections in that regard were well known. As to the second part, Stoker did think it unlikely that Edward would have been able to steal a key from Grafton and then take the girl down to the cellar – knowing the dangers of the gas – and that the youth's assertions in that regard might well be true. But then why would the Guv'nor lie about such a thing, saying that Edward had stolen the key if he hadn't, and thus implicate the young man? Stoker traced his lip in momentary contemplation then, noting the hour on his fob watch, picked up the brown paper bag, extinguished the lamp, and left for home.

CHAPTER II

ST LEONARD'S TERRACE

It was half past ten in the evening and Stoker was in his study, sitting at the oval desk where he chose to attend to his private affairs – the bills and correspondence that did not pertain to his work at the Lyceum. Among the missives scattered across the desk was yet another rejection from *The London Magazine* for one of his short stories, several letters from family members – including one from his mother in Italy reporting on the fluctuations of her health – and another letter, as yet unopened and previously unremarked. This appeared to bear the spidery writing of his mentor, Jacob Henstridge, at Bagfleet Chambers, where for some years Stoker had been using the library in desultory preparation for entry to the Bar – a seemingly respectable profession towards which his wife had increasingly been encouraging him.

While Stoker had visited Chambers only a few days before, he had missed Henstridge, who had been at court prosecuting for the Crown in a notable case, the details of which the clerks had refused to divulge but whose silence had been amply compensated for by the efforts of the gutter press. Stoker was reaching for his letter knife when suddenly the doorbell rang, startling him with its uncommon lateness.

'Emma, will you please see who it is?' he called out – loudly enough to be heard but not so loud as to disturb his sleeping son and early-to-bed wife. He heard the patter of his housemaid's feet through the hallway towards the vestibule, and then the gruff but amiable tones of his brother as the front door opened. Immediately, Stoker's mood improved as the dimly lit contours of his study, with its desk littered with papers and its crammed bookshelves, became the potential backdrop of an entertaining hour or so. Why George should be visiting him so late Stoker could only imagine, but his joy after such a perplexing day overrode any such anxieties.

The door creaked open and in came the diminutive form of his housemaid.

'Sir, Dr George Stoker here to see you,' she announced with a barely suppressed smile on her face: the young doctor was popular with everyone.

'Good evening, frater,' said George, striding into the room. Stoker stood up to shake his brother's hand, the two men chuckling with childish glee.

'Emma, will you fetch the decanter of whiskey and two glasses.'

'Certainly,' came the reply, the servant now bustling out of the study to complete her task.

'So, young man, what brings you here so late of an evening, great and unexpected boon though it may be?' resumed Stoker, seating himself once more behind his desk.

'Well,' said George, sitting himself down on a small button-backed armchair adjacent the desk, 'I just wanted to ask you what took you careering into Trafalgar Square earlier this evening...'

'Bejesus!' returned Stoker, exaggerating his habitual brogue. 'Will my little brother mind telling me how he knew I was there?'

'I saw you come, like Murrough through the Danes at Clontarf, scattering a fair few pickled Vikings on your way. I should know, I was almost one of them!' George graciously accepted the glass now offered by Emma and added, 'Well, in my case, not pickled, of course,' before taking a large gulp of his whiskey.

'Ah, so you *were* at the rally,' retorted Stoker.

'Too right I was. New ructions from the Russians and Gladstone once more urging us to dodge the shindy.'

'Well, although I must admit a certain partiality for the Grand Old Man, in this case I sympathise with your cause, as you know, and not with Gladstone and our prime minister, Salisbury. Sadly, I could not attend the rally myself, as we theatre people work night and day, unlike you loafers in the medical profession.' George grunted.

'Still, anyway, Bram,' resumed George. 'Do tell me what you were doing, going at such a speed?' Stoker gulped. He had left the bag of druggist's wares on the corner of his desk and could see George eyeing them suspiciously. He did not want to lie and so chose to be glib.

'Oh, one of the girls at the theatre fainted,' he answered at last. 'She didn't revive for some time, so Irving sent me to get some medicine.'

'A girl?'

'Yes, just a girl… an actress… at the theatre.'

'And didn't you call a doctor?' asked George, angling his tumbler in the desk's lamplight.

'Well, I did suggest it. In fact, I suggested you.'

'Well, it's just as well you didn't call for me as I wasn't in my surgery,' snapped George, failing to disguise his irritation.

'Well, indeed. And I doubt any other of you loafers would have been available at that time of a Saturday evening!' George laughed good-naturedly at this, although Stoker suspected his younger brother was somewhat perturbed by his equivocation.

'There's a fair few in Harley Street at that time, but they cost a pretty penny, I can tell you that. What happened in the end?'

'Oh, nothing much,' replied Stoker. 'By the time I got back, the girl was much recovered and had left. We never used any of the medicine, so I brought it back for safe keeping,' and here he pointed at the brown paper bag.

'Yes,' said George. 'Probably one of those narcoleptic seizures common in hysterical young girls, if she was out for that long. There are some things, I'm afraid, that my fellow loafers and I will never cure.' He got up to look inside the bag. Taking out then replacing the bandages with some curiosity, he then picked up one of the phials and guffawed.

'What's wrong?' asked Stoker.

'Turkey rhubarb? Who on earth gave you that?'

'Irving asked for it, and I got it from that druggist at the top of Whitehall.'

'Oh,' said George, rolling his eyes, 'not that dreadful quack who mocks the Irish.'

'The very same,' conceded Stoker, suddenly trying to feign interest in his correspondence. George returned the phial to the bag and settled back to his whiskey.

'You might as well have asked Merlin for a remedy, or even some alchemical order – just humbug in today's world!' Suddenly, Stoker dropped his papers and got up from his desk.

'What's the matter?' asked George.

'That's what it was!' exclaimed Stoker, tapping his top lip excitedly. He moved towards where the bemused George was taking another sip of whiskey and pulled a leather-bound volume out from the bookshelf behind his head. Opening it up, he started leafing through its pages.

'What will-o'-the-wisp has taken your fancy now, frater?' asked George. Instead of answering, Stoker simply showed the book's cover to his brother.

'Johann Andreae, *The Chymical Wedding of Christian Rosenkreutz*,' pronounced George. 'What the devil has that got to do with that bigoted quack in Whitehall?' Stoker found the image he was looking for – a red, many-petalled rose, printed between the third and fourth chapters – and handed the opened book to his brother.

'Not very much, in truth, little brother; but you have just helped me solve an annoying little mystery.' He walked back to his desk, sat down, and took a slug of whiskey.

'What mystery is that? How to turn base metal into gold? I'm surely no help with that,' quipped George.

'Not that exactly, but close. When you talked about alchemical orders, it reminded me of that book. I bought it some years ago as research for a possible short story. Anyhow, today I saw the strangest black carriage hurtling down Wellington Street; it had a peculiar red rose embossed on its back. Something made me think I had seen its like before, but where – and, indeed, what it meant – I could not fathom. And now you, little brother, have brought it back to me!'

'I see,' said George. 'The red rose of the brotherhood of the Rosy Cross,' he now read out from the page before him. 'What the devil is that?'

'It was an alchemical order – the Rosicrucians – founded before the Thirty Years' War. The carriage owner might even be a member. If he is, shows they still exist, I suppose – like the Masons.' Stoker stroked his beard thoughtfully. His brother shut the book and placed it on the desk.

'Bram, you're still the same incorrigible investigator you always were – must solve every mystery, no matter how small. Like when that litter of kittens appeared out of nowhere in our garden in Dublin, when you were twelve, remember?' Stoker chuckled but was in secret somewhat miffed: he would have preferred it if George had praised his scholarly exploits instead.

'Well,' said Stoker, 'sadly, my detective work only succeeded in getting poor Katharine released from her position, when it came out that she had a secret cat, so I'd have done better to have left well alone!'

'Talking of Dublin,' said George, his tone now changing from flippant to sincere, 'has Thornley written to you recently?' From this point on the conversation turned to family matters: the brothers' widowed mother's health problems; how much they wished their brother, Thornley (himself a surgeon), would leave Dublin for Italy to help out; how little time the two of them had to make a visit to either Dublin or Italy, and how much they needed to; and finally, as ever, how tiresome the political situation was back home in their native isle.

As always, Stoker studied his brother's face, not least because he could never quite get over how similar it was to his own, as though George was a displaced twin rather than a mere brother. As George sat there before the bookshelves in his white shirt and cravat, his jet-black waistcoat with its gold fob watch and chain, Stoker saw the same close serious eyes, long square jaw and short straight nose that met himself in the mirror every morning. When seated, George stooped over in the same cumbersome way as did Stoker, his knees arching awkwardly upwards (they were both too tall for commonplace furniture). It was only the greater length of George's beard and moustache, a bronzy gold in the half-light, that seemingly set them apart. And, of course, the fact that George was a little slighter, partly owing to his younger years and partly to Stoker's athleticism while at Trinity College, which had built up his now-powerful frame after a childhood of invalidism.

Stoker contemplated his brother with admiration – a man who by the age of thirty had already qualified as a surgeon, accompanied several armies on campaign, and patented a number of medical inventions. It would surely not be long before George received a knighthood; an impossible dream for a mere theatre man like himself! And yet he begrudged George his fame and brilliance not one jot. Still, Stoker was the senior sibling, and always tried – if not always successfully – to show more restraint than George in their exchanges, usually maintaining their conferences like this, from behind his desk, and taking care occasionally to pause powerfully before responding to his brother's questions.

The conversation now began to draw to a close, the halo above the lamp on Stoker's desk growing ever smaller, indicating its fuel was failing fast. George checked his watch and sighed.

'Frater, I must thank you for the whiskey and make speed to Agnes, back home in Pimlico,' he said, making to stand up.

'Well, it's been a pleasure to see you after all these weeks,' replied Stoker, rising to his feet. 'I'll call Emma to see you out.' George extended his hand to shake that of his brother and then withdrew it sharply; his brow rippled like the sea, suddenly troubled.

'Bram, there was one more thing I wanted to ask you.' Stoker felt a stab of fear: would his brother return to questioning him about his trip to the druggist?

He looked at George, and then, with as much calm as he could muster, replied, 'Please, by all means, little brother.'

'Well, it's maybe more to ask your advice about something – and I'm sorry, but it's a bit of a long story.'

'Go on,' replied Stoker, signalling that they should both sit back down.

'Well, a very odd thing happened to me some few days ago – Thursday before last, in fact. It was about eight o'clock in the evening, and already dark. The surgery was closed, and I was on the ground floor, checking stock; not something I normally do myself, but my nurse and assistant surgeon had both gone home and, to be frank, it doesn't hurt if I attend to these things myself occasionally.'

'I should imagine not,' replied Stoker, relieved to hear that his own activities were to escape George's further investigations.

'I heard a rustling sound, like the feet of a small animal, so looked up to see whether some cat or rat were there. Then, from behind me, I heard a cough, making me nearly jump out of my skin. I turned round to see a man. He was immensely tall, with a full head of hair – completely grey – and a pale, lined face with an aquiline nose. He was wearing what looked like some form of evening dress under a black cape. "How the devil did you get in?" I spluttered, and he replied, quite coolly, "Please, Dr Stoker, don't be angry. Your door was unlocked, and so I came in." While his English was excellent, he was not, I thought, a native Englishman, as his accent and intonation were clearly Slavic; I could tell that from my time as a surgeon in the army – when I was stationed in Danzig. "Well, you must leave immediately!" I shouted. The man did not budge, however, and just looked at me mockingly. I went to move him on, but he gripped me with prodigious strength and held me as I stood. "Please, Dr Stoker," he repeated, "I have only come for one of your famous vapour pipes. I will gladly pay you for it." And then, with his free hand, he removed some gold sovereigns from his trouser pocket and let them fall onto the floor. I looked into his black eyes, curiously restless and mobile, and wondered what he would do next. And then he let go of me, as suddenly as he had taken hold of me, so I walked briskly to the cabinet behind my desk where I keep a few of my vapour contraptions. Once there, I heard the clank of metal and turned to see the man prising open the locked medical chest where I keep my phials of blood.'

'Phials of blood?' queried Stoker with some astonishment.

'That's right,' replied George, 'blood.'

'Why in the name of our Maker do you keep blood? Surely it's not permitted – and won't it simply deteriorate anyway?' George was visibly shaken, his bravado beginning to falter. Stoker reached down behind his desk to retrieve a carton of cigarettes and a silver cigarette-holder.

'Well,' replied George. 'I have actually been taking part in some informal experiments with Sir Arthur Bowman of King's College Hospital, to see whether we can keep it preserved under certain conditions.'

'And can you?' asked Stoker, charging the holder and lighting the cigarette before handing it to his brother; an infrequent smoker, Stoker did not normally allow smoking anywhere except the drawing room, but he could see that George needed some relief from his agitation.

'Thank you, frater. I have no way of knowing whether we can do or not since this man swiftly opened, and then downed, the contents of one of the phials, as if it were merely water. He then bundled up the rest of the phials and leapt like a cat out of the window. I rushed to said window and leaned out over the sill but checked myself from shouting, "Stop thief!", since I had no wish to explain to the peelers what it was the man had stolen.'

Stoker looked at his brother closely as the lamplight grew ever dimmer, seeing his own trim-bearded visage reflected in George's eyes, and then shook his head. He felt tempted to confess the strange goings-on of his own day but resisted.

'Well, it sounds like this man was just some lunatic, nothing more,' he pronounced at last. George coughed on his cigarette and shifted back on his armchair.

'Oh, he was certainly a lunatic. One sees them all the time. Indeed, I thought little of it until I read the *Gazette* earlier this evening. When I heard of that second horrific murder, I thought, well…'

'Well what?' demanded Stoker, his heart pounding.

'Well, I was wondering whether the two incidents might be connected in some way, you know.'

'Oh, come now,' laughed Stoker, clapping his hands in false mirth. 'How many loonies are out there in London, I ask you?'

'Yes,' said George, 'but you remember when I was in the Balkans, among the Bulgars?'

'Of course I do. I helped you publish your memoir.'

'Well, I came across lunatics just like that man back then: men who would drink blood before committing murders of just that insane kind – attacking a woman, cutting up her body.' Stoker shuddered at the thought. 'Often they would drink each other's blood – *pobratimové* or blood brothers some called them – before going off and accosting Pomak or Turkish women in that way. This man was clearly from that part of the world; he may even have been one of the loons who used to attack our hospital periodically, in search of blood.' Stoker was looking at his brother intently, his feelings convulsed.

'Are you saying this man was some kind of vampire?' he asked at last.

'Well, no,' returned George skittishly. 'No; *pobratimové* are ordinary men with a crazed fixation on blood – a fixation too primitive for most of my fellow sawbones to credit! Anyway, I did wonder whether this man might be one of them, coming back for me from that time to exact some kind of revenge.'

'I doubt that,' replied Stoker swiftly; it amazed him that his brother, a man with so much physical courage as both doctor and soldier, could be susceptible to such fearsome speculations.

'Well, that's as may be, but after this second murder I thought perhaps it was my duty to tell the police about what had happened – though, to be frank, I was somewhat worried, lest they accused me of having perverted the course of justice, because of my delay.' George now sighed and took a puff of his cigarette as Stoker looked on in the half-light, the desk lamp having by now entirely failed, the streetlamp outside offering the only illumination.

'Well, anyway, Bram, I was wondering what you thought I should do,' resumed George.

'Well,' replied Stoker, 'first, you can only be accused of having perverted the course of justice if you knew that this man was guilty and thus delayed with intent. This individual seems like any other common lunatic to me, and you yourself cannot be blamed for making a none-too-speedy surmise.' Stoker paused. 'However, I would advise you *not* to go to the police, George. There is nothing to connect these two horrific murders with the actions of this man. In any case, the Whitechapel culprit will surely be caught soon.'

'Perhaps you are right, Bram,' said George, stubbing out his cigarette as both men now stood up.

'Besides,' said Stoker, hoping to turn his brother more firmly towards this course of inaction, 'you would have to explain why you keep phials of blood to the Board of Health. They might close down your surgery, not to mention inflict quite some damage on Sir Arthur's reputation. Would you want to be responsible for that?'

'Well, no,' muttered George. 'Yes, I'm sure you're right, frater.' Stoker opened the study door and let a stream of light from the hallway reveal the swirling patterns of the Persian rug on which they were standing.

'Emma,' he called, 'please escort my brother to the door.'

'Good night, Bram,' said George, shaking his brother's hand. 'I shall take your advice.'

'Have a safe journey home,' said Stoker, patting his brother on the back as he was ushered out by the housemaid.

Once his brother and Emma were out of sight, Stoker refilled his desk lamp with oil and shut the study door. He had deliberately not replenished the lamp while George was making his revelations, so as to hasten his departure.

Seated once more behind his desk, now bathed in a full globe of light, Stoker sighed deeply. George's story had genuinely alarmed him, not least because he could discern plausibility in his brother's conjectures. What if this lunatic had followed him from the Balkans and was indeed the murderer of the two prostitutes in Whitechapel? Had he perhaps discovered George's relation to himself – and might that explain why the girl had been attacked in so bizarre a fashion in the cellar of his own theatre? After all, lunatics were capable of all sorts of abominations, of that he was sure. This whole nightmarish scenario was becoming more vivid, and louder, in Stoker's mind – like the sleigh bells continually jangling in innkeeper Mathias's ears.

Stoker shook himself. No, this whole scheme was impossible, surely? There was no sign of a break-in at the theatre, and would a lunatic really have the foresight to steal, copy and return a key unseen into his own, the Guv'nor's or Grafton's pocket? No, he was spinning webs without spiders. George's encounter at the surgery and the attack in the Lyceum were chance events, no more – and he had surely been right to tell his brother not to go to the police; something which made his own silence about the girl in the cellar feel somewhat less painful.

He took up his letter knife once more and opened the missive from Henstridge.

6 September

Dear Mr Stoker,

I was wondering whether you would like to attend court at the Bailey sometime this week.

As you may know, I have recently been prosecuting for the Crown in a case which has sparked not a little interest, and which, I believe, will soon draw to a satisfactory conclusion. Clearly, it is not appropriate for me to discuss details of the case in a missive such as this, but if you were to find some spare day this week to attend, it might improve your prospects in your forthcoming Bar examinations, as I believe this case may constitute food for much digest in the Law Society for years to come, given the remarkable circumstances under which the trial has so far progressed.

I look forward to your response.

Yours most sincerely,

J.R. Henstridge

Stoker stared at the note. He understood it immediately as a veiled threat: he had not attended court in some time, and Henstridge had clearly taken umbrage at his neglect over this trial – the most significant so far in his mentor's career. Through it Henstridge was finally establishing himself as one of the luminaries of the criminal Bar, whose cases filled the pages of *The Pall Mall Gazette* and *Star* for the delectation of a blood-starved audience, long deprived the public executions enjoyed by their neighbours across the Channel in France.

The trial was most notable on account of the high-handed way in which the young defendant, whose many titles included a lairdship in Berwick-upon-Tweed, had tried to invoke an archaic byelaw which granted him immunity from prosecution – a law never revoked owing to the continual change of sovereignty in that tightly walled town, that had been hurled to and fro between England and Scotland for centuries. This vestige of droit du seigneur had delayed the trial, as the Commons and then the Lords had had to meet hastily to repeal the law before the case could proceed.

The trial related to the murder of a young housemaid in the defendant's Bayswater home and was considered to be an open-and-shut case; the murder involving – as far as most of London was concerned – a rather clumsy attempt by an aristocrat to conceal a shameful dalliance with a young woman well below stairs. Until the Whitechapel murders, London had been in uproar about the crime, so soon after the 'Liza affair' and its shocking revelations of the aristocracy's exploitation of girls. William Stead, the doughty journalist behind that notorious exposé, had lost no time splashing headlines about the young lord's trial all over the *Gazette* in his pioneering New Journalism style. Henstridge was no doubt delighted to have netted such a prominent case.

Stoker looked at the note again and suddenly felt a sense of unease. After all, did he really have any right to attend court and sit alongside honourable men sworn to see justice done when he himself had just vowed to turn a blind eye to the dubious events of earlier that evening, in the theatre? Still, he knew that Henstridge and his fellow lawyers were more than capable of being economical with the truth, but did that really make it any more acceptable for him to join their ranks? Perhaps he himself had too much conscience to be a barrister! Stoker sighed, then, taking up a clean leaf of paper, jabbed his pen in the inkpot.

Dear Mr Henstridge,

It really is most kind of you to remember me at such a time, when your energies are surely turned to more pressing matters.

As you know, my energies are also much diverted at this time, with the opening of a new season of 'The Bells' – for which I have reserved tickets for you and your wife in the week after next. Nonetheless, I shall endeavour to find

a means to abscond from my duties this Wednesday, as I
understand the importance of the case in hand.

I look forward to seeing you at the Bailey.
Yours truly,
Bram Stoker

He turned the piece of paper over and sealed it in an envelope before leaving it in his out-tray for Emma to collect the following morning. Having locked the brown paper bag away in a drawer and extinguished the lamp, Stoker rose from his desk and fumbled through the darkness to join his wife upstairs in bed – an event he found himself putting off until later and later each evening.

CHAPTER III

THE OLD BAILEY

The first night of *The Bells* for that season was drawing to a close. Thankfully, smooth performances from Miss Terry, Irving, Mr Alexander and other members of the cast onstage had been matched by the smooth performances of Grafton, Loveday and a raft of stagehands offstage (young Craig having been replaced by Loveday's enthusiastic son, causing the usually reticent Telbin – 'Quiet' Telbin – to emit a few resentful grunts at the loss of his protégé). The orchestra too had been accomplished, the musicians blowing and sawing deftly before the Prince of Wales who, as usual, did not stay beyond the interval, presumably finding the company of other 'actresses' more agreeable.

After the curtain fell, Stoker made his way up to the Beefsteak room, where Irving and Miss Terry were receiving an array of notables at drinks, to make his request to attend court the following day. Everyone, including the Scotsman, Conan Doyle, and the grey-headed poet, Coventry Patmore, was complimenting Miss Terry on the particular pathos of her performance that evening – something which Stoker could tell was making her less lauded leading man somewhat disgruntled. Perhaps this was not a good time to approach the Guv'nor? Still, he had little choice, as he had not found a convenient moment before.

'Upon my word, Bram,' laughed Irving tetchily on hearing Stoker's request, 'what a deuce of a chance; to see the trial of the hour in its closing Act, and on such a stage as the Bailey – second only to the Lyceum!' Here everyone laughed. 'Be sure to write one of your fictions on it afterwards!'

Stoker said nothing.

'Not every day the murder of a young girl like that takes place,' declared Conan Doyle, his bristly red face blaring through the lamplight.

'You are certainly right in that, Sir,' replied Irving, wiping away a dab of greasepaint from his face.

'I'd have been going myself,' continued Conan Doyle, 'if I didn't have that wretched deadline from *The Strand* hanging over me like a guillotine's blade,' and with this he took a petulant swig of his Champagne. 'I'd make a much better report of it than that sensationalist, Stead.'

'Steady on Stead!' quipped Patmore, looking nothing so much like a gentleman scarecrow, in his loose-fitting tails. 'He's got more courage than the rest of us put together.'

'That I concede,' said Conan Doyle, his vexation seeming to subside. 'I wish he could match it with his prose style, that's all.' An awkward silence fell upon the group. They all still felt guilty at having not spoken up when, in a scoop as notorious now for its revelations about the exploitation of young girls as for its effects on the man who had made them, Stead had 'purchased' thirteen-year-old 'Little Liza', supposedly for prostitution, and then been charged, convicted, and carted off to Holloway for a crime he was merely seeking to expose rather than commit. Hounded by the very aristocrats whose vices he had been seeking to reveal, Stead's moral standing had been high ever since.

'You are sure you will not be needed tomorrow, Mr Stoker?' Miss Terry's eyes were two watery pools beneath the brim of her bonnet; unlike Irving and the other players, she rarely changed out of her costume for receptions, frequently retaining her onstage accent as well, as though she inhabited any character she played, and the character her.

'Mr Loveday can answer any urgent requests on behalf of the theatre. All boxes and tickets for this week and next have been booked, and I can take any pressing correspondence home with me, if need be,' Stoker moved to assure her.

'It will be fine, Nell,' said Irving, affording her a not-quite-casual stare.

'I could always stand in,' piped up the aged Patmore, raising a glass to his hosts. 'I've always wanted the chance to work close to the boards!' Despite being a small, and astonishingly wizened, man, Patmore's presence was invariably jovial and served to lighten the mood.

'I don't think Bram could bear the competition,' said Irving. 'His correspondence can't quite match your shining terza rima for style!' Everyone now laughed, except Stoker, who understood the tacit rebuke in the Guv'nor's remark. But soon even he was smiling. After all, he had achieved his aim: a chance to mollify Henstridge, and his wife, and reach ever closer to the Bar – if that was what he truly wanted.

The next morning dawned clear and sunny; colder than preceding days and most definitely announcing autumn. After breakfast, Stoker put on a green frock coat, donned his familiar brown bowler, and picked up his cane, before bidding both Emma and his young son goodbye – his wife, as ever, being still abed. Turning out of the house, he strode towards the King's Road to hail a cab. A young driver perched at the back of a hansom quickly drew reins and Stoker clambered aboard the cab's leather seating.

'Where will you be going, Sir?' asked the youngster.

'The Old Bailey,' said Stoker, craning his neck. The boy took off his blue bowler and scratched his flaxen head.

'The Bailey, Sir?' For a moment Stoker feared he might not reach his destination. Would he have to guide this novice? He himself still felt a stranger in parts of London and was not convinced he could manage its navigation.

'Between Chancery and St Paul's.'

'All right, Sir, I know where.' The boy tugged the horse's reins and off they went, in a considerably more ramshackle fashion than Stoker was used to with the likes of Jonas and Tinder, and at a brisk – and not always comfortable – pace.

Leaving behind the mundane haberdashers, milliners and grocers of Chelsea's King's Road, they were soon zig-zagging over the sawdust and setts of the Mall and into Trafalgar Square. Fearful lest they crashed into an omnibus – or, worse still, some aristocrat's carriage – Stoker kept the cabin's sidebars firmly in his grasp, his cane between his knees; an awkward pose that made him hope no one he knew would notice him. Outside, he could hear the sound of newsboys screaming, 'Read all about it! Read all about it! Drayfield case closing! Case closing!' As the cabbie drove on like the classical Phaethon, past the barrow-boys and hawkers gathered outside Charing Cross Station, and along the Strand, Stoker was seized with surprise. Was the trial really coming to a close so quickly? Did this mean the defence had no real case to make, or little with which to combat Henstridge?

'Oi, Bert,' yelled the cabbie, reining in his horse. 'Which way to Chancery?'

'Second on the left and all the way up to the crossroads, then right,' yelled back another driver, travelling in the opposite direction. They had already passed the entrance to Wellington Street when they made a perilous swivel left, almost turning the hansom onto its side. Stoker was too shocked to remonstrate, bewildered clerks and barrow-boys standing agape at the sight of this careering juggernaut on a chill Wednesday morning. Stoker wondered whether he himself might be the subject of the next headline in the newspapers: 'Manager of well-known theatre impaled on railing by careless cabbie'.

'I say, young man, do you think you could slow down a bit?' shouted Stoker through the roof's trapdoor. 'I wouldn't want to see you fall and break your neck.'

'I can't, Sir. Only one speed with this beast, Sir!' shouted the boy back at him, his pimply face contorted with fear.

They spun wildly at the crossroads and the boy drew the reins right, this time seeming to know where to go. Then, after another few minutes, and with an almighty pull and a screech, he brought the horse to a halt, exactly in front of the Bailey. Shaken, but relieved to be alive, Stoker looked up at the boy's face through the trapdoor. He was now smiling down at him – almost maliciously.

'That will be three shillings, please, Sir.' Stoker rooted in his coat pocket for his money pouch and withdrew the coins, which the boy took up greedily. The boy then released the cab door and Stoker climbed out, dusting off his frock coat once his feet were safely on the ground. He looked around to see whether his uncommon arrival had drawn any unwanted attention, but no; the crowd outside the Bailey – reporters, sketchers, the idle and the cruel – were all too busy jabbering to one another to notice. He turned to the boy, resplendent in his blue frock coat and bowler.

'Good day to you,' he said curtly. 'I might advise you to pursue another trade.'

'Good day to you, Sir. Always a pleasure to be of service to a gentleman, especially an Irish gentleman like yourself.' And with that the boy cracked his whip and drove off slowly, and in a perfectly straight line, no doubt to play more practical jokes on the unsuspecting.

∽

Stoker looked for Henstridge in the scrum outside the Bailey but could not find him. All of a sudden, he felt a tap on his elbow and turned to see the familiar face of a small, wiry man some fifty years of age, with thinning sandy hair and sideburns. He was wearing a short black coat with wide lapels and a pale green tie tucked behind a dark green waistcoat. He was uncomfortably close to Stoker, both men being pressed on all sides by the crowd.

'Good to see you, Mr Frobisher. I have heard the trial is almost at its end. Am I too late?'

'Good morning, Mr Stoker,' said the man in a reedy voice, his bright eyes twinkling. He paused before continuing, like an actor trying to recollect his lines. 'The prosecution, the defence and the judge will all be summing up today.' He stopped and smiled. 'But we do not know whether the verdict will come.' He paused again, this time to sneeze, and then twitched his ferret-like blue eyes – an annoying habit Stoker had remarked in him before.

'I'm told the evidence is conclusive, and the papers are confident,' submitted Stoker. 'I'm sure that the jurymen will not be deliberating long over their verdict after so incisive a prosecution as Mr Henstridge's.'

'My employer does entertain such hopes,' confirmed Frobisher with a tight grin, 'for reasons that he will soon make clear to you. Please follow me.' He now started pushing, if not shoving, Stoker through the crowd of reporters, sketchers, top-hatted idlers and monocled sadists, many already reeking of brandy or gin, eager to see the noose tighten an inch or two further around Lord Drayfield's arrogant neck. Coughing through the cigar smoke, Stoker noticed clusters of toothless Gipsy women in straw hats selling late-blooming roses and nosegays close to the walls of the Bailey, the blue-suited policemen making no attempt to move them on.

The accused must have already arrived and be waiting in the cells beneath the court, presumed Stoker; the judge, however, must be running late, if the crowd were still waiting to scramble for seats.

'Mr Frobisher, will there be room?' Frobisher did not reply. Stoker tried humour. 'Did Mr Henstridge reserve me a box or a seat in the gallery?' Frobisher grunted.

'Only the jury and witnesses get boxes in this theatre, Mr Stoker – and, of course, the accused! Don't worry, we will find a place.'

Sure enough, once Frobisher had shown his papers to the policeman at the door, they advanced along the stone floor of a wide echoing corridor – passing a flurry of lawyers and attendants on their way – then up some steps and into a courtroom largely devoid of people. From the two men's vantage at the front of the gallery, Stoker had an excellent view of the ground floor. Here he noted some four or five policemen standing against the heavy oak-panelled doors of the court, while across from him, facing where the judge would be seated, were the counsels for the prosecution and defence, the prosecution being closer to the jury box, down to his left. There was Henstridge – a portly figure in his black gown and white wig, his jowls making a curving slope from his chin to his silk necktie. Beside him was the tall, skeletal form of his solicitor, James Arbuthnot. Together, they resembled nothing more than the figures of Greed and Want from a medieval church mural. The two men were known not to like one another, but to make a formidable, and thus expedient, team. The counsel for the defence looked worn and appeared to be mopping his brow; he was clearly not anticipating a good day.

Looking down to his right, Stoker could see the accused, wearing a bright blue suit and a florid purple tie, seated haughtily in the dock. With his Roman nose, large eyes and shock of wavy, reddish-blond hair, he looked a prime example of the type Stoker so often found securing some of the best seats at the Lyceum: aristocrats from the Midlands and the North, down in town for a week or two to escape their estates; or young officers from the more fashionable regiments, back home on leave from India, hoping to impress a would-be fiancée. In short, the best stock of Old England, with no need to engage with the likes of himself, Irving or Conan Doyle, all three of whom mere mongrels from the Celtic periphery, trusting furiously to their talents, not their birth, once at the centre.

It was remarkable, though, reflected Stoker, to see such a noble specimen in the dock, charged with such an ignoble crime, and the confidence which the young lord exuded (he could be no more than thirty years of age) could only be due, Stoker assumed, to his total incomprehension of his plight.

Looking now at the benches below him, at the small group of press men there assembled, Stoker noticed the bespectacled figure of William Stead. Elegantly dressed in a white cravat and Eton collar (strange, thought Stoker, for such an enemy of the privileged), Stead was standing up, his bearded jaw jutted towards the dock, his eyes fixed on the accused, like a ravenous bird of prey. The young lord's composure now impressed Stoker even more, for he himself knew how terrifying a stare from Stead could be, having once had to endure the same after making an unthinking remark in the Beefsteak room.

'I see Stead is eager for the denouement,' said Stoker. 'Clearly has no fear of a final twist in the plot by the looks of him.' Frobisher turned to look at his companion but made no reply.

Suddenly, the doors behind Stoker opened and there was a rush for seats. All too soon Stoker found himself uncomfortably packed on his bench, a stout fellow with greasy sideburns squeezing up beside him. The courtroom was now filled with the clamour of spectators jostling for standing room and the frustrated cries of policemen forcing late-comers back. Weren't such folk called 'penny stinkards' in Shakespeare's time? The reek of gin was now harassing Stoker's nostrils as the stinkards laid ghoulish bets on the verdict, as all the while the young lord continued to stare silently ahead, with apparent unconcern.

At last the doors were creaked shut and a court usher led in the jury: twelve bored-looking men; the only people in the whole of London, it seemed, who had no interest in this trial. Once in the jury box, one – who looked a little like Loveday, minus his smoking hat – started inspecting his pocket watch, as though anxious to get proceedings over with; another began doodling, perhaps sketching, on some loose leaves; still others were merely slumped in despond. All looked faintly resentful at having had their time taken up with this trial when they could have been using it more gainfully, trading on the 'Change or otherwise attending to their affairs. From their temper, Stoker suspected a verdict might be delivered that day.

Another usher now stood up and screeched, 'Silence in court!' The rumpus behind Stoker abated. 'All rise for the judge, Mr Justice Hawking!' There was a shuffling of feet and a scraping of chairs as in came a short fat man wearing a scarlet robe and long rolling white wig that reached almost to his waist. Quickly seated, the judge tapped his gavel on the sounding block with his pork butcher's hands and, in a surprisingly deep voice, declared the court in session. For an instant Stoker detected a faint sneer on the judge's lips that reminded him of Irving.

'Well, Mr Johnson,' began the judge, 'do you have any more witnesses for the defence?' The old lawyer twitched but said nothing.

'I repeat,' demanded Hawking, 'do you have any more witnesses?' Johnson shook his head.

'No, your Honour.'

'Look harder! Look harder!' Stoker turned to his right to see the accused, now on his feet, and shaking visibly. 'I'm telling you, look harder! Where is he, you fool?' he continued with increasing agitation, and it seemed the young aristocrat would have jumped over the wood panelling which enclosed the dock had it not been for the two policemen who grabbed him then pinioned him on the floor. The penny stinkards were now agasp as the press men muttered frantically among themselves – all except Stead, whose now-seated profile Stoker could clearly discern from his vantage. 'I'm telling you!' screeched Drayfield. 'Look—'

'Silence in court!' roared the judge, battering his gavel on the sounding block. 'Do not add contempt of court to your charges, Lord Drayfield!'

'What kind of lawyer are you, Johnson? He's here – in London! Why is he not here, in court?' continued the lord regardless. And now Drayfield was hauled up by his minders, his hands cuffed behind his back, his mouth stifled by a third policeman with conveniently large hands. Still he attempted to scream. The judge once more addressed his defence counsel.

'Mr Johnson, can you vouch for the accused's good behaviour throughout the rest of this session?' Johnson again shook his head, in a gesture of abject defeat.

'I cannot, your Honour.'

'Very well then,' he continued, 'the trial must go on without him!' A startled murmuring overtook the gallery, the judge banging his gavel once more to silence the crowd. 'Take the accused down to the cells!' The jury, it seemed, was at last showing some interest, a few of them even hurriedly penning notes to one another.

Suddenly, Stoker heard a loud yelp: Drayfield had bitten the hand of one of the policemen. 'Look harder! Where is he, you fool?' the lord continued to scream as the two policemen now bundled him down the steps of the dock and into the cells, like the devilish Mephistopheles dragging the desperate Faust into hell. A murmuring, accompanied by the renewed waft of gin, recommenced from the benches behind Stoker.

'Silence in court!' roared the judge again. 'Now, if the defence has no more witnesses to call, I would like to call upon the prosecution to sum up its case.' Stoker saw Henstridge beam and the curving slope that connected his chin to his neck tauten inwards as he raised his portly frame, turned to Frobisher up in the gallery to make some obscure gesture which had the clerk grinning, then walked up to the jury box and began to address the jury.

Henstridge laid out the details of the case as follows. The body of the housemaid had been found at Lord Drayfield's Bayswater home in Dawson Street by his butler and housekeeper when they returned for work on the morning of Tuesday the third of April, and they had alerted the police. The housekeeper – a Mrs Prism

– had been away in Hackney, and the butler had, most unusually, been dismissed for the night. So, all had perfect alibis, did they not? Only his lordship had been in the house with the maid – a sure sign he had been planning some wicked offence against the unfortunate victim. And what an offence! The poor maid's body had been discovered with its head completely severed, a bizarre symbol like a rose carved on the forehead (here Stoker's ears pricked up); a symbol of the Freemasons, it transpired – an order of which his lordship was no doubt a member, and whose import he alone in the house would have known. The murder had been witnessed by a Mr Ponsonby, an engraver and man of most high repute – contrary to the defence's preposterous assertion that he was the same Ponsonby who had been accused of coining up in Aberdeen some fifteen or so years prior – who had been passing the house that evening and seen a kerfuffle, the curtains having been left open and the interior lamps blazing. He had assumed it was some amateur dramatics at play and so had not thought to inform the police until the true nature of events was revealed later, in the newspapers. Then there was the testimony of his lordship's doctor, who had broken professional confidence to disclose that the young aristocrat had approached him about illegally terminating the young maid's pregnancy – showing a clear and radiant motive for her murder. And then there was his lordship's attempt to blame an obscure cousin in far-off West Prussia for the crime. This gentleman, who Lord Drayfield claimed had been in London, and whom he had witnessed murdering the maid, had been unable to attend the trial owing to pressing business at home, but had in any case been quickly eliminated from enquiries as his description by the lord as being a lined and grey-headed individual had been revealed to be wildly inaccurate by officers from Scotland Yard, who had interviewed the man in Krakow – a city not too far distant from his native Danzig – just weeks after the murder. Finally, and most heinously (and here Henstridge grinned at Stead before reassuming his combative air), his lordship had tried to invoke his hereditary privilege of immunity from prosecution as Laird of Berwick-upon-Tweed. If that were not itself an admission of guilt, then what was?

Henstridge now turned triumphantly and waddled like a pantomime dame back to his seat. His immediate audience was well pleased with his performance, judging by the smiles on the jurymen's faces, but it was the penny stinkards behind Stoker who let forth a ripple of applause, soon quelled by the judge.

Was Stoker the only man in court to have seen how flawed Henstridge's summing-up had been? His reliance on testimonies by servants who could easily have murdered the girl themselves – the lawyer had not established that they had no motive; his failure to investigate the Rosicrucian order to which the lord belonged – mistaking it for the Masons; and his ill-judged reminder to the jury that Ponsonby was, according to the defence, a counterfeiter. Really, it was a complete farce, and Stoker was seriously beginning to question whether he wanted to remain in this buffoon's pupillage.

The defence counsel, Alfred Johnson, was met with sterner looks from the jury than Henstridge, but nevertheless attempted to be clear and spirited. The allegations against the accused, he asserted, were based on wholly unreliable and circumstantial evidence. The housekeeper's testimony could be countered by the fact that he himself had discovered that it was nigh on impossible for her – or indeed anyone else – to have left Hackney at three quarters past seven in the morning and entered the back door of his lordship's house in Bayswater some twenty minutes later, to discover the crime. As for Ponsonby, he was indeed the same man who had been arrested and accused of coining in Aberdeen some fifteen years prior; that he had never been prosecuted was on account of the principal witness, his partner, having drowned in suspicious circumstances before the police could apprehend him, and it was only to be regretted that these same police had not bothered to take a photograph of the suspect – as was the protocol in England – and had spelled his name P-U-N-S-A-N-B-A-Y, as could only be expected from people who spoke the Doric tongue (here some members of the jury managed a chuckle, despite the feeble nature of the joke). It was also to be regretted that none of the police who had arrested Ponsonby fifteen years before was still alive to bear witness to his detention, the last having died in an unfortunate accident in Scotland just before his client's trial had begun. His lordship's visit to the doctor, admittedly, had been an error of judgement, but there was no suggestion that his lordship was the father of the unborn child, as the doctor himself readily conceded when questioned. Indeed, there was no suggestion that his lordship was doing anything other than trying to help a young, wayward servant – and he certainly had no record of violence against women. As to the symbol incised on the dead maid's forehead, this could easily have been reproduced by someone who wished to cast suspicion on the lord himself, whether that were her real lover – who had not been traced – the butler, or even Ponsonby himself. Who knows, they might all have had a motive!

And here Johnson sighed as he saw the jurymen's faces harden. He did regret, he now continued, that his client had insisted on blaming the crime on an obscure cousin who, living in a country far from fair Albion, had felt no obligation to abandon his business affairs and speed to London to clear his name. That the lord insisted on blaming this man, when his description so clearly did not tally with that provided by the officers of Scotland Yard sometime later, after they had interviewed him in Krakow, or the artist's impression produced by their draughtsman – an impression which revealed a much younger man than the lined and grey-headed individual described by his lordship – was simply due to his lordship's whimsical understanding of the world and his own high-spirited youth, making him exaggerate the years of others. While the defence no longer believed that this man, his lordship's cousin, was responsible for the murder, this did not validate the flimsy argument put forward by the prosecution, which had failed to establish any proof beyond a reasonable doubt – let that be remembered, *a reasonable doubt* – as to the guilt of the accused; a fact that could surely not in any way be dislodged from the minds of the members of the jury who were, he was sure, all decent, law-abiding Englishmen, with honest hearts and open minds.

The barrister turned, with some resignation, to regain his seat, as the hubbub rose again. Frobisher now turned to Stoker and gave him a thumbs-up, his ferret-like eyes twitching. It beggared belief, thought Stoker, that neither the prosecution nor the defence had investigated the possible motivation of the servants – and was the housekeeper's arrival at Lord Drayfield's house in such record speed in itself not deeply suspect? Was that not obvious? Both sides had been utterly blindsided, he could tell: the prosecution by its easy reliance on the circumstantial evidence, the defence by its easy reliance on Drayfield's testimony regarding the cousin from Prussia. But it was not just the lawyers who had been blindsided; the whole of London had been. The desire to skewer an aristocrat in retribution for the Liza affair had obsessed the do-gooding middle classes to the point where no one – not the press, the police, the judiciary or rabble of stinkards behind him – was prepared to look at the evidence objectively or entertain the possibility that the arrogant young lord might be innocent.

Under such circumstances an unbiased summing-up from the judge might have gone some way towards supporting Johnson's plea to the jury to maintain a reasonable doubt, but Judge Hawking was not prepared to allow any such fair judicial practice to hinder his performance – and played to both box and gallery. Stoker could see the upturned corner of Stead's mouth as he listened approvingly to the judge's support for Henstridge's argument: who says that a woman in a speedy hansom cannot reach Bayswater from Hackney in twenty minutes? What proof was there that Ponsonby was the same Ponsonby who had been arrested for coining in Aberdeen? And why would a man seek to avoid prosecution by invoking some archaic byelaw if he believed himself to be innocent, etc, etc? The judge was playing to the crowd like one of the ham actors at the

Adelphi, and Stoker felt ashamed to have seen any resemblance between this ridiculous individual and his governor at the Lyceum.

Once the judge had restated the case for the prosecution, he adjourned the court with what amounted to firm directions to measure a length of waxed rope for the accused. Henstridge swiped a pen from a begrudging Arbuthnot, signed some papers, and then turned round to look up at the gallery, his eyes popping out at Stoker and Frobisher with a look of triumph. He made an eating gesture at the two men and Frobisher smiled broadly.

'Care to partake of some luncheon over the road, Mr Stoker?' he called up to the gallery. 'You too, Mr Arbuthnot,' he added, turning back to his solicitor. Being famished, Stoker readily agreed, and soon all four men were making their way down the steps of the Bailey, pushing through the raucous crowd of top-hatted idlers and monocled sadists in their path.

CHAPTER IV

THE RED LION

The eating room upstairs at the Red Lion was a haven of calm after the excitable scenes that had greeted Stoker, Frobisher, Arbuthnot and Henstridge as they left the Bailey. Nonetheless, it was no doubt to the good that there were coloured glass and mahogany dividers to sequester the small snug in which the men were now established, tucking into pork chops and parsnips, washed down with glasses of claret. Greed and Want were attacking their food in keeping with their exemplary appearances, with Henstridge picking up the pork in a most indecorous fashion (well, there were no ladies present) and Arbuthnot cutting up tiny morsels before placing them into his narrow mouth. The two men had so far said nothing to one another; indeed, Henstridge had been uncharacteristically subdued – his feelings of relief now perhaps equal to those of triumph. Frobisher, meanwhile, was smiling on blithely, twitching his eyes and occasionally sneezing into the back of his chair. He knew when to speak to his master, and when not.

As he gorged himself, Henstridge became visibly livelier, his eyes lightening. Eventually he heaved a contented sigh and pushed his plate away, then reached over and poured himself another glass of claret, draining the bottle. Arbuthnot looked on with a glimmer of contempt in his eyes but said nothing. Stoker, meanwhile, offered Henstridge some snuff, in an attempt to engage his attention (he hated the stuff himself, keeping the box purely as a social ice-breaker) – an invitation predictably declined. He then asked his mentor a question.

'Tell me, Mr Henstridge, when do you think the jury will deliver a verdict?' Henstridge laughed out loud.

'Well, I don't mean to sound cocky, Bram, but I am hoping for a positive verdict today.'

'Indeed?'

'Yes, of course! You heard my closing argument,' he replied, taking a swig of wine. Arbuthnot simply kept his thin lips pursed. Perhaps he shared the same misgivings as Stoker?

'But surely,' persisted Stoker, 'this man Ponsonby was an unreliable witness, and the servants might have been lying also? Isn't that at least grounds for reasonable doubt for the jury?' Frobisher threw a ferret's glance towards Stoker, looking as though he might for once offer a few words and be the conciliatory Coventry Patmore of the hour. Henstridge, meanwhile, merely removed a silver case from his jacket pocket and, without offering its contents to any of the others, took out a cigar, lit it from the candlestick in front of him, and let his frog-like throat convulse at the inhalation of smoke.

'You are absolutely right, Bram,' he replied at last. 'This is all not beyond the bounds of possibility. It is certainly not beyond a man like Ponsonby to have been a coiner in his past and wish to deny it now, although that does not mean he did not see what he saw; a man who lies in one situation may not necessarily mouth untruths in another. And it is certainly possible that the housekeeper's testimony has some holes in it – well, if she were to lose her position now, would she, or indeed the butler, want it known that they were in any way unreliable? That would hardly speed them into new employment after the loss of their present employer, would it?'

'Oh, come now, that cannot be the reason—'

'But, I grant you,' resumed Henstridge more forcefully, 'you are right in thinking that their testimonies do not quell any reasonable doubt that Lord Drayfield is guilty.'

'Well then,' said Stoker, leaning forward and clasping his hands together in a gesture of assertion, 'why are you still so certain the jury will convict?'

'Because,' said Henstridge, flopping his jowls in a most disagreeable manner towards Stoker and fixing him in a bulbous stare, 'one thing that is *not* beyond reasonable doubt is that Lord Drayfield himself is lying! He has attempted to blame the crime upon some obscure cousin who has likely been nowhere near London for years, and whom he cannot even describe accurately. If a man is claiming that another man has committed murder, when he clearly has not, it is worse than saying he knows nothing at all. This has destroyed his lordship's credibility and leaves the jury with no choice but to convict!'

Here Arbuthnot uttered a hollow laugh and looked most uncomfortable, while Frobisher returned quietly to eating his meal. Shapes were moving past the coloured glass dividers of their cubicle like phantasmagoria in a magic lantern show, giving form to the unspoken agitation Stoker had unleashed on the party.

'Was this other person the man whom his lordship was referring to when he was in contempt of court, when he was telling his counsel to "look harder"?' ventured Stoker. Henstridge choked on a large slurp of wine, and even Frobisher could not suppress a snigger.

'My word, Bram, what kind of barrister-in-waiting are you?' spluttered Henstridge. 'Have you really not even been reading the newspapers? He was referring to his cousin's name, *Lucarda*, spelt L-U-C-A-R-D-A, the man he is blaming for this bizarre, cult-style death. He could not even describe him properly, getting his age completely wrong.'

Stoker was momentarily confused.

'So, are you suggesting the two men never met?' he resumed, hoping the others had not noticed his discomfiture.

'Well, clearly, they have not,' replied Henstridge.

At this point there was a tap on a mahogany divider and there appeared Stead, his cheeks as gleaming with joy as his eyes behind the lenses of his little round glasses. His frame was wrapped entirely in grey flannel below his Eton collar, and he looked for all the world as though he were off to the races.

'What a performance, Henstridge!' he announced, nodding to Stoker out of recognition as he did so. 'Care to—'

'Now, now,' interrupted the barrister, with cheerful remonstrance, 'you know the law, Will. Won't be saying nowt till the trial's over.'

'Well, let's hope the jury comes up with a verdict today. Wouldn't want that madman in Whitechapel bumping you off the front page, now would we?'

'Heaven forbid!' exclaimed Henstridge, stubbing out his barely touched cigar and making a grab for Stoker's snuff box. 'Can't think I'll be getting a case as eye-catching as this for some time if he does!' So, this was what Frobisher had been talking about earlier when referring to Henstridge's hopes of a swift verdict. The clerk gave Stoker a knowing smile, as if to confirm his apprehension.

'Anyhow, a capital performance. Capital!' Stead now cocked his walking stick to his brow in mock salute and left.

'Yes, capital,' muttered Stoker beneath his breath once he had gone. His thoughts now returned to Lord Drayfield, counting down the minutes in his cell. 'I suppose, gentlemen, there'll be only one sentence in a case such as this.'

'Afraid so, but none of our concern,' returned Henstridge, taking a pinch of snuff from Stoker's box and arching his neck as if in readiness for a sneeze.

'Perhaps it is,' came a voice to Stoker's left. Want had finally spoken, just as Greed was about to turn sideways and clear his nostrils over the back of his chair, instead of which he now sneezed out the candle before him, wobbling the candlestick in the process.

Henstridge began choking out the words, 'Eh? What do you mean, Mr Arbuthnot?' Arbuthnot's thin lips parted.

'Now I must defend Mr Stoker by accusing *you*, Mr Henstridge, of not reading the newspapers.'

'I don't understand you, Sir.'

'What I mean is that, apparently, another solicitor acting for Lord Drayfield has identified a second law relating to his status as Laird of Berwick. This is no immunity from prosecution, but another law, stating that he, as Laird, cannot be "punished by the Sovereign of Scotland".'

'Well, what of it?' breathed Henstridge, with the artless assurance of a general who believes a thick forest can be magicked away before his advancing army. 'This does not relate to English law – unlike that other absurd piece of legislation we got the Lords to repeal.'

'I'm afraid that it does. If the "Sovereign of Scotland" should still exist, any archaic byelaw from Scots law that covers an area within what is now England can be argued to be legal within English law. And that is the argument Carruthers will be presenting to the High Court tomorrow – or so this says.'

And here Arbuthnot produced a crumpled newspaper article, torn from an inside page of *The Star* – a piece the editor had clearly considered insignificant compared to the trial itself. Henstridge grabbed the article and read it aloud in a monotone. This latest defence was presented, even by the journalist himself, as a last-ditch attempt by Lord Drayfield to save his neck – the law in question bound to be repealed, however unamused the 'Sovereign of Scotland' herself might be at seeing a peer of her realm sent to the scaffold.

'Even if this law does exist,' now declared Henstridge, laying the article aside, 'and even if the High Court rules that it does apply, as the paper so rightly says, the Commons and Lords will repeal it just like they did the last one. We'll just have to wait a little longer for the sentence to be passed, that's all.' He took another swig of wine, seemingly unconcerned about the possibility of staggering into court or slurring his words before the judge. 'Not really a problem, do you think, Mr Frobisher?'

'None whatsoever, Sir,' replied the clerk, for once not hesitating to reply.

'After all, if they don't hang him, it will enrage the hoi polloi,' resumed Henstridge, his eyes now turned towards the ceiling. 'And all the more limelight for us, don't you think, Bram?'

Stoker looked at his mentor with ill-concealed disdain, but before he could muster a reply, a sudden rap on a snug divider announced the arrival of a court usher, who informed the party that the jury had reached a verdict. The four men immediately got up and hurried downstairs, to discover the whole of the Red Lion in uproar – tipplers at the bar jostling to shake the two lawyers' hands, like spectators at a cricket match looking to greet two batsmen out of the pavilion after tea, all set to finish off the opposing side. Having finally gained the cloakroom, Henstridge donned his wig and gown while Stoker and the others put on their coats and retrieved their various sundries. Soon all four men were stepping across the road towards the Bailey, desperately trying to dodge the penny stinkards now too far gone on gin to be admitted back into court.

Once inside, Stoker and Frobisher found seats next to each other in the gallery, close to the jury – not one of whom had his eyes directed towards the accused; himself restored to his former calm. The usher now announced the arrival of Judge Hawking, who trotted in and slammed his gavel on the sounding block, demanding silence from the unruly crowd.

'Is there a spokesman for the jury?'

A tall man in a striped waistcoat stood up and announced that it was he.

'How do you find the accused charged with murder: guilty or not guilty?'

The man paused to glare at Lord Drayfield. He then turned back to the judge.

'Guilty, your Honour.' A wave of joy erupted across the court, with hats thrown into the air in a display of contempt so widespread that, for once, Hawking did not attempt to restrain it. Stoker saw Henstridge make a grab for Arbuthnot's hands in a surge of triumph, only to see the solicitor reject this advance by muttering something indecipherable and wrapping his arms tightly around his bony frame. Drayfield himself remained unmoved, save for a faint quivering of his nostrils, as if from anger.

At last the cheering subsided, and the judge slammed down his gavel. He seemed keen to bring this rumbustious trial to an end, and Stoker felt sure that he – unlike, no doubt, Henstridge – would not be dining out on the day's proceedings in a gentleman's club later that evening.

'Very well,' declared Hawking. 'Take the prisoner to his place of confinement until the day of his sentencing.'

'It was Lucarda, you fools, not me!' screamed Lord Drayfield suddenly. 'He said that she would live again! I tried to stop him, but he pushed me away saying that she would surely live again – and now he cannot be found and has left me to face the rope! It was not me, your Honour. I did not kill her!' Drayfield showed no fear, only the righteous indignation of an aristocrat who feels he has been wronged by his inferiors.

'Take him away, before he sullies his name further!' commanded the judge. And with that the policemen once again bundled the lord down the steps of the dock, this time meeting no resistance from the accused.

Stoker wasted no time in leaving this macabre theatre, with its morbid spectacle and barbarous audience, for the more sympathetic one in which he worked – happy to attend to the business that awaited him there and relieve Grafton and Loveday of their duties.

From the wings that evening, having earlier finished a mountain of correspondence and personally greeted several distinguished playgoers, including the Duke of Edinburgh, Stoker took the opportunity of watching Irving once more in the final Act of *The Bells*, when Mathias is confronted in a dream by an imaginary judge charging him with the murder of Koveski. As always, Stoker marvelled at the proficiency with which the Guv'nor performed his role – the spasms in his cheek every time he was accused, and the sweat which seemed to arrive at will when under imagined scrutiny. Observing Irving like this convinced Stoker of Drayfield's innocence all the more, the Guv'nor's portrayal of Mathias's attempts to conceal his feelings of guilt being so far removed from the complete lack of guile that Henstridge's victim had displayed. Taking a peek from the wings at the auditorium was also salutary: here were the Lyceum's playgoers watching the Guv'nor with compassion and awe, and none of the barbarity that he had witnessed from the carrion-baggers at the Bailey earlier.

As ever, his life at the theatre was instructive, and he took this thought away with him as he headed home after another long day.

Back in his study, answering mail around half past ten that evening, Stoker noticed once again his copy of *The Chymical Wedding*, edging its way out of the bookshelf. He got up from his desk and went to retrieve it, the day's events having piqued his interest for a particular passage. Soon he was rereading the allegorical account of Rosenkreutz's experiences on the fourth of his seven days of initiation. This described how, having been summoned to the Castle to attend a royal wedding, Rosenkreutz witnesses six royal persons – both old and young – being beheaded, their bodies then being sent on ships by the Virgin of the Castle to the island tower of Olympus where, on the sixth day, the young king and queen are reborn. Stoker had dimly recollected this passage when he heard Lord Drayfield shout from the dock, 'He said that she would live again!' What if this Lucarda really had been with Drayfield, and in similar fashion beheaded the maid, he himself being a Rosicrucian? Indeed, what if he had framed his cousin for the crime? That would fit Lord Drayfield's version of events. He certainly believed that Drayfield was innocent of the actual murder – 'I did not kill her!' – and was, in whatever way possible, telling the truth, despite all the evidence to the contrary.

Suddenly, Stoker's train of thought was interrupted by the loud 'ting' of the doorbell, and he heard Emma patter through the hallway towards the vestibule. Who could be so unthinking as to call on him at this hour? He put the book back in its slot on the shelf and sat back behind his desk, assuming a posture of earnest labour over his correspondence. He was determined to hurry off his visitor with a show of industry, and purposefully dimmed his lamp.

His humour quickly improved, however, when he found himself shaking the hand of his brother, still clad in his overcoat and clutching his hat, indicating that this would be a short visit.

'My word, frater,' exclaimed Stoker. 'What brings you back to fair Chelsea so soon? Emma, could you bring the decanter of whiskey?'

'No need, Bram,' said George, waving his hand in dismissal. 'I won't be staying long this time. Just came to tell you what happened today.' He settled his tall physique on the small button-backed armchair adjacent his brother's desk and exhaled. 'Before I forget, though, did you have a good day yourself?' The door shut behind the retreating Emma.

'Not really,' replied Stoker, returning to behind his desk and scratching his beard. 'Believe it or not, but I was at what proved to be the last day of the Drayfield trial.'

'My word,' cried George, half-laughing. 'Did the Guv'nor really let you have a day off? I thought he had you chained to your desk!' Stoker was a little taken aback by the tone of his brother and, for once, did not respond.

'Tell me, was it a fine experience?' George now continued, more seriously.

'I can't say that it was,' replied Stoker, turning up his lamp. 'To see an innocent man go down with all the wolves of London baying for his blood.'

'You don't really believe that he's innocent, do you,' said George leaning forward, 'after all the evidence against him?'

'I'm afraid that I do,' replied Stoker after a brief pause. 'His defence did not do its job properly – and he had no chance in the court of public opinion!'

'Ah,' said George. 'Well, I'm afraid he'll get no mercy, that's for sure.'

'Indeed not,' said Stoker. He was about to mention the curious matter of the Berwick-upon-Tweed lairdship that might yet spare Drayfield the rope but thought better of it; he'd had enough of this shameful affair for one day.

'Anyhow,' he continued, 'tell me your news, George. Off on any new campaigns? Been asked to take your expertise back to the Himalayas?'

'No, no, nothing like that,' laughed his brother. 'Just to let you know, though, that I went against your advice, Bram – and don't regret it one jot!' Stoker joined nervously in the laughter.

'Well, it wouldn't be the first time, young man! What did you do?'

'Well,' said George, 'I finally let my conscience get the better of me and went to Scotland Yard.'

'What?' said Stoker, trying to suppress his anxiety. 'Did you tell them about the blood?'

'Yes. And because I mentioned Sir Arthur's name, they were assured I was a gentleman, and the sergeant promised not to put anything down in his pocketbook. The name of a gentleman goes a long way, it seems, even in these reprobate times.' Stoker looked at his brother with a growing sense of relief: it seemed the police were not going to investigate matters further. Still, even if they did, he was beginning to feel that the events in his theatre and his brother's surgery were less and less connected.

'Anyway,' continued George, 'I described the incident and the man's appearance, and they assured me that it could not have been the man who committed that last Whitechapel murder.'

'They're sure?'

'Positive. The report the police made public withheld a vital detail on purpose: the last victim had traces of the culprit's hair in her fingers when they discovered her corpse – dark hair, dark as the night. My villain had grey hair, grey as iron.'

'Well, that's a relief,' said Stoker.

'Good to know I haven't been protecting a murderer... well, not that murderer anyway!'

'Yes,' said Stoker slowly, running his finger over his top lip. George had been expecting a more enthusiastic response from his brother and felt somewhat crestfallen.

'Well,' he said at last, consulting his watch, 'I'd better see if I can get the last of those stinking Underground trains back to Pimlico.'

'George, it's been most pleasant to hear your news. Some comfort, at least, on a day that I have otherwise found most wretched.' Stoker rose, followed by George, and the brothers shook hands. He walked to the door then ushered George out into the hallway, pausing to give the long-bearded man a firm but silent handshake.

'Take care, Bram. Shall we meet again soon?' asked George.

'I certainly hope so,' replied Stoker. 'I'll let you know, by post.'

Once George had gone, Stoker returned to his desk and tidied his correspondence away. It had been a most depressing day; a reacquaintance with the ignoble theatre of justice.

'He said that she would live again!' A pity that she hadn't, mused Stoker, before extinguishing the lamp and once more climbing the stairs to join his beautiful, but increasingly morose, wife.

CHAPTER V

A PECULIAR BARBER

A week or so later Stoker was entering the theatre when he came upon an unexpected visitor. Sitting on the plush red velvet seating in the foyer, close to the stairs to the gallery, was a small but immaculately dressed young man with round glasses, an oval face, and winged collar. He was perched over his cane, whose tip was inserted between his heels, his knees slightly parted, making him appear quite symmetrical. His whole comportment was apprehensive, betraying the importance with which he judged his presence there. Beside him, next to his hat, was what looked like a blue leather file. The visitor's face lit up the moment he saw Stoker, just as Stoker's own face fell – for he did indeed know who the young man was. What favour was he going to ask of him now? Placing his cane on the velvet upholstery, the man stood up and approached Stoker to shake his hand.

'Good morning, Mr Stoker. It really is a great pleasure to see you – and looking so well.'

'Likewise, Mr Zangwill, likewise,' said Stoker in return, releasing his hand from the young man's grip.

'I have been meaning to pay you and Mr Irving a visit for some time but, as you know, I have been rather busy. You have heard of the success of my latest novel?' Stoker recalled that Zangwill's second book had indeed been greeted with a few positive reviews in arts magazines edited by the likes of Henley – and had even made a few shillings for one or two booksellers. But this was of little concern for a man such as he, who dined regularly with the likes of Tennyson and Patmore.

'Yes, yes, most impressive. I wish you all the best,' he replied.

Zangwill now allowed his narrow mouth to form a wide crescent – clearly failing to grasp the faintness of Stoker's praise. 'You know I have had a play accepted at a theatre in Stepney. I was wondering whether you and Mr Irving would like to see it.'

'Which theatre is that?' replied Stoker briskly. 'I'm not sure the Yiddish one—'

'No, no,' said Zangwill, flushing with embarrassment. 'This is a *new* theatre, dedicated to new and more challenging works – in English! Please do come and see my play if you can.'

'I'm afraid it's unlikely that either myself or Mr Irving will have the time,' replied Stoker, pointedly consulting his fob watch. 'And, as you know, we only ever put on performances by writers who are, how shall I put it, already of some renown.' He looked back at Zangwill to see the young man's mouth collapse in disappointment. A pang of compunction stabbed Stoker: he was at heart no bully and it pained him to cause distress in others.

'Of course,' he went on, 'I am sure that in a few years' time we will be knocking furiously on your door, competing with London's most illustrious theatres for your plays.' Zangwill's eyes lit up from under the thick glass of his spectacles.

'Well, Mr Stoker, why not make an advance on those competitors by reading my latest work now?' To Stoker's annoyance, the young man spun round and picked up the blue file from the velvet seating before practically thrusting it into his hands. His countenance was beaming anew. 'It is based on my novel, *The Premier and the Painter*.'

'Well, I suppose we could take a look,' replied Stoker, trying not to reveal his disappointment at his own indiscipline.

'You will, I say with quite some confidence, Sir, be most impressed,' continued Zangwill, his face now embarrassingly close to Stoker's own, the pupils of his eyes forming two black pits behind his glass lenses – an impression that unsettled the acting manager enormously.

As Stoker was searching for something to say, he suddenly noticed a dark figure, like some monstrous bat, loom as a reflection in Zangwill's glasses. He turned to see a tall man with a glowering face, jet black hair protruding from under a felt top hat, and a leather bag from under a cloaked right arm, flapping his way precipitously down the gallery stairs into the foyer. So violent was his demeanour that the red-headed man in the box office, Mr Palfrey, and the two workmen mending part of the skirting board further off, could not help but stop what they were doing and watch as the outsized bat scurried out of the foyer into the street, affording one of those rare occasions when onlookers can be sure they have been touched by a rare shade of evil. After the man had gone, Stoker turned back to see Zangwill's face contorted with fear. The young man made a pitch to grab Stoker's arm, which Stoker deftly avoided.

'Mr Stoker,' he said in a quivering voice, 'do you know who that creature is?'

'Well, Mr Zangwill,' replied Stoker. 'I've not yet met him, but I imagine it's Mr Irving's new barber, whose services he asked me to procure recently. Why, do you know him?' Zangwill nodded earnestly.

'Yes, yes,' he replied in an agitated whisper. 'And I can tell you that Mr Irving must dismiss him, immediately!'

'Why so?' asked Stoker, rubbing his top lip with his finger nervously: he was dreading some new aggravation.

'Sir, he is a most dangerous man; quite possibly mad. His name is Aaron Kosminski. He used to attend our synagogue in Bethnal Green, but he attacked two women of the congregation in the vestibule on two separate occasions and has been forbidden from ever worshipping there again by our rabbi, Samuel Breslau.'

Stoker felt the blood in his veins tingle: having such an individual in attendance was the last thing he or the theatre needed.

'Have you told the police about him?' asked Stoker all of a sudden. Zangwill's mouth crumpled.

'That is for the rabbi to do, not me,' he replied.

'Yes, well,' said Stoker, recalling his and the Guv'nor's own recent omissions in that regard, 'thank you for letting me know. I shall tell Mr Irving.' The two men shook hands, as Zangwill now returned to his former cheer. He wished Stoker goodbye and, grabbing his hat and cane, stepped lightly through the foyer doors and out into the bright September sunshine, leaving Stoker with yet another tiresome play to read, and doubtless reject.

Back up in his office, as Stoker's eyes once more met those of the monstrous Metal Man in the harbour at Rosses Point, his thoughts returned to the monstrous bat he had just encountered in the foyer downstairs. Suddenly, Stoker determined to ask Irving why he had made him procure the services of such a villain as a barber. He marched down the corridor and, having rapped on the Guv'nor's dressing room door, was beckoned by a drawling 'En... ter!'

Stoker crossed the threshold to see Irving sitting at his dressing table, his head buried in a battered-looking book. The room contained the usual paraphernalia of props crammed in chests, tubs of greasepaint on shelves, and numerous costumes, including that worn by Irving's character in *The Bells*, Mathias, hanging from wheeled wooden trellises. What was less usual, Stoker noted, was a peculiarly patterned blue and orange shawl he had not seen before, lying half-crumpled in front of an ottoman. Despite the general clutter of the room, Irving rarely allowed anything to litter the floor and, among the few garments he did maintain close to him, none was usually out of place. Stoker could see that the shawl had been used by Kosminski to catch the Guv'nor's hair – and had probably been discarded by him in his apparent haste to leave. The thought of the bat Kosminski applying scissors to the Guv'nor's head – to any man's head – rattled his entire being. Stoker cleared his throat.

'Is everything set for tonight's performance, Bram? No double-bookings, I trust?' asked Irving, setting down his book on the dressing table to admire his new haircut in the mirror, and not remotely deigning to turn round and face his acting manager or invite him to sit down on the small plush armchair he habitually reserved for visitors.

'None whatsoever, Guv'nor. I have even made sure that the Prince of Bulgaria is several boxes away from his sworn enemy, the Russian Count Oblovsky. Neither man need ever know the other is there!' Here Irving laughed and swivelled round in his chair towards Stoker.

'Good! We don't want to get involved in brokering yet more peace treaties – like we did between the Russians and the Ottomans – do we? Yes, I think that one in Berlin some years back should do for now!' This time Stoker laughed. There was a pause as Irving swivelled round again and went back to admiring his new cut; Irving only rarely wore wigs, his sloping 'plume of pride' being one of his most cherished features.

Stoker decided to broach the matter at hand.

'Look, Sir, I was meaning to ask you why you made me procure the services of that peculiar barber from Bow.'

Irving turned around abruptly in his chair. 'I mean,' continued Stoker, 'I was just talking to Israel Zangwill in the foyer—'

'Oh no, not Zangwill!' exclaimed Irving, rolling his eyes ceiling-wards. 'Still trying to foist his worthless scribblings on us?'

'I'm afraid so,' replied Stoker, shaking his head. 'However, he did have some useful information to impart.'

'There's a first time for everything, I suppose. What might that be?'

'He was telling me some rather disturbing details about your new barber, Aaron Kosinski.'

'*Kosminski*,' corrected Irving. Stoker thought he heard the costume trellises tremble.

'Yes, Kosminski. Well, the Israelite wanted to warn us—'

'Bram, will you please refrain from using that term, common parlance though it may be!' Irving's stare was now more than emphatic, betraying both steep irritation and anger. Stoker flushed with embarrassment, then immediately flushed again as he recalled the Guv'nor's particular sympathy for the Jewish people – a sympathy which had informed his revolutionary portrayal of Shylock as tragic victim, not villain.

'Sorry, Sir,' continued Stoker. 'I did not mean to offend. I mean the young man.'

'That's better. Pray continue.'

'Well, the young man tells me that this barber is a most dangerous individual, possibly insane; that he has attacked two women of the congregation at his synagogue and been forbidden from ever worshipping there again by the rabbi. He certainly looks as though he is of unsound mind to me.' Irving now laughed, slapping his hands on his knees.

'Really, I would not believe the gossip of an excitable fellow like Zangwill.'

'I do not believe him to be lying, Sir,' continued Stoker, feeling the need to back up his assertion.

'Oh, come now, Bram. He's probably made a pass at some ladies and the rabbi has taken offence. I'm sure he is a damn sight better behaved than most of the players in our company – and he's a damn fine barber, I can say that! It was Gatti who alerted me to him, having used his services at the Adelphi for some years. He seems to have all sorts of techniques for adding lustre to my sadly greying locks.' Stoker now looked at the Guv'nor plainly. Setting aside his surprise at Irving's mention of his rival, Gatti, and the Adelphi, as far as he could see, the Guv'nor had received no more from the barber's two-handed exertion than a levelling of his grizzled mane. Stoker's resolve was, however, wavering, and he decided not to pursue matters further.

'Besides,' continued the Guv'nor, swivelling back to his dressing table and picking up his book once more, 'we have far more immediate worries.'

'Of what kind, Sir?' asked Stoker.

'I will let Ellen tell you when she comes in, as they more closely concern her – or rather, her son.'

'What might they be?' persisted Stoker.

'Bram,' responded Irving with some irritation, setting down his opened book and turning around again, 'I am currently occupied with some urgent research, as you can see. Please go and attend to your correspondence!' And with that he swivelled back to his dressing table, determinedly smoothed down the thin page of heavy Gothic print before him, and resumed reading.

Back in his office a few hours later, Stoker was attending to some requests for seats and boxes by notables for the last week of *The Bells* when there was a sharp rap on the door. He opened it to see the grey-bonneted form of Miss Edith Craig, Edward's older sister, the tight lace collar at her neck and tight-lipped smile on her face immediate signs of *noli me tangere* – signs as apparent to a middle-aged married man such as Stoker as to a man-about-town in his twenties. Edith – a serious, somewhat gruff young woman, who preferred the company of her female 'best friends' (as Miss Terry called them) to that of her male suitors – stood in marked contrast to her mother, who often seemed quite perplexed by her only daughter.

'Good afternoon, Mr Stoker,' she said, stepping unbidden over the threshold. 'I really need to speak with you.'

'Good afternoon, Miss Craig,' Stoker replied, shaking her hand. 'Well, this truly is an unexpected pleasure. How may I help you?' Without removing her gloves, Edith withdrew an envelope from her coat pocket and handed it to him. The envelope bore the unmistakeable handwriting of Miss Terry, and appeared not to have been sealed.

'This is a letter from my mother, who cannot herself come in before the performance, and needs your assistance, urgently!' She snorted and gave him a look of what seemed like defiance.

'Can I not discuss it with her after the performance?'

'No. You must act at once, I fear.' Edith pursed her lips; and then she spoke again. 'It concerns Edward.'

'Really?' said Stoker. 'What has the young rascal done now?'

'I am afraid that he has left the school where he was confined after his latest... escapade, and we are not now sure where he is.'

'Well, what am *I* to do about it?' asked Stoker, stroking his beard as he studied Edith's pelican-like face, ensconced in its lace collar and grey bonnet. He could sense that she was already losing patience with him.

'That will all be explained in my mother's letter; I do not wish to detail it myself,' replied Edith with a huff. And then she continued. 'Are not men, particularly young men, tiresome beasts when it comes to their dalliances?' Stoker cringed at the effrontery of this young woman, imposing herself so brazenly in his office.

'Shakespeare did have something to say on the matter of men before their twenty-third year... although, with all due respect, women can cause their parents problems of a somewhat similar nature.' The quick fury with which Edith looked back at Stoker was like the rasp of a viper's tongue.

'You should have had the privilege of being raised by parents as frivolous and feckless as mine, Mr Stoker, before you have sympathy for them!' she declared, with all the righteous indignation of youth.

Stoker frowned.

'But, enough of that,' she continued. 'I'm afraid I cannot tarry as I need to attend an urgent meeting at the Women's Political Union – about the vote.'

'Well then, I must thank you for your time, Miss Craig,' said Stoker, trying not to sound sarcastic. 'Please don't let me delay you further.'

'Ha!' she tutted. 'If you only understood how important my work is – as does even Mama – you would not be so scornful.' And with that she turned on her heel and marched out of Stoker's office. Yes, poor Miss Terry, mused Stoker. What it was to have two such difficult children!

Stoker took the envelope to his bureau and released its contents, noting as he did so that it had in fact been torn open at its top rather than simply left unsealed. Why someone as meticulous as Miss Terry would have used such an envelope was baffling. Looking down, his puzzlement quickly resolved, for now he saw the envelope contained not one, but two, missives, by two different authors – one evidently stuffed in after the other. The larger piece of paper was touched with the crowded handwriting of Miss Terry herself; the smaller piece, in a hand he also recognised. Yes, it was Edward's! There was clearly one young man in this world whom Edith did not find tiresome, whatever her public protestations.

Out of a sense of protocol, Stoker picked up Miss Terry's letter first, to read the following.

My dear Mr Stoker,

It is with a heavy heart that I must inform you that Edward has absconded from Sedbergh and is now somewhere only our Maker knows. I am so disappointed in him, words almost fail me. I realise that the fault lies largely with myself for the somewhat bohemian way in which I brought up both him and his sister, but his lack of obedience is nonetheless quite astonishing.

Please, Mr Stoker, he must be found before he commits some new outrage which further imperils my name and that of the theatre. Can you please not discover him (I am sure that you can – having a gift for such things, I know, from Henry!) and then find him some work at an establishment in Dublin? I know that he would find it so much harder to behave badly there, what with the upright standards of our fellow Churchmen in your country, and the smallness of the town, depriving him of the opportunities London – a city to which, I fear, he may now have returned – so liberally affords to pursue his interests.

Please, we must act quickly!
Yours with gratitude,
Ellen Terry

Stoker put down the letter and rubbed his beard. He understood very well what Miss Terry meant by his 'gift'; indeed, the Guv'nor had asked him to keep an eye on the movements of his own teenaged son, Laurence, while at Marlborough College, just the year before. But why Miss Terry presumed he would be able to discover the whereabouts of her own son was, Stoker assumed, on account of his being Irish, and her belief that this afforded him some magic gateway to the most dissolute regions of London – this despite her professed regard for the upright standards of their 'fellow Churchmen' in his native isle.

Stoker now turned to the second missive. Edward's handwriting was scrawling, but the turquoise letterhead, 'Mr William Telbin, 5 Hereford Road, W.2', clearly legible. Stoker began to read.

Monday, 24th September

Dear Mr Stoker,

As Edith has probably told you, I have run away from Sedbergh. If you had suffered the treatment that was meted out there, it is my firm belief that you would have done just the same!

As you can see from the above address, I am staying in Bayswater with Mr Telbin, who is taking a huge risk by housing me – so please do not tell Mater that I am here, as I do not wish to be the cause of upset between my mentor, Mater and Mr Irving.

I know that you have visited Mr Telbin before, and that on a Tuesday or Wednesday mid-run you are not usually so busy, so could I possibly meet you here tomorrow, before you go to the theatre? Edy intimated that Mater thought you could find work for me outside London; and while I really

want to stay where I am, with Mr Telbin, I have no desire
to see Mater or Mr Irving for some time, particularly as I
understand from Edy that Mater has recently developed
some quite peculiar beliefs about me.

So, please do come and see me – and believe me when I
say I do not wish to be the cause of more trouble for you or
the theatre.

I remain yours respectfully,
Edward G. Craig

Stoker sighed. It seemed most unfair that a youth such as Edward was barred from the theatre he loved on account of his natural, if sometimes overzealous, passions while a monster such as Kosminski was welcomed into it with open arms. He glanced through the letter again and reflected that he might well find time to make a detour to Bayswater the following morning, before reaching the Lyceum, as planned, at noon. He opened his bureau drawer and withdrew some unheaded paper, then penned a quick reply to Edward, saying he would arrive in Hereford Road around ten the next morning. He sealed the note in an envelope and addressed it to 'E.G.C.' – Edward Gordon Craig – at Telbin's, and then affixed a stamp. If posted immediately, he realised, the note would reach the youth later that day, so hurriedly donning his frock coat and hat, Stoker set out to put it in a letterbox himself – not trusting any theatre flunky with the task, even with Edward's name curtailed to initials.

The Strand was washed in weak September sunlight as the usual cries of barrow-boys and hawkers rent the air. Having posted the letter, Stoker bought a copy of *The Star* from a newsboy screaming about a new twist in the Drayfield case. It seemed that the Lords had unexpectedly delayed debating the motion passed in the Commons some days before which would have finally allowed the 'Sovereign of Scotland' to condemn Lord Drayfield to the rope. Stoker's mouth relaxed into an involuntary smile:

perhaps fate would play an obliging hand in the young lord's fortunes after all.

~

Back up in his office, Stoker was attempting to complete his correspondence when there was a knock on his door – one he knew well.

'Come in, Mr Loveday,' he called out from behind his bureau. In came his stage manager, his grey head crowned by his trusty Armenian smoking hat, his hand clutching a lantern. He was wearing his familiar 'Soho' attire – a paisley satin waistcoat over bright green slacks – his extravagant clothes, as ever, belying his temperate nature. Stoker got up to shake his stage manager's hand, then stepped back a pace, conscious of his own superior height and eager not to intimidate his visitor.

'What can I do for you today, Sir?' asked Stoker.

'Have you heard about the rats in the cellar?' began Loveday.

'What do you mean? Haven't those traps killed them off?' replied Stoker (some five traps had been laid in the cellar by Grafton since that painful night some weeks before when Stoker had discovered the girl).

'There's dead rats aplenty, but not from those traps! I borrowed the key from Mr Grafton this morning, as I could smell something odd, and found about a dozen of them strewn all over the place. There was blood and brains everywhere, as if they had been dashed on the hard floor.'

Stoker was aghast – not just because of the rats but because Grafton was not allowed to lend his cellar key to anyone, not even Loveday.

'My word, I wonder what's killing them like that,' he replied at last.

'Well, maybe some cat, or even some super-rat. Whatever it is, as I say, it's not those traps!'

'Well, we'd best go down and take a look,' declared Stoker, still trying to assimilate Loveday's admission. 'But first, let me…,' and now he unbuttoned a waistcoat pocket and emerged with a long brass key.

Once downstairs, the two men made their way to the cellar and Stoker unlocked the door. Immediately, his nostrils were assailed by the noxious smell of musty air mingled with rotting flesh. Fighting a sudden desire to retch, he quickly withdrew a handkerchief from his trouser pocket and placed it over his mouth and nose before grabbing the lantern from Loveday and descending the few steps into the gloom. Loveday was right! The traps were all empty. As he waved the lantern further in, he saw that there were dead rats all over the floor – many with their brains dashed out, blood splattered around their necks. As he held the lantern higher, he noticed what looked like an assortment of blankets piled against a wall. Had these items been there before? He could not remember, but the stench from the rats gave him no desire to investigate further. Turning to leave, he saw Loveday in the cellar doorway, shaking his head solemnly. ''Pon my word, Mr Stoker,' he began, 'it's the strangest thing I've seen in all my years working in the theatre. It bodes no good, I can tell you.' Stoker shook his head; he had never succumbed to the superstitions in which virtually all other members of his profession, even Loveday, indulged.

'No,' he replied through his kerchief. 'As you say, it's probably some cat, or even some rat that's grown big on its grim diet. I'll get hold of some arsenic; that will kill them off and drive any others away.' Loveday looked genuinely shocked and scratched his brow beneath his smoking hat.

''Pon my word, Mr Stoker, how do you intend to do that?'

'Don't worry, Mr Loveday,' replied Stoker. 'I have my ways and means. Now, will you kindly ask a couple of stagehands to come down and clear up the carcasses – and make sure that they don leather gloves and kerchiefs. Let me know when they are finished, as really this catacomb should never be left unlocked, because of the gas.' Loveday shrugged his shoulders and nodded before turning to head back to the stage. Stoker, meanwhile, ascended the cellar steps and headed up to his office – determined to address the matter at hand immediately. Established once more at his bureau, he pulled out some unheaded letter paper for the second time that day and began writing.

Dear George,

I am writing in confidence about acquiring some arsenic poison. We have an unusual infestation of rats in the lights cellar, and no normal means will cure it. Please trust me on this; this is to kill rats, not humans, and we have no plans to ask Miss Emery to play Lucrezia Borgia any time soon!

Please write to me at my Chelsea address – not at the Lyceum, as this is private business – as soon as you are able and advise me; the theatre's survival could depend on it!

Yours ever,

Bram

Having placed the note in an envelope, Stoker's mood darkened as he recalled Loveday's admission: Grafton had betrayed both Stoker himself and the Guv'nor by giving the stage manager the key. And perhaps it was not the first time he had done such a thing? Perhaps he had given the key to young Edward? Whatever the case, this particular lapse could not go unremarked.

That evening Stoker was standing next to Grafton in the wings as he managed the gas pipes for the lights, his timing impeccable. Looking out into the auditorium, Stoker could distinguish the Prince of Bulgaria's box – the arrogant fool having draped his country's crest over its brocaded front to announce his presence. So much for trying to keep the prince's attendance unknown to his enemy, Count Oblovsky! Stoker now looked back at the stage, at Irving. Here was the Guv'nor, once again in the dream trial scene, pinioned by a solitary limelight as he attempted to evade the mesmerist who would bring him to reveal his crime. Once again, Stoker marvelled at the Guv'nor's performance, his low West Country tones exerting an almost hypnotic effect on the audience. The day was appearing to end well, and Stoker felt relieved.

Once the curtain had fallen and the players retired to their dressing rooms, the stagehands and flunkies busying themselves packing away the props and clearing the auditorium, Stoker tapped his lights manager on the shoulder as he bent over a footlight.

'What is it, Mr Stoker?'

'Aloysius, may I have a word with you?'

'Of course,' replied Grafton, peering anxiously through the lenses of his beloved pince-nez: summonses like this from the acting manager were rare, and thus troubling.

Having led the lights manager through to a space deep within the wings, so as to be out of earshot of any of the hands, Stoker wasted no time in making his complaint.

'Why did you lend Mr Loveday the key to the cellar today?' Grafton looked up at him with parted lips and wide eyes.

'Well, he wanted to go down there, he said, because he could smell something odd. I was busy with a leaky float, so I lent him my key. What is the problem?'

Stoker could barely contain himself.

'You know full well that only three people have the right to use those keys: you, me and Mr Irving. No one else, not even a man like Loveday, has the right to even touch them!' He could see Grafton's brow puckering in the half-light.

'But, Mr Stoker, I was busy, and someone had to attend to the smell,' he said. 'And you know how trustworthy he is.' Stoker now surprised himself with the vehemence of his tone.

'That is not the point! Only you, me and the Guv'nor know the layout of the pipes, and how dangerous the gas can be. If Mr Irving were to find out about this, you would be thrown out the door!' And with this he made a sweeping gesture with his arm, as if to reinforce his assertion. Grafton now looked as though he would cry. His lean face was cast down towards the floor as he wiped some steam off his pince-nez.

'I'm very sorry, Sir; it won't happen again.' Stoker sighed.

'And has it ever happened before?'

'No, just this once, and just today,' Grafton averred.

'Are you sure you never lent the key to Mr Telbin… or young Edward?' Grafton now looked back at him with near anger in his eyes.

'Bejesus no. To that young scoundrel? Of course not!'

'Are you sure?' Stoker pressed.

'Too right, I'm sure. As I say, it's just been this once I've lent the key out, always keeping it on my person – in my waistcoat or jacket pocket – as you told me to.' The conversation paused.

'Well, I'd like to believe you but I'm not sure that I can after what has happened today.'

The lights manager frowned.

'Yes, Mr Stoker, but while I may have broken house rules, I have not once lied, have I? Nor would I.' Stoker scratched his beard and reflected: Grafton certainly appeared bitterly offended that he had not believed him. He shook his head and laughed softly.

'No, that much is true. Well, let's hear no more on it, then. You'd best go back to your duties.'

Taking his cue, Grafton shrunk silently away. The bridge that Stoker had sought to build between the two of them, both from the same isle but from opposed peoples, had been destroyed with one unavoidable blow; he would have to work hard to repair it. Still, it would be worth the effort, he reflected, especially as he did in fact believe Grafton was telling the truth. Of course, the question of quite how the girl had got into the cellar remained. But that was a puzzle for another day, and within half an hour Stoker was in a cab, heading home to Chelsea.

~

As Stoker entered the dimly lit vestibule of his house at St Leonard's Terrace and handed his sundries to his beaming housemaid, Emma, an unexpected but familiar voice called to him from the drawing room.

'My dear, is that you?' The light brogue of his wife tingled disagreeably in Stoker's ears; he could not now avoid conversing with her.

'Yes, Florence,' he replied. 'You are not yet abed, then?' He moved past the staircase and turned the floral knob on the door adjacent his study. Behind it lay a refined but cluttered space, with numerous small tables and green armchairs arranged around a velveteen chaise longue, upon which his wife was now seated, wearing a favourite royal blue dress with satin frills. Her beauty was, as ever, astounding, and Stoker marvelled at it with the same sense of pleasure as he did the reproduction Rossetti on the wall. In the ten years they had spent in London, his wife's red hair had lost none of its lustre nor had her grey-blue eyes become any less clear – making her a fitting incarnation of the 'Blessed Damozel' who looked down at her from the canvas above. It was at moments such as these that Stoker keenly recalled the bright love that had enthused him as a young man – the love that had inspired him to take Florence for long walks along the sands at Clontarf in a bid to win her heart; the same love that had inspired him to take on the brilliant Wilde in a bid to win her hand. How fondly he remembered the light in those fine eyes as she smiled longingly at him, her wry sense of humour punctuating the sweeter words they spoke, as the waves crashed upon the shore.

And yet this full tide of happiness had soon withdrawn to reveal a trail of emotional jetsam, following years of disappointment and debt that had threatened to drive the pair almost entirely apart. He touched the silver fob watch in his waistcoat top pocket – how sadly distant the joy of receiving it seemed!

For now, here was Florence. And here, the familiar red-topped bills – which usually she would leave for him on his desk to peruse at his leisure of an evening – splayed in a fan across her lap, as though she were a rebellious courtesan. His wife observed him, or so it seemed to Stoker, with her now-habitual look of reproach. He went over to peck her on the cheek in a show of affection, but she swiftly withdrew her head beyond the headrest of the chaise longue. Stoker chuckled and went over to the walnut drinks cabinet in the corner.

'Did you take the Underground back from work, like I suggested?' asked Florence. Stoker poured a whiskey into a crystal tumbler and gulped it down in one.

'My dear, you should know that I cannot be seen in such a place. If a playgoer were to notice me there, it would damage the reputation of the theatre.' Florence sighed and threw the bills onto the little mahogany table in front of her.

'Well, my dear, Emma and I have to take it several times a week, when we go in search of necessaries. It would greatly contribute to our household economy if you could do the same, as cabs are so expensive!'

'It is *I*, not you, who brings in our daily living, Florence. And it is *I*, not you, who understands what is necessary for us to maintain our way of life!' replied Stoker sharply. He turned towards his wife, trying to fix her in a stare, but was merely met by her unmoving profile against the low light of a lamp on a nearby table. Again he was reminded of her ethereal beauty – the same beauty that had dazzled the Dublin of his youth and elicited jealous jibes once the pair were pledged to be married. Florence turned back towards Stoker, creating a curious chiaroscuro effect which, for an instant, lent her the same troughs in her face as the Metal Man at Rosses Point. Suddenly, Stoker felt sickened at what he deemed his wife's unseemly penny-pinching.

'Bram,' said Florence slowly, still not meeting his gaze, 'if you do not begin to exercise greater thrift soon, we will not be able to secure a position at the Varsity for young Noel – not even in Dublin, at Trinity.'

'My darling, everything will be fine if you simply don't interfere!' Stoker poured himself another drink, gulped it down in one again, then set down the glass and turned around, rubbing his hands together ostentatiously. 'Indeed, I think my luck may at last be turning, as I have just been promised ten pounds for two short stories in *Lloyd's*, and next year my share in box office receipts at the Lyceum will increase, on top of my regular salary. In a few years' time, we will have no money worries – none!' he added emphatically. He was hoping his wife would look at him, but she simply pointed at the bills on the table.

'The demands for Noel's last term at Haberdashers' won't even be covered by that,' she replied. 'Indeed, the headmaster is becoming quite impatient. Do you want me to read you his letter? Its tenor shows that he's in no way intimidated by your powerful friends, I can assure you.' She now looked at Stoker directly. 'The sooner you pass out as a barrister and leave that dreadful theatre business the better!' Suddenly, Stoker spun back towards the drinks cabinet and shook his fist, silently, by his side.

Then suddenly, he cried out – still with his back turned, 'Ah, to hell with you! You... you want to ruin everything I love... simply because what I love no longer loves you! Even when I do join the Bar, I'll never leave the theatre. Never, you witch!' And then he stormed out.

'Then we'll all three of us end up on the street!' she called out after him, but the door had slammed shut before he could hear her rebuke. Florence felt a tear run down her cheek; it appalled her that her husband, so meticulous in his habits, so careful with the accounts of his theatre, was so cavalier with the accounts of his family – dining out at the Garrick and entertaining patrons most nights of the week, with no expenses provided for this by his 'Guv'nor', Irving. It was she who had had to buy school clothes for Noel second-hand; it was she who had had to stop his allowance. Too scared to tell her son the reason why, the young boy had begun to hate her. Little did her husband know that it was her own father who had paid Noel's school fees for the previous year – but now even his patience was wearing thin. Poor Noel would have to seek a profession rather than attend college. It was the only way to save him from the vicissitudes of his father's fortunes in this city.

How she now hated London, remembering bitterly the joy with which she had anticipated her arrival there. And how she hated the theatre! True, she herself had once wished to try for the stage, taking minor parts in some of the early productions in Bram's tenure. At one time it had seemed that she too might be another Miss Terry… but Bram had too quickly yielded to the overtures of the English actresses who had Irving's ear and had ceased to fight her corner.

Profoundly frustrated with meeting famous writers and actors, and with having her beauty admired in the privacy of her drawing room while not being able to disclose it publicly, onstage, Florence was heartily sick of the theatre business, and yearned for their old life in Dublin, when Bram had had a steady job with the civil service – and she all her family around her. Lord how she missed and needed them! And how she had loved Stoker then! She suffered her worries entirely alone, and had made few friends among English women, who tended to mock her accent out of jealousy for her beauty.

She looked once more at the red-topped bills before her and shook her head. She then reached for the little bell that now lay half-buried beneath the mass of papers on the little mahogany table and rang it. Within a few minutes the housemaid appeared, beaming at her in the doorway.

'Emma, can you please make up the bed in the spare for me tonight. I shall be sleeping alone.' After throwing her mistress a puzzled look, the housemaid's generous face recomposed itself into a smile.

'Certainly, Madam. It will be ready in ten minutes.'

'Thank you.' Once the servant had left, Florence leaned her head on a cushion and began to sob as she recalled the changes that had come over her and Stoker's love, once so pure and passionate, since they had come to this unhappy town.

CHAPTER VI

DAWSON STREET

The following morning arrived cold and crisp. With some hastily consumed spoonfuls of porridge lining his stomach, a green frock coat covering his frame, and a black top hat adorning his head, Stoker walked down to the cab stand on Sloane Square and – despite the admonitions of his wife – ordered a hansom to take him all the way to Bayswater. As they set off, a copy of *The Morning Post* purchased from a shrieking boy outside the Underground brought to his attention the alarming disappearances of three young children on successive nights in the vicinity of his own theatre. The culprit for at least one of the disappearances, as described by local witnesses, was a girl with long blonde hair and dishevelled appearance – a girl whom no one so far had been capable of apprehending. There were apparently some mutterings among the hoi polloi as to whether this girl might in some way be linked to the Whitechapel murders, but the police were dismissing this line of enquiry, given the strength and ferocity of that particular attacker. Even though there was no mention of the Lyceum itself, Stoker knew that such events so close to the theatre were never good for business.

The cab rattled over the sawdust and setts of Hyde Park Corner then up Park Lane and into Edgware Road. The chill of the morning made Stoker press his knees and arms together as they moved at speed past the flat-fronted Georgian edifices that always reminded him of Harcourt Street back home in Dublin. As they came towards the junction with Marylebone Road, the cab stopped abruptly. A whole cart full of flowers had overturned, making it impossible for traffic to pass in either direction, and turning the road itself into a patchwork of colour.

'What's happened here?' cried Stoker's cab driver to one of the cloth-capped men attempting to set the shattered vehicle back on its wheels.

'Some loon in a carriage did a sharp turn down Dawson Street, quicker than Old Nick 'imself – tipped this cart right over. Luckily the 'orses weren't 'armed.' Stoker could see the cart driver holding his horses tightly by their bridles to the side of the road; most of the flowers would be unmarketable now, and he could understand the look of concern on the man's face.

'Sorry, Sir,' said the driver, now addressing Stoker. 'We'll 'ave to make a detour, down Dawson Street. Sorry for the inconvenience; the fare will be the same.'

'It's no problem,' called back Stoker.

As they turned left into the narrower, and less familiar, Dawson Street, Stoker recalled that he had heard its name before. Tripping past its brightly painted facades and iron railings, he realised that this was the same street whose name he had heard in the Drayfield trial – the same street in which the murder of the housemaid had taken place! At the end of it, parked up outside one of the large townhouses, he could see a black carriage.

'It's that crate wot turned the flower cart over, I'll wager,' announced the cabbie. 'I think I'll give its driver a piece of my mind, if you don't object, Sir.' Stoker was about to reply when he noticed a red, many-petalled rose embossed on the back of the carriage. Was this not the same carriage he had seen hurtling down Wellington Street on the night he had discovered the girl in the cellar?

'Please, can you slow down, my friend,' Stoker called up to the driver.

'Very good, Sir,' came the reply.

As they drew closer, the double doors at the back of the carriage suddenly sprang open to reveal two men – both of whom looked like Gipsies. They jumped out onto the pavement to join a tall bald man in a long coat wearing a monocle, a grey-headed man in butler's attire, and an old woman with a crumpled face dressed in a maid's uniform – although she more had the air of a housekeeper. The monocled man was looking furtively up and down the street.

Suddenly, Stoker made a decision.

'Can you stop here a while?' he called up to the driver. 'I will pay you for the delay.'

'Certainly, Sir,' came back the somewhat baffled reply. As the cabman drew reins, twenty or so yards from the carriage, Stoker carefully positioned his newspaper halfways in front of his face, then peered discreetly past it. The back of the carriage was now fully open, and Stoker could see that, apart from some velvet benching lining its sides, all it appeared to contain was a long wooden box. The two Gipsies now grabbed the box and started dragging it towards the back of the carriage. Once it was almost out, they lifted it up by its ends to reveal what it actually was: a coffin. So, the carriage with the symbol of the Rosicrucian order on it was being used – at least on this occasion – as a hearse! A hearse like no other Stoker had ever seen. As the men proceeded to carry the coffin up the steps towards the front door of the house, led by the butler, the monocled man suddenly started bawling at them, in a rolling Scottish accent.

'Be careful, ya fools! Ya duz nat wish to wake the maister.' Why they might be in danger of waking up the master of the house was utterly beyond Stoker, who was struggling to comprehend this whole mysterious interlude.

The butler now led the two men with the coffin into the house, the housekeeper and the tall Scotsman remaining on the pavement outside, talking.

'You do think the baron will be 'appy 'ere?' asked the housekeeper in a Cockney accent so broad Stoker found it difficult to decipher.

'Baron Cadwall'der wull be mair than happy,' replied the Scotsman with an arrogant laugh. 'Just like he waz when he came back from Danzig in the summer, before he decamped ta Soho a few weeks back, resting up during the day in that there coffin. Yes, he'll be mair than happy, especially now he can rest mair comfortably, back in his iron tomb.'

The housekeeper nodded.

'Just let him pursue huz whims unperturbed, as before,' now continued the Scotsman, 'and he will be mair than happy and ya'll be handsomely paid!' The housekeeper now laughed, or rather cackled – her crumpled face erupting like lava.

'Yes, Mr Ponsonby, I'm sure you're right.'

Ponsonby! Stoker could barely repress a shiver on hearing this name and buried his head in his newspaper in fright. When he looked up, the two individuals before him appeared to be trembling with his own white fear – like humans dissolving into devils – the arrogant laugh of the Scotsman now seeming as infernal as the cackle of the housekeeper. As Stoker grappled with what was happening, and why this Ponsonby – surely the same Ponsonby whose unreliable testimony had helped secure Lord Drayfield's conviction a week or so earlier – was in the same street, surely in front of the same house, as where he had supposedly witnessed a bizarre murder, the horse of the hansom suddenly reared up and bolted, carrying him, the astonished cab driver, and any hope of further observation along with it.

'I'm awful sorry, Sir,' shouted down the driver. 'This 'orse 'as a mind of its own – but a good one, I can tell you that. Sometimes it seems to see and 'ear things we 'umans don't. Got me out of scrapes and barneys no end of times!'

'It's no problem, I assure you,' shouted Stoker through the cab roof's trapdoor. 'I need to get on anyway.' The chill he had felt when hearing Ponsonby's name had been matched, it would seem, by the horse's own sudden sixth sense.

As the cab finally slowed to a more settled pace, Stoker tried to gather his thoughts: Dawson Street, a Rosicrucian carriage, Ponsonby, a butler and a housekeeper (most likely the Mrs Prism mentioned at the trial!) – all seemed to point to some wicked plot against the young lord, instigated most likely by the owner of the black carriage. But why? And why was this Baron Cadwallder... Cadwallader moving in? Did he simply want Drayfield out of the way so he could take possession of his house? And did this baron perhaps have some connection to the cousin from Prussia, whom Drayfield had blamed for the young housemaid's murder – were they perhaps in league? After all, they were seemingly both Rosicrucians. And what about the coffin? Did this baron, like some ancient aristocrats, take the remains of his ancestors with him to any new abode? If so, this removal was clearly no temporary measure, and Drayfield must have permanently forfeited his home...

The questions whirled in Stoker's mind, and as the cab now moved calmly across Norfolk Square, he began to wonder whether Scotland Yard knew of this activity, and that one of the key witnesses in the Drayfield trial seemed to have an undeclared interest in his lordship's house. He resolved to write to the Yard forthwith, no matter how much his mentor, Henstridge, might disapprove of such a move.

Soon the cab was advancing further into Bayswater, past the white-fronted houses with coloured bay windows that advertised the painters, sculptors and men of letters who inhabited the district. Before long, Stoker was outside Telbin's house in Hereford Road. He paid the driver and asked him to wait – a request to which the cabbie readily agreed, for an extra two shillings. Two shillings! Stoker momentarily winced at his extravagance, his wife's cold stare returning to menace him. He shook his head as if to dislodge Florence from his mind, then started climbing the shallow, clay-tiled steps that led to the wrought-iron porch – an artistic tour de force in leaf pattern, contrived, no doubt, according to Telbin's own meticulous design.

Stoker pressed the doorbell. Within moments the door opened to reveal the kind but somewhat idiotic features of Telbin's housekeeper; a woman of about forty-five who spoke in a broad Welsh accent. She smiled slowly, revealing gapped front teeth.

'Ah, Mr Stoker. How nice to see you.'

'A pleasure to see you too, Miss Jenkins,' replied Stoker, stepping over the threshold and handing her his top hat and coat.

'Mr Craig is expecting you,' she said, once she had shut the door behind him.

'I should hope so,' replied Stoker with an air of comic authority. 'After all, he asked me to come, and here I am! Is Mr Telbin in?'

'Ah, no,' she said, cocking her head to one side uneasily. 'I'm afraid he's out somewhere... working.' Stoker chuckled.

'It's all right, Miss Jenkins. Mr Irving and I do not expect to command Mr Telbin's complete loyalty. If he needs to do a little work at the Princess by the "light of the moon", as they say, we understand. Now, please, where is young Edward?' Miss Jenkins' long face now contracted into a smile of relief.

'He's in the morning room, Sir,' she said, ushering Stoker towards a door at the far end of the corridor leading from the vestibule. The corridor itself was a tribute to Telbin's skills, its walls lined with exquisite violet and gold-petalled wallpaper hazing into doorways rimmed with patterned wood, the younger Telbin – 'Quiet' Telbin – clearly having inherited his father's considerable talent.

But Telbin was not Stoker's target today. Miss Jenkins pushed open the door and there, standing in profile against the light from a netted window, was the figure of Edward Craig. The youth seemed not to notice the entrance of Stoker as he was engrossed in a sketchbook of some kind, whose pages he was continually turning over and examining. His spectacles were rammed right up the ridge of his beaky nose, and his collar stud was fixed firmly into his collar. Stoker could hardly remember the youth appearing so adult in his demeanour. Perhaps his sojourn in the North had done him some good after all? Stoker now coughed.

'Oh, Mr Stoker, it's you!' exclaimed Edward, called suddenly from his reverie.

'It is indeed,' came the reply. 'Exactly as promised. Although, I must admit,' and here Stoker took out his fob watch to consult the time, 'some ten or so minutes later than I had intended.' Edward laughed.

'I remember Mater telling me you were never late for anything!' Stoker chuckled and sat down, uninvited, on a convenient ottoman.

'For once I had a compelling distraction...'

'And what was that?'

'Oh, nothing for you to worry about, young man! Now, tell me, what was so bad about Sedbergh that you ran away?' Edward sighed, then pulling up a green velvet armchair to be opposite Stoker, put down his sketchbook on the low table that now lay between them and sat down. As he settled himself, Stoker glanced around the room: every inch was covered with paintings, many by Telbin himself and still others by his famous, now long-dead, father – the older Telbin's romantic vistas clearly influenced by Turner.

'It was truly awful, Mr Stoker. I could not bear it,' now began Edward. 'They made us take runs and cold baths every morning, and stuffed Latin and Greek down our throats. At sixteen, I was one of the oldest there, since the school was mainly getting boys ready for commissions in the army. There was little for me to do, and no one for me to befriend.'

'You do realise that you have greatly upset your mother by your actions.' Edward ran a hand through his mop of dark hair and sighed.

'Yes, yes. Edy has told me everything. But with her own reputation, who is Mater to judge?' he replied, with unwonted boldness.

Stoker said nothing for a few moments. Edward did indeed have a point: Miss Terry's colourful love life had scandalised London town on more than one occasion. He thought it time to turn the conversation to more pertinent matters.

'You asked to see me, Edward, but, as you know, I would have had to see you anyway. Your mother has plans for you which are really quite sensible.'

'Yes, yes,' said Edward, pulling out and lighting a cigarette (he offered none to Stoker himself, knowing he seldom indulged in the habit), 'she wants me to find some work in Dublin – or rather, you to find work for me!'

'Well,' said Stoker, 'finding a position in Dublin will no doubt placate your mother – but that aside, I think you will like it there, as the Irish are somewhat more friendly than the English, although somewhat less civilised.' Edward puffed on his cigarette.

'Well, according to Edy, it might take more than this to placate Mater as she is apparently upset with me for another reason… According to Edy, she let slip one night after dinner that she believes I am responsible for the Whitechapel murders!' Stoker laughed out loud.

'You're not serious?' he cried.

'I am,' replied Edward, flicking some cigarette ash into a glass ashtray. 'You know how melodramatic she can be!' Stoker knew only too well, but the thought that the slight, bespectacled Edward could have run all the way over to Whitechapel to launch a ferocious attack on a hardened prostitute – nay, two prostitutes – before returning late at night to his mother's house in Belgravia, to work at the theatre the following morning, was preposterous. A shaft of sunlight shot through the net curtains, lending the youth a bizarre halo, as if to confirm his innocence.

'Well,' said Stoker, shaking his head, 'I must find a moment to calm your mother.' Edward smiled.

'But first, I must write a letter of introduction for you to take to Gunn, the manager of the Gaiety in Dublin, recommending you as a scene painter at his theatre. He owes me quite a few favours and will surely find work for you there. The letter will no doubt secure your appointment.' Edward smiled again and took another puff of his cigarette.

'Thank you, Mr Stoker. I am sorry to have put you to so much trouble.'

'It's no trouble, young man. Just make sure you behave yourself while you're there. The Irish, both Protestant and Catholic, are a more conservative lot than the English. And whatever you do, don't run away, like you did from that school!'

'I promise not to, Mr Stoker. In any case, I doubt I will feel the need; the ten days or so in Sedbergh were utterly miserable, but being in Dublin affords me no terrors. I was so miserable at Sedbergh, indeed, that I took to sketching furiously to ease the pain.' Stoker now looked down at the sketchbook on the table.

'May I take peek?' he asked.

'Certainly,' replied Edward, handing him the book, then stubbing out his cigarette. 'They're mainly local scenes – the hills, the moors... I was thinking of using them for backdrops in *Lear*.' Stoker took the book from the youth and leafed through the mass of drawings. What he saw made no sense to him; it just seemed like a set of oblique lines and faded blurs, even less defined than the continental art that had made such a splash in recent times. He scratched his head and showed one of the sketches back to Edward.

'What is that supposed to be?' he asked with a look of purposeful confusion.

'That?' replied Edward. 'That was the scene outside my study. You can see the trees and the river, here,' and he moved his finger over the lines. Stoker frowned.

'I'm sorry, Edward, but I just can't see them. I think you would be better off copying the older Mr Telbin.'

'Well, believe it or not, but the *younger* Mr Telbin is most enthusiastic about my... my... innovations. Like me, he believes that theatre audiences are tired of sets cluttered with naturalistic detail and, like me, sees no future in that so-called Impressionist movement from France either. No, we both want to reinvigorate the stage with geometric designs of the kind seen in the art of the oldest civilisations: the pyramids of Egypt, the ziggurats of Sumer – something to take us back to our rawest and most primitive feelings!' He reached over and took back the sketchbook from Stoker, pursing his mouth in a way which betrayed his irritation.

Stoker was nonplussed.

'Well,' he said at last, 'it just seems very impersonal to me, that's all. I prefer the work of people like Mr Burne-Jones.'

'Ha!' snorted Edward. 'If I am able to do designs like this at the Gaiety, I will soon make my mark!'

'As I said,' replied Stoker, 'the Irish are somewhat more friendly than the English, but they are also more conservative; they will not take kindly to innovation.' Stoker looked once more at the oblique lines which Edward had traced over the pages of the sketchbook, now lying open on the young man's knee; there was something quite repellent about their lack of human sympathy. Could 'Quiet' Telbin really be endorsing this art from the hand of his protégé?

Stoker parted company with the youth (assuring him he would not reveal his exact whereabouts to his mother), collected his sundries from Miss Jenkins, then climbed back into the hansom, giving orders to go straight to the Lyceum. Stoker now recalled that, until recently, Edward had performed child parts with aplomb, before begging to go backstage. Perhaps it would be best to ask Gunn to employ him as an actor instead, not least because his other artistic talents appeared to be going so badly awry!

Back in his office at the Lyceum, once more attending to his correspondence, Stoker noticed an envelope bearing the rare but familiar handwriting of an old friend. He smiled and smoothed back his moustache. This was surely a missive from Edward Dowden – Professor Dowden, in fact – his old mentor from Trinity. The envelope was postmarked London, from earlier that day. He opened it to remark the headed paper of the Great Eastern Hotel.

Tuesday, 25th September

My dear Bram,

I have decided to check up on you and make sure that you're still thriving in your illustrious position at the theatre! I am staying at the Great Eastern – an establishment you know well – until next Monday, and am currently free from both research and talks, having finally delivered the last of my lectures on Shakespeare at University College. I would very much like to meet you and Florence for luncheon at my temporary abode, either this Saturday or Sunday. Please respond as soon as you are able.

Very truly yours,

Edward Dowden

P.S. I tried to invite Johnny Yeats, but my timing was completely topsy-turvy. Apparently, he took the Liverpool to Dublin ferry just as I was landing in the mainland.

Stoker put down the letter and smiled. Apart from being a fabulous raconteur, Dowden was one of the few Dublin associates whom he truly missed – the prospect of lunch with him was a joy! He took up a pen and started writing.

My dear Edward,

What a wonderful surprise, that you have been in London! Yes, I would be delighted to meet you at the Great Eastern. Shall we say half past twelve, this Sunday the 30th? Florence, sadly, will not be able to join us, as she is seeing one of her brothers-in-law up in Bloomsbury, and has pledged to take our boy Noel with her.

How long must it have been since I last saw you – in Dublin, when we were last there on tour!

Until Sunday.

Yours truly,

Bram Stoker

He hastily sealed the note in an envelope and put it in his out-tray. Next was another missive, in the familiar stationery of his brother's Fitzrovia surgery. He opened it, eagerly.

Dear Bram,

I have to tell you in no uncertain terms that your enquiry regarding acquiring some arsenic cannot be entertained on my part. As a registered surgeon, I, like many in my profession, have the right to use this substance under certain strict conditions, but I have no right whatsoever to issue it to anyone without a good medical reason. If you have a problem with rats, I suggest you employ a professional rat-catcher. Such fellows do exist, I assure you, and would be happy to clear your cellar of vermin.

I am sorry to have to send such a frank rebuff to you.

Yours ever,

George

Stoker scowled. How dare his little brother address him so – and ignore his particular plea to send this response to Chelsea, not the theatre? He rubbed his top lip anxiously as another thought assailed him: could it be that he was somehow now diminished in George's eyes, the measured sense of seniority he had tried to maintain in their dealings of no account? The thought grieved him, but after a few moments he set his brother's letter and anxieties to one side and turned his attention to more pressing, and distracting, matters.

After answering several requests for boxes at the theatre, Stoker finally got round to writing Edward's letter of introduction to Gunn at the Gaiety, recommending the youth as a budding actor (surely a better path for the young man to follow!) and subtly reminding his friend that he, Stoker, had helped him pack out his theatre over several summers by persuading Irving and Miss Terry to tour Ireland during that most unfashionable of seasons. He sealed the letter in an envelope upon which he wrote the name 'Michael R.T.

Gunn, Esq', then further sealed it in another envelope, addressing it to Edward at Telbin's, again using just the youth's initials.

Were there any other letters he needed to write? Yes! the Rosicrucian carriage – Ponsonby – the coffin. He really should write to Scotland Yard and tell them about what he had seen in Dawson Street. Even if his witness proved to be nothing, it was, he understood, his civic duty to report such events, especially if they might shed light on such an important case as Drayfield's. He took a piece of unheaded paper from his drawer and was about to jab his pen in the inkpot when a knock on the door interrupted him. He answered with a loud 'Enter!' and looked up to see the sheepish face of Aloysius Grafton.

'Er, Mr Stoker, Sir, Miss Terry has asked to see you in her dressing room.'

'What is it she wants?' returned Stoker briskly.

'I have no idea, but she is insistent,' replied Grafton, conspicuously avoiding eye contact with his boss: the bridge between the two men had clearly not yet been repaired. Throwing down his pen in irritation, Stoker followed Grafton out of the office and went to speak with Miss Terry, who was simply seeking assurance that Stoker was trying to find work for her son in Dublin (whatever his exact whereabouts were now!) – an assurance Stoker was glad to give, with regards to Gunn; and that this Gunn would keep Edward under close scrutiny, not allowing him out of his sight – an assurance he was less glad to give, as he knew this was practically an impossibility. Stoker was, in truth, a little taken aback by the urgency of Miss Terry's tone; still, he knew that Miss Terry, while the finest actress of her generation, was not above melodrama, including when it came to matters pertaining to her son.

The conversation concluded, Stoker was headed back to his office when his mind suddenly turned to the multitude of tasks that awaited him downstairs before that evening's performance: checking the lights, inspecting the backdrop, and whatnot. Before he knew it, he was back onstage, his plan to write to Scotland

Yard regarding Dawson Street and Ponsonby forgotten, his good intentions disintegrating like the wrappings of a mummy in a ruptured tomb.

CHAPTER VII

THE GREAT EASTERN HOTEL

Sunday brought mild but hazy weather. As Stoker's hansom trundled past Liverpool Street Station towards the Great Eastern Hotel, he noticed that, among the usual Sabbath-breakers trying to sell fruit, and ranting preachers trying to upbraid them for their sins in so doing, newsboys were beginning to invade the streets like swarms of rats, squealing their headlines – although about what, Stoker could not discern. The dailies were not normally sold on a Sunday; some uncommonly great event must have taken place overnight, and Stoker shuddered to think what it might be. The papers being sold were thin, no more than dispatches. What could it be? Yet more ructions with Russia? Had Prussia invaded France again? Was his own country in the grip of another convulsion, like the devastating famine or Cholera epidemic in Sligo his mother had so vividly described to him when a boy?

As they pulled up outside the Great Eastern, Stoker consulted his watch and realised that he was late; most unusual for him, and quite an affront, he feared, to a man such as Dowden. He galloped up the steps of the hotel and quickly deposited his sundries with the cloakroom attendant, admiring as he did so the Byzantine-style mosaic which adorned the foyer ceiling, lending it the genuine lustre of the Turkey-land which his brother was so fond of recalling in their conversations.

Stoker felt no need to announce his arrival to the flunky at reception, and soon found himself striding along a purple carpet, past arrays of vases crammed with orchids and hollyhocks, towards the atrium, where a smiling maître d' directed him towards a table in the corner. There, backdropped by the atrium's curved glass window and the street behind, was the familiar form of his friend, Edward Dowden – one of the finest literary scholars of his day. Dowden's chalk-coloured hair was falling loosely over his chiselled features as he pored over a book. He was occasionally sipping from a glass of what looked like sherry, judging by its golden colour. Stoker did not wish to break Dowden's concentration, and so, pressing his finger to his lip, winked at the maître d', who sniggered quietly and slunk away. Stoker took a few paces towards the unmoving man, then, clearing his throat and summoning up his best Cockney accent, exclaimed, 'Professor Dowden, a Mr Whitman 'ere to see you, Sir!' This seemed to electrify Dowden, his face first shooting up towards Stoker with a wide smile, then falling immediately, then recovering again as he appeared to take in the object of his gaze. And then Dowden laughed, stood up, and hugged the somewhat taller Stoker heartily across the table.

'Bram, it's so good to see you. Sorry, I thought that perhaps it was somebody el—'

'Sorry to disappoint you,' riposted Stoker. 'There's nothing I'd like more myself than to meet the old wizard in the flesh – but I'll have to make do with correspondence, and we'll both have to make do with being each other's second bests for the day!'

'Ha!' laughed Dowden, sitting back down. 'To be a creditable substitute for Walt is an accolade, I assure you. Do you remember the joys we had reading his poems at Trinity all those years ago?'

'Do I indeed,' replied Stoker, pulling back a chair and signalling behind him for a menu. 'It was you who put me on to the great man. I shall never forgive you for it – took up all of my time when I should have been practising my hammer throws for the Games! And what about all those public recitals we did at the Hist. and Phil? I'm surprised I got anything else done at all!'

'Well, all those recitals got you well and truly noticed, as far as I can see – taking you to the *Mail* and, ultimately, to the Lyceum; wasn't it your review of Irving as Hamlet in that paper which caught the great man's eye, and effectively secured your current position?'

'It was indeed,' laughed Stoker.

'Well then, I don't feel so bad about distracting you after all!' Dowden raised his perfectly featured countenance and downed the rest of his drink in one. 'Let's order some more sherry, eh, Bram?'

'Why not?' replied Stoker. Dowden snapped his fingers with all the authority his renown as a scholar could muster, and the waiter was soon trotting back with two glasses of the golden liquid that promised to relax their tongues still further.

The two men now started chatting at length about shared acquaintances, particularly those they knew back in Ireland: both men looked after the impecunious Yeats – Stoker by searching far and wide among his celebrity friends for commissions for his paintings and Dowden by promoting his son's inscrutable verse; various women were still contesting the will of the libidinous Isaac Butt, years after his death; and Willie Wilde, older brother to Oscar, was publicly drinking himself to oblivion in whichever holes of Temple Bar he did not owe credit in. The tittle-tattle of Dublin was the same tired study of Anglo-Irish families such as the Balcombes and the Wildes, whose lives of unchecked eccentricity, far from the Empire's centre, was aptly summed up, observed Dowden, by the title of Stoker's first, unnoticed novel, *The Primrose Path* – a quip that had both men chuckling uneasily when they considered Willie Wilde following that same path to his destruction.

While Dowden poured forth more gossip and amusing anecdotes about Dublin, Stoker's mind turned to London, and the tribulations he faced there: the constant need to impress patrons and to flaunt unowned wealth – and the painful row this had caused between him and his wife some nights before. And yet it was all still worth it, he told himself: life in Dublin for a cultured man was intolerable for all save the literary god before him – the only man he knew in that forsaken town whose reputation had transcended its provincial location.

After an hors d'oeuvre of potted crab, Dowden had the waiter open a bottle of Chablis. Stoker was now observing Dowden as one would a bust of the Emperor Constantine, and just briefly he had the sensation that he was in a museum rather than a restaurant, the shafts of light through the curved glass behind the professor illuminating his friend's face most agreeably. They clinked glasses as Dowden resumed the conversation.

'So, tell me, Bram, are you still living in Southampton Row?'

'No, no,' laughed Stoker, 'not for some years. We are now at St Leonard's Terrace, Chelsea; one of the best districts in London, let me add.'

'Good. Glad to hear that you and Florence are some distance away from Whitechapel, with all its murders.'

'Well away. Although the last murder was several weeks ago now, so let's hope the culprit has himself been killed or moved on.' Dowden's fine face tautened and his pupils dilated.

'What? Haven't you heard?' he exclaimed, taking a sip of his wine. The light now struck Dowden's silver cigarette case and blared into Stoker's eyes, causing him to flinch and push it towards his friend.

'Heard what?' asked Stoker, taking a swig of his wine.

'Why, there were two new murders in Whitechapel in the small hours of this morning. The bellboys are abuzz with it. All the hallmarks of the last two. The slit throat, the bre—'

'Yes, yes,' breathed Stoker, genuinely shocked. 'Please, spare me the details, Edward. Have there really been two more murders in Whitechapel?'

'Yes. As I said, the hotel is abuzz with it. Most of the newspapers have been caught out on a Sunday and are now busy playing catch-up.' With that Dowden produced a thin dispatch and offered it to Stoker, who promptly waved it away.

'By Jove,' exclaimed Dowden, 'you seem positively delighted by the news, Bram! Did you place a bet on it or something?' Indeed, Stoker was smiling – even if he didn't realise it. The events in Whitechapel were truly appalling, but at least now he could convince Miss Terry of her son's complete innocence in relation to them: Telbin had sent him a telegram just the day before reporting that he had put Edward on the first train from London, to make his ferry connection for Dublin at Liverpool – so the youth was well away from town. The absurdity of Miss Terry's beliefs always guaranteed the difficulty of dissuading her of them, and a hysterical leading lady was a bane for all at the theatre, as he well knew; he could do without her histrionics.

But with the mention of more murders, other troubling events returned to Stoker's mind. There was the trial of Lord Drayfield, at which the young lord had been imperfectly – but successfully – prosecuted by Stoker's own mentor, Henstridge. And then there was his encounter with Ponsonby and the coffin in Dawson Street – an encounter, he recalled with a pang, he had meant to report to Scotland Yard but had failed so far to do. What should he do? But now here was Dowden, ever a figure of respect in his life, his *true* mentor, right in front of him! Stoker resolved to confide in his friend.

'Edward,' he ventured, picking up and turning the professor's cigarette case around in his fingers, 'did I tell you that I was training for the Bar?' Dowden looked at him quizzically, and with not a little disdain.

'You did not, my friend. Don't tell me you are thinking of leaving the finest theatre in the world to become a hired tongue-padder?'

'No, no,' replied Stoker, putting the cigarette case back on the table, away from the awkward shaft of light it had been reflecting into his eyes. The sunlight outside had got stronger and there was no sign of the fog that had been intimated earlier in the day. 'No, it's just that it might help me if, as I fear, the theatre's fortunes begin to falter in coming years – too many competitors.' Dowden smiled and recharged their glasses.

'Well, I can't see the Savoy outdoing the Lyceum for some time, but if you wish to have a second string to your bow, I quite understand.'

'Anyhow, as part of my studies, I was at court for the end of the Drayfield trial. Have you heard of it in Dublin?' Dowden almost choked on his wine and put down his glass.

'Have I heard of it?' he replied. 'For two whole days the Catholics were getting drunk on it around O'Connell Street. South of the Liffey, we kept a much lower profile, I can tell you. A peer of the realm facing the rope, especially one seemingly trying to invoke some obscure hereditary privilege to avoid prosecution? Delighted every priest and horse-coper from Kerry to Connemara!'

'Well, anyway,' continued Stoker, 'I have to say that the case against Lord Drayfield was actually pretty weak. It depended on evidence from witnesses who were plainly lying, and it was only the fact that Drayfield blamed another man – a Prussian cousin, who is likely a Rosicrucian, but who did not fit his lordship's description – that he was found guilty.'

'Well, not even the *Mail* reported it quite like that, I must say,' replied the professor. 'It just went on about how his lordship had given false testimony, and how the evidence against him was conclusive. Indeed, even an ivory tower fellow like me can see that someone trying to blame an innocent man merely directs suspicion upon himself.' Dowden's handsome countenance was now observing Stoker closely. 'Tell me, what else do you know?'

'Well, Drayfield's housekeeper claims that she arrived early in Bayswater from Hackney by hansom in twenty minutes, to discover the maid's body – which his lordship's defence counsel has proved is simply impossible – and the key witness is almost certainly a man wanted for coining in Aberdeen… although, unfortunately, all the original peelers who arrested him are dead. Ponsonby, his name is.'

Dowden looked thoughtful and stroked his beard. The glass wall behind him was revealing a flurry of starlings, moving like a quick squall of rain through the railings – a sudden violence which Stoker found most unsettling.

'Hmm… well, that's as may be. But if Drayfield *is* innocent, why did he try and invoke hereditary privilege – that byelaw – to avoid prosecution? As I said, the priests, horse-copers and every drunken ring-kisser was baying for his blood back home when they heard about that!'

'Yes, but I'm not so sure they should have been. You see, the other day I was in the exact same street where Lord Drayfield's townhouse is… in fact, where the murder took place: Dawson Street. Outside one of the houses was a tall man with a monocle haranguing two servants – Gipsies, by the look of them – who were attempting to carry a coffin inside; yes, a coffin! His name, as I heard it, was the same as that of the unreliable witness: Ponsonby.'

Stoker paused to see whether any shock registered on Dowden's face, but no; the professor was gleefully looking over Stoker's head, his eyes fixed on some distraction.

'I say, Bram, do hold off for a moment. Our knight-of-the-napkin is returning with a mouth-watering epitasis, so let's let him perform.'

The smiling waiter, in a pink-banded waistcoat and black bow tie, and sporting a waxed 'French' moustache, wheeled in a little silver trolley and began piling slices of roast beef from the carvery onto their plates, all the while deferring to his customers as 'Monsieur' in a Cockney so faultless that both men had difficulty supressing their laughter. Once the waiter had left, Dowden having ordered another bottle of wine, the professor entreated Stoker to resume his story.

'Well,' said Stoker, 'not only was this Ponsonby almost certainly the same man who was at the trial, and a supposed witness to the murder, but the carriage from which the servants removed the coffin... I had seen it before; it had a red, many-petalled rose embossed on the back.'

Stoker paused.

'Do you know what that might mean?' he added suddenly, and somewhat triumphantly, reasoning that, for once, his learned friend might not know the answer. Dowden smiled.

'That the owner of the carriage is likely a Rosicrucian,' he replied. 'The rose will have had some seven petals, representing the seven days of initiation in *The Chymical Wedding of Christian Rosenkreutz*. Some more Chablis?'

'How do you know that?' spluttered Stoker; he had wanted to pique his friend and intellectual superior but had signally failed so to do.

'Most Shakespeare scholars know that, Bram. For what it's worth, I've read the text in the original seventeenth-century German.' The flurry of starlings behind the glass was now indistinguishable from the sudden murk that had befallen the street that formed Dowden's backdrop. 'But what is your point, Bram?'

'Well, I just think that the collision of all these things is very strange, if not downright suspicious, don't you?'

'Well,' said Dowden, lighting a cigarette from his silver case directly over the beef, 'there are probably a hundred such carriages rattling all around London, so I doubt it was the same one you saw before. Anyway, even if it was, I still don't understand what might be the connection between this collision, as you put it, and the Drayfield case.' His eyes now drilled into Stoker's.

'Well, Ponsonby, of course; though there's more to it than that. I have in fact been wondering whether Lord Drayfield might have been framed by this Prussian cousin, this Lucarda, as he claimed. After all, he is, like the owner of the carriage, most probably a Rosicrucian. I wondered whether he and Ponsonby might be in league…' Now Dowden laughed, pouring smoke over the table.

'Speculation, Bram, mere speculation,' he chortled. 'There is no proof that this Ponsonby is the same man as appeared at the trial and, as I say, there are probably a hundred carriages like the one you saw all over London. Occultism has become an obsession for these young aesthetes. I should know; they attend my lectures in Dublin.'

'Yes, but—'

'Tell me, Bram, do you know the name of the man who owns the carriage?' Stoker sat back and tried to look nonchalant.

'Well, as a matter of fact, I do. I heard Ponsonby and the housekeeper mention him: it's a man called Baron Cadwallder… Cadwallader.' At this Dowden burst into guffaws of laughter that were quite unseemly for a man of his position.

'Cadwallder, you say?' he queried.

'Yes, Baron Cadwallder.'

'Then, Bram, let me assure you that you have seen nothing suspicious – just a little yellow, perhaps.'

'What do you mean?' asked Stoker.

'Well,' replied Dowden, taking another puff of his cigarette, 'I actually know this Baron Cadwallader – *not* Cadwallder; he was a student of mine and, as I say, quite an outrageous one at that!'

'Really?'

'Yes. He was sent down from Oxford for throwing some peculiar party and ended up in my tender care. A decadent young gentleman with a penchant for green carnations, but otherwise quite harmless.' The coincidence seemed too near to be believed, but Stoker's trust in Dowden was not easily shaken. 'I wouldn't put it past the baron to get involved in some arcane order; a man as wealthy as him can often find little useful to do.'

'Still, I find the whole connection with Ponsonby a bit odd,' pressed Stoker, 'given his role as a witness.'

'Well, if he is the same Ponsonby, coiner or not, he may have legitimate cause to be there,' returned Dowden, glass in hand. 'Maybe he's a letting agent for the street.'

'And the coffin? Surely *that* is a bit odd?' Stoker then pressed.

'Well,' laughed Dowden, 'perhaps Cadwallader now fancies himself a vampire. I wouldn't put that past him either!'

'A vampire?' exclaimed Stoker.

'Why not?' shrugged Dowden, stubbing out his cigarette and tucking into his food. 'They reside in tombs and coffins by day, then prey on their neighbours by night, sucking their blood – or, more often, their daughters' blood – to return their strength and youth.' Here he picked up his napkin and wiped his mouth before smiling wryly. 'I should know; it was me who helped old Joseph write that novella.'

'Which Joseph are you referring to?' asked Stoker, feeling, in spite of himself, faintly irritated.

'Your former employer, Joseph Sheridan Le Fanu.' Stoker dropped his fork.

'My word, did you really meet that old recluse?'

'I did indeed,' laughed Dowden. 'In fact, I helped him with many of his finest works. As you know, he never left his house in Merrion Square after his wife's death, sending all his articles for the *Mail* by trusted messenger boy; didn't even talk directly with his senior partner, Maunsell. The only person he saw was me.' And here Dowden gave a slow, meditative smile. 'Did like the theatre reviews you wrote for his newspaper, though, you'll be glad to hear – as indeed did Irving!'

'So, what was the vampire novella he wrote? I can't remember reading it, I must say.'

'Oh, it was a most curious tale, about a young woman who is attacked by a monstrous black cat. It was me who gave him the scholarship he needed, since I could filch almost anything from Trinity Library in those days... and still can.' Stoker was about to ask his friend another question but Dowden, after taking another sip of wine, simply carried on. 'Yes, old Joseph would never even go near the front of the house – which looked out onto the square – and took all of his meals alone; apart from perhaps when he dined with his daughters, whom he rarely spoke to, and who themselves couldn't get out of the house quickly enough. I would ring the bell, usually in the evening before supper, and then be led quite silently by his old servant, Tilly, through the house to his study. The room was full of the most macabre collectibles, I must say.'

'Such as?'

'Oh, he had painted skulls from Austria, and death masks – some of fellows who had swung; he even had a model gallows on his mantelpiece. He claimed he needed such items to fire his imagination and write his tales – his tales being his only sizeable source of income at that time, since his newspapers were doing so badly. He had a lean face, which I never saw properly because of the low light and his long unkempt hair.'

'What scholarship did you give him?' asked Stoker.

'Only a treatise for his vampire novella. A work by a man called Christmas, I believe, or at least translated by him, from another man called Calmet – *The Phantom World*.'

'I have that treatise, or rather, book!' declared Stoker. 'A most grisly reportage of spirits and revenants from what I recall – and yes, I do remember it talking about vampires!'

'As I said,' returned Dowden, 'Joseph had an eye for the macabre – and the supernatural. He also gave me some scholarship – on the occult – in return.' Here Dowden laughed again, letting his sculpted countenance crease agreeably. 'It was old Joseph who gave me books on Rosicrucianism – the seven stages of initiation, the use of Kabbalah, sacred anagrams. He was a firm believer in it, you know. I think you'll find that, in contrast, young Cadwallader is just a dilettante.'

'And did he write anything on it?'

'Well, he was going to but died before he had the chance. He wanted to write a novella about how Shakespeare and Marlowe, as travelling players, had founded a Rosicrucian lodge with Dr Dee in Bohemia.'

'Sounds preposterous!' exclaimed Stoker. Dowden looked at him archly.

'Not as preposterous as you might think, Bram,' he replied. 'We know that London players performed Marlowe's *Faustus* on the Continent at that time, and that Shakespeare could easily have been one of them – and that Dee was performing his own mischief nearby, Rosicrucianism arising from his symbology.'

'Still, it all seems very far-fetched to me,' maintained Stoker.

'Again, perhaps not. I have been researching whether Marlowe's play is in fact about the whole Dee and Kelly scandal. Do you know of it?'

'Yes, of course,' answered Stoker. He had indeed read about the work of the great alchemist and demonologist Dr John Dee, who, along with his dubious associate, Edward Kelly, had been drummed out of England at the time of the Virgin Queen on account of his magical investigations.

'Still,' sighed Dowden, reaching for his glass, 'nothing ever came of that novella – as I said.'

Talk of Le Fanu and Merrion Square led Stoker to recall Dublin, and his own lucky escape from that town. What might old Joseph himself have achieved had he entered society in London!

Soon the French-speaking Cockney was back, removing the men's plates and offering them dessert, which they both declined in favour of retiring to the spacious smoking room, where they carried on their conversation over brandy: news of George and Thornley; of Irving and Miss Terry (and when, if at all, they might tour Ireland again); of Stoker's sadly unsung novels and Dowden's unsung plays (which Dowden hoped Stoker would read, causing the meeting's only embarrassed silence).

By the time Stoker had shaken hands with his friend in the Byzantine foyer, having without demur settled the hefty bill left on their smoking-room table, dusk was falling on London, and with it traces of autumn fog. As Stoker rode home in his cab, he felt a sense of relief on two counts: first, thanks to Telbin, he would now have no trouble countering Miss Terry's belief that her son was the Whitechapel murderer (he must find time to do this!); and secondly, thanks to Dowden, he could now rest assured that the mysterious scene he had witnessed outside the townhouse in Dawson Street was entirely innocent – there could be no connection between this Cadwallader and the dark deed performed at the house earlier. Trust his mentor to clear matters up; well, in the first case, inadvertently so, as he could have known nothing of Miss Terry's views on her troublesome son. Still, insight of any kind always tasted sweeter coming from Dowden, even though there were times when Stoker felt jealous that his friend seemed to understand everything so much better than himself.

The fog was now descending rapidly on London and the streetlamps being lighted, making the constantly shifting tableaux of the city appear like a series of Impressionist paintings – an effect which afforded Stoker an unexpected, and not entirely unwelcome, sense of detachment.

As the fog descended, so the cab slowed, and Stoker was glad when he at last found himself outside his house in Chelsea. Having located his key, Stoker was about to let himself in when a sudden screech, like the cry of a young child, pierced the gloom. He turned round to see two great bats wheeling about a nearby streetlamp, their pinched countenances catching the light at fleeting intervals, making them look like flying devils. Stoker turned back and hurriedly unlocked his door.

Later that evening, safely back in his study, Stoker was once more attending to his correspondence when his eyes wandered in momentary apathy towards his bookshelves. Immediately, his conversation with Dowden about *The Phantom World* returned to command his attention. How that work had consumed his interest ten years prior, just before he had set off for London! He got up and, discovering the tome on a top shelf, released it from its high position and returned to his desk. He turned to its second volume and started thumbing through its grim reportage of documented cases from the early eighteenth century, all relating to the particular phenomenon of vampires. Vampires! Dead people, often buried in unhallowed ground, who would return at night to suck the blood of the living – turning them into vampires too. People such as Arnold Paole or the son of Millo; Hungarians mainly, but some Serbians as well. These wretched individuals could not be killed, except by being staked through the heart while prayers were being recited – vampires being called the 'Undead'; neither alive nor dead, neither in heaven nor hell, but doomed to roam the earth endlessly. The reports were utterly gruesome despite the matter-of-fact way in which Christmas had translated his source. It was indeed this very matter-of-factness, Stoker realised, that had turned his stomach and made it so difficult for him to turn tales on such subjects himself. It was perhaps because of this that he had never read old Joseph's novella either.

As he browsed through the accounts of these peculiar people, his mind returned unbidden to the peculiar people he had tried so hard to leave behind, in Ireland – the degenerate circle of Anglo-Irish back home in Dublin. And then he thought of the monstrous Metal Man at Rosses Point, whose statue had scared him so much as a boy. Yes, his fear of the monstrous all stemmed back to that first fear, he was certain; and while he knew that he might have to embrace such terrors if his hopes of becoming known as an author were ever to be achieved, he had held back from doing so. Le Fanu, he knew, had not; indeed, he had created his own macabre menagerie in order to fire his imagination, bringing forth terrifying tales such as *Madam Crowl's Ghost* and *Green Tea*. But he had clearly paid with his sanity, from what Dowden had told him. Stoker did not wish to do the same.

As Stoker read grim account after grim account, he must have lapsed into a deep dreamless sleep, as his next conscious apprehension was the clatter of draymen outside his study window at dawn.

PART II

CHAPTER VIII

THE WOMAN IN THE CASTLE

Wladyslawa looked out from her promontory and smiled. The castle walls held no allure for the common observer, but for her they were the object of continual fascination – their aspect sheer, their stonework close, they provided not a single foothold for anyone ever tempted to assail them. Looking now down at the gatehouse, she noted that the wooden drawbridge remained upright, like a mouth shut tight. Yes, her instructions were to keep the castle enclosed until her master returned – and this was exactly what she and the other servants had done for the past few months now, not having wanted for beef or maize or beetroot, or even Rhenish wine, during this time. Still, she was glad that her lord would be returning soon!

Wladyslawa now headed out of her boudoir at the base of a turret, climbing first a single flight of spiral staircase, then creaking open the oak door that led out onto the ramparts. Looking now out over the battlements, across a plain of scorched September stubble, she could discern the crossroads that lay just outside the castle, while further beyond, the grey snake of the sea, and the docks she had known all her life. She smiled wistfully. It was some ten years since she had drifted, friendless, to the very same crossroads she was observing now – in the year 1878, when she was not much more than a girl. Cast out of her father's inn in Danzig after he had caught her abed with one of the guests, Wladyslawa had spent the whole day wandering south in search of the road to Königsberg. As evening had begun to draw in, she had thought salvation was at hand for she had found herself approaching this very crossroads where, she reasoned, she would likely meet some travelling wagon which might carry her to some nearby town, where she could find work. Beyond the crossroads lay a vast castle with crenelated towers and turrets – a building the like of which she had never seen in the confines of her native Danzig – seemingly shrouded in dark clouds of its own making.

Yes, how well she could recall that time, but how different her salvation would turn out to be!

Wladyslawa stopped and removed a small flask of water from her bag; she had been wandering south all day and was tired and thirsty. As she did so, a group of peasants in grey pantaloons and caps suddenly appeared, pulling a cart. They stopped at the crossroads and a couple of men proceeded to pick up shovels from the cart and start digging a hole. As she approached them, she could see that there were also two old women in the group, their faces shrouded by black shawls. The women had the look of ordinary Polish peasants, the kind her Ruthenian father had always warned her against conversing with – country people, who would come with their meagre wares of lace and over-ripe apples to set up shop in the Scottish district, where the silver sellers would attempt to shoo them away. The women now began to howl and recite dirges as the men, who had stopped digging and returned to the cart, began edging out a coffin, which they then dragged to the hole and began to let down clumsily with ropes.

Suddenly, one of the women noticed Wladyslawa. She stopped howling and called out something in her Polish tongue, the gist of which the girl could just make out through the earpiece of her own close language.

'*Odejść z tobą!* Be off with you!' the woman screamed. 'Don't come near the *przeklęty!* Away from the accursed!' Wladyslawa froze as the men, who had now begun piling earth on top of the coffin, stopped what they were doing and glared balefully at her. '*Odejść z tobą!*' screamed the woman again as the men now put down their shovels and began to approach Wladyslawa at quite some speed. Wladyslawa backed away slowly, wondering what she should do next.

As her indecision hovered, she heard a loud crack: the drawbridge from the castle had fallen with an almighty thump, and over its planks now came a horseman on a dark stallion. At the sound of the drawbridge crashing the peasants all turned and began scurrying back to their cart, not bothering to pick up their shovels – and leaving the burial incomplete.

Again Wladyslawa was caught in indecision, not knowing whether to flee or stand her ground; but her fear was too great to give wings to her feet and so she had little choice but to await the mysterious horseman – and any fate that this might bring.

As the rider came nearer, he stopped and looked down at the half-filled grave. He laughed, then, having allowed his horse a tremendous rearing over its hind legs, jumped off the beast with consummate skill, grabbed its rein, and started soothing it by stroking its nose and whispering something into its ear. Then he quietly led the animal towards Wladyslawa, a gracious smile lighting up his face. She noticed that he was wearing peculiar-looking breeches, bottomed by long socks, and a black coat atop a cross-patterned waistcoat – of the kind she had seen some of the families in the Scottish district of her hometown wear. The rider was immensely tall, with black hair and a thin handlebar moustache that trailed his jaw. All Wladyslawa's fears evaporated as she observed this force of nature – a man who had expelled the loathsome peasants with his presence alone, and who was now approaching her with the unmistakable gait of a gentleman.

'So, young lady, may I know what has brought you here?' he began in a high German she knew only true aristocrats spoke.

'Sir, I have come in search of work.'

'And where do you come from, may I ask?' he laughed.

'From the town yonder,' she replied, pointing back in the direction she had come. The man now began to circle around her, leading his horse as though tracing a charmed ring.

'And what is your name, young lady?'

'Wladyslawa Sienkiewicz,' she replied. He stopped in front of her, patted his horse's nose, and smiled. She had never in her life seen a man more majestic or refined.

'Well, well; a Ruthenian ruby, with bright red hair. Quite a treasure,' said he. Wladyslawa smiled – as ever delighted when a gentleman commented on her charms. 'Allow me to introduce myself. I am Baron Vassil Drayfield-Lucarda, Prince of Prussia and Count of Mestre.'

Wladyslawa curtseyed and lowered her head. Again he laughed.

'Well, you are certainly a well-mannered young thing, I must say! How old are you?'

'Sixteen, Sir.'

'Can you launder, clean and wait at table?'

'I can indeed, Sir.'

'Well, I happen to have a dearth of servants at present,' he continued. 'If you were willing to work for fifteen marks a month, I could give you board and lodgings here.' She now looked up at him with sudden trepidation: did his handsome aspect conceal some Bluebeard heart? She knew that once the drawbridge was pulled up, she would be at his mercy – like a slave in a seraglio.

'Can I trust that you are a man of honour, Sir, and will behave in accordance with the customary dignity of an aristocrat?' Yet again he laughed.

'You have my word as an Italian count. However, I can judge from your situation that your recourses are few.' Wladyslawa bit her lip in recognition of this truth.

'If you are willing, join me up here on the back of my mount and I shall take you to my castle.' He leapt with ease into his horse's saddle and reined the steed sideways for Wladyslawa to climb up. After a few seconds, she tended her left hand towards him and placed her foot on the stirrup, swinging her slight frame onto the horse's haunches. Her fate was sealed.

As they passed the crossroads, Wladyslawa's curiosity got the better of her.

'Pray, Sir... your Lordship. What were those people doing?'

'Wretched idiots,' he exclaimed. 'Bane of my life! Some three hundred years ago a ramshackle band of English Catholics landed here, hoping to get away from their Virgin Queen after King Philip of Spain had failed to liberate them. Unfortunately, they brought their wretched customs with them also. Now none are left... they all married Polack women, their descendants speaking that language and not a word of the old Anglo-Saxon tongue. But they still observe their forebears' ridiculous rituals.'

'What do you mean, your Lordship?'

'In England, suicides get buried at crossroads, so that their spirits will not know which way to turn, and so cannot rest. Whatever body is in that box down there, its owner took its own life – and now these peasants come and land it at my feet!'

'My God!'

'Yes, it is superstitious nuisance that visits itself on myself periodically,' he continued. 'The road from Danzig to Bialystok crossing the one from Königsberg to Warsaw just outside my castle.'

The word 'Danzig' caused a lozenge of despair to implode in Wladyslawa's stomach – it was a town she might never see again; her family ties severed, her reputation shattered by the irresistible force of her lust.

The sound of the horse's hooves now changed from the bright clip-clop over hardened mud and stone to the dull thud over wood as they travelled up the drawbridge. Soon they were in an immense cobbled courtyard surrounded by high stone walls, carved into which were strange, goblin-like creatures. Wladyslawa shuddered. The baron now leapt off his horse and took her hand. In one swift movement she was placing her feet on the sand and sawdust beneath her, like a sailor reaching terra firma.

As she glanced about her, trying to absorb the unreal dimensions of the courtyard, her attention was drawn to the sight of a handsome youth in black jodhpurs and a blue waistcoat, some few years older than herself, running towards her and the baron. The man stopped a few feet away from his master, then smiled and lowered his eyes.

'Ivan, this young lady is called Wladyslawa, and will be joining the servants. Please take Bucephalus back to the stables, while I myself show her around.' As the youth went to take the horse's rein, Wladyslawa smiled at him – but he purposely ignored her, much to her chagrin.

'Once you have done that, please go and fill in the hole at the crossroads, while there is still some light,' continued the baron. 'I am afraid the Polacks have been troubling us again.' Ivan nodded his head dutifully.

Then the baron led Wladyslawa beneath an ornate arch featuring roses, crosses and other bizarre symbols and into a great hall with a fine wide staircase. The walls of the hall were bedecked with portraits whose sitters all bore the same distinguished looks as the baron. The baron now turned to Wladyslawa and smiled, his eyes flashing with a preternatural light that simultaneously thrilled and terrified her.

'Through there you will find Roxana, the mistress of the house in place of my poor darling wife, who died some years ago. Go to her now and discover your duties!'

Some ten years later here stood Wladyslawa, looking out again over battlements and scorched September stubble. She smiled as she recalled the naive impressions that had attended her all those years before, and how glad she now was that she had been banished from her father's inn, as since that time she had discovered new talents – talents which had bestowed on her immense power. The discovery of such talents had become the joy of her life – she had truly been saved!

Pulling her tartan shawl close, she fingered the brooch she had worn for most of the past ten years: the brooch with the seven-petalled rose. Suddenly, a gust of air assailed her cheek, and with it a sudden recollection of her duties. She turned to open the oak door and hurled her voice down the echoing stairwell.

'Ivan,' she screamed. 'Come here immediately!' Soon faint footsteps could be heard, becoming ever less faint until the same young man she had first admired all those years ago was before her. His blond moustache now drooped over a slightly chubbier face, but he wore the same black jodhpurs and blue waistcoat that formed his master's livery as he had done when they had first met, some ten years prior. How foolish she had been to have noticed him! He stood with the same idiot's gait that she had once mistaken for shyness, and which she found so repellent now.

'Mistress, you called?' he mumbled from beneath his moustache and downcast eyes.

'Have you checked the stables today?' she asked, her green eyes flashing. 'I may ride out later, should it please me.'

'Which horse would Mistress like to take?' he replied. She slapped his cheek.

'You know very well which one! I'll take Bucephalus, as your master always permits me when he's away.' Ivan stood stock still, although began blinking rapidly.

'Very well, Mistress, I shall prepare him now.' He bowed his head then turned to perform his task.

'Oh, and Ivan,' she called after him. 'You will leave a bottle of Riesling in my rooms with my meal this evening; the 1858.'

'Very good, Mistress,' he replied, before returning down the spiral staircase.

She turned to look again over the scorched stubble before her, her breast swelling with the exhilaration that bullying Ivan and the other servants always afforded her. She was now their mistress, Roxana having long since been dismissed.

She now recalled how, some months after starting in service to the baron, she had noticed that Roxana – a somewhat plain woman, with a baggy face and pouchy eyes – was becoming notably jealous of her. Whether it was because of her relative youth (Wladyslawa was some ten years younger) or because Roxana was intent on maintaining her exalted position, Wladyslawa could not be sure, but whatever it was, it had led to a great deal of trouble.

◊

Wladyslawa was attending his lordship in the smoking room where, clad in his purple velvet smoking jacket, he would retire after lunch. Propped up in a leather armchair, he was, as ever, poring over some esoteric book, his concentration intense as he puffed on a pipe shaped like a treble clef. As Wladyslawa knelt down to stoke the fire, the smoking room's door burst open, like a cabin door breaking inward from a wave.

'You fiend!' screeched a voice. Wladyslawa dropped her poker before the grate and turned sharply. In the doorway stood Roxana, quaking, her face scarlet with rage. 'You fiend!' she cried again, launching towards the Ruthenian like a genie escaped from its bottle, only to be caught by the baron, who had shot up from his armchair to trap the woman in his arms. 'Let me at her, my Lord, let me at her!' Roxana screamed.

'Compose yourself, woman!' ordered the baron, throwing her into the armchair and pinioning her with his hovering gait.

Wladyslawa was now standing up, the poker newly grasped in her hand.

Folding his arms regally before him, the baron tried to calm the two women.

'Tell me, Roxana, what brings you to accuse Wladyslawa so?'

'My Lord, she is evil. She has killed my family!' A spasm of fear and self-doubt shook Wladyslawa, as shakes even the most innocent when confronted with unexpected, and unwelcome, intelligence.

'How... how can I have done that?' she stammered. 'I have been here all along, and don't even know who your family are, or where they live!'

'It was your curse that killed them,' screamed Roxana. 'The other day when, for some trumped-up reason, you cursed me and my entire family. The baron knows!' At this Roxana rose again and leapt at her foe, but the baron secured her in a lock and held her over his shoulder, her fists beating futilely on his back.

'Tell me what's happened, Roxana,' demanded the baron. He let the woman fall back into the armchair but did not fully release her, knowing full well she was primed to attack her foe once more if she could. Wladyslawa bit her lip – pins and needles coursing through her frame.

'My father, my brother, and my sweet little sister, all were discovered yesterday by my father's woodcutter. All were slumped on the kitchen table, having drunk hemlock. My cousin arrived today, to take me to their funeral.'

'I'm so sorry, Roxana,' exclaimed Wladyslawa, slackening the grip on the poker. 'Such terrible news. But how can I be to blame when they took their own lives together?'

'It was you who cursed them, you witch!' Roxana screamed, her cheeks candescent. 'My Lord, you must dismiss her.' Roxana rose to launch herself at her enemy once more, but Lucarda again restrained her, then threw her onto the floor.

'I am truly sorry for your grievances,' said he, with little sign of sorrow, 'but you cannot blame Wladyslawa.'

'My Lord, she has the evil eye,' cried Roxana. 'I will not work with her anymore.' She struggled up and pointed at her enemy, her eyes wild with anger. Lucarda now grabbed Roxana again and threw her against the open doorway. Visibly shocked by the baron's lack of sympathy towards her, the mistress of his house, Roxana looked at him mutely, her blue-black apron miserably torn.

'If you cannot abide Wladyslawa, then I suggest that you leave – now! Here,' said the baron, taking some crumpled notes out of his smoking-jacket pocket and stuffing them into her hand, 'this is two months' pay. Leave with your cousin, and don't come back!' Roxana's lips quivered. She stared at Wladyslawa, and then at the baron, in evident disbelief.

'But, my Lord,' she cried, 'surely you cannot be supporting her over me?' her rage now withering into humiliation.

'Roxana,' continued the baron, narrowing his dark eyes, 'I have come to believe that you have been harassing the other servants, to get them dismissed, and maintain your own position.'

'My Lord, that is not true,' replied Roxana.

The baron shook his head. 'I am afraid I do not believe you. Indeed, I believe you have been doing this for some time. Now, go quickly – and don't come back!' he repeated, folding his arms before him. 'And be sure not to bury your wretched family near the crossroads either, or they will be disinterred and burned – that is, if they really are dead, and this is not some ruse to have your rival dismissed!'

Roxana glared at Wladyslawa then slapped her forehead with her palm. 'And have my loved ones near where that witch can gloat over them? Never, you fiends!' And with a sudden lurch she made to attack the baron with her fist but was easily restrained, then propelled bodily through the doorway.

'Go now,' the baron shouted after her, 'or you and your cousin will face the whip and the brand!' Roxana now glared at the baron then began edging further backwards into the corridor. Then, all of a sudden, she turned and fled, her sobs receding with the patter of her soles along the passageway.

Lucarda closed the door and turned to face Wladyslawa, his features impassive in the light from a flickering oil lamp.

'My Lord, thank you,' said Wladyslawa curtseying. 'If Roxana speaks truly, then I am truly sorry for her, I am. But you must know I could never have had anything to do with her family's demise.'

'No, that is not entirely correct,' replied Lucarda calmly. 'You most certainly have.' Wladyslawa dropped the poker on the floor with a clang.

'My Lord, you surely cannot believe—'

'Come now,' he resumed, in a mollifying tone. 'I am not blaming you, but I have heard you cursing Roxana because of her poor treatment of you, and now this is the result!'

'But, my Lord,' spluttered Wladyslawa.

'Yes indeed, Wladyslawa; you clearly have talents of which you are fain aware.' Wladyslawa bit her nether lip as he said this, feeling simultaneously appalled and thrilled: appalled by the baron's belief she had anything to do with such violence, thrilled by the sheer closeness of his lithe, demonic energy.

'Yes, you clearly do not know it, but you can summon up evil spirits at will.' Wladyslawa shook her head and started backing towards the fire.

'No, no, no...'

'Do not be afraid,' continued the baron. 'You can do good with your powers, and will be of use to me, like Prospero's Ariel.' Wladyslawa now stared into the baron's black eyes, the fire bouncing its reflection in his pupils; her excitement increased.

'Who is Ariel, my Lord?'

'You are, my spirit of mischief.'

It was then that the baron had sat Wladyslawa down and begun a long discourse on his devotion to Rosicrucianism and what he understood to be its goal: spiritual oneness with the divine; the return of Christ in a new world order; and immortality in a paradise on earth. He explained the use of Kabbalah and Theurgy in ascending through the seven stages of initiation that led to immortality, and the rituals entailed at each stage. Picking up the book he had been reading earlier, Lucarda explained that he himself had passed to the third stage, and was now trapped there, since he could not control the hostile spirits that impeded his advance – and that even the Seal of Solomon was no protection against them. How could he progress?

He then got up and took another book from a shelf to the left of the fireplace and, having blown away some dust and sat back down, explained that it was *The Lesser Key of Solomon*, a work that described the sigils of various evil spirits which could be used in invocations, including that of Gamigin, the great Marquis of Hell; the sigil they would come to use in all their communications, as if it were Wladyslawa's own personal seal.

'You must learn to master the invocations surrounding these sigils, Wladyslawa, and so protect me as I advance,' announced the baron. Wladyslawa was not sure how to respond – why would the baron ask her to forfeit her immortal soul?

'Is this not a great blasphemy and danger, my Lord?' she asked. 'I do not wish to offend my God.' He looked at her and slammed the book shut.

'You have already been claimed by the devil, Wladyslawa!' he declared sternly.

Wladyslawa gasped.

'And it is only now in service to me that you can be saved!'

The baron's words offered Wladyslawa some reassurance, but quite in what way she did not know. Nonetheless, she cleaved to them, the events of the past few hours having unsettled her more than anything that had happened her entire life.

Lucarda now extinguished the oil lamp. It was twilight, and the glow of the sunset flecked the room, obscuring her master's features. 'Come,' he said, standing up, 'let me show you my temple. You will learn.'

It had been a marvellous education, she reflected. She had become adept at conjuring evil spirits, which communicated with her through symbols and dreams. Thanks to these spirits, she could now protect her master through her control of Gamigin. She could also now read minds through scrying, her repute keeping the Polish peasants away from the crossroads for many a year and allowing her to control the servants with a flash of her fearsome green eyes. A demon vixen, she needed no husband or lover. The longings for men which had troubled her before were now sated with the cruel thrill of her power and the adoration of her lord – with whom she enjoyed a passionate but celibate union, his devotion to his dead wife being absolute.

Once again, she clutched her rose brooch – it felt more natural to her now than any rosary. And then she reflected that she had one more task to perform before riding out in the warm autumn sunshine – her first such foray since her lord had ordered the drawbridge to be kept up on his departure. She pushed open the oak door and descended the spiral staircase to her boudoir. Here there were more steps. Down she went, counting some three flights of winding stair before gliding through a long passageway carpeted with Persian rugs and lined with strange, eastern-looking statues on podiums. At the end of the passage she stopped and pulled back a panel of tapestry to reveal another, narrower, stairway. She now moved down this until she reached an elaborately carved wrought-iron door within a pointed arch – a door through which only she and her master were allowed to pass.

Retrieving a key from beneath her petticoats, she opened its padlock and entered. She lit one of the braziers beside the lintel – and now the marvellous gold and red tiles of the temple of the Rosy Cross were before her. In the centre of the wall opposite her, behind an altar, stood a large gold cross, itself centred by a red, seven-petalled rose. To its left, painted on the wall, a tableau of demons and their symbols; to its right, the four archangels, Raphael, Uriel, Michael and Gabriel. She held affection for them all, but what commanded her greatest love was the open stone tomb or sarcophagus in the centre of the chamber where, since passing, as the baron had told her, the stage of silver, he had slept during the day when at the castle. He would, she thrilled to think, soon be immortal – and so would she, once he was, never to die and suffer her soul to burn in hell! Wladyslawa looked again at the cross, its glorious gold resplendent against the red of the rose. For some reason, since returning from Krakow, the baron had insisted the cross be covered up while he had lain in the temple, and she was glad to see it restored.

It was time to see his thoughts – a ritual the baron had instilled in her before his return to London, back in the summer. Wladyslawa nodded her head briefly before the cross then knelt down on a footstool which stood before a shallow pool of water housed within a small wooden cabinet at the foot of the sarcophagus. As she knelt, she kissed the sigil of Gamigin on the pool's rim. 'Oh, Gamigin,' she declared in the perfect Enochian of Dee and Kelly, 'show me your limitless darkness and light! Show me my master's mind!' As she did so, a whirring sound started up and a light came sparkling through the water. Images that she now knew well congealed at the bottom of the pool: the man with the imposing brow and mane of grey hair; the woman, younger, with the long fair hair – both the man and woman strangely familiar from her youth; and then the building with the grand white portico where these reprobates spent so much of their time – their theatre, no doubt.

Yes, she knew all about them, and their betrayal – the baron had told her. And now the baron was back in London, and they would now suffer, as she knew that they must. And then he would be coming home!

CHAPTER IX

THE TROLLOP RETURNS

It was Monday afternoon and Joseph Harker was behind the red velvet curtain of the Lyceum fixing the canvas backdrop – first with some clever stitching, then with some lightly applied paint from his pot. An impressive-looking man in his braces, strong and sporty, the stagehands knew not to trouble him with enquiries or make too much of a commotion around him while he gave the finishing touches to the intricate outlines of snow dunes and black branches which imbued the backdrop's spare elliptical design with its otherworldly aura. Frankly, Harker did not care much for the design himself – a creation of Telbin – but he knew how well limelight could show up poor workmanship, even to those members of the audience seated far away, and so was concentrating with firm and quick precision on the job.

He stood back and admired his work. It was, he reflected, an honour for a scene painter such as he, still green in his trade, to be working at Mr Irving's theatre, and he relished the opportunity of showing off his skills to those more highly orbiting in London's theatrical cosmos than he. Recent days and recent contacts seemed to be advancing his career, and he was glad, most glad, that he was taking the path which he had elected to follow by joining an eminent occult society.

Harker's cricketer's forearms rested on his knees as he now bent down to examine the canvas bottom in the light of an oil lamp positioned some two feet behind him. There was no time to lose – he must finish painting the backdrop then move the lamp somewhat closer to the canvas to give it some drying time; everything must be ready before curtain-up at eight o'clock. Suddenly, he called out.

'Mr Loveday, pray tell me the hour!'

'It is half past five exactly, Mr Harker,' came a straining voice behind him.

'Thank you, Sir,' he replied. 'I shall be ready in no more than two shakes of a dodo's tail!' – an attempt at jocularity that drew but little response.

A few minutes more and Harker was closing up his paint pots, wiping down his brushes, and then putting all inside his leather Gladstone – an unfortunate name, he reflected, for so useful a bag; he would have preferred it to be called a Canning, given his strong Tory leanings. He signalled to Lovejoy to bring an extra oil lamp before placing first it and then the other lamp some six inches before the canvas. The offstage lights were low, and once the two globules of light were safely in position, they created the not-unpleasant impression of a small campfire in the gloom.

'Now, Mr Loveday, you must stay and watch over these lamps for some time. Please make sure no one knocks them over and causes some conflagration, the like of which I am sure Mr Irving would not recover from!'

Loveday sighed.

'Well, I'm afraid I cannot stay here and watch them for much longer, Mr Harker. Of course, if you had come when you were expected...'

'I did not receive my summons from you until late in the day, Mr Loveday,' retorted Harker. 'And then the steamer was delayed for over an hour, owing to some mechanical problem. Of course, had your acting manager shown his usual punctuality, you would not need to be watching over these oil lamps now!'

'My apologies,' came a low voice from behind him, 'but it has been a most trying afternoon.' Harker turned round to see a tall figure with bowler and cane, centre stage.

'I am so sorry, Mr Stoker, I did not mean to harm your reputation,' said Harker, approaching the acting manager to shake his hand.

'No harm done,' said Stoker dully.

'You don't seem your usual self tonight, Sir,' ventured Harker. 'Can it be these latest Whitechapel murders have perturbed you?' Stoker frowned. 'I'm afraid I know little of their details,' continued Harker, 'having heard of them just this morning. Would you know anything more?' Stoker took the newspaper he had bought earlier from under his arm and gave it to the younger man.

'It's all in here, should you wish to read about it. Please keep the paper for yourself – I've read as much as I care to.'

'That's very kind of you, Sir,' replied Harker, trying to sound cheery despite the awkwardness of the conversation. 'Saves me forking out for a copy.'

'Anyhow, Mr Harker,' resumed Stoker with more vim. 'It looks like you have done a fine job here. Now, here's your cheque.' He pulled out a folded piece of paper from his coat pocket and thrust it into Harker's hand. He then stepped past the scene painter to join Loveday. 'You may go now.'

'Thank you, Sir,' said Harker, talking hesitantly to Stoker's long back. 'You know, I am always available for whole commissions, and my most recent work at the Adelphi—'

'Yes, yes,' breathed Stoker, waving his hand dismissively behind him. 'We will be in touch again soon.'

'Thank you, Sir, thank you.' And with that Harker went to pick up his Gladstone then, turning his back on the lights and shadows of this pre-performance stage, set off for the foyer.

Once outside, he noticed that the fog was peculiarly thick,

like in an Impressionist painting. As a painter, if only of sets and scenes, he had already rejected the novelties of this continental movement, and their depictions of London in the murk had simply made the reality of it all the more miserable for him. He could see no cabs in the offing; in fact, he could barely see anything at all, the fog occluding any sun. Stationing himself beneath a convenient gaslight, he decided to wait outside the theatre until a cab came along. He opened up the newspaper and began, with some difficulty, to read.

The paper was full of the double murder in Whitechapel the day before. Although the crime scenes were described obliquely, Harker's keen visual fancy could not help but make him wince as he took in allusions to bizarre incisions and mutilations, and the description of one of the victims – her petticoat bloodied, her bonnet and blouse horribly ripped. As he read on, he was surprised to come across an unusually precise account of a shawl that had been left at the scene of one of the murders; a shawl of a most unusual design – part a deep blue, part a bright orange, with peacock-feather motifs – and which had seemingly not belonged to the victim herself, owing to its likely exotic origin. As Harker squinted under the lamplight, he noted that this description had clearly caught Stoker's eye as well, as he had circled it with a charcoal crayon and underlined it further, as if in a fit of excitement, judging by the increased thickness of the second stroke. Strange, thought Harker, that this should have intrigued the acting manager so.

Before he could read further, Harker was disturbed by the jangling of a horse's bridle: a vehicle had pulled up directly alongside him. He threw the newspaper onto the pavement and was about to call out to the driver when he saw that the vehicle was in fact a private carriage, a dour-looking man with a moustache at its helm. He determined to walk on and hail a hansom – but the carriage's horse suddenly neighed violently, stopping him in his tracks. The driver now bellowed thick rings, like smoke, through the yellowing fog.

'Mr Harker, is it not?'

'Yes… but who are you?'

'I am the baron's driver. Please go to the back of the carriage and join him. He demands to see you.' Harker gulped – he had not expected his vows in the temple to draw such immediate duties. He strode to the back of the vehicle where, embossed on ebony doors, he faced the symbol he had so recently kissed in the mystique-riven room in Soho: the red, seven-petalled rose. He was about to knock when the latch within rattled and the double doors were pushed open. Inside, illuminated by gas lamps, were two velvet benches, flanking the interior, on one of which was seated the baron, clutching a cane. He was immaculate in black evening dress with tails, a white cravat and pin. A silk top hat lay to his side.

'Please, Phoenix-not-Dove, come in.'

'Of course, Baron—'

'You must call me by my order name,' snapped his mentor.

'I mean, Lord Rosy Cross.'

'That's better,' responded the baron. 'I am here on official business.'

Harker climbed up into the carriage, taking care his Gladstone did not touch the velvet seating lest any stray paint brushed off and annoyed his mentor.

'So, Phoenix-not-Dove,' the baron continued, 'how has your week been since you took your vows in my temple?'

'Excellent, Lord Rosy Cross,' replied Harker, 'excellent. Fortune favours the adept. I have been inundated with requests for work, and my skills have increased tenfold already. I really feel as though the Pansophia—'

'You are but a virgin, Phoenix-not-Dove, in the roots of the Pansophia,' interrupted the baron. 'A mere sapling hoping to entangle itself in the mesh of the Pansophia's many branches. You are still only at the stage of Malkuth on the tree of life.' The baron's voice was quiet but menacing, his handsome moustachioed face radiating a power of such magnitude that even the strong cricketer

Harker felt he could be overwhelmed.

'You are right, Lord Rosy Cross.'

'Tell me, will you be working at this theatre again?'

'I hope so, Lord.'

'When?' The baron's tone had become insistent. 'Tomorrow?'

'I am afraid not, Lord Rosy Cross.' The baron sighed, evincing disappointment for some unfathomable reason. There was an awkward pause.

'You know them well?' he now continued.

'Who?'

'Why, Mr Irving and this Mr Stoker.' Harker shrugged his broad shoulders.

'Tolerably well, I suppose.'

'So, you know where their offices are – somewhere upstairs…?'

'Yes, up on the second floor, Lord Rosy Cross – at the back.'

'And Miss Terry's dressing room, where is that?' Harker thought for a moment.

'I believe it is right next to Mr Stoker's office.'

'And it faces towards the back, away from the street, you say?'

'I've never been there, but yes, I believe so.'

'Very well. You may go.'

'But, Lord Rosy Cross?'

'Go! I have no more use for you!' And with that he struck Harker's nose with his cane and snarled, revealing hideously long incisors. Harker slid violently off his seat, his weight knocking open the double doors as he then tumbled out of the carriage – his precious Gladstone, with all its precious paints and brushes, left to the mercy of the baron.

The carriage now moved off into the darkness, as though driven by a horseman of the apocalypse. Harker got up and, finding himself unbloodied, dusted himself off and headed down towards the river. As he made his way along the Strand, his shock starting slowly to resolve, he realised with a pang that his recent inauguration at the temple in Soho – his hobnobbing with men such as Conan Doyle and Dowden in their gold and red robes – had probably all been part of some elaborate deception; the whole thing not so much about the order helping him as about him helping the order! How could he have been so naive? He stamped his foot on the setts and howled, before coughing and trying to compose himself. And then he realised with another pang that not only had he betrayed himself, but he had also betrayed others, imparting details about the layout of the Lyceum to an unscrupulous party – who might do Lord knows what with it!

As Harker was making his way down the Strand, shaking with shame and indignation, Stoker was reviewing preparations for that evening's performance at the theatre, as being overseen by Loveday. He had counted the number of stagehands as one short – and one, Mr Bluedale, was decidedly reeking of gin. Grafton, meanwhile, was creating a slow kaleidoscope over the stage, testing the row of lights suspended from a wooden ceiling batten in careful sequence. As Stoker looked on from the wings, his mind wandered into another heaven – to the peculiarly patterned blue and orange shawl so precisely described in the newspaper. Was it not the very same shawl he had seen discarded on the Guv'nor's dressing room floor a week before? Could it be that Kosminski, the barber, was somehow involved in the Whitechapel murders? Or could it even be that the Guv'nor was himself somehow involved? No amount of speculation could end in a clear conclusion, and Stoker was appalled. As he continued to ruminate on this, a sudden shaft of light from behind him shattered Grafton's carefully sequenced kaleidoscope. Stoker turned round to see the imposing silhouette of the Guv'nor, the unmistakeable cast of his long mane falling over his shoulders in the shape of an upside-down fan.

'What brings you down here this evening, Bram?' growled Irving. 'Surely you have tasks aplenty up in your office?'

'Oh, I had to pay Harker for some work,' replied Stoker quickly.

'Ha!' responded Irving. 'Well, I hope you paid him in accordance with his deserts rather than what he imagines them to be!'

'Yes indeed, Guv'nor.' Stoker was trying hard to control any facial tics as his boss advanced towards him, but Irving was not one to overlook such cues.

'Bram, you seem somewhat out of sorts tonight.'

'A little, Guv'nor. I read *The Star*!' responded Stoker, with some boldness.

'Ah,' said Irving, sighing and tossing back his long mane, 'the degenerate has struck again. A most distressing story, I agree.'

'Did you read the description of the crime scene?' pressed Stoker, looking at the Guv'nor for any signs of self-betrayal.

'I did indeed,' replied Irving, revealing none. 'Very upsetting. Glad I don't have a daughter, I must say.' He now strode past Stoker to inspect Harker's work by the two drying lamps, which were now being withdrawn by the stagehands. Was Irving so assured that he did not query this line of questioning, wondered Stoker, or was he simply bluffing? He was certainly a consummate actor, that he and everybody else in London and the wider world knew well. Or was the shawl's presence in the Guvnor's dressing room not suspicious, its origin not as rare as he supposed it to be? That seemed unlikely, though, given its singular design.

Stoker was in a quandary: should he pursue his suspicions of the Guv'nor or let things pass? Before he could follow these thoughts through, a screech assaulted his ears. He turned around to see, of all things, a young girl, her teeth bared, her hands splayed like the paws of a cat. Suddenly, like the flash of a bursting gas lamp, a drunken Bluedale was thrown across the stage, followed by shouts and exhortations as two of his fellow hands rushed to gather him up. The girl was lashing her arms about her, whining like an animal, her eyes red with demonic energy.

'My God, it's her,' screamed Grafton. 'She's come back!'

'Quick,' cried Irving, as Stoker now rushed onstage, 'we must restrain her; she's mad with the rabies!' Together with Grafton and the remaining hands, they formed a circle around the girl, whose tousled blonde hair looked like a tangle of luminous seaweed. She wore the same skirt and tatty red shawl (now even tattier) that she had been wearing when Stoker had rescued her from the lights cellar all those weeks ago – as if she had worn nothing else since.

'What are we to do, Mr Stoker?' squealed Grafton, as yet another advance was met with a vicious snarl and a violent slice of the air. 'This is no ordinary girl!' Her head turned rapidly from side to side as if she were a furious Cerberus, her eyes shining with the heat of Hades over her hollow cheeks.

'Just keep her checked,' shouted Stoker. 'Don't move!'

He now faced the girl.

'Why are you harassing us like this, young woman? Why have you returned?' he asked, brandishing his brass-tipped cane before him.

'I don't think she understands you, Bram,' rasped Irving. 'The rabies has clearly rendered her bestial! Perhaps if we throw some water over her...?' At this the girl parted her lips to reveal long canines and leapt high towards Irving, aiming for his neck. Before Stoker could act, Irving had jumped screaming into the canvas backdrop, tearing the outline of a snow dune. The girl crashed against the side wall, stage right, with a force that would have crippled any ordinary being.

'My goodness, is she concussed?' cried Loveday, the others crowding in behind him.

'Keep back,' shouted Stoker. 'She's not concussed and is still dangerous – mark my words!' His warning was well timed, for no sooner had he said this than the girl was up again, primed for attack.

'My God!' cried Grafton. 'Who would have believed it?' At this the girl wrenched open her mouth once more, ready to launch.

'Get away,' cried Stoker. 'Get away, all of you!' And then the girl lunged high into the air towards the acting manager. Stoker crouched and held his cane instinctively out before him, like a lance. And then he fell backwards blindly onto the floor. He felt a mass slam onto his chest, then a quivering vibration, slowly losing its force, accompanied by a long low wail.

'For the love of Christ!' screamed Grafton. And then the mass was inert; slumped across Stoker's body. Stoker opened his eyes to see the girl's tousled blonde hair and shoulders next to his face. Then, in a moment of preternatural horror, he realised that the lower part of his cane was protruding out of her back: he had impaled the girl right through her heart; she was dead.

'Are you all right, Bram?' now demanded Irving, seemingly recovered from his encounter with the backdrop. For a while Stoker said nothing. He looked up at the ceiling and tried to focus as thoughts squalled through his mind.

'What have I done, Guv'nor?' he whispered at last.

'I'm afraid you've just made a ghost,' replied Irving. Stoker pushed the girl's body off him then immediately turned onto his side and retched onto the stage. After a few moments, Grafton stepped forward and helped the acting manager onto his feet. Stoker now came face to face with his boss.

'It was not your fault, Bram,' said Irving. 'Purely self-defence. The girl was clearly in the last throes of rabies – and would have died anyway.'

'That was not rabies!' shrieked Grafton. 'And that was no human, but some supernatural creature. What ordinary girl has strength like that?'

'Come now,' said Irving, trying to calm his lights manager. 'Mad people have all kinds of strength; I know that from my days doing character sketches at the asylum.'

'Look at her, will you?' shrieked Grafton once more. 'She's dead but not bleeding!' The three men now looked down at the girl, Stoker atremble with the hope that, somehow, she might still be alive. The girl lay on her side, Stoker's cane protruding almost a foot past her spine – and yet there was no sign of blood. Grafton squatted down beside her, then wrenched out the cane to reveal just the faintest crimson spots along its length.

'Astonishing,' murmured Stoker.

'It's the same girl Edward seduced in the theatre,' continued Irving. 'Must have been bitten by a rabid dog and come back here deranged, looking for him.'

'I swear,' breathed Grafton, 'that whatever she may have been then, she came back now either a banshee or a vampire.' Irving laughed dismissively.

As Stoker eyed the body, he noticed that the girl now looked like a wax doll. All of a sudden, he felt no remorse over killing her. Surely Grafton was right, and this was no ordinary girl, but some other being – yes, quite possibly, as he knew from his study of Calmet, a vampire!

'Aloysius, I know little of what banshees in your country do, and what spirits haunt your glorious peat bogs of a winter's evening, but this rabid wretch was no supernatural creature,' said Irving. 'Indeed, she is nothing but a common trollop!' he added grimly. Loveday now approached Irving.

'With all due respect, Sir, we must work out what to do. Should we call the police?'

Irving glared at him, suddenly furious. 'Police? Are you mad?'

'Well,' Loveday replied, tremulously, 'it *was* just an accident. There are many witnesses here who can testify it was clearly self-defence on Mr Stoker's part.'

'No, a thousand times no!' screamed Irving. He stepped over the girl's body and took Loveday by the shoulders. 'We cannot – *must* not – risk the theatre's reputation over this matter.'

'But, Mr Irv—'

'But, Mr Loveday,' continued Irving, 'while we do not know who this girl is, we do know that Edward seduced her. If we were to tell the police, heaven knows what other skeletons they might find in young Edward's closet – as we all know he is capable of some rough and tumble. And then, think of Miss Terry. No, we must all – myself included – keep our silence on this!' And here he turned and looked determinedly at the stagehands as Loveday nodded meekly. It was not the first time, Stoker noted, that he had seen how Irving's natural authority could override the conscience of others – indeed, it had overridden his own.

'Now, Mr Loveday,' continued Irving, 'let us see if we can patch up the backdrop with some paper and glue while you, hands, put the girl's body in an empty props basket behind the stage. I will have it disposed of later, after the show. Come, everybody, we must act quickly!'

Loveday nodded again, slowly.

'Aloysius,' said Irving, now turning towards the lights manager, 'be sure to say nothing of what you have seen tonight; I wouldn't want your blarney scattering wisps of rumours over the fair fields of London.'

'No one would believe me anyway,' replied Grafton, shaking his head and sighing deeply. 'Not every day you see a vampire or suchlike. Ah well, at least we now know what was wanting the blood out of them rats in the cellar! Mind you, as they say in Connemara—'

'Enough of that!' commanded Irving. Then, with a clap of his hands, added, 'Come now, clear away those lamps, will you? We have only forty minutes till curtain-up, and I must speak to our acting manager!' As the hands started to busy themselves with their chores, Irving approached Stoker, who had remained stuck to his spot – his only movement the furious unconscious fondling of his beard.

'I can't believe what I've just done, Guv'nor,' said Stoker in a low voice.

'Don't worry, Bram,' replied Irving. 'As Aloysius said, your actions were clearly self-defence. Anyone would have done the same. Besides, as I told you, the girl would have died of her derangement anyway. You have no need to reproach yourself, and certainly no need to say anything to the police!' Irving's black eyes were now burrowing unblinkingly into Stoker's own, as if weighing his soul. 'You had better spend tonight and most of tomorrow away from the theatre,' he added at last, before heading purposefully offstage, brushing past his acting manager on his way.

Stoker shook his head in resignation, and was about to head towards the wings himself, when a thought seized him.

'What about *The Star*, Sir?' he called out to his retreating boss. 'All those details in the newspaper, about the shawl and yesterday's Whitechapel murders? A shawl just like the one I saw on your dressing room floor. Things look rather suspicious, don't you think?' Irving turned round and glared at Stoker, before curling his lip cruelly.

'The only suspicious-looking thing I have seen is the death of a rabid prostitute in my own theatre at the end of your cane!' Stoker took an involuntary step backwards. Was this a veiled threat from a guilty man? 'Now go home, Bram, and don't feel you need to come back until tomorrow night. You need to take some rest.'

The steamer journey home that evening was mercifully quick, and once back in his study, Stoker immediately returned to his copy of *The Phantom World*. Here he read again the infamous case of Arnold Paole, and of how vampires needed to suck the blood of the living to renew their Undead existence. He shut the book. Yes, surely Grafton was right. The creature that had attacked him, this wax doll with scarcely any blood in it, might once have been the girl Edward had seduced in the theatre, but was no longer human by the time he himself had dispatched it – of that he was certain.

He mopped his brow, and then suddenly buried his head in his hands and began to sob uncontrollably. The last few weeks had been truly hellish, what with the farce of the Drayfield trial, the horror of the murders in Whitechapel, the inference of Irving's guilt, and now this – the worst of all. But he knew that if he were to report his fears about the Guv'nor to the police, his own 'killing' of the girl, or whatever she was, would come to light. And if she was indeed a vampire, who would ever believe him? His long-held silence over the girl he had first discovered in the cellar would seem most culpable. Even the testimony of Grafton, Loveday and the others would not be believed. Like a desperate Faust awaiting Mephistopheles, he was trapped. How could it have come to this? Stoker now let his head collapse on the desk, and out of sheer nervous exhaustion, fell immediately and profoundly asleep.

CHAPTER X

THE BARON ATTACKS

Stoker had taken the Guv'nor's advice and stayed at home most of the following day, until half past four in the afternoon, when he donned his frock coat and bowler, and left his house at St Leonard's Terrace. It had not been a restful day in Chelsea, his mind running amok as he agonised over whether to write to the police. And yet, each time he had resolved to do so, his fears had overcome him. He would find himself reflecting on the gravity of his suspicions and attempt to write again, only to feel renewed foreboding about the confession he would have to make over skewering the rabid girl's heart; no rabid girl surely, but a supernatural creature of some sort – yes, he was sure Grafton's suspicions were correct, even if they did conflict with all the rational beliefs he had acquired while at Trinity. Were he not currently distanced from his brother, he would have consulted his opinion as a man of science, but the stinging rebuff he had recently received from that quarter had left him unwilling so to do.

As Stoker was making his way towards the river for the steamer at Cadogan Pier, he noted that the earlier fog had lifted, and the air was crisp. The leaves from the trees were forming patterns of gold and red along the pavement, like scattered Rosicrucian designs. As he passed the bottom of Radnor Street and headed on towards Flood Street, he saw a carriage coming towards him, rattling swiftly over the setts. He stopped – the driver atop the carriage cracked his long whip – a Cheshire cat's face turned and glared at him as the vehicle passed – Ponsonby? – the Guv'nor? And then the spasm of untruth passed, and Stoker was left marooned in its wake.

As he stood there, passers-by streaming round him like water around an eyot, Stoker tried to collect himself – it was just a harmless carriage, after all... After a few moments, he took out his watch and consulted the dial: five o'clock. Sighing deeply, he put his wife's gift safely back in his waistcoat pocket and set off once more for the river.

He arrived at the pier to discover that the steamer was running late; he would have to wait at least half an hour before it arrived. As he loitered near the jetty, he was seized with the desire to rush up to the King's Road and hail a cab, but he had no desire to encounter that carriage again – harmless though it may be – and, for once, resisted the temptation.

At last the steamer came. Once on board, standing on deck (there was no room in first class), Stoker found himself among a crowd of overly bustled barmaids and flat-capped lamplighters off to their evening's work. The brass rays of sunlight were colouring the currents of the Thames, making it appear like a rippling vat of whisky. Soon they were passing beneath Chelsea, Vauxhall, Lambeth then Westminster Bridges, the steamer seeming to pierce through an ever-duskier light.

At Embankment Pier Stoker disembarked. To his relief, at the top of the gang plank, was a figure he recognised; yes, there was Jonas, standing at the back of his cab, his whip dangling over the top towards the rump of Tinder. Stoker moved swiftly to hail him.

'My word, Mr Stoker,' exclaimed the cabbie, turning his head in the direction of Stoker's long halloo. 'What brings you here at this hour?'

'Work, as always,' replied Stoker breathlessly. 'Starting late tonight, I'm afraid.' He clambered into the hansom and shut the cab door behind him.

'The Lyceum, then, Sir?' asked Jonas, smiling reassuringly at Stoker through the cab roof's trapdoor.

'As ever, please, Jonas. I'm in a bit of a hurry, so please don't spare Tinder.'

'Ha!' responded Jonas, and with a crack of the whip they were circling round the emptying courtyard outside Embankment Station. Soon they were trotting up a side street past assorted warehouses, and then past assorted public houses, where horse boys and traders late from the 'Change were bandying gossip on the news of the day. On they went into the Strand, past Charing Cross Station with its usual clutch of barrow-boys, hawkers and soldiers on leave, then past the Adelphi, with its gaggle of gin-sodden stinkards queuing up to see the latest spectacle of 'sensation gone mad'. As the hansom pushed on in the murk, Stoker once more becoming lost in his thoughts, Jonas suddenly drew reins as he turned into the bottom of Wellington Street, jolting him from his reverie.

'Oi, Sir,' he shrieked. 'It's that daft foozler again!'

'What do you mean?' asked Stoker.

'I mean that lunatic driver and his cart wot almost crashed into us a few weeks back, when I took you to that druggist's.' There, right in front of them, was Baron Cadwallader's black carriage, its seven-petalled rose looking as blood red as if it had been painted just that morning. It was stationary, and Stoker could see the form of its saturnine driver skulking from his promontory.

Deciding to settle up with Jonas there and then, Stoker delved in his coat pocket for his money pouch before handing two shillings to the cabbie and bidding him and his brave war horse goodbye.

Stoker now approached the black carriage to observe it in more detail. As he did so, a wave of nausea came over him, as if he had kissed the hand of a corpse. Could this really be the carriage of a harmless misfit and fop, as Dowden had assured him? He was about to draw closer when the driver turned his moustachioed face towards him and snarled, baring crooked incisors – a sight which left Stoker reeling.

Without waiting to see what unfolded next, Stoker rushed to the Lyceum's stage door. As he ascended the narrow wooden stairs that led up to the second floor, Stoker realised that he was dreading seeing his boss again; indeed, he wanted to keep out of the Guv'nor's way at all costs, at least for that evening. Once past the Beefsteak room and down the corridor, he noticed that light and voices were pouring from the doorway of Irving's dressing room. He resolved to tiptoe past, but before he had gone even a few paces, he heard a cheery exhortation. 'Bram! Do come in, pray. How are you this evening?' He turned to see Irving and Miss Terry, both already in costume – the Guv'nor sporting the brown and cream-striped waistcoat and knee breeches of a half century ago, and Miss Terry in her bonnet and pale blue Swiss pinafore. Their make-up was thick, as always, and in the confines of this Aladdin's cave they looked more like marionettes than players.

'So, Bram, did some rest serve you well?' asked Irving.

'It did, Sir,' replied Stoker glibly, clasping his hands together in an attempt to control his nerves, and remaining on the threshold.

'I am glad,' declared Miss Terry. 'Yes, Henry told me all about that accident with the backdrop last night. So fortunate to have had Mr Loveday around to patch things up.' Stoker looked at the Guv'nor and then back at his leading lady. So, Irving's vow of silence really had been observed.

'Yes, it was most fortunate,' he replied. The nausea he had felt outside had just about washed from his body, and he did not wish it to return.

'Well,' said Irving, 'it's only three quarters of an hour till curtain-up, so you had better get to front of house. We have some very important people coming to the theatre tonight – including, as you know, the Duke of Buccleuch – and I would be most grateful if you could greet him personally on mine and Ellen's behalf.' Stoker laughed weakly.

'Yes, of course, Mr Irving,' he replied. And then, with sudden boldness, added, 'Indeed, I believe we may have another aristocratic visitor – although I don't remember dealing with his tickets, I must say!'

'And who might that be, Bram?' asked Irving, casually tossing his long mane behind him.

'The eccentric Baron Cadwallader no less. A Rosicrucian famed for his reckless driving.'

'Baron Cadwallader? A Rosicrucian, you say?' queried Irving.

'Yes. My friend, Professor Dowden – whom you met, some years ago – taught him in Dublin. Do you know of him?'

'Never heard of him, I'm afraid,' replied Irving, somewhat skittishly.

'He rides around London in a black carriage with a red, seven-petalled rose embossed on its back. That very carriage is outside on the street now!'

Stoker finished this pronouncement to see the strings of the marionettes tauten. Irving and Miss Terry exchanged glances, then, all of a sudden, Irving pounced past Stoker and out into the corridor to look through an arrow slit that gave light to the passage during the day. Suddenly, he uttered a short shriek of fear, the like of which Stoker had never heard from the Guv'nor before, save through the pretence of play-acting. Irving now returned through the gloom, fierce despair shining through his greasepaint. He stepped past Stoker into the dressing room and approached Miss Terry, now atremble with apprehension, then breathed a heavy sigh – as though pieces of slate were dropping from his mouth.

'There is a carriage outside, Nell,' he said softly. 'It must be him.'

'Are... are you sure?' she stammered.

Irving nodded dolefully.

'The baron has kept his infernal promise, and come to London. I knew that he would.'

'Baron Cadwallader?' broke in Stoker. 'What does a man like him mean to you?'

'Cadwallader?' scoffed Irving. '*Curdala*, that is the man's name. A Prussian baron come seeking revenge.'

A sob issued from Miss Terry, who now fell into the arms of her leading man for solace. He patted her on the back and sighed once more.

'This is most strange. I myself heard the name Cadwallader, outside his house in Bayswater.'

'Bayswater, you say, eh, Bram?' said Irving, now more energised. 'Is that where he resides?'

'Yes, but his name is Cadwallader, as I heard it. Indeed, Dowden himself confirmed this for me.'

'Dowden's not to be trusted, Sir.' Stoker started at the voice sounding powerfully behind him. He turned around to see a familiar figure materialising through the gloom.

'What the mercy brings you here, Harker?' now barked Irving.

'Guilt and fear,' replied Harker simply. Harker now addressed Stoker again. 'Your Professor Dowden is, like myself, in the Rosicrucian order. He and this man, Lord Rosy Cross – the same man as in that carriage – are close associates. Curdala is one of the names he goes under, another is Lucarda – Baron Lucarda; L-U-C-A-R-D-A being the letters used in both names.'

'Lucarda?' exclaimed Stoker. 'The same man as in the Drayfield case – the Prussian cousin?'

Irving raised a massive eyebrow.

'That I cannot vouch for,' replied Harker. 'Just do not expect Professor Dowden to be honest, Sir. I am breaking my vows by informing you of this, and perhaps also signing my death warrant. But,' and here he glanced at Irving and Miss Terry, 'I know Curdala – or Lucarda – means ill.' Stoker gasped: these revelations were almost too much to bear. So, Baron Cadwallader, otherwise known as Curdala, the man he had seen being taken in a coffin into Lord Drayfield's house on Dawson Street, and Lucarda, Drayfield's

Prussian cousin, were one and the same! Stoker could barely credit it, or that Dowden could be an associate of this individual. He was about to question Harker further when Miss Terry spoke.

'What are we to do, Henry?'

'We must go on as normal, Ellen, and arouse no suspicion.' Irving's eyes were now liquid, his brow robbed of its usual self-command. And then he seemed to collect himself, and spoke again.

'Maybe we can forestall Curdala in some way... maybe even dispatch him? Harker, you know what the baron looks like. Go with Mr Stoker and waylay him front of house.'

'I had sooner walk into the jaws of hell, Sir.'

'There's no need to worry, Harker. Curdala need never know you are there. Wait in the foyer, in disguise, and alert Bram when he comes in. Bram, tell the baron you are taking him to the best seat in the house and then lock him in the broom cupboard behind the box office. We can deal with him there.'

'I am not taking part in any murder or suchlike,' protested Stoker. Irving looked at him venomously.

'Some might say you already have!' Stoker gulped. How could his governor speak to him so? Nonetheless, he decided to press on.

'I would truly love to know what your relation is with this man, Sir – and what you may have been getting up to in Whitechapel!'

'Whitechapel?' gasped Miss Terry. 'Bram, surely you cannot suspect Henry—'

'Oh yes, Miss Terry, I have reasons for my suspicions, I can assure you.'

'Well, Bram, your suspicions are wrong,' growled Irving. 'But you shall know all in good time, I promise. Now, go and forestall the baron. The show must go on!'

Some ten minutes later Stoker found himself front of house, in the foyer of red velvet and gold. Beside him stood Harker, a harlequin mask obscuring his face, a plume of peacock's feathers adorning the crown of his head. Couples in evening dress were emerging from the descending London fog like headlamps, one after another, into the foyer. Most came to shake Stoker's hand and extend their good wishes before joining the queue to collect tickets at the box office or walking up to the gallery. None enquired about the strange fellow standing to Stoker's left, although a few old military types did cast the occasional bemused look.

'I must say, I must look a tad ridiculous, Sir,' said Harker out of the side of his mouth.

'Well, no one knows who you are, Harker, so there's no need to feel self-conscious. Do you see the baron coming?'

'Not yet,' replied Harker.

'Mr Stoker!' boomed a voice suddenly, shattering both men's attention. There, beneath a glossy top hat, was the lobster-red face of the Duke of Buccleuch. Behind him was his dark-haired wife, dressed demurely in a green taffeta dress.

'My apologies for not noticing you sooner, your Grace,' began Stoker. 'Welcome to the Lyceum. I trust you shall enjoy the performance.'

'I'm sure that I shall,' replied the duke. 'Now, Mr Stoker, if you would be so kind as to lead my wife and me to our box, I would be most grateful.' Stoker hesitated.

'I am afraid I am unexpectedly detained here, your Grace. Can you not—?'

'No, please, Mr Stoker,' boomed the duke again. 'I insist!' Stoker glanced at the harlequin.

'It's all right, Sir,' said Harker from behind his mask. 'You can trust me.'

Stoker smiled wryly.

'This way please, your Grace,' he continued, making a small bow to the imperious duke and his silent wife. He then led them towards the stairs which issued into the box closest to the stage – a box of far ampler size than was required by just two people.

Despite his apparent eagerness to gain his seat, the duke was as lobster-like in his movement as he was in the colour of his face, and took his time climbing the stairs, all the while indulging in his usual prattle about the scarcity of game on his estate and the need to give the Russians a good kicking. Stoker had to fight hard to hide his frustration; he did not entirely trust Harker and was keen to get back to him. Once Buccleuch had settled himself in his box (the duke contenting himself with staring contemptuously through his opera glasses at the hoi polloi below), Stoker made his excuses and dashed back downstairs to front of house.

By now the incoming playgoers had all but dispersed, with just a few late-arriving couples drawing towards the box office under dimming lights. Harker was still stuck to his spot, his peacock's plume now dangling precariously over his right shoulder. After exchanging nods and pleasantries with a few late-comers, Stoker sidled up to his charge once more.

'So,' he asked, 'has Curdala come in? Did you manage to accost him?' Harker shook his head.

'No, Sir, not a peep from him.' One of the ushers now abruptly rang a hand bell to announce the closing of front of house.

'Are you sure?' Stoker persisted, unconvinced by the younger man's words.

'Trust me, Sir,' muttered Harker, keeping his eyes turned towards the foyer entrance.

'I trust that I can,' replied Stoker wryly.

'Why would I have come here tonight if the case were otherwise?' retorted Harker. 'I am putting myself at grave risk by helping you.' Stoker coughed awkwardly then consulted his watch.

'The performance will begin shortly. Let's go backstage now; I must speak to the Guv'nor.'

Once in the dark of the wings in the final minutes before curtain-up, as Harker busied himself removing his disguise, Stoker quickly apprised Irving and Miss Terry of their news.

'So, there is no news as such? Are you sure he did not come?'

'Positive, Sir,' said Stoker.

'Well, Nell,' said Irving through the eerie patterning of his make-up, 'we can be relieved.'

'Yes, I suppose we can,' she breathed, before quietly stepping onstage to take up her position by her character's spinning wheel.

'Thank you, Joseph,' said Irving, shaking the scene painter's hand. 'I appreciate your loyalty. You may go now.'

'Thank you, Sir,' replied Harker, before turning to leave. He had not taken more than a few steps, however, when suddenly he turned back, as if he wanted to add something; but Irving had already disappeared. 'There was something else I wanted to tell you and the Guv'nor, Sir... it may be important,' he declared.

'Leave it till tomorrow, Harker,' returned Stoker. 'Disaster averted for tonight, it would appear.' A light flush rippled across Harker's cheek.

'Very well, Sir. I shall drop by first thing,' he replied, then nodded briefly. 'Good night, Mr Stoker.'

'Good night, Harker.'

In another ten minutes Stoker was up in his office, surveying his in-tray. Quite a few missives were stacked there, many in stationery he recognised, and many no doubt containing the now-customary demands for boxes for the coming season. Just by looking at them he could anticipate his various responses – the agreeable, 'Dear Mr Conan Doyle, we are most happy to oblige your request', and the not so agreeable, 'Dear Mr Lloyd George, I am afraid we cannot on this occasion...' etc.

As he contemplated his correspondence, his mind turned to Irving and Miss Terry. What was their relation to this Baron Cadwallader, Curdala, Lucarda or whatever his name might be – and why might the baron be seeking the revenge Irving had alluded to? Still, rather than viewing the Guv'nor with dread, Stoker now looked to him for relief. After all, their long association should not count for nothing, and Irving had promised to explain all. He should reserve his judgement.

Turning his attention back to the missives before him, Stoker discerned the distinctive oblong form of a telegram. He picked it up to read the following. *'Dear Bram Stop Confirming Edward*

Craig arrived this morning with your letter Stop Hope he has talent like his mother Stop Yours truly Gunn Stop.'

Stoker could see that the telegram had issued from a post office on Grafton Street (one he had had cause to use himself on many occasions) that very morning. Strange, he thought. Surely Edward would have reached Gunn before now, as Telbin had dispatched him to Liverpool for his connection to Dublin some days ago? Still, it was possible his passage had been delayed, as there had been storms in the Irish Sea. Or perhaps Gunn was simply being muddle-headed. Thinking no more of it, Stoker stuck the telegram under his paperweight and allowed himself to be drawn once more into the work of the theatre. The following night was to be the last performance of *The Bells*, and they would soon be rehearsing for the winter season's performance of 'the Scottish play'; there was much to do.

It was not long before the sound of muffled applause was heard from the auditorium. Usually at the interval Stoker would go front of house, meet playgoers, and generally maintain the bonhomie for which the Lyceum was renowned. But that was not to be the case tonight; his pressing work duties, coupled with his desire not to encounter Buccleuch, were enough to keep him well away from the foyer. He looked down again at his in-tray and now noticed a missive in the stationery of his brother, George. He frowned, then opened it, tentatively.

My dear Bram,

I feel I must apologise for my brusque response to your recent enquiry regarding acquiring some arsenic. I was, in truth, somewhat riled that day as some peelers had – on the orders of the Board of Health – come to confiscate my phials of blood. I did in fact curse them like a Fenian as they wrenched open my medical chest, and I was lucky not to be arrested!

Perhaps unsettled by my own transgression (and indeed its discovery!), I was only too quick to make severe judgement

of your own and made what I now realise was a most rude
response to your enquiry. Despite this, I am afraid I still
cannot issue you any arsenic – most certainly not now, after
my finger-wagging from a policeman – but would love to meet
you for luncheon in the near future should you happen to be
in Fitzrovia. Needless to say, I would be happy to foot the bill.
　　Yours ever,
　　George

Stoker laughed out loud with relief – it seemed his sibling seniority did count for something after all, even though George had persisted in sending correspondence to the theatre, not Chelsea. He was about to set the missive aside when suddenly the nausea returned. Looking up once more at the glowering features of the Metal Man, they seemed suddenly to move – the mouth to open – the entire thuggish face to vibrate – the lightless eyes to oscillate into one, like that of a fearsome Cyclops. What was happening? Was he losing his mind? Stoker stood up and moved towards the painting. He now realised that it was not just the painting that was vibrating, but the whole room. And now the Metal Man was speaking to him – or so it seemed. He seemed to be mouthing, 'Go next door! Go next door!' And within a second there was a shrill scream. Miss Terry!

Stoker ran out into the corridor and banged on the actress's dressing room door.

'Are you all right, Miss Terry?' he shouted. His response was another shrill scream, just as the familiar presences of Loveday and Irving came crowding in behind him.

'For God's sake, man, go in!' screamed Irving. Stoker now turned the knob, threw open the door – and gasped. Lying on the floor, limp and lifeless, her carefully coiffed hair a tangle, was Miss Terry. Standing beside her was a formidably tall man with fine but cruel features and a thin handlebar moustache, wearing a black cape. The man said nothing as Stoker and his fellow theatre men looked on with astonishment at the scene. The man then snarled to reveal two abnormally long incisors that gleamed viciously, like those of a viper over its prey.

'My God,' cried Loveday. 'The scoundrel has bitten her neck!' Two thin streams of blood were issuing from above Miss Terry's lace collar, depositing trickles of crimson on her pinafore.

'You filthy swine!' shouted Stoker, who now leapt at the villain, only to find himself thrown back against a wooden costume trellis. Again he heard a shrill scream – not from Miss Terry, but from someone closer to him. He looked up to see the actress's dresser, her hands cupped around her quivering face.

'Rose, are you... are you all right?' stammered Stoker, attempting to get up and extend her a comforting hand. But the girl merely recoiled and started to whimper. Stoker now hauled himself up but, detecting a painful dent in his thigh, decided to remain standing where he was.

Now, in the ochre light of the dressing room, set against the trellises of costumes and shelves of greasepaint and make-up, were Lucarda and the Guv'nor, facing each other across the supine body of Miss Terry. In profile, Stoker could not help noticing the fine features and aquiline nose of the villain, who towered over Irving by almost a foot. To his surprise, Irving was looking coolly at his foe; there was no sign of the spasms in his cheeks he could conjure at will onstage. A sudden wave of admiration swept over Stoker, recalling his earlier esteem. Perhaps the Guv'nor was a man of good character after all?

No one spoke, the room silent except for the convivial hubbub of the audience front of house, enjoying their interval drinks. After what seemed an eternity, Irving addressed the baron.

'What do you want from us, Curdala?'

'What do I want from you, blackmailer? What do you think I want?' came back the reply in a thick Slavic accent.

'If you want your diary back, then I can give it to you. We have no further use for it, and once you have it, you will be safe from detection, and we will be safe to go home – and sleep sound in our beds.' There was another silence. In the dim light Stoker could see that Irving was breathing heavily. Now Lucarda broke into a hellish cackle and bent over double, his gaze meeting the now-open eyes of Miss Terry. As he straightened up, Stoker noticed a peculiar blue and black crest adorning the collar of his cape.

'Ha, ha, ha!' he screamed, shaking his head. 'No, it is too late for that! Like the character Macbeth you play so well onstage, my fine thespian, I am "in blood stepped in so far that, should I wade no more, returning were as tedious as go o'er". No, I shall continue with my crimes, no longer afraid of what you – or the diary – might reveal.'

'And if the police catch you,' cried Irving, thrusting his long jaw towards his opponent like a dagger, 'you have a surer guarantee of the gallows than your kinsman, Drayfield. You were best to return now.'

'Ha! If the police catch me, then they can hang me, place me in a coffin, and bury me in the English earth… but then my minions and familiars – my cats, dogs, and even the wolves from London Zoo – will come and dig me up! But you, my mortal friend, and this floozy at my feet,' and here the baron cast his eyes once more on Miss Terry, 'will be revealed for the blackmailers you are, and will languish in jail – your reputations in tatters, your future obscurity assured!'

There was yet another silence, and then Loveday spoke.

'Mr Irving, should we really not now call the police?'

'Police?' scoffed Lucarda. 'I do not believe, Mr Loveday, that you know Mr Irving as well as I do. I have a letter back at my castle, written many years ago by this fine thespian, that will cause him and his leading lady to be of interest to the police on their own account, not mine!' And with this he spat on Miss Terry's face.

'How dare you treat the lady so!' shouted Loveday with unaccustomed vigour. He made to lunge at Lucarda but Irving moved swiftly to bar his way, in what Stoker took to be another sign of confidence from the Guv'nor. Irving now snorted and turned to face the baron.

'Tell me, Curdala. Are you responsible for these horrific Whitechapel murders? Are these the crimes to which you refer?' Lucarda's moustache twitched momentarily. He shifted to his left and turned quarter profile towards Stoker, giving the acting manager another chance to observe his features in all their fine, if depraved, glory.

'I will neither confirm nor deny that, blackmailer – nor any other crimes! You shall no doubt find out all in due course. For the moment, one half of my revenge on you is complete,' – and here he pointed at Miss Terry, now roused to full consciousness on the floor – 'the rest is to follow!' And with these words he swung his cape with infernal speed in front of him, clipping Irving's nose in the process, and then jumped through the open window.

Immediately, Loveday and Irving fell about helping Miss Terry, while Stoker hurried to the window, hoping to espy the baron – surely collapsed on the ground, if anything like a normal man. But no; there was no one – nothing except the baron's carriage, its double doors swung open, and a black cat that sauntered towards it then jumped high into the back. The doors slammed shut and the carriage shot like a virago's arrow out of the alleyway and out of view, away no doubt to other sites of crime for its demonic owner.

Stoker was now convinced, the rational beliefs he had acquired while at Trinity now in ruins – for here was surely a vampire; one of the Undead, who mocked the hangman and the grave, who sucked the blood from the living, and could change his form at will to that of an animal. Indeed, had he not just seen the baron turn himself into a black cat? Stoker shook his head. How he wished he had met his old employer, Joseph Le Fanu, all those years ago and questioned him on such matters!

'Are you all right, Nell?' Stoker turned to see Irving cradling Miss Terry in his arms with unforeseen tenderness, his sang-froid against Lucarda entirely vanished next to the glow of his wounded leading lady. Miss Terry sighed, then sat up and took the mug of water offered her by Loveday, who now began dabbing her wound with a dun-coloured shawl. Irving's massive eyebrows were twitching preternaturally against the effect of his heavy make-up.

'I am so sorry, Henry, so sorry,' said Miss Terry softly, as Loveday continued to dab blood off her still-bleeding neck.

'There is nothing to be sorry about, Nell,' replied Irving. 'It all happened many years ago, and the fault is largely my own.'

'No, no, Henry. Had it not been for my own recklessness, none of this would have occurred, I'm sure.'

The bells marking the start of the final Act were now being rung by the ushers. Irving looked around anxiously.

'Nell, shall I call off the performance? You are in no fit state to perform.' Miss Terry now stood up, glanced at Stoker as if in plea for support, and then looked back at Irving.

'No,' she declared. 'The show must go on – as you know!' So saying, she tied the dun shawl about her neck and went to retrieve her bonnet from the floor.

'Nell,' said Irving, 'you are, as always, an example to me, to Bram, to us all!'

'I owe it to you, Henry,' she replied solemnly. 'And besides, we must not let Curdala ruin our present and future, as well as our past…' With that she sighed deeply then walked out the door, headed for the stage.

'Mr Irving,' coughed Stoker, now confounded by this apparent confession from Miss Terry, 'I really would like…'

'Yes, yes, Bram,' said Irving, fixing his eyes on his acting manager. 'I have some explaining to do, I know.'

Watching from the wings some half an hour later, Stoker observed how particularly impassioned was the Guv'nor's portrayal of Mathias that evening, as though the thin veil between play-acting and reality had been torn asunder, and character and actor melded into one. The constant fear of discovery, the desperate confession of the dream trial scene, the sudden terror as the sleigh bells were shaken by Loveday – 'The bells! The bells!' – it was one of the most powerful performances Stoker had ever seen from the Guv'nor, and he only hoped Irving would be able to distinguish fantasy from reality when it came to explaining recent – and perhaps not-so-recent – events, as he had promised he would do.

It was just as well, indeed, that the Guv'nor was at his most powerful that evening, as Miss Terry now seemed to be failing – starting to slur her words. Stoker remarked a trickle of blood meander down her pinafore. Unable to attend to her himself, Stoker signalled frantically to the hands to revive her with water when she rested offstage. But this proved to be but a temporary salve, and as the play reached its finale, Miss Terry fell to the floor at exactly the same moment as Mathias, causing a gasp and then rapturous applause from her adoring audience at the unscripted innovation – the startled prompt, Mr Allen, having to utter her final lines in her place. As the curtain came down, every hand came rushing to Miss Terry's aid. Shooing them away, Irving knelt down and pressed his leading lady close to his bosom.

'Don't worry, Henry. I'm just a little weak, I suppose.'

'Let me call for a surgeon,' choked Irving, breaking the precedent of previous occasion.

'Don't be stupid! How will I explain what has happened? It was just an attack, leaving but small injury.'

Miss Terry now called for more water and took a swig. 'No, my private carriage is waiting outside. I shall go home immediately and rest.' She sat up and took off her bonnet. Grafton and one of the hands then stepped forward and helped her to her feet. 'I can remove my costume and clear my make-up at home,' she continued. 'I have no need of my dresser.'

'Very well,' said Irving, pursing his lips with concern. 'Good night, my dear.' And with that Miss Terry was led off by Grafton, his pince-nez askance with the effort of supporting her.

Irving ran his hands through his grizzled mane and sighed. 'Come, Bram, I shall explain all.' And so saying the two men left the astonished stage crew to their clearing up against the murmurings of an equally astonished audience in exit.

CHAPTER XI

THE DANZIG DAYS OF HENRY IRVING

Irving's dressing room was much as it had ever been, with its array of wheeled wooden trellises and chests, and pervasive smell of greasepaint. On the dressing table lay the same battered book Stoker had seen Irving thumbing through a week or so earlier, but with several pages now poking out of its cover, having seemingly come loose – a sure sign he had been reading it avidly. Irving signalled to Stoker to seat himself on a small plush armchair next to a low mahogany table, hung up his antique costume jacket on a trellis, and went to pour two drinks from a crystal decanter sitting somewhat precariously on a mantelpiece.

'Here, Bram,' he said, 'you may need to let this settle in your bones before I begin to relate my – *our* – sad and sorry tale.' The Guv'nor now dragged an ottoman from the back of the room to beside the low table and sat down. In his brown and cream-striped waistcoat and old-fashioned knee breeches, he looked nothing so much like a shade resurrected from a former age; as uncanny, even, as their earlier vampiric visitor. Both men downed their Cognacs in one, and then, almost simultaneously, set down their tumblers on the table. Irving shifted back on the ottoman and took a deep breath.

'It was almost twelve years ago, Bram; the November of '76. You may recall that, just after Ellen and myself had first begun to draw a flurry of good reviews from the newspapers, moving from the back towards the front of the *Gazette, The Times* and *The Star*, we disappeared from view for some time on tour, in an attempt to establish our reputations on the Continent; a foolhardy and dispiriting enterprise if ever there was one, and quite unlike our triumphant tours to America and Canada some years later.'

'You forget, Sir,' replied Stoker, 'that I was in Dublin at that time. We had not yet met, and your exploits first in London and then abroad were for me still unknown.' Irving laughed and shook his head with a look of acknowledged humiliation.

'Yes, well, we were jeered off the stages of Paris and Brussels, and ignored in Antwerp and Amsterdam, our voices echoing helplessly in empty auditoriums. We had never appreciated how strange and provincial we might seem to these cosmopolitan audiences, how backward our stagecraft, how primitive our acting, and how little our mother tongue would be understood by these people. It was a rude awakening, I can tell you.' Irving sighed and offered Stoker a cigar from a box on the floor, which he refused, and then lit one himself, blowing the smoke conscientiously to his right.

'Despite these setbacks, I learned a great deal, I must say, and so did Ellen. We took time to study the techniques of the great Flemish players, as well as the staging of the theatres themselves, in Hamburg and Berlin. Indeed, it was in Berlin that I first started to realise that I wanted – *deserved* – a theatre of my own, where I could fulfil my destiny, and so could my darling Ellen.' He sighed once more, now blowing smoke above Stoker's head, his long jaw looking like a blunt stiletto at this angle. 'In truth, the more I travelled through Europe, the more I craved a theatre of my own – a desire I shared with Ellen, and which she then shared with me.

'Our tour of scenes from Shakespeare and Congreve – they were only scenes as we could not take a full company at that time and were accompanied by but one dresser and just a few fellow players – muddled on until we reached, in late December, the port of Danzig, high up on the wintry coast of West Prussia. There we found an astonishing town of red-bricked towers and houses with red-fluted rooves over wood-framed gables. A town of thin alleyways and alcoves where rich merchants in mauve and blue-plaited coats crowded in coffee houses while Tatar and Kazakh women in colourful shawls hustled their wares to passers-by outside. A town where, for the first time, I saw real sleighs being pulled by dogs through the streets at night, as Polacks and Ruthenians came in from the outlying villages to prepare for market, riding through the contrasts of light and shadow cast by braziers high on the walls. Everything was so very different from the wide, open streets of our Strand and Mall, and yet somehow it agreed with me. Our cold receptions in Paris and Amsterdam receded from our minds as the real ice gathered, and we both felt our aesthetic sensibilities sharpen and refine.'

Irving took a puff of his cigar and laid it in an ashtray.

'It was here also,' he continued, 'that we had our only success of the tour. Thanks to the enthusiasm of some local amateurs of semi-talent, we were able to put on a week of *Faust* in a small circular theatre made of creaking timbers that seemingly had whole centuries of woodworm running through them – a theatre like our own Bard would have known. Despite having neither curtain nor roof, still the audience would come to the round, so enthralled by our performances as to ignore the patinas of snow that formed on their bonnets and caps. Indeed, I have neither before nor since met with such appreciation for that play, my Mephistopheles drawing raptures from every inch of that antiquated structure. With each performance, my eagerness vaulted for a theatre of my own, where I could perform this work and others, using the same primitive colours and chiaroscuro with which Danzig had inspired me. As each night came to a roaring close, so the light and shade of this town, which I perused with ever more wonder, more firmly filled out the canvas of my – *our* – own future theatre; the one you find yourself in today!'

Stoker listened to Irving's paean to this faraway town with a degree of irritation. He knew that beneath his veneer of metropolitan sophistication, the Guv'nor was in essence a primitive Cornishman – more at ease in the shambolic, far-flung reaches of Europe than in the civilised heart of London. And yet, as intriguing as this apprehension might be, Stoker sincerely wished that Irving would stop setting the scene and get on with more recent action.

'Each performance ended with a standing ovation, with notes of praise and invitations to dinner constantly being pressed on our dresser. On the advice of the local players, we only accepted invitations from the most eminent of local luminaries – all of whom seemed to be blessed with English and Scottish names. Not long into our run, Ellen and myself found ourselves seated around a table spread with a tartan tablecloth in an eating house atop a tavern – one of many built by Scottish merchants from the Hanseatic days – being feted by a diminutive merchant named Slawek Ross; a man with a ratty red face and an equally ratty, red-headed wife. They were in their fifties – well-to-do whisky importers – and afforded most delightful company, congratulating us, in perfect English, on the power of our performances. Indeed, they themselves seemed most delighted by our company and, at one point – as we clutched glasses of a delicious Madeira – Ross made a most unusual toast.

'"Welcome back, friends," he declared. "We have wanted you to return for so long!"

'I started at this remark. Had our host perhaps mistaken us for two other players, or had he perhaps misread the wording of our hastily printed programme – myself and Ellen having but a smattering of German? I looked at Ellen – my, how beautiful she was then – to see her lips parted by the same startled unease. I resolved to broach the matter immediately, so as not to prolong any misunderstanding.

'"My dear Sir," I said, "I'm afraid this is the first time Miss Terry and I have been here." At this the red-faced little merchant laughed, as did his wife, and they patted each other's hands.

'"No, my fine compatriot, that is not what we mean. We mean that you follow *him*," and here he pointed at a reproduction of the Droushout Shakespeare, suspended next to some candles burning from brackets on the wall. "And him," and here he pointed at a copy of a Marlowe portrait. "And, of course, him!" And now he was pointing behind us, at a painting next to the stairwell. The painting was a poorly executed daub of a man with an auburn beard, receding hairline and elaborate ruff. So lifeless was it that it could have been anyone, including some of our rivals at the Adelphi!' Stoker met this joke with a momentary chuckle: the Guv'nor's oration was beginning to entertain him.

'Who was it, then, Guv'nor?' Irving smiled and shook his head.

'I turned round and asked Ross the same question. He seemed puzzled that I should ask. "Why," he replied, "the great King's Men actor, and sponsor of Shakespeare's First Folio, Henry Condell. Who else?" I turned to Ellen who, like me, appeared to be wondering whether this were not all some elaborate joke.

'"Mr Ross," I ventured, "there is only one portrait of Condell – well, as far as we know, it's of Condell – and the likeness is in no way that of this man." Ross simply touched his red nose and winked.

'"Exactly – as far as you know," he replied. "But our English and Scottish forebears actually knew Condell well, from the visits he made with his company. One of my ancestors even received letters from him, which I hold to this day." And at this he pulled out some grimy pieces of parchment featuring some elaborate squiggles, apparently thanking a certain Tadeusz Ross for his hospitality and the pleasure of sitting for his fine portrait painter. "That is why I know that the painting behind you is of the real Henry Condell!"'

'Did you not copy those letters for posterity?' broke in Stoker, the scholar in him suddenly piqued.

Irving stood up and crossed the room to pour two more glasses of Cognac. He then returned to the ottoman, handed a tumbler to Stoker, and cleared his throat loudly.

'I am an actor not a scribbler, Bram. Such things inspire me, but unlike you I have little desire to put pen to paper, whether for research or mere storytelling!' Stoker shook his head as Irving took a sip of his brandy and then resumed his tale.

'On the last night of our run, the snow was falling thick and fast, and yet still did nothing to deter our audience. I noticed several members of the crowd whom I had seen at least twice before, but a new one – an aristocratic-looking gentleman in a silk top hat and cape with dark spectacles, at the front of the gallery – now invariably drew my gaze. He sat leaning over the balcony, applauding rapturously each time my Mephistopheles accosted poor Faust for his diabolical deal, reminding him of its inexorable terms, and pressing him to abandon his beloved Margaret. When Ellen lay dead upon the floor in that role, and our German actor playing Faust – I forget his name, but he was equal to Mr Alexander, I can assure you – was weeping over the corpse, waiting for myself as Mephistopheles to drag him off to hell, I saw the gentleman lift up his spectacles to reveal eyes swollen with tears. I somehow felt that this man must be a kindred spirit to myself – and longed to meet him.'

'And did you meet him?' asked Stoker.

'Yes,' replied Irving, 'that very night. And now so have you!' Irving chuckled uncomfortably, as though mocking his own former enchantment. 'In the chill wooden cell that we called our dressing room, there was a knock on the door, and then appeared a youth in peculiar blue and black livery with a bottle of Krug Champagne and a card from a man named Baron Curdala. We both immediately guessed – for Ellen had been equally taken – that this was the aristocratic-looking gentleman we had observed in the gallery. We wasted no time extending the baron an invitation to the theatre's makeshift green room, only to be told that the baron was himself inviting us to Danzig's most celebrated restaurant – the Spatif, in the old Scottish district. Both sensing a potential patron – possibly for my, *our*, own theatre – Ellen and myself immediately accepted his offer then rushed out of our costumes.'

'You and Miss Terry shared the same dressing room?' exclaimed Stoker, almost choking on his Cognac; this was too much!

'We shared a dressing room as well as a bed, I must confess,' replied Irving casually. 'I thought it was no secret that in those days Ellen and myself were lovers. My wife had already left me by then, and Ellen herself was relatively free. How our love was later strained by events will be explained by the ensuing story.' Irving picked up his cigar and took a puff, followed by another mouthful of brandy.

'I'm listening, Guv'nor.'

'We were soon in the baron's carriage seated upon plush benches inlaid with mother-of-pearl. The carriage was lit with gas lamps and decorated with erotic designs such as one sees in the *maisons closes* of Paris. Had Ellen been of a different nature, I might have felt abashed at the loucheness of our host, but I saw that she, like any creative spirit, was intrigued by this most aristocratic of men, who liberally poured Champagne from out of an oversized bottle propped up in a bucket of ice.

'It was not long before we found ourselves in a beautiful eating house, festooned with chandeliers and golden ornament – far superior to the establishment Ross had taken us to. The baron complimented myself and Ellen on our bravura performances and then proceeded to interpret the play. Intriguingly, he understood *Faust* not as a tale of individual hubris but of a man seeking knowledge that could bring immortality to the whole of humankind – an idea which seemed to inspire his very being. In the baron's estimation, Mephistopheles was not a tempter and betrayer, enticing Faust to sell his soul to the devil, but an intermediary between earth and heaven and hell, who could make these last two realms equally paradisiacal, and eventually merge them with the earth itself. In his understanding, those who crossed into this realm would enjoy the bliss of eternal life in such a way that would make the Last Judgement a mere footnote in human history, as the living and the dead would be the same.

'He seemed a man much afraid of the finality of death, and

when, in the politest of ways, I enquired whether he were not a bit anxious about the possibility of his own extinction, he pointed to a black armband – almost unnoticeable against the rich black of his dinner jacket – and told us about the demise of his beloved wife, and his hopes that the two of them would one day be reunited, in a paradise reunited with earth.'

Stoker frowned.

'And then,' continued Irving, 'he began to talk about his own blood family, and his connections with our own country. How, although he had Prussian, Russian and Italian political allegiances, his ancestry was in fact English and Scottish, going back to sixteenth-century aristocracy. Finally, he declared that his full name was Baron Vassil Drayfield-Curdala.'

'Drayfield?'

'Yes, Drayfield,' replied the Guv'nor testily. He laid his cigar down in the ashtray. 'He asked us whether we would be prepared to come and humour him at his castle, a dozen miles outside the city walls, in some informal performances, and we agreed – not least because he assured us that his castle possessed a fine private theatre. We were so dazzled by our host, with his fine features and fine sensibilities, that we quite overlooked the fact that we barely knew anything about him at all. Although we were booked to take the train back to Berlin in two days' time, and then on to Paris, we knew that Mrs Bateman would not need us back at the Lyceum for at least another week, and so we asked the surly Ruthenian who owned the tavern where we were staying to send our costume and prop chests back with our fellow players and dresser, but to cancel our own tickets – which he did, having greased his palm with a few marks. In truth, both Ellen and myself were relieved to be spending one less night under his roof, not least because his young daughter – whom he made clean and wait at table – was clearly a floozy!'

And here Irving picked up his cigar and took a number of puffs, as if readying himself for the most difficult part of his story.

CHAPTER XII

THE CASTLE OF BARON DRAYFIELD-CURDALA

'The following afternoon we found ourselves once more in the baron's carriage, being whisked past the fortress walls of Danzig and out into the countryside. Drawn by four black horses, the carriage made a mockery of the receding snow as the baron himself pointed out the less obvious delights of the country through a partially opened shutter, all the while knocking back glasses of Champagne. Soon we had sped through several Ruthenian, then Polack, villages, weaving here and there past churches with slanted crosses atop onion-shaped domes, then churches with square crosses atop cupolas. Curdala seemed indifferent to all, despite the fact that many of the villagers, often staggering drunk from their various inns, would cross themselves in their assorted ways at the sight of his carriage.

'The baron's conversation was much less voluble than it had been before; a change which I now ascribe to the fact that Ellen and myself were already his prisoners, and he had much less need to exercise his superficial charm in securing us for the forthcoming... festivities.' Irving laid his cigar back down in the ashtray.

'Soon we were on the road of a darkening plain. We saw nothing through the shutter except, at last, a crossroads lit with a hanging oil lamp, illuminating what looked like an empty gibbet. I felt Ellen – who was attracting more than an occasional leer from our host – shrink beside me; to which Curdala simply laughed, allowing his fine jaw to crease in a most Mephistophelean manner.

'"Relic of a bygone age, I assure you, Madam; Count Bismarck preferring to copy us English rather than the French. So much for the Revolution!"

'Soon the dull trundling of the wheels over mud and snow was replaced by a bright clattering as we ran upwards across what sounded like wood, and then drew to a stop. The baron smiled and finished off his glass of Champagne – none the worse for the copious amounts of alcohol he had consumed.

'"Welcome to my house!" he declared. The carriage door was opened and Ellen and myself alighted to discover an immense courtyard surrounded by high stone walls, which seemed to reach up and scratch the cloudless, now star-lit, sky. A number of servants in blue and black livery – the baron's colours, we understood – were in attendance, awaiting instructions. The baron himself now alighted then quickly issued some orders which had the men bundling up into the carriage to retrieve our trunks. He then gave what seemed like more orders to a rather plain woman with pouchy eyes – inducing a curtsey from her – before turning to us.

'"I shall leave you in the capable hands of my Polack servants," he announced, before setting off across the now-freezing snow. The pouchy-eyed woman smiled, curtseyed again, and then led us through the courtyard, under an ornate arch, and into the castle.

'The great hall, awash with darkness visible from its many braziers, was vast and imposing – and not a little dispiriting. But once Ellen and myself were in our separate rooms, Bram, my spirits lifted. For here, in my room – aside from an excellent supper laid out on a tray – was a fine bed next to a fine looking-glass, and walls lined with rare and antique books, all illuminated by a magnificent crystal chandelier. I was about to explore one of these volumes when a knock on the door brought my beloved into my arms.

"'Nell,' I said after a warm embrace, "what a fine old world we find ourselves in!"

"'I do not find this world so fine,' she replied. "And I do not trust this baron either. I think we should leave, tomorrow morning!'

"'How? We have no means of transport. And besides, the baron is no more than a harmless eccentric!' My response did not convince her.

"'I do not like him. He looks at me in a way that is most unsettling – and unwelcome.'

"'The man who is blind to your charms is indeed that, Nell – blind,' I retorted, trying to make light of her fears. She looked back at me, her mouth curling downward. "No,' I continued. "Here we have the opportunity to impress a potential patron.'

'My darling stared at me mutely.

"'I wonder what the performances he wishes to involve us in are,' she said at last.

"'Probably just a few scenes from Shakespeare, no more,' I replied. Suddenly, Ellen threw her arms around me and asked whether she might stay the night; but I declined, as the baron must know we were not married and might, in my estimation, have been angered.

'The next morning we were summoned to breakfast early by the woman with the pouchy eyes and were soon rolling through the frozen countryside, with its stalagmite birches and poplars, on a tour of the baron's estate. The sights that we encountered were most deplorable. I have never seen an estate so poorly maintained, with lopsided cottages and emaciated peasants in rags, all furiously doffing their bonnets and caps as their master passed, their fear of him palpable. As the baron now detailed, with some passion, his benevolence towards his workers, my glances towards Ellen returned ever more censorious looks, as though the potential trap into which we were being drawn were solely the result of my own cupidity, and not hers.

'Later, in the oak dining room, curiously adorned with sceptres and crosses placed at hexagonal points, we were served a lavish luncheon of duck with syruped cherries. After some inconsequential chatter, the baron began to expand upon his English connections.

'"You have perhaps heard," he declared, "of the great Dr Dee from England, who performed feats of alchemy before the Emperor, and whose work so inspired our other great compatriot, Kit Marlowe?"

'"I cannot say that I have," I lied cheerily, hoping to turn the conversation to more gainful, theatrical matters.

'"It's thanks to him," resumed the baron, "that both our spiritual and theatrical traditions are so fine." Seeing a chance to ingratiate ourselves with our host and his bulging purse, I lost no time in encouraging him to talk further on this subject, winking at the still-anxious Ellen.

'Soon the baron was detailing how, not long after Shakespeare and Marlowe, and possibly even the great Alleyn himself, had toured these northerly regions as players, Dee and his associate, Kelly, had come – two men who had been thrown out of England on account of their magical investigations, conjuring spirits through a new symbology, but who were eventually welcomed on the Continent, and indeed, even in faraway Danzig. I listened to this with little interest. I did in fact know of these men through my own associations,' and here Irving pointed at the square and compasses on his ring, 'but had always been warned by our Grand Master to avoid Dee's works as being those of a malevolent Prospero who would ruin our association... by association.'

'So, you are, as I always presumed, Sir, a Mason?' Irving smiled weakly then resumed his tale.

'And then the baron became much more voluble, his glee practically glinting off the various metallic baubles that were arranged about the room, for he was talking with unbridled passion about the Bard, Marlowe and Greene, and how a new order – the Rosicrucians – had arisen from Dee's symbology. How, sometime later, some from this order had come from England and settled – in Prague, Danzig, even Catholic Krakow – and had written plays, in imitation of Shakespeare and Marlowe. How they had formed theatres and performed these plays – based on the ideas of Dee and other mages – for their temples and orders, to enhance the spiritual life of Europe and bring, or so the baron believed, eternity back to earth. How they had rediscovered the path of the knight, Father Christian Rosenkreutz, who would be resurrected at the apocalypse to help Christ reign again on earth with – and I am not making this up, Bram – a red rose blooming on the cross at Golgotha!' Irving swept back his hair in the ochre light, his cynical laugh wheezing through the cigar smoke. Stoker smiled; so old Joseph's plan for a new novella had not been so fanciful after all!

'Faced with such absurdity,' resumed Irving, 'my fears about the baron's nature began to recede. He was indeed a harmless eccentric – or, at least, simply a Rosicrucian; although, as we soon discovered, one who took his own interpretations to extremes.'

With this Irving frowned and took a long draw on his cigar before stubbing it out.

'Anyway, at this point both Ellen and myself were sufficiently reassured that, when the baron suggested we take part that very evening in a playlet of his own devising, we both readily agreed. We were now to go to our rooms, where costumes and a set of stage directions and lines would be awaiting us, and in a few hours, having memorised the short scripts, we would be led to the baron's private theatre. The baron's zeal and excitement were alike infectious, and I believe both Ellen and myself felt genuinely eager to take part in the performance.

'Back in my room, I found waiting for me on the bed a red robe with the sign of the sceptre, sun and moon on its back. A slim booklet lay atop it. Sitting down on the bed and opening up the booklet, I discovered numerous scribbles and annotations as well as what appeared to be hastily written directions over the blocking for some sort of stage. Beneath this, a short text, whose couplets my character was directed to pronounce after first the baron and then Ellen had given their short recitations. All was in English, and I faintly discerned the imagery of Shakespearean sonnets in the baron's invention. Having finished with the booklet, I donned my robe to remark a veritable decadent cardinal in the long looking-glass provided.

'My attention then turned back to the shelves of books, where my eye was taken by a leather-bound volume adorned with mother-of-pearl, sticking out at the bottom. I bent down to retrieve it then sat back on the bed and started leafing through the text; it was all in French! Although my gift for that tongue has never been as powerful as yours or Ellen's, even I could make out that it seemed to be nothing more than a set of overblown confessions – a diary, recorded by the baron in his younger years. But as I leafed through further, and time went on, I became more intrigued, as here were references to identifiable people, intimations of whose peccadillos, as detailed by the baron, had later seared the pages of the press, offering convincing proof of his close connections with them.'

Stoker looked quizzically at his boss but said nothing.

'Yes,' continued the Guv'nor, 'the baron's life in London some years earlier, while I was yet a green actor in Manchester, brought forth well-known people whose crimes, shining like limelights on the stage of our host's past, were now... well known. People like Arthur Orton, the fraudulent claimant for the Tichborne baronetcy, whose villainy it appeared Curdala, and indeed the wife he alluded to, had abetted – and worse, much worse, like murder!' Here Irving paused and looked at Stoker, as if hoping to elicit some exclamation of shock, but still his acting manager said nothing.

Irving continued.

'Soon I was being led through a long passageway, then behind some sort of tapestry screen and down some steps until we faced an elaborately carved iron door. Once through this, I saw a most peculiar theatre – if you could even call it that – and certainly one totally unlike what Ellen and myself felt had been promised. Facing me, at the back of the room, behind some sort of bizarre altar, stood a large gold cross centred with a red, many-petalled rose – a symbol of the Rosicrucians. On the floor was a cross tessellated in brick, like a crossroads. Behind the altar stood the baron himself, wearing a robe of green satin, with a red rose emblazoned on the front. I gasped when I saw his firm features, now knowing the depravity of the man, and had to exercise all my powers not to convey my fear to him. And then I turned to see, on my left, the figure of Ellen. Like myself, she was dressed in a ridiculous outfit – like that of a silver fairy, topped with a brass crown – though even this ridiculousness could not detract from the beauty of her liquid eyes and delicate mouth.'

Stoker shook his head slowly and took a large gulp of brandy.

'The baron motioned us to stand opposite him, some few spans apart from each other. He crossed his arms over his chest and intoned some words in Latin before suddenly closing his eyes and chanting in English:

> *"Ever shall be winter days,*
> *Ever shall be happy lays."*

And here Irving stood up and crossed his own arms, launching into an impression of the baron's monotonous dirge:

> *"Ever shall be berries bright,*
> *With blood, their thorns have brought to sight.*
> *Ever shall be sunsets gold,*
> *Which aye renewal God has foretold."*

'My word,' broke in Stoker suddenly. 'The Baron's certainly no wordsmith!' Irving pursed his lips in irritation, before solemnly recalling the verse:

> *"Only where the roads are joined,*
> *Can life renew and life with death be e'er entwined."*

Now Irving released his arms and allowed them to move like sails through the air, as if delineating the crossroads tessellated on the floor. The Guv'nor was seriousness itself, the baron's corrupt spirit seeming to inhabit his entire being.

> *"'What say you, Queen of the Midnight Waters,*
> *Whose pale face lights the mobile quarters?'"*

Irving now stopped and cleared his throat.

> *"'I say 'tis good that you should try,*
> *The future life within me scry!*
> *My waters shall so near reveal,*
> *The balm which can cold death unseal.'"*

The shrill falsetto with which Irving mimicked these words from his leading lady was not one of his more edifying performances, and Stoker was relieved when the Guv'nor leapt back into the character of the baron.

> *"'And you, who blaze on every path,*
> *A truth unmissable as death.*
> *Cannot you with silver moon combine,*
> *And harness the fickle whore of brine?'"*

'And here, Bram, he gave me the cue for my own words, which I fail to remember, about a monad and a hierophant, or something like that.'

'The "Monas Hieroglyphica" – a symbol of Dee's.'

'Yes, that was it, I should think. Anyhow, the baron now continued with other such tawdry rhymes, Ellen and myself responding in unison from our own scripts, until two doors, one either side of the large gold cross at the back, were suddenly flung open, letting in fierce draughts of cold night air. The baron splayed his arms and, with a roll of his wrists, signalled the entrance of two terrified peasant girls, who were then brutally pushed forward by his henchmen until they stood either side of the altar. Their heads were shaven, and they wore simple diaphanous robes of silk. They would have looked like priestesses at the Temple of Artemis were it not for the gags that stifled their mouths and the ties that constrained their hands. Their large eyes looked at both of us with a sense of doom, as each was pinioned by the baron's liveried servants. The baron now raised his arms and practically shouted:

"'Behold – I Lord Rosy Cross will bring,
On this fourth day the dead to sing.
Those brought unto the place of shades,
Soon unearthed by angel spades!"

'And with this, through the same doors either side of the altar, were wheeled two contraptions, the like of which Ellen and myself were hardly expecting, given the baron's earlier remarks about Count Bismarck – for here was the wooden frame and metal blade that had become so feared in France during the Revolution! But what startled me the most was the sight of the man pushing one of the dreadful contraptions, weaving his aproned form past the servant and struggling girl on the right-hand side.

"'Ross!" I exclaimed. "What—"

"'Quiet!" snarled Curdala.

"'And so as every year begins,
With blood, new sacrifice and sins.
Expunged, we of the Rosy Cross..."

"'Ross," I remonstrated, "you're not about to commit murder?" At this the little merchant simply glared at me and snorted.

'The rest of the ceremony was mercifully short but too pitilessly cruel to recount in detail. Suffice to say that the girls were forced down into the infamous frames and their heads sealed in the deadly rings. Before I had time to connect each part of this horrifying phantasmagoria or protect my ears from the muffled screams of the girls, there was the sound of Ellen falling to the floor next to me and the sight of my own vomit puddling beneath me. It was a ghastly scene, I can assure you, Bram; just ghastly.'

'Did you not try to stop them?' asked Stoker all of a sudden. Irving's grimace slackened momentarily.

'There was nothing that myself or Ellen could do. They were too many and we too few; and besides, we did not realise what was happening until too late.' He smiled feebly, as if half-acknowledging his guilt.

'So, what happened next?'

Irving ran his hand through his hair.

'After Ellen's body had fallen, so with two wet slices, both of the girls' shaven heads fell to the floor, blood gushing over our costumes. I screamed – called the baron a villain and a murderer – one of the girl's heads bounced, its eyelids still flickering, and splashed in the pool of vomit at my feet. My last memory was of the baron's mad stare, and his words, "They shall live again! Trust me; trust me!" But whether it was the choking of his henchman or my own delirium, soon all was a blank.'

Throughout this denouement Irving had been pacing continuously, right to left, mimicking at one point the fall of Miss Terry, at another the fall of the blades, at another his own remonstrance – as though the whole event were no more than the dream trial scene in *The Bells*.

He now stood panting, as he looked directly at Stoker, as if for affirmation. Stoker, however, merely held out his tumbler to be refilled. After a few moments' awkward silence, Irving obliged. He then sat down, exhaled deeply, and resumed his tale.

'I revived some hours later to find myself lying on a bed, my head aching, not knowing at first where I might be. The magnificent crystal chandelier above me soon recalled my grim plight to me, and I shot up from the bed and tried to open the door: locked. A wild feeling began to engulf me as I thought of myself and Ellen, confined in the close labyrinth of a madman. I ran to the window and pushed open the shutters, only to be scuffed by the wintry embrace of high winds. I ran back to the door and tried to ram it with my shoulder, and then with a chair, but it was no use. I was trapped.' Here Irving stood up again, as if reliving his agitation.

'I flung myself onto the bed, the diminishing light from the chandelier making the contours of my room appear ever more like those of the condemned cell. So preoccupied was I that I almost missed the judder on the bolt that presaged the opening of my door. In the doorway was the outline of the pouchy-eyed woman who had shown us to our rooms. She was labouring beneath the weight of a seemingly intoxicated servant, whose body she let fall to the ground. Throwing a set of keys next to the man, and pressing a finger to her lip, she then turned and beckoned to some other in the dark of the corridor. Out of the shadows, dressed in a winter fur and hat, emerged a shivering Ellen. I jumped up and moved to embrace her, but she thrust her hands out before her, as though the experiences of earlier had riven our love asunder.

'"Go now, you both," said the Polack woman in halting English.

'"How?" I asked. "How can we get out?"

'"There is a way, Henry," replied Ellen. "Roxana assures me."

'I did not stop to think why we should trust this Roxana, or indeed why she would help us. I sensed her plan was more to do with framing the servant for our escape than anything else – though for what reason I did not know, or care.

'"Show us the way, quickly then," I exhorted her. The woman smirked, stepped over the servant's unmoving body, and then slid aside a wooden panel to reveal a secret door. Opening it to a sudden gust of chill air, she pointed to a narrow staircase and smiled.

'"Quick, Henry!" said Ellen. "We must leave."

'"And walk in the freezing cold back to Danzig, in the dark?"

'"What other recourse do we have?"

'I ran to my wardrobe, and with no concern for propriety, rushed out of my costume and into my breeches and thick fur coat.

'"We must hurry!" said Ellen, her liquid eyes imploring me. The Polack woman was nodding in agreement.

'"Come, then," I replied. But, as I was about to leave, I noticed the baron's diary on my pillow and reached over to grab it.

'"What's that?" exclaimed Ellen.

'"Something that might keep the baron off our backs in years to come," I replied. I kissed the Polack woman's rough hand – so unlike my beautiful Ellen's – snatched a lantern from a shelf, and soon Ellen and myself were careening down the stair. At the bottom we creaked open a door and found ourselves directly out on the plain – thankfully, well outside the castle's demesne.

'"Are you a strong and fast walker, Ellen?" I asked.

'"Necessity will make me so, Henry," my beloved replied.

'We were just passing the crossroads, trying our best to keep up our spirits despite our desperate plight, when luck came in the form of a group of Gipsies, who graciously allowed us to climb into the back of their caravan as they made their way through the night to the morning fair in Danzig. The breath of pigs and the constant clucking of chickens, not to mention the sweet smell of excrement, made this one of the less comfortable rides of our tour, but in all other ways it was by far and away the most agreeable.'

Irving allowed himself a half-smile and then took a swig of brandy, draining his glass.

'Back in Danzig, early the next morning, we wired Gatti, asking him to purchase tickets to take us by steamer along the coast to Stettin – the fastest passage available. Once at Stettin, we felt more at ease, and were soon able to take an advance from Coutts bank. It was not long before this whole escapade seemed nothing but a dream – a nightmare – the baron far from our thoughts and concerns.'

Irving now stopped and wiped the sweat dramatically off his brow, before dropping unceremoniously onto the ottoman and burying his head in his hands.

CHAPTER XIII

THE DIARY

It was some time before Stoker felt able to disturb the Guv'nor. What a fine act it had been! One in which the Guv'nor's own guilt had been successfully thrown into the character of the baron, Irving's powers of performance surely proof of his powers of deception. Stoker was dismayed, particularly so as he realised he still lacked answers to so many important questions – not least of which being why it was that Lucarda-Curdala had come seeking revenge on Irving and Miss Terry, and how it was that the peculiarly patterned shawl he had seen discarded on the Guv'nor's dressing room floor had come to be at the scene of one of the Whitechapel murders. Still, the Guv'nor had provided some clues. Stoker cleared his throat.

'This diary you mention is, I presume, the one to which you were referring earlier, when speaking to the baron in Miss Terry's dressing room?'

'It is indeed, Bram,' replied Irving, now apparently recovered, and sitting up on the ottoman.

'And when the baron referred to blackmail,' continued Stoker, 'it was this same diary you used, blackmail being the reason why he is seeking revenge?'

'It was hardly blackmail, Bram,' replied Irving briskly.

'Then what was it, Sir?' Irving sighed and clasped his hands together.

'Once the dust had settled, once we were back in the run of our daily lives, both myself and Ellen realised that we were no nearer to achieving our desires... And then it occurred to us that the baron had probably forgotten us by now, and possibly knew nothing of my purloining of the diary. We realised that the diary contained enough evidence to destroy him, and others in his circle, and so would be something he would wish to conceal. Such a man would pay dearly for such concealment, we presumed, and with such payment the two of us could wrest control of the Lyceum from Mrs Bateman and create the theatre we so craved – and deserved!'

'So, you did blackmail him?'

'No, not blackmail, Bram, not blackmail,' insisted Irving, now wagging a reproving finger and shifting uneasily backwards. 'I simply sent the baron a letter informing him of our possession of his scarlet testimony, demanding money to secure the theatre, and threatening to reveal the diary's contents should he refuse. We also made arrangements for the contents of the diary to be revealed by a third party, should he in any way try to harm us – a provision which I also communicated to him in this letter. Soon a thousand pounds or so were appearing each year in my Coutts account... and the rest is history. A great theatre, the greatest in the known world, was born!'

'You were extorting money from him by threatening to expose his secrets. If that is not blackmail, Sir, I don't know what is; elementary, as Mr Conan Doyle's detective might say!'

'That is perhaps how others might see it, I agree,' replied Irving, running a hand through his long mane, and shifting uneasily on his ottoman. 'But I cannot seriously equate our actions at that time, devoted as they were to the high interests of art, to the low interests of blackmail. Myself and Ellen knew that we were the finest actor and actress in London, and we also knew how the public longed to see us fulfil our destinies, especially when shysters like Barrett and Boucicault were busy making hay. It had to be done, in the interests of art – in the interests of the public's edification!'

'So,' continued Stoker, emboldened by the Guv'nor's discomfiture, 'if your conscience is so clear, why have you gone to such lengths to avoid the baron, and regard him still with such fear? Is it because you knew he was out for revenge, for you stealing the diary?' Irving sighed and shifted awkwardly once more, his countenance moving from messianic to demonic in the changing light.

'Bram, as I have said, I am fully aware that others – Philistines, no doubt – might not see things quite how we do, and thus might drag mine and Ellen's names through the proverbial mud – banishing us from high society and destroying the most successful theatrical partnership of all time!'

'Or even sending you to prison, indeed?'

'Indeed, Bram,' conceded Irving, his bravado beginning to falter. 'Anyway, the money came through regularly for quite some years. But then, all of a sudden, it stopped, and we assumed – or rather, hoped – the baron was dead; or, something we dreaded, perhaps no longer afraid of what we might reveal. Then in January this year, *this year*, our hopes that he might be dead were dashed as I received a letter from him, at the Lyceum – my fame no doubt having reached his shores – promising to come to London and unleash a reign of terror on our capital. He said that he would come and kill and rampage and do whatever he pleased until the police arrested him; and then he said that we would be exposed, for he still kept the letter I had sent him all those years ago.'

'So, you did not want to report him?'

'Good God no, Bram!' exclaimed Irving in a stage whisper. 'And risk to ourselves exactly what he had threatened to us – exposure, humiliation, ruin… worse than the hanging he himself courted?' The moral cowardice of his boss now plunged Stoker's esteem back to its nadir. 'Anyway, once those wretched murders began in Whitechapel, I could positively smell the reek of the baron's foul hand. It was only a matter of time, I knew, before he would be caught – and ourselves revealed.'

'Your blackmail, you mean?'

'Yes... er, no.'

'And your complicity through silence presumably also?'

'Well, we would of course have denied everything, and the police could never have proven our knowledge of the baron's threats, as I took the precaution of destroying his letter. But we knew that such outrageous crimes would lead to his discovery sooner or later, and the discovery of the small part we played in the whole affair.' Irving was now cupping his brow in self-pity. He wiped his forehead and leaned forward.

'I came up with a plan to throw the police off his trail – or at least those peelers not sworn to loyalty to me through my lodge. I had heard about the shameful activities of the barber, Kosminski. If I were in some way to implicate him in these crimes, I could divert the police from the baron, saving both the theatre and ourselves.'

Here Stoker cringed as he observed Irving's joy at this seeming stroke of genius.

'I invited the fiend to cut my hair, then, by distracting him – not difficult to do with one so insane – managed to let him forget the peculiarly patterned shawl on which he gathered my hair. I handed it to one of the Whitechapel peelers who attends my lodge so that he could include it in the inventory of evidence the next time the murderer struck.'

'And frame an innocent man?'

'And frame a public menace, Bram, who would only have committed more attacks on women, and ultimately murder as well! After all, the best way to treat a mad dog is to run it over a cliff before it can do serious harm!' Stoker was shaking his head in disbelief. After a few moments, he broke silence once more.

'And Miss Terry? Does she share your opinion of the baron's culpability?' Irving frowned at this.

'Well, I understand from Edith that she has begun to believe there may be another culprit… Absurdly so, for it is surely Curdala.' He smoothed down his trouser legs and sighed. 'But no, I am sure she will see sense soon and come back to our original shared opinion.'

Stoker shook his head again, then continued.

'I'm afraid you need not have bothered to frame Kosminski. Whoever killed those poor women in Whitechapel was not your baron, of that I can assure you.' Irving's massive eyebrows now twitched, as if in hope of redemption. 'If they had been attacked by him, they would, like the girl I accidently skewered last night, and whom the baron must have attacked, have become vampires – the Undead – and not the forlorn corpses being inspected by the police.' For a moment the Guv'nor simply stared at Stoker, and then he exploded into uproarious laughter, vaulting himself into a fit of coughing.

'My word, Bram, you're as bad as Grafton! Do you really believe such tommyrot?' Stoker sat back in his armchair and folded his arms.

'I wish I did not, but the evidence points towards it – certainly in terms of the girl – does it not?'

'Oh please, my paddywhack friend, no more of your nonsense.'

'So, tell me, Guv'nor,' said Stoker, 'what really happened that first night, when the girl was attacked? Did she really get up and leave after you and Miss Terry paid her off?' Irving's guffaws stopped abruptly.

'No, no. To be frank, neither of us was in the Beefsteak room to see her go. As soon as you had set off for the druggist, I ushered Ellen out into the corridor, thinking perhaps we might discover Curdala in the theatre… for, in truth, I knew it must be him, and not young Edward, who had inflicted such vile wounds. And when we returned, the girl had gone.'

'And yet you still pointed the finger of suspicion at Edward?'

'Edward was not entirely without blame in this episode, Bram. Anyway, as it happened, it was in fact Ellen who first decided to point the finger.'

Stoker scoffed and took a slug of brandy.

'You should have to deal with a charge as difficult as Edward; you might not censure us so. No, the girl left of her own accord, thank heaven – and then we had the perfect excuse for dispatching Edward northwards.'

Stoker looked unimpressed.

'And what about tonight? I saw the baron jump out of Miss Terry's dressing room window and disappear, a black cat taking his place. I saw Miss Terry collapse onstage, and then her unstaunchable wound. Believe me, Guv'nor, this was no ordinary attack!'

'This is just speculation, Bram… speculation, embellished by your fanciful Irish mind.'

'That sounds just dandy coming from a Cornish Mason, I must say!' returned Stoker with some boldness.

'No, no, Bram; the baron is mad, not supernatural – here,' and now he got up and retrieved the battered-looking book from his dressing table. 'This is what inspires his moves.' Irving now sat back down and handed the book to Stoker. It was none other than the work he himself possessed: Andreae's *The Chymical Wedding of Christian Rosenkreutz*.

'I have been studying it again to see what the baron might do next. My understanding is that he believes he is now on the seventh day of initiation, and that he will now attain eternal life, if only he is able to unite silver with gold – whatever that might mean in his own interpretation of this ridiculous allegory.' Stoker thumbed through the book, shook his head, then put it down on the low mahogany table.

'No, Guv'nor,' he declared. 'I doubt this book will help you. It seems to me that the baron has forsaken his attempt to attain eternal life through reaching the summits of spiritual alchemy, through the magic of Dee and Kelly – whose significance to visiting English players he held forth to you about all those years ago – and has instead willingly and willfully succumbed to the teeth of a vampire, his desire for immortality now not to be frustrated, even at the cost of not being joined again with his wife in a paradise reunited with earth. He has now become one of the Undead, but has kept on his gullible Rosicrucian minions, like Dowden. Now that he is doomed to survive all attempts to kill him, being Undead, it seems he has become emboldened to exact his revenge. He has gained his revenge on Miss Terry, and let's hope that might be enough, as that vengeance holds ruin for us all!'

'Ha, Bram!' exclaimed Irving. 'That is an excellent tale, and I wish I could believe you but I cannot. The baron will commit new outrages, of that I am certain. If you don't believe me, let me give you this.' And now Irving stood up and ducked beneath the costumes on the trellis behind him, emerging with a volume adorned with mother-of-pearl. 'Here is the diary written by this madman. I am afraid it bears witness to many terrible crimes. But there is nothing in it, thankfully, that could ever stand up in a court of law – except in relation to the baron himself. Otherwise,' he went on, 'I would never have had the courage to have used it as I did.' Stoker was aghast: his boss's moral recklessness had been more complete than he could ever imagine.

'Why do you keep it here?'

'Why should I not?' retorted Irving. 'Does our friend Conan Doyle not talk about it being best to hide things where they are not concealed? The baron had every reason to believe that this was the last place the diary would be, and despite his considerable learning, he is a creature of little animal cunning. Since he no longer wants the diary, it can now only serve as a barometer for his future crimes.' Irving let the book dangle in the air before Stoker, who now rose to take it.

'Come, Bram,' said Irving, 'let us meet tomorrow and consider what to do. As I say, I do not believe we have heard the last of this madman.'

Angry and revolted in equal measure, Stoker was about to ask Irving why he took his loyalty for granted, but the Guv'nor was already halfway out the door, and within moments Stoker himself had quit the dressing room and was striding down the corridor towards his office, ready to collect his sundries and take himself, and his curious cargo, home.

∽

Later that evening, back at his desk in Chelsea, Stoker opened up the diary. A glass of water sat to his right, his fob watch, released from his waistcoat top pocket, and a French dictionary (in case he needed to decipher the baron's no doubt esoteric lexicon) to his left. But he need not have worried about the baron's language, for as he started leafing through the diary's entries, he soon realised that his own facility in that tongue far exceeded that of the vampire's. Vampire – how odd that word sounded when used by a man of his own liberal education!

In the trilling lamplight, jutting out of the bookshelf, he saw the two books that had helped him understand the events of the past few weeks: Andreae's *The Chymical Wedding* and Calmet's *The Phantom World*. From *The Chymical Wedding* he had learned about Rosicrucian tenets and beliefs (recalling Lord Drayfield, 'He said that she would live again!') and from *The Phantom World* about vampires, and that Lucarda-Curdala must now be among their number. How strange that these two volumes, originally intended as sources for diverting fictions, had become guides to disturbing realities – the most disturbing of these being the depravity of his boss, Irving. Indeed, Stoker reeled with far greater horror now at the revelation of Irving's deliberate, shameless behaviour than he did at the recollection of his own accidental violence against the girl – or whatever creature she was – just the night before. He sighed as he recalled how his greatest fear over the past few weeks had been that the Guv'nor – *his own Irving* – was somehow involved in nefarious activity, and how he, like the poacher's wife who only wishes the charcoal concealing her husband's face is soot fallen from a nearby chimney, the deer around his neck a gift from his liege, had only hoped his fears would prove unfounded. But now his hopes lay in ruin – and while the Guv'nor had cleared up some matters for him, he still retained some fears, not least of these being that Irving could still be hiding something. After all, had not Miss Terry – whose behaviour at the castle Irving had portrayed as entirely blameless – apologised for some perceived 'recklessness' the night Lucarda attacked her? What could that mean? Still, one thing he knew for certain – she had indulged in blackmail.

Ah, blackmail! He returned to the diary, reading now more systematically.

Starting with the entries detailing the baron's earliest escapades, Stoker, like Irving, found little that pointed to his later depravity: here were overblown accounts of tussles in the bierkellers of Berlin, of masked duels in the student guilds, and of liaisons with aspiring actresses.

Then, after a few pages, came the declaration of true love, in the March of 1861 – an event that put a speedy end to all the bravado and revealed the baron's finer sensibilities: tales of romantic walks on his estate, strawberry-picking; of impassioned readings of Goethe's *Werther* and Shelley's *Queen Mab* in the long spring grass; of ardent metaphysical debates on the nature of the universe and the possibility of eternal life, as the baron and his love sought refuge from the late summer rain in a musty barn. A long gap in the September of that year was followed by an ecstatic account of a holiday on the Lido in Venice, in the baron's own palazzo – descriptions of elaborate games in costume over the Rialto as the baron indulged his new bride's whims for the exotic.

It slowly transpired that the soulmate for the baron was a beautiful, red-headed Irish woman, and Stoker could not help but recall the lineaments of his own wife as he read these entries. Stoker sighed as he anticipated the death of this beloved wife, the bitter grief of the baron, and his turning to Rosicrucianism in search of eternal life.

But no; it soon became clear that it was in fact this wife who had introduced the baron to the ways of Rosicrucianism – an order to which her whole family belonged. It turned out that she, like Stoker himself, was a member of the established Church, and that the baron had forsaken his Catholicism to marry her. It was she who had introduced him to occult ideas – and soon alchemical symbols and Hebrew letters were peppering the margins of the diary. It seemed that the couple were convinced of their own imperviousness to damnation, and it was not long before it became clear that the two were involved in the random killings of nameless drunks and prostitutes in the worst quarters of Bruges and Liège, Paris and London, the baron's description of these events embellished by strange verses involving sun, moon and mercury.

As the diary progressed for some years, for the baron now only recorded the more notable points of his existence, Stoker noticed, as had Irving, the emergence of identifiable people and events – not just the likes of Orton and the Tichborne baronetcy, but far-reaching events, playing out on the world stage. As Stoker read on, he noticed that each of these events was framed by specific symbols, as though the entries were seconds or minutes in one of the seven days enjoyed by the Rosicrucian initiate passing from base lead to pure gold – from physical materiality to spiritual alchemy and eternal life in a paradise reunited with earth. He began to look for further clues about the baron's fellow initiates – what they did, where they met – but, as Irving had intimated, he found nothing that could condemn anyone but the baron himself. A pity, for he would have loved to have known how long Dowden had been in league with the baron, or whether he himself had committed any of these crimes. But no; even if he had been involved in such barbarities, there was no proof of his involvement – not that proof had seemed to matter much when it had come to Drayfield.

Like a bolt of lightning, it struck him – proof, Drayfield! Was not the diary before him proof of the nefarious nature of the Prussian cousin, as Lord Drayfield had more than alluded to? Well, if not exactly proof, being circumstantial, would it not at least help

Drayfield's case for an appeal, and go some way towards mitigating his own – and the Guv'nor's – silence concerning Lucarda?

He took up a piece of headed paper and was about to jab his pen in the inkpot when a slight scuffing sound accompanied by a shaft of light made him look up.

'So, Bram, did you take the steamer home tonight?' The silhouette of his wife was framed in the study doorway. In outline, her body was intricately detailed, as though traced from a camera lucida.

'Yes... both there and back... the last one, coming back,' he sputtered. Why was she so very late to bed? 'The King's Road was just like Grafton Street.'

'In what way?' asked Florence. 'Full of drunks?'

'No; just Salvationists trying to save them!' Florence lifted her head up high and laughed, showing off her fine white neck. For a moment Stoker wondered whether the red-headed woman with whom the baron had committed so many crimes might be a relative of the Balcombes – a genuine possibility, given the smallness of their community back home. His wife looked at him with her grey-blue eyes, then down at the watch on his desk, and smiled. Suddenly, a surge of desire overtook Stoker, drawing him from behind his desk, across the floor, and into her arms.

'My fine, thrifty, abstemious husband!' whispered Florence, resting her delicate head upon his chest.

'Soon to be a barrister, I promise,' replied Stoker. She jerked up her head and looked into his eyes.

'And give up that wretched theatre business?' He laughed.

'In the long run I will, I promise.' She squeezed his hand.

'Come, then, my darling, come up to bed; it is so very late.' He kissed her on her forehead and pushed her away from him gently.

'I will do soon. Just a few things to tidy up first.'

Florence walked off into the brighter light of the hallway then turned. 'Bram,' she called, 'I shall be waiting!' And with that she turned again and climbed up the stairs.

Back at his desk, Stoker took up the piece of headed paper once more and jabbed his pen in some ink. Boldly, perhaps rashly, he began to write.

Dear Mr Johnson,

The enclosed diary is the ignoble testament of Baron Drayfield-Curdala of Danzig – also known simply as Lucarda or Curdala – the Prussian cousin of Lord Drayfield. I believe it will go some way towards clearing your client's name should he be granted leave to appeal (indeed, I believe it will, at the least, help his case for appeal) as the baron's handwriting is easily verifiable, and the events he describes – even if in French and not directly related to events in Dawson Street – clear evidence of his reprobate character.

Please handle the intelligence it contains wisely, and discreetly. Indeed, I would be most grateful if you would keep the provenance of the diary itself a secret, as it would be most unfortunate if Mr Henstridge were to learn of my involvement, since I am – as you may be aware – currently undertaking my pupillage in his Chambers.

Yours truly,

Bram Stoker

Opening a drawer in his desk, he brought out some manila paper, some scissors, string and glue, then placing the letter inside the diary, wrapped the whole package up neatly before addressing it to 'Alfred Johnson Esquire, Buxton and Hulse Chambers, 34 Lincoln's Inn, W.C.'

Stoker sat back and yawned; it had been a long day, and the package still needed to be franked at the post office. But that was a task for the morrow, and within half an hour he found himself in bed, his wife in his arms, enjoying feelings of tenderness and moral relief he had not known for many a long London year.

CHAPTER XIV

THE DOCTOR HAS VISITORS

The following morning George Stoker was in the midst of examining a patient when there was a knock at the door. The knock was the usual long-spaced series of four which he had trained his nurse, Gertrude, to employ, just in case he might have to ask one of his clients in an embarrassing state of undress to rebutton a corset or replace a chemise, or simply in case they were in the throes of some intimate confession – an increasingly common occurrence in recent times. Despite not having a fashionable Harley Street address, George's reputation for good medical practice (which seemed to consist as much in his good looks and exciting past in Turkey-land and the Himalayas as in his pioneering use of oxygen therapy) had ensured that some of the wealthier, younger, and more aristocratic society ladies were lengthening his list of patients.

Such a patient was occupying his attention at that very moment, as the Marchioness of Anglesey – a woman whose husband was gaining an increasing reputation for his frequent 'aways' – was bemoaning her unhappy lot and trying desperately to persuade the doctor of the merits of him accompanying her and her inattentive husband on a tour of the Swiss Alps that spring; an invitation he was politely attempting to decline.

'But you simply *must* join us,' the Marchioness exclaimed. 'Only you of all doctors know my particular needs – and the contours of the mountains are quite exquisite at that time of year!' she added, breathlessly.

It was with some relief, therefore, that George made his excuses and attended the summons at the door.

'Gertrude, what can I do for you?' he asked, ushering the nurse out into the corridor.

'Your brother and Mr Irving are waiting downstairs to see you,' she replied.

'What the devil do they want?'

'They say that it's urgent and must see you immediately. Apparently, an actress is gravely ill.'

'Well, can't they get another doctor, one not detained with the Marchioness of Anglesey and other hysterical patients for the next few hours?' George assumed Gertrude would smirk, but she merely shook her head.

'I'm afraid they are quite insistent.'

'Which actress is it, pray?' now asked George. Gertrude pursed her lips.

'One whose name common decency does not allow me to repeat,' she replied with a huff. George sighed: sometimes Gertrude's Presbyterian leanings annoyed him, but she was generally a most reliable and efficient nurse, and he was glad to have her.

'All right,' said George. 'Please tell them to wait a few more minutes, and I shall send the Marchioness on her way.'

Having apologised to the Marchioness, and assured her of her charms, George was about to head downstairs when three, not two, men came bursting into the surgery, barging past the Marchioness in a most ungentlemanly fashion. Before George had time to voice any complaint, he heard the distinctive brogue of his brother.

'Frater, you must come with us, immediately! Miss Terry has been attacked and is now gravely ill.' Before him now stood the three men: his brother, Bram, in his green frock coat; Irving, his top hat skew-whiff; and another, sporty-looking fellow, with bristles and curly brown hair tufting at the side of his bowler – some ten years younger at least than the other two.

'Why me? If Miss Terry is ill, surely another surgeon closer by can see her.'

'I'm sorry, Dr Stoker, but this will require some discretion… the like of which your brother assures me only you can provide,' replied Irving.

'And there may be a degree of expertise which you alone among doctors in London can bring to the case,' added Stoker.

'Well, it's a bit much, I must say,' replied George, ignoring Irving's and his brother's blandishments. 'And I have appointments until noon at least.'

'Please, George,' continued Stoker, 'I really would appreciate you coming. This would appear to be no ordinary attack – or illness.'

'Well, all right. I will ask Gertrude to dispel my remaining patients and prepare a medical bag. I do hope this is no fool's errand!' Irving now came up and clasped George's arm encouragingly – an impromptu gesture which more than bolstered the doctor's resolve.

Soon the four men were in two hansoms, bundling down the Charing Cross Road. The newsstands of *The Morning Post* were gleefully announcing that the Lords would finally be debating the motion which would allow the Sovereign of Scotland to punish the Laird of Berwick-upon-Tweed. George noticed that his brother was shaking his head mournfully.

'You wouldn't be wasting any tears on that murderous cut-throat Drayfield, would you, Bram?'

'Drayfield is no murderous cut-throat!' retorted Stoker. 'Everything he said at the trial was true.'

'How do you know?'

'Because both myself and Mr Irving have seen proof – or, at least, compelling evidence – that he is innocent of murder, though not perhaps of gullibility,' replied Stoker. 'Indeed,' he continued, 'I think you will find that Miss Terry's attacker is the same man as killed Lord Drayfield's maid!'

'Sounds fanciful to me, frater, I must say,' replied George. And so, as they once again passed the top of Whitehall, close to the obnoxious druggist Bartholomew, Stoker began telling his brother about the baron – and what he knew about his relations with Irving and Miss Terry: how the baron had kept an occult diary detailing nefarious activity which revealed him to be more than capable of committing the murder of which his own cousin, Drayfield, had been found guilty – despite Drayfield himself repeatedly protesting that it was the baron, not he, who was the culprit; how Irving had purloined this diary from the baron's castle in Prussia many years before – when he and Miss Terry had been on tour – and then used it to blackmail him; and finally, yes, how the baron, in an act of revenge, had attacked – indeed bitten – Miss Terry with the uncanny strength of a vampire the night before, leading to her collapse onstage and unstaunchable wound. He explained how, Miss Terry having insisted on going home after the performance, Irving had been woken early that morning and called to attend her house in Belgravia, and that his alarm had been so great at what he had seen there that he had summoned both Harker – an individual who also knew the baron – and himself to attend (a demand which, Stoker privately acknowledged, he could fain ignore, despite his misgivings about the Guv'nor and his leading lady).

George had continued to look unimpressed throughout this whole account until he heard one detail which made him sit up.

'What did you say was on the collar of the baron's cape?'

'The Drayfield-Curdala crest: a blue and black heart topped with a coronet.'

'Are you sure?' asked George, speaking more loudly to overcome the din from a nearby organ-grinder.

'Absolutely sure. Why do you ask?'

'Well, that was the self-same crest the lunatic who raided my medical chest and stole my phials of blood had on the collar of his cape, I've just remembered!'

'Well then, it must have been this Lucarda-Curdala scoundrel. What did you say he was called? One of the *pobratimové*, or blood brothers?' George laughed nervously.

'That's one possibility,' he replied. 'But I really only mentioned that Balkan tradition to conceal my real fears as to what he might be.'

'What do you mean?'

'I am afraid his love of blood may have another, more disturbing, cause.'

'Because he is a vampire, you mean?'

Before George could answer, the cab had pulled up outside an impressive, whitewashed building: Miss Terry's Belgravia abode. As the brothers made their way towards the steps leading up to the front door, George asked Stoker a question.

'Tell me, frater, what did you say the baron's name was? Curdala?'

'Yes,' replied Stoker. 'Lucarda-Curdala, he goes by both names – possibly to frustrate detection; they're anagrams of one another.'

'I see,' muttered George, as the brothers now hurried to join Harker and Irving at the top of the steps as they waited for Miss Terry's maid to let them in.

Miss Terry's vestibule was an airy feast of lilac and white wallpaper, leading onto a marbled hallway bedecked with sprays of chrysanthemums, punctuated by photographs and daguerreotypes of the actress as Ophelia, Portia and other celebrated roles that had enabled her to purchase both this house in town and her beloved Smallhythe in Kent for the off-season. Stoker had never been inside the house before (Miss Terry was almost always dining out and rarely entertained at home), but he was hardly surprised at her exquisite taste, and marvelled that such wealth could have been garnered by one woman. He looked across at George, now removing his hat and gloves, and was pleased to note that he too seemed suitably impressed.

'Come,' said Irving. 'Let us go and see Ellen.'

The maid now led the men up two flights of green Wilton carpet, then down a corridor until they arrived at a white-painted wooden door. With a degree of self-consciousness suggesting that what lay beyond was rarely privy to visitors, the maid turned the knob to reveal a scene reminiscent of an operating theatre.

There, on a powder blue counterpane over a plump white bed, was Miss Terry. She was dressed in what appeared to be pink silk pyjamas, her golden hair splayed in all directions over the blanched pillows. She was breathing weakly, almost as if not alive. A nurse in a starched blue uniform stood silently in the corner. The men exchanged knowing glances.

'Perhaps the beginnings of consumption,' said George of a sudden. 'But I shall divine further. Gentlemen, could you please turn your heads.' Along with the others, Stoker turned to face the damask curtains. He could hear the rattling of a stethoscope and presumed that his brother was inspecting Miss Terry's chest.

'Mr Irving, Sir, can you please divide the curtains?'

'It upsets her greatly, Dr Stoker. Are you sure that we should?'

'Please, just do as I say.' Irving took a few paces and thrust the damask apart, letting in the weak October sun.

'Aaah!' screamed the patient, and then there was the sound of a loud thud. Stoker and the others turned round to see Miss Terry sitting bolt upright on her bed, her pyjama top indecently exposing, her blue eyes like saucers. 'No,' she cried, 'no, not that! Please, Henry, please!' She was now turning over and desperately burying her face in a pillow, as though trying to block out the light. George, meanwhile, was slumped in the corner, the force of Miss

Terry's fit having flung him across the room. After a moment, the doctor got up and approached the bed once more, his expression strangely unperturbed.

'Please close the curtains again, Mr Irving.'

Miss Terry now appeared to have returned to the same state of inertia she had displayed when they had first come in. Gently, George turned her onto her back and did up the buttons on her front.

'Any idea what might be the matter?' asked Harker. George looked up at the anxious faces of his companions.

'I have some idea, but there is one more necessary test.' As Miss Terry lay unconscious, George slowly opened her mouth and appeared to look intently inside, before shaking his head and withdrawing from her quietly respiring form – the only other sound being that of Irving, muttering, 'My poor, poor Juliet.'

'Gentlemen,' whispered George, 'will you please join me outside?' They all now tiptoed out of the room, leaving the drained form of Miss Terry lying, as before, on the bed.

Once outside, George beckoned the men along the corridor towards the stairwell then gathered them close. He looked at each man in turn before addressing the group.

'Miss Terry has little blood left in her, her incisors are beginning to lengthen, and she has developed a profound photophobia.'

'A what?' demanded Harker.

'A fear of light,' responded Stoker.

'And what has caused this?' asked Irving, irritably. George shook his head and sighed.

'My brother tells me that Miss Terry was attacked last night by a vicious aristocrat... a Prussian baron, no less, whose nefarious nature is quite well known to you, Mr Irving – is that right?' Irving scowled at Stoker and then sighed heavily.

'Yes, it is. The attack happened during the interval.'

'That he bit her in the neck, where the marks from his incisors are still evident now, and that the blood could not be staunched, leading to her collapse onstage.'

'That again is true. But please, Dr Stoker, can you not cure her?' We have our last night of *The Bells* tonight.' George took a deep breath and drew himself up to his full height. A sudden squall of rain rattled the window behind him.

'I regret to inform you that I believe Miss Terry has been bitten by a vampire.' Immediately, Irving scoffed, while Harker gasped. Stoker alone remained silent.

'She has been startled by a madman, affronted and shocked, that's all,' huffed Irving.

'This must be the result of some Rosicrucian ritual,' broke in Harker. 'We can reverse it by following other Rosicrucian rituals, I am sure.' Again Irving scoffed.

'She has been bitten by a vampire,' said Stoker quietly, echoing his brother. 'Of *that* I am sure.'

'Yes, the initial ceaseless bleeding, which follows a first attack, has stopped, and she is now drained of blood,' continued George. 'She is on her way to becoming one of the Undead. Trust me, gentlemen, however strange this may seem, it is true. I have seen this sort of thing before, in the Balkans. Her fear of light – particularly sunlight – and lengthening incisors are further typical symptoms.'

'And I refuse to believe you!' declared Irving, folding his arms defensively.

'I believe you!' piped up a woman's voice from the direction of the stairwell. Stoker turned to see a pelican-like face looming towards them up the stairs. Edith seemed unusually buoyant, perhaps comforted by the men's discomfiture, and seemingly unconcerned by the plight of her mother.

'I believe you,' she repeated as she now reached the top of the stairs, 'as my mother told me all about the other strange goings-on at the theatre, including,' and here she looked directly at Stoker, 'an attack by a bloodless young hussy on Mr Stoker just the other day!' For a moment Edith looked almost coquettish, as though she were intimating an affair between the acting manager and some girl of the theatre.

'Did you tell her about that, Guv'nor?' asked Stoker swiftly.

'Not Edith, no; but Ellen, yes.'

'How could you?' burst out Stoker. 'I thought you said we men of the company should keep our silence about that terrible incident!'

'I had to let Ellen know!' shouted Irving and turned away sharply.

'What incident are you alluding to?' asked George to nobody in particular.

Stoker groaned.

'Two nights ago,' he began, 'I was attacked onstage by a young girl whom I had had cause to rescue previously.' And with that he related the sorry tale of the girl in the lights cellar and how she had returned and attacked him, and how he – yes, he – had accidentally impaled her on his cane, but how she had seemingly contained no blood, like a vampire; like Miss Terry was fast becoming now.

'And did you report this incident to the police?' asked George.

'No,' replied Stoker.

'Why not?'

'Because,' growled Irving, 'we reasoned that they would not understand the delicacy of the situation.'

'Ah, I see.' Edith was now openly smirking at the others' awkwardness, much to Stoker's annoyance.

'But Miss Terry does know, you say, about this… this vampire hussy?' continued the doctor.

'Yes,' replied Irving curtly. 'As I said, I had to tell her.' Harker, now flanking George as the squall pelted the window behind them, seemed dumbfounded by the whole admission.

And then suddenly he spoke, with some urgency.

'I have my own confession to make,' he declared. But George was unmoved.

'Please leave it till later, Harker. We have enough on our plates already! Now, does anyone know where this Curdala lives?'

'Yes,' said Stoker. 'Dawson Street, in Bayswater.'

'Well, we must go there at once! I shall write a note to my friend at St Thomas' Hospital to come and transfuse Miss Terry some blood – and collect my medical bag for safe keeping. Edith, can I entrust you with delivering this message, and with arranging for some garlic to be strewn around your mother's room?'

'Garlic?' queried Stoker.

'Yes, Bram, garlic. It warded off vampires in the Balkans and will doubtless work here too. Edith, can you do this for me?' Edith scowled.

'Oh, can you not ask her maid, Betty, or her nurse to do it?' she replied with a huff. 'I have an important meeting at the Union in an hour's time, and I really cannot miss it.'

'But your mother is gravely ill, Miss Craig,' asserted Stoker. 'Her nurse is needed here!'

Edith frowned momentarily, and then shook her head.

'No, no,' she now continued, 'I really am sure Betty could manage – and Mama is so very prone to histrionics!' And with that she spun on her heel and moved her bustled and booted self down the Wilton-carpeted stairs, off to see her campaigning friends and various other New Women. After a moment's shocked silence, George addressed the group.

'We must visit Dawson Street. The surest way to cure Miss Terry is to find the culprit while it is daylight and then stake his heart.'

'Stake his heart?' exclaimed Irving. 'Are you serious?'

'Entirely serious. It is the only way the baron will be truly dead – and Miss Terry truly free. Anyhow, we must get there as soon as we can, before the light diminishes and the baron's powers inevitably increase. Shall we take the Underground?'

'The Underground?' said Stoker apprehensively, as the men made their way downstairs. 'Are you sure that is a good idea?'

'Of course,' responded Irving briskly. 'I myself never travel otherwise if I can help it.'

'I cannot believe this, Sir – that you take the Underground!' resumed Stoker, as he, Harker and Irving now assembled in the vestibule, George hurriedly scribbling his note in the hall. 'Why would a man such as you risk his reputation so?'

'Because, Bram, it is the only place I know where I am unlikely to encounter that vile Jezebel whom I know, or once knew, as my wife!'

George now joined the others and summoned Betty. He explained that she must deliver a message to his doctor friend at St Thomas' for him to come and transfuse some blood (although not a cure, George hoped she would be better soon, but quite when he could not know), but that Betty herself would be responsible for strewing some garlic around her mistress's bedroom. Evidently puzzled, the maid nonetheless swore to follow the doctor's instructions, before opening the door and letting the men out onto the street. The sun was illuminating the whitewashed colonnades of Belgravia, giving the street the appearance of a fanciful mausoleum, as there was no sign of any people anywhere. There was no sign of the earlier rain either, except a glistening from the cobblestones, or indeed of any fog, although Stoker knew this would likely descend later that day; a prospect he silently dreaded.

As they made their way from Miss Terry's house, past Eaton Square and towards Victoria Station, George took the opportunity to say a few words to his brother.

'It's just as well you didn't tell the police about the girl in the lights cellar, Bram – they would never have believed you. You have to have lived where I have lived to know the truth of these things.'

'That may be so, but the Guv'nor still doesn't believe Miss Terry has been attacked by an actual vampire,' replied Stoker. They were now near the porticoed entrance to the station, close to the steps that would lead them down into a temporary Hades.

'Well,' replied George, 'as I say, you have to have lived where I have lived to know the truth – or one of the truths.'

'What do you mean by that?'

George laughed. 'I think you will find there are as many untruths as truths in this affair, Bram.' And with that he slapped his brother on the back, almost making him slip on the stone steps as they descended into the Underground.

CHAPTER XV

THE BARON'S LAIR

It was not the first time Stoker had endured the smoke, heat and stench that possessed the platform of an Underground station, but he had spared himself the indignity for many years. After all, it was not an experience that a gentleman, even a gentleman of the theatre, would rush to repeat. Stoker and George were seated on a bench, while Harker and Irving were standing a few yards in front of them, close to the platform edge, talking – the older man listening intently to the younger. Beyond them, on the far side of the track, Stoker could make out the lettering of bills advertising Pears soap and Fry's cocoa, and then, to his wry amusement, a playbill advertising Mr Henry Irving and Miss Ellen Terry in *The Bells*. Now casting his eyes towards the end of the platform, Stoker noticed the figure of a shortish man, dressed head to toe in what looked like tweed, seemingly staring at them. He looked back at Harker and Irving to see the older man pat Harker on the shoulder, as if acknowledging some sort of intimacy. What might that be?

Soon the rhythmic heave of train wheels compelled Stoker's attention. The whole platform shook as the sound became louder, dark smoke pushing itself into the void, like dragon's breath. The din became shriller and shriller until it climaxed with the long screech of a horn, and the train's many carriages came rolling before Stoker's eyes, like the slides of a magic lantern show – a succession of lights and little lives moving before him in a display so ephemeral it made Stoker feel quite unsteady.

As the train drew to a halt, Stoker got up and beckoned George and the others to walk further along the platform, away from the shortish figure in tweed.

'I think we may be being followed,' he began once he and his companions were settled in a compartment.

'What of it?' replied Irving. 'My celebrity often draws well-wishers, and sometimes simply the curious.' Stoker cringed.

The train was now chugging through the penumbra into Sloane Square Station, where the rude mechanicals of Chelsea – the workers in scruffy bowlers and flimsy bonnets who, along with countless others across the city, allowed more affluent Londoners to stroll untroubled through the park of a Sunday afternoon – were gathered together on the wooden platform, ready to undertake their orchestrated chores, like prop hands backstage at the Lyceum.

Soon they were passing through Gloucester Road, then the sooty bricks of High Street Kensington, before finally arriving at Paddington, where they would make their ascent from this Hades of peeping monsters and infernal smoke into the yellower mists of a returning London fog.

As they left the station, Stoker became aware once more of the short, tweed-wrapped figure, now climbing the steps behind them.

'I am *sure* we are being followed,' he told the others in a passing whisper. 'And not by one of Mr Irving's admirers!'

They were soon in the hubbub of Bayswater, surrounded by the habitual cries of barrow-boys and hawkers that echoed through the streets near stations. Indeed, the only difference of note between this district and Charing Cross or Waterloo was the sight of brightly dressed young aesthetes, already the worse for wear for absinthe, shifting aimlessly between the estaminets that they had begun to make their own. Stoker recalled that this was the district Telbin and his associates called home.

'By whom, Bram, do you think we might be being followed?' asked Irving.

'By a suspicious-looking fellow in tweed.'

'By me, to be precise,' came a voice from behind. Stoker turned round to see the dapper figure of Edward Dowden, his jaw immediately dropping for what seemed the umpteenth time in as many weeks.

'What the devil brings you here, Dowden?' barked Irving before Stoker could collect himself.

'A pleasure to meet you again, Sir, after all these years,' replied Dowden with a smirk. Irving harrumphed.

'And you too, George,' continued Dowden. 'Still a brilliant sawbones, I hear!'

'I try my best,' replied George glibly.

He now turned to Stoker. Not knowing what to say, Stoker merely gestured towards Harker.

'It's all right, Bram,' said Dowden. 'If you didn't already know it, Harker and I have met one another before – and have both decided on the same course of action, it would seem.'

'What might that be?' responded Harker.

'Come now, we are both close to the house of Lord Rosy Cross – not a place an initiate would normally be approaching in broad daylight with an apostate, would he? I presume you have come for the baron.'

'An… an apostate?' stuttered Harker.

'Now, Joseph, don't play the jobbernowl. I have broken with the brotherhood and come to help Bram discover Lucarda – just as you have.'

'And how did you discover *us*?' asked Stoker, suddenly finding his voice.

'I went early to the Lyceum and found out you and Harker had been summoned by Mr Irving to see Miss Terry. I waited outside her house in Belgravia then followed you all on foot to the Underground – a most unusual locale for you, Bram, I must say!'

'But what made you break with the baron?' pressed Stoker, ignoring the jibe of his erstwhile friend.

'When I told Lord Rosy Cross that you had seen his carriage in Dawson Street, he told me he would hasten his revenge on Irving and Miss Terry; and then I became worried he might embroil you, Bram, so decided I had to do the right thing – tell you what I know!' Dowden said this with a degree of dramatic fervour, as though hoping his confession would induce exclamations of gratitude from the acting manager. But Stoker could only disappoint him.

'So… the story about Baron Cadwallader… Curdala?'

'A spontaneous invention to help protect Lucarda from your investigations,' replied Dowden. 'You had misheard the name Curdala – as you know, another form of his name – so I made up the details of a fictitious Baron Cadwallader there and then.' Stoker groaned.

'Come now, Bram,' said Irving briskly, 'it's no good crying over spilt milk.' And here he turned to Dowden. 'So, Professor, you now wish to help us not harm us… by helping us discover Curdala?'

'Yes indeed, Mr Irving. Indeed, since it is only I who has been inside his London lair, I believe I am indispensable to this little expedition. Come, let us confront the baron!' Stoker looked at the firm features of his governor and his brother, and then at the smirking features of Dowden. It seemed their course was set, and he had little choice but to follow it.

Soon all five men were outside Lord Drayfield's townhouse – the very same house outside of which Stoker had seen Ponsonby and the housekeeper talking just over a week before, and into which Stoker had seen the two Gipsies carry the coffin. Now the house had the air of being empty. In fact, the whole street was strangely still, as though a gossamer net had descended on the vicinity. Irving coughed, eyeing Stoker.

'Well,' said Stoker, tapping his moustache nervously, 'I suppose we had best start by ringing the bell.'

'You can try, but I doubt you will get a reply,' said Dowden. 'Mind you, the times I was here it was never in daytime; the baron only ever entertained at night.'

'That makes sense,' muttered George. 'Avoiding the sunlight.'

Stoker walked up the steps leading to the front door and pulled on the bell cord, releasing a shambolic clatter but no sound of stirrings within. He pulled on the cord again. Still no stirrings within. Stoker turned round to see Dowden smiling wryly at the bottom of the steps.

'I have another idea. Please follow me.' Stoker shrugged his shoulders and soon he and the others were facing a sunken basement window at the back of the house. There were some shards of broken flowerpots strewn on the ground, as well as the remains of fallen hydrangea blooms. Brushing aside the shards, Dowden knelt down before the window and wrenched it open – just wide enough to allow the men to pass through. Dowden turned, triumphantly doffed his hat, then slid feet first into the basement, Stoker and the others following his lead.

Inside, Stoker discovered the most peculiar room he had ever seen. It was lit dimly with three gas lamps shaped like roses, spreading their aureoles in an isosceles triangle on the ceiling. At the back, on the wall, was a painted, seven-petalled rose, and before this, what looked like an altar, with images of a sceptre, sun and moon embroidered on its cloth covering. Before this stood an elaborate wrought-iron coffin, engraved with crests and escutcheons. As Stoker gazed in some amazement at this scene, he heard a contemptuous harrumph from behind him. Irving, clutching his top hat in front of him, now spoke.

'Not a square or set of compasses anywhere to be seen. Sheer bogusry.'

'Nor a cross either,' observed George, edging around the gloomy space with a clinical eye.

Harker was shaking his head. 'Nor a decent brush stroke. Painted by some amateur, no doubt!'

'So, you never came here, Harker?' demanded Stoker.

'No. I only ever saw the Soho temple,' returned the scene painter, looking at Dowden, whose self-satisfied smile was annoying Stoker intensely.

'So, you have never seen this coffin before?' asked George.

'Never,' replied Harker.

'And you?' he asked Dowden.

'Of course,' said Dowden. 'This is the tomb of Lord Rosy Cross.'

'What did he do here?' asked George.

'Lucarda was the Father Christian Rosenkreutz, Lord Rosy Cross – well, his representative at least. He used to provide certain services from here during the hours of darkness – for the inner circle... a circle to which, sadly, young Harker here was not privy.'

'Services?'

'Yes; using his name to garner favour in high places, such as with the Prince of Wales.'

Dowden now smiled sardonically at Harker.

'Spared my artist's soul this visual cacophony at least, not being privy to this circle,' responded Harker tartly. 'And besides, as we both know, the baron was certainly no Rosenkreutz in his dealings!'

Dowden's face fell at this remark, and he turned silently away.

'Come now,' said Irving, 'this bickering takes us no nearer to saving Ellen. How, Doctor, do you suggest we proceed?'

'Well, I think we should open the coffin and see if the baron is in there.'

'You are joking?' exclaimed Irving. 'How could the baron be in there? He would have suffocated, surely? It is shut tight.' Indeed, the coffin lid looked securely fitted over its base, if seemingly unsealed, and suffering from some deep cracks along its top.

'Not if he were a vampire – a member of the Undead,' replied George. 'The Undead have no need of air, food or water to survive, any more than the dead do; just blood.' Stoker nodded in support of his brother.

'You are, I hope, not being serious,' returned Irving. 'I find this whole vampire idea preposterous!'

George now strode to the corner of the room where stood a large vessel, sealed with a brass cap. He prised off the cap, looked inside, then turned to the others.

'Tell me, Professor,' he asked, 'is it customary for Rosicrucian temples to house pots of earth? Is there any passage in the *Fama*, *Confessio* or *Chymical Wedding* which calls for such additions? I ask not just because you are an initiate but because you are a literary man who has surely read such texts with much acuity.' Dowden turned, his eyes now glistening with tears of seeming humiliation.

'No; there is nothing in such texts that calls for such things.' Harker was looking at the famed scholar with curiosity, as though still relying upon his novice's instinct for learning more. The roseate light from the gas lamps was flickering across the ceiling, auguring some imminent climax.

'And would such earth, do you think, require such a thing as this?' And here George plunged his hand into the urn and pulled out a white object, seemingly shedding bits of yellow cloth, and held it up to the others. Suddenly, Dowden screamed, as he and the others suffered the same psychic shock. For here was a human jaw, shedding scraps of dead, jaundiced skin.

'Who could that be?' gasped Irving.

'Probably a suicide; one from off the baron's Prussian estate. Look!' And here George pulled out a round metal object from the urn and threw it towards his brother. Stoker caught it and turned it over in his hand. He could make out faint Teutonic lettering on one side.

'An old German mark,' he declared. 'George is right. The baron clearly took the earth back with him to London.'

'Why would he do that?' asked Irving. George laughed.

'Tell me, Mr Irving, as you have visited his castle, did the baron have a burial ground there?'

'Not that I saw. There was a crossroads with a rather ghoulish gibbet beside it, so I suppose there could be such a ground nearby.'

'A crossroads, you say?'

'That's right,' confirmed Irving.

'Where suicides are buried,' said George triumphantly. 'Unhallowed ground – a necessity to the lair of a vampire!'

'I still don't believe all this nonsense,' declared Irving. 'I know Curdala had his Rosicrucian bogusry, but vampires do not exist!'

'Well, there is only one way of deciding the matter,' continued George. 'Come on, gentlemen!' And with this all five men set about lifting the lid of the coffin, George and Stoker kneeling down then pushing upwards until the lid itself sprang suddenly upwards, like a tight felt cap off a fusilier's head.

'My God, he's gone!' cried George. Indeed, as Stoker peeped into the coffin, he saw nothing more than what appeared to be velvet, flickered by the roseate light reflecting off the ceiling. As he looked closer, however, he could make out dark trails containing what, to his horror, looked like splinters of human bone – unhallowed earth! But there was something else: an envelope, trimmed in blue and black. Harker let his corner of the coffin lid hang in the air to edge inside and pick it up.

'Shall I open it, Guv'nor?'

'Please do,' said George, interrupting Irving before he could reply. 'But first, let us lower this coffin lid to the ground.'

The task accomplished, Harker tore at the envelope and drew out a sheet of paper. He moved to beneath one of the gas lamps, then scratched his chin.

'What does it say?' asked Irving.

'Most strange.'

'What does it say, Harker?'

"You who have fallen to my place of earth,
Where gnomes abound and sylphs have dearth.
I ride upon the winds so strong,

And soon shall 'light where wolves yet throng.
And you, Faustus, shall desert,
Your friends and acolytes and revert,
To bloodless roaming, and your Queen,
Will prey upon your very spleen."'

Despite the low lighting of the temple, Stoker and the others could not fail to notice Irving blanching at these final two lines. Harker stopped reading and looked up at the Guv'nor, perhaps worried his painter's rendition of the verse had not impressed the great actor.

'Well,' said Irving, his bravado appearing to return, 'is that all?' Harker coughed then resumed.

"'I now return, and live forever in the shade,
At night where bats and demons raid.
Eternal Unlife my reward,
Confined within the Ryssocord."'

'Ryssocord?' queried George. 'What the devil can that mean?' Harker passed the sheet of paper to the doctor. After puzzling over it for a few seconds, he passed it over to Dowden, who seemed eager to contribute his linguistic expertise to proceedings.

'It's an anagram... not a very good one,' he asserted, after a moment.

'What's the solution?' asked Irving impatiently, reaching over to snatch the note from the professor, who simply shied away and held the paper closer to his chest.

'Dowden?'

'I think,' said Dowden, his fine face turning to them in the roseate light, 'that it could mean "Rosy Cross" – the baron's own name, if we follow the rules of one letter substitution, the *d* at the end replacing an *s*.'

'Or else his temple in Prussia,' said Irving, 'which I – to my shame – have seen.'

'Or,' continued Dowden, ignoring Irving's failure to appreciate his cryptic interpretation, 'it could, by the same rule, mean crossroad, the *y* substituting an *a*; both are possible.'

'A crossroads, you say,' responded Irving, now successfully snatching the paper from Dowden.

'So, since he is a vampire,' broke in George, 'it could mean at the crossroad, or crossroads, where suicides are buried – which you have also seen, have you not, Mr Irving?'

Irving sighed and waved his hand towards the empty coffin.

'If he is indeed a vampire, as you say, Dr Stoker, then surely he would have to be transported around London – or, indeed, back to his estate – in this very coffin, at least during daylight hours?'

'He has another coffin – a wooden one,' announced Stoker. 'I have seen it, in his carriage, outside this very house!'

Before anyone had time to question Stoker further, the men were startled by a noise: muffled cries were issuing from the floor above them.

'There *is* someone here,' whispered Irving urgently. 'We must leave immediately.' George laughed.

'Mr Irving, we happen to be a company of four – sorry, five – fine fellows; we have little to fear. And besides, we have just cause to be here.' So saying, he moved boldly past the coffin and marched up some narrow steps Stoker had failed to notice in the gloom until he reached a wooden door. He pulled back the door's bolt with a clang and, beckoning the others to follow, stepped through.

The men now found themselves in the hallway of Lord Drayfield's house. The room was unfurnished, except for a number of crates and boxes which were stacked, in seeming preparation for removal. The voices were issuing from an adjacent room. A man and a woman, or more precisely a Scotsman and a Cockney, were arguing furiously.

'I tell you, I ain't doin' no more for you and that awful man! He seems to have taken over 'is lordship's 'ouse entirely – and done Gawd knows wot else!'

'Ya'll duz as yaa're toold, ya wee Sassenach!' shouted the Scotsman.

Stoker started, instantly recognising the same two voices he had heard in Dawson Street just the week before. He beckoned the others towards him.

'The man talking is Ponsonby, the woman, I believe, a Mrs Prism – Lord Drayfield's, and now the baron's, housekeeper,' he whispered. 'I heard them talking outside this house before – when I saw the carriage and the coffin. They are the same two individuals who committed perjury at the Drayfield trial.'

'Well then,' said George loudly, 'let's go and confront the little liars!' And with that he strode purposefully into the adjoining room. The dialogue gave way to gasps, and then screams of astonishment, but before either the Scotsman or the Cockney could respond otherwise, Stoker and the others had crowded in behind George, forming a veritable posse.

The sight of Ponsonby was utterly repulsive: he looked something like a giraffe, Stoker now noticed, his bald head too small for his long body. He wore a brown duffel coat over black breeches, and a monocle next to a roman nose. His whole presence was unsettling, like a creature from the pages of a medieval bestiary, his outlandish proportions like those of an Irish Formorian. As Stoker and the others looked on in silence, Ponsonby's shock turned suddenly into laughter – laughter of the most hellish kind.

''Oo the devil is you lot?' asked the housekeeper.

'It's all right, Mrs Prism,' said Ponsonby. 'I think I knaa who thuz coowards are; the baron told me. So, Mr Irving, ya finally plucked up the courage ta vusit huz lairdship?'

'Yes indeed, we have been trying to catch up with him,' replied Irving, without a trace of irony.

'Waill, ya'se too late.'

'Then tell us, where is Curdala now?' demanded Irving. Here Ponsonby's small head arched downwards, his narrow eyes fixed on the Guv'nor.

'No, Mr Irving, ya'll nat be finding ma maister here,' he sneered. 'He's where ya and your vagabond crew cannae touch him. Now naiver ta die... now one of the glairious Undead!' He sniggered hideously at this point. 'As wull soon be Miss Tairry!'

'I see your master confides in you a lot,' replied Stoker drily. 'When did you see him last?'

'Laast nait, if ya moost knaa, Mr Stoker; but he's now fair, fair away!' Ponsonby folded his arms in triumph.

'You must tell us where he's gone,' cried George. 'If not, we will have you arrested!'

'I fear none uv ya... especially not ya, ya wee leprechaun.' Instinctively, George and the others, excepting Dowden, attempted to pounce on the revolting creature, only to be repulsed by his arms, which catapulted them into the furthest corners of the room.

As Stoker lay dazed next to a panting Irving – their attempt to restrain Ponsonby seemingly hopeless – he heard a thud followed by a yelp and saw the Scotsman crash to the floor. Rubbing his eyes, Stoker made out the figure of the housekeeper, holding a poker, her watery eyes alive with the glee of newly acquired vengeance.

'Oi, you be'er tie 'im up quick, before 'e come round,' she announced, before skipping past the men into the hallway, returning with some ropes. George and Harker scrambled to their feet and stepped forward to restrain the unconscious Scotsman, who now bore a large red mark on his pate. Harker used his cravat as a gag and made sure that the knots around his ankles and wrists were tightly tied.

Stoker got up and looked around. Where was Dowden?

'Should we not wait for Ponsonby to come round so we can quiz him more about the whereabouts of the baron?' he now asked no one in particular.

'There's no need, dearie,' piped up the housekeeper. 'I can tell you that the baron was taken out early this mornin' in that coffin of 'is – wot a loon 'e were, travellin' round inside that thing – before settin' sail from India Docks.'

'And do you know where he's setting sail for?'

'Back to Danzig – or so I 'eard him tell this swine last night.' And here she spat on the motionless Ponsonby.

'Well, we have to stop Ponsonby telegraphing him,' said Stoker, now addressing his companions. 'So, where can we keep him confined?' The Scotsman was now beginning to struggle against the ropes, like a line drawing coming to life.

'Let's put him in the temple. We can pile some boxes against the door and the window outside, in case he escapes his bonds,' replied Irving. As George and Harker carried Ponsonby out, guided by Irving, Stoker addressed the housekeeper again.

'Why did you implicate Lord Drayfield at the trial,' he demanded, 'saying that you were away in Hackney?' The housekeeper's face twitched in irritation as she seemingly searched for a reply.

'Well, I *was* away, if a tad closer than 'ackney; and in any case, I thought it was 'im wot killed poor Lily, 'e were be'avin' that strange at that time. It was Ponsonby who made me stay away that night, tellin' me to say I was over in 'ackney, which is why I just—'

'Yes, yes. But you must have known Drayfield was telling the truth about the baron!' She shook her head slowly.

'I niver knew the baron; niver saw 'im back then. His lordship must have only brought 'im round late at night, after I'd retired. But when the baron returned to the 'ouse, after his trip to Danzig, I could see from 'is ways that 'e meant to keep 'old of it – and realised it must have been 'im not 'is lordship wot killed Lily.'

'So why did you not go to the police then?'

'Too scared. Ain't none of my business neiver.' Stoker smiled wryly: there was no escaping the woman's logic.

'And what will you do now, Mrs Prism?' he asked finally.

'I'm off out of 'ere. Got a place in Bucking'amshire wot no one knows about.'

Irving was now back in the room, followed by George and Harker, dusting off their hands.

'Is Ponsonby secure?' asked Stoker.

'For a good two days, I reckon,' answered George. 'He will eventually wriggle out of his bonds, but not before we have completed the second phase of our plan.' He glanced around the room. 'I see Professor Dowden has already taken his leave.'

'He has then gone?' queried Stoker glumly. George nodded.

'What is the second phase of our plan?' asked Irving suddenly.

George glanced at the housekeeper.

'Ain't none of my business, is it?' she replied, and scuttled out of the room.

'You will have to cancel your last night, I'm afraid, Mr Irving,' now resumed George.

'What do you mean?'

'Well, Miss Terry is in no fit state to perform, and I doubt the audience will be happy with two understudies in the lead roles.'

'Two, you say?' Irving was astonished.

'That's right. You would have to find a replacement for your own part as well as Miss Terry's, since you must come with us. We must now all four make haste to Danzig!'

'Are you serious?' asked Stoker. George was nodding his head emphatically.

'Never more so, I'm afraid, Bram. We need to stake the vampire's heart as soon as possible... it is the only chance Miss Terry has.' Stoker could not remember seeing his brother appear more grave.

'I have never cancelled a last night before,' resumed Irving. 'Can I not leave you three—?'

'Of course not!' spluttered George, scandalised at the Guv'nor's lack of urgency. 'You are the only one among us who has visited the castle before, and who can guide us to the temple. We really must set out now... not least because we can't be sure that Dowden will not inform the baron we are on his tail, despite what he says about having broken with the brotherhood.' Irving sighed and rubbed the lapels of his jacket uneasily.

'Well, the castle is almost impenetrable, we should perhaps try and waylay the baron first.'

'All the more reason to leave now, Mr Irving,' responded George.

'Very well, I agree,' replied the Guv'nor. 'Yes, perhaps this vampire thing is real after all, however daft.' He sighed deeply and shook his head before continuing. 'In any case, I can see no other way to proceed. Bram, we must send word to Grafton and Loveday to man front of house and refund people's tickets. We will say Ellen is indisposed, to allay suspicion, as this is bound to reach the press. Are you game, Mr Harker?'

'Sir, anything I can do to atone for my earlier indiscretion with the baron will please me.'

'Good,' said George, solemnly extending his hand to shake first Harker's and then the other men's hands. 'Now, let us go our various ways and meet at Victoria Station in three hours' time. We can take the train to Dover then the ferry on to Calais. Then there is a train from Calais to Amsterdam, from where a sleeper continues to Danzig – at least there was, when I was in the army. Make sure you have your travel documents with you.'

And with that the men made their way to the front door, stepping down onto the street with a renewed sense of mission.

PART III

CHAPTER XVI

THE BARON RETURNS TO THE CASTLE

Wladyslawa was pacing the ramparts of the castle, inhaling the crisp October air, when suddenly she stopped and gazed towards the crossroads: she had received word that the baron would at last be returning – and she was excited. Deprived of her master's company, the last few months had taken a heavy toll on her discipline as mistress of the house. Increasingly, her temper had been frothing over after guzzling a bottle of hock, leading to spontaneous acts of violence against the servants, invariably followed by squalls of frustrated tears. She needed her master back, his guidance a necessity in her daily life.

Things would have been better, she reflected, had she been able to scry the pool in the temple as before, but in recent days the images had been dark and sluggish in the water, her master's thoughts no longer the bright screen of impressions she had known. The man with the long grey hair and the woman with the long fair hair – who she knew were enemies of the baron – seemed to return repeatedly, making her wonder whether the baron had not been able to exact the revenge upon the pair they so richly deserved – or, perhaps, that he himself was marooned in his contemplations, incapable of transcending these impressions. She was worried lest her powers of second sight were deserting her, or that her master's powers were deserting him, just as he was about to reach the seventh stage of initiation and the attainment of pure gold.

As the sun now started to set, turning the plain a delicious pink, she detected the unmistakable puffs of dust, accompanied by the dull pounding of hooves and whistling of wheels, that marked the arrival of some vehicle. The recklessness with which the vehicle was speeding through the empurpling landscape betrayed some agitation on the part of its driver. Wladyslawa hesitated. Perhaps it was some bandit's cart? But once it had passed the crossroads, she recognised the distinctive form of the baron's carriage – the baron's driver, Geronimo, at its helm. Wladyslawa ran to the turret, pushed open the oak door, and ran down the spiral staircase, then on down three more flights of winding stair, crying, 'Ivan, Piotr, open the gates! Open the gates!' As she sped towards the great hall and into the courtyard, she was relieved to see that the wheel which let down the drawbridge was already in motion. Slowly, the view of the plain began to widen and deepen past the gate, showing the ever more detailed lineaments of the baron's carriage making its return. As the lip of the drawbridge crashed down onto the ground, the hooves of the carriage's three-horse coffle began to clatter then race up the planks, the carriage thundering onto the cobblestones of the courtyard, terrifying Wladyslawa with the prospect of a crash and cartwheeling the bewildered Ivan onto his side. Miraculously, like the devil's own horseman, Geronimo reined in the horses just before the apocalypse, making all four animals rise high on their hind legs and neigh furiously, before settling down askance one another, like dominoes tossed high in the air and then shuffled back inside their box.

Wladyslawa advanced towards the carriage, preening her long red hair in nervous expectation of seeing her master. The seven-petalled rose split asunder as the back doors opened – and there, to her surprise, was not the baron, but his personal retainers, Bertoold and Brennus, who had accompanied the baron to London along with Geronimo. The men were hunched either side of a wooden coffin, which they now began inching out of the carriage and onto the ground. Wladyslawa began screaming as she realised whose body it must contain.

'Hush now!' cried Brennus, the taller of the two men. 'It's not what you think, Mistress. Wait until sundown and all will be well.'

'The sun is almost down now!' exclaimed Bertoold, raising a finger to the sombre sky. Then from inside the coffin came the muffled tones of a voice Wladyslawa, to her joy, knew well.

'Is it safe, Bertoold? Is it safe to get out?'

'One minute more, your Lordship, and dusk will become night.' The drawbridge was still down, and looking across the plain, Wladyslawa could see the reddish-orange glow of the sun's last rays. Then that disappeared and the silver light of the moon began to shadow the landscape. She looked again at the coffin, her joy evaporating as she took in the bizarre nature of the baron's homecoming. She had of course seen the baron lie in his sarcophagus in the temple many times before, after he had returned from Krakow some months previously – but never in a coffin like this: completely sealed, apart from, she noticed, a couple of crude holes on either side, each about an inch across; the result of a rough passage, she surmised. All at once the sky darkened further above her: things really were not right.

'Tell me, Brennus, why is the baron shut up in a coffin, and why have we had to wait until sundown?' she demanded.

'All will soon become clear, Mistress.' Now, with greater firmness, came the baron's voice again.

'Is it safe?'

'Yes, my Lord,' said the wiry Bertoold, bending over to lift up the coffin lid. With a single burst, that catapulted the lid back into the carriage, the baron now appeared, sitting bolt upright, his back to Wladyslawa. She yelped with delight.

'Oh, Master,' she trilled, moving towards him, 'you have returned!' But the baron made no response as the two servants helped him out of his narrow casket and onto his feet. He now turned towards Wladyslawa and offered a feeble smile.

'How now, Wladyslawa? How goes the castle? How goes your scrying?' Despite the baron's hair being far darker than she remembered – at least around the temples – he looked pale and failing.

'My Lord, all is well; but you... you look so weak!'

'I shall be fine in a day or two, don't worry,' he snarled, revealing two abnormally long incisors she had not seen before; a sight that horrified her.

The baron then spoke again.

'Wladyslawa, have you covered up the cross in my temple as instructed?'

'Yes, my Lord, it is done. Your sarcophagus awaits you.'

'Good. I shall repair there and rest; you must direct Bertoold and Brennus.'

'But, my Lord,' said Wladyslawa, circling in front of him, 'why are you so weak?'

'I need blood,' he replied simply, his arms now resting on his two retainers' shoulders. Wladyslawa frowned.

'Was it that evil man and woman, the play actors, who have harmed you?'

'The villains have played their part, yes. But don't worry; after some time on my estate I shall be renewed, and as lithe as you remember me. Come.' As the baron staggered forward, helped by his two retainers, Wladyslawa noticed that he was depositing drops of blood on the ground. She shook her head in disbelief.

Once in the great hall, Wladyslawa directed the two servants to help the baron through to the long passageway carpeted with Persian rugs, then behind the tapestry screen and down the stone steps which led to the wrought-iron door. Taking a key from beneath her petticoats, Wladyslawa opened its padlock. Bertoold and Brennus gasped in amazement as they saw the temple within, its rich ornament illuminated by braziers; but the baron was not to be delayed.

'Quick,' he declared, 'take me inside and place me in my sarcophagus!' Without further ado, the two servants lifted the baron up and carried him to the tomb, their charge panting as they did so. Once laid within the velvet lining, the baron sighed, as if with relief, and became more composed.

'Wladyslawa?'

'Yes, your Lordship?'

'Equip Bertoold, Brennus and any others we trust with blunderbusses from the arsenal; I can at least count on my Gipsy retainers' loyalty, unlike some other servants I have known. Quick now – we may soon have some unwelcome visitors...'

'And you do not need me to first call a surgeon, Master?'

'No; no need, no need! My tomb, my temple and my estate are the only salve I require to make me whole again.'

'Very well, your Lordship,' she sighed, touching the rose brooch on her shawl for reassurance.

'Go now. We'll need some sentinels on the ramparts, to ward off the intruders.' With this the baron closed his eyes and seemed as if ready to enter a long deep sleep.

CHAPTER XVII

AMSTERDAM

Stoker was eyeing the outskirts of the city through a gap in the blind of his train carriage window. Once in Calais, the four men had initially been unable to obtain a carriage to take them through to Amsterdam, but Irving's calling card had brought an obsequious station manager running down from the ticket office to breathe all manner of compliments over '*le grand acteur*', and a carriage next to the dining car had miraculously been secured. Like the steward on their ferry across from Dover beforehand, the manager had made no enquiry as to what lay inside the trunks accompanying the travellers, and might have been amazed to discover an array of pulleys and ropes, a mallet and stake, as well as a crucifix and King James Bible – all in preparation for the men's attempt on the Undead life of Lucarda.

Stoker must have dozed off for some hours during the dreary journey across northern France, as he had awoken to discover scenes of strangely gabled houses – like ziggurats – by narrow canals, and inns with lanterns swinging beneath wooden awnings. He had visited Paris on many occasions, but Amsterdam was rare, and he wished he could have had time to explore its various canals and byways. But as he looked across at his companions, slumped and snoring in their assorted scarves and overcoats, he realised that time was not something they had in abundance. The baron was probably tucked up in his coffin on a ship some way towards the Baltics, and so, he reasoned, they must get a train direct from Amsterdam to Danzig to have any chance of waylaying him before he reached his castle.

As the train now pulled into Westerdok Station, alive with the early-morning commotion of a busy metropolis, the other three men started out of their sleep. Stoker checked his fob watch: half past seven. He raised the blind to see a pitifully narrow set of platforms, crowded with workers jostling to stay off the tracks.

'No chance of a porter in this bedlam!' exclaimed Irving. 'I suppose we must shift for ourselves and take our chances in the madness.' Soon the men were hauling their trunks, their Gladstones atop them, out onto the station's wooden platforms. Indeed, everything here seemed to be made of wood, including the canopy above the ticket office, to which the men now made their way. The office was crowded and smoky, and they had to spend an uncomfortable half an hour among bonneted girls in aprons (lacemakers from the Frisian Islands, George informed them) and rough-hewn labourers before they reached the front of the queue. Once at the window, George used his faultless German to address the man behind the glass. After a few minutes of animated discussion, he turned to his companions with a wry smile.

'I'm afraid the first train isn't until eleven o'clock – but it will take us straight through to Danzig, via Stettin.' Irving groaned.

'What time will it arrive?' Stoker asked.

'Not till tomorrow afternoon.' Stoker looked at Harker and shrugged his shoulders.

'I'm afraid there is no hope of waylaying the baron,' continued George. 'We will have to go to his castle.' Irving now produced a large leather pouch and poured out a stash of guilders, which he had hurriedly obtained from a street seller next to the jetty at

Dover. George paid the ticket man and then he and his companions started lugging their trunks through the crowd to deposit them at the baggage office.

'Well, we have nothing to do except be the beggars of time for a few hours,' said Irving.

'Well, I am in no mood for sightseeing,' declared Stoker.

'Nor me,' said George. 'Indeed, we should really not distract ourselves with such amusements – and set about making a plan.' A cough issued from Harker, who had retrieved a pad and some charcoals from his trunk before passing it over to the baggage collector.

'I had been hoping to do some sketching,' he ventured. 'I can't think I'll have many opportunities to visit this city again.'

'Well, from what I have seen so far, it has little to intrigue us,' said Stoker, looking around the chaotic, miserable station.

'Come, there are wonders aplenty in this town,' said Irving. 'But they are far from the station and the docks where we are now… and,' he added, looking purposely at Harker, 'as George says, we do have less trivial things with which to occupy ourselves… But as for now, let's occupy ourselves with finding some breakfast!'

Within ten minutes all four men were seated in a small estaminet sipping coffee as they waited expectantly for plates of waffles, fried eggs and ham to line their empty stomachs. The air was thick with the smell of rum and absinthe from the now-thinning crowd of navvies and bargemen, hurriedly imbibing the last of their necessary anaesthetic before leaving for their work of the day. Soon only the four travellers remained. George took it upon himself to address the others.

'Well, we now know that we cannot stop the baron before he arrives at his Prussian lair. May I ask, Mr Irving, if there is any way we can get into the castle without being seen.'

'I believe that is almost impossible – unless I can find a way to the secret stair I practically threw myself down all those years ago. But, in truth, I doubt whether I'd find it again; Ellen and myself were in such a hurry to leave I didn't think to fix in my mind where it might be located. One thing I don't doubt, though, is that we must approach the castle in daylight… and we must not admit any further delay!'

'We will need firearms,' announced Stoker suddenly. 'Where can we get hold of some?'

'There are places I know of in Danzig where we can get some,' replied George coolly.

'How do you know that?' asked Irving.

'From my time in the army,' laughed George. 'I even once had occasion to procure some myself, when I was stationed at one of the local barracks some years ago and we fancied some boar-hunting… army ordnance being strictly off limits for such pursuits.'

The conversation quickly drew to a halt as the men tucked into their food, now finally arrived, and finished their coffee. After some time, their appetites appeased, Harker brought out his sketchpad and began drawing the others – an action which Stoker saw was irritating Irving intensely.

As Stoker contemplated his companions, his mind turned to the bizarre series of events that had brought him and his companions to this continental estaminet on a cold autumn morning. First, the lights rehearsal at the Lyceum, when he had discovered the girl in the cellar; then his brother's revelation of the theft of the phials of blood by a man who both now knew to be Lucarda – or Curdala; then the trial, at which he had seen Lord Drayfield convicted for a crime he now believed to be the baron's doing. There was Irving's association with Kosminski – an association he now understood as complicit in Irving's attempt to frame the barber and thus protect the baron, and himself, from exposure; and then the attempt by Dowden to keep Stoker off the trail of the baron, and the subsequent revelation that both he and Harker were Rosicrucians. There was his suspicion of the Guv'nor's involvement in the Whitechapel murders, and then, most terrible to Stoker's mind, his own killing of the girl he had not long before saved – the girl in the cellar; one of the Undead, he knew, but an action that grieved him mightily. And finally, the baron's attack on Miss Terry, Irving's confession about his and Miss Terry's relations with him, and the inevitable vampirism of Irving's leading lady. Deep in his soul, Stoker was appalled.

He looked across at the Guv'nor as Harker continued to sketch – the scene painter still unaware of how much he was antagonising a man he desired so much to please.

'I can't say this is the best time for you to be sketching, Joseph, what with Miss Terry so ill!' barked Irving, slamming his coffee cup down on his saucer. 'After all, it was your indiscretion with the baron that revealed the whereabouts of her dressing room!' Harker looked up from his pad and fairly snorted. He hurriedly put his pad back in his bag and began trying to engage the Guv'nor in small talk about his knowledge of Amsterdam – a tactic that elicited but the glibbest of responses from Irving, who was clearly still preoccupied with the fate of Miss Terry.

As Stoker looked on, and George buried his head in a German-language newspaper, he realised that, although he was no doubt clearer about certain matters, certain mysteries remained: there was Miss Terry's apology to Irving for her 'recklessness' on the night of her attack, seemingly blaming herself for both the attack and what provoked it; and then there was her bizarre, almost unnatural, belief that her own son had committed the Whitechapel murders – a belief fostered, it seemed to Stoker, by Edward's quite natural attraction to women, even if he was sometimes a little overzealous in his attentions, and they invariably of the wagtail class.

It was all most disturbing, and Stoker was relieved when, half an hour later, the bill was settled with the last of the guilders and he and the others started making their way back to the station, ready to collect their luggage and board the train to Danzig.

~

The men were delighted to find themselves in a more salubrious carriage than the one they had occupied before: gone was the garlic whiff of creton (an unfortunate consequence of travelling next to the dining car), and in its place the lavender scent of an altogether more refined situation. All four were nevertheless impatient for their destination, and watchful – constantly alert to the arrival of one of the baron's minions.

As the train passed the spires and bridges of Hamburg and began to move towards the coastal plains of Pomerania, and on towards Stettin, Stoker noticed that each station was becoming more barracks-like, the atmosphere more like that of an intensely militarised society, as the workers of Holland and Frisia in their clogs, caps and wide pantaloons were replaced with soldiers in boots, helmets and gabardine overcoats. Much to his and his companions' frustration, checks were now being made more frequently, at each of the borders to Germany's different regions. Harker seemed particularly perturbed by these interruptions, pretending to be asleep whenever an officious square beard burst in on their calm to point violently at the trunks secreted beneath their seats, the man's curiosity only assuaged by George's faultless German and the production of papers from his time in Danzig – papers which fortunately still bore the appearance of currency.

'Do you think we will be able to get to the castle before sunset tomorrow, Guv'nor?' asked Harker, as the men turned in to their sleeper wagon.

'The castle is not far with fresh horses,' came the reply.

George, however, was shaking his head.

'At this rate, we won't pass through Stettin until around eleven o'clock tomorrow morning, and then we still need to get along the coast to Danzig,' he said. 'We have not made sufficient progress and will have to find ourselves a hotel, as there is no point assailing a vampire at night – when his powers are greatest.'

'I just hope we can enter his castle unseen when we do get there,' said Stoker. Irving grimaced.

'That might be difficult. Still, for Ellen's sake, we must try.'

The mood in the sleeper wagon was now tense, and as the train chugged and whistled through the solid darkness of a moonless night and the fleeting glow of passing night-time stations, Stoker's dreams were of his wife, Florence, seamlessly seeping into the image of the red-headed woman of whom he had read in the baron's diary. It appalled him that these two Irishwomen – one his own wife, the other the wife of Lucarda-Curdala – could become confused, the melding of their features, both real and imagined, making him jerk awake at several points in the journey. His fob watch recorded the hour – four o'clock, five o'clock – until finally chinks of light began to peep through the carriage window's blind, announcing the day of their arrival in the faraway town the Guv'nor had professed so recently to love.

CHAPTER XVIII

DANZIG

The carriages slunk through the weak rays of early evening towards their final destination, the Baltic Sea gleaming a pale bronze. All four men had prepared themselves well, cleaning their teeth with gin and pulling down the carriage window's blind in order to discreetly change vests and garters.

Once out on the station platform, coughing in the engine's final flourish of steam, a group of men in what looked like jodhpurs and old sailor caps came running across the platform to scoop up their luggage and deposit it in a cab. 'Ruthenians,' remarked George to the others. 'Trustworthy, as long as well paid.'

The Ruthenians were as good as the doctor's word, and soon all four men were seated in a comfortable carriage as George gave the order: 'The Prinz Friedrich Hotel!' As the carriage started across the uneven cobblestones, Stoker noticed that Harker, his bristles appearing darker than usual from under his slanted bowler, seemed to be looking out hopefully for scenes worthy of his sketchpad. But Stoker could sense the younger man's disappointment – the brick towers and houses of Danzig recalling nothing so much as the mercantile provincialism of his own Waterford or Sligo. How anyone, even the Guv'nor with his known predilections, could have been enthused by this far-flung town, with its poorly built gables and crumbling plaster, was beyond him. But as Stoker now looked across at Irving, he noticed that smiles of nostalgia were animating his face as he too peered through the carriage's open hatches, his eyes darting eagerly from street corner to street corner.

'I only wish Ellen were with me now, she so loved this town,' he breathed, as they at last approached the hotel – a remark to which Stoker did not deign to respond, so inappropriate it seemed.

Having deposited their luggage at the hotel and hurriedly refreshed their hands and faces, the men now found themselves making their way through the narrow cobbled streets, Irving in the lead. After some fifteen minutes, he stopped, and within moments the men were sitting inside an eating house atop a tavern. The walls of the eating house were dotted with an assortment of portraits, which the Guv'nor began surveying knowingly. Indeed, it seemed that Irving had seen them before.

Remarking first on portraits of Shakespeare and Marlowe, Irving proceeded to declare the poorly executed daub next to the stairwell to be none other than a likeness of Henry Condell – an opinion swiftly rebuffed by Harker, who swore that it was in fact a reproduction of a portrait of the Duke of Buckingham, the original of which he had once been paid to copy himself. Irving's sense of humiliation after so grandly launching this surprise was clearly too much for him to bear, and before any of them had had time even to order a drink, he had stormed down the stairs and out of the tavern, the tails of his frock coat flapping furiously behind him. Stoker looked at his remaining companions and wrung his hands.

'My word, I never meant to…' spluttered Harker.

'Come,' said George. 'Let us leave before we embarrass ourselves further.'

Soon they were out in the street, once again following Irving over the cobbles. The evening air was crisp, the red-bricked buildings clear in the lamplight, and yet everything felt utterly gloomy to Stoker. He looked across at his brother, whose eyes were fixed on the ground – the Danzig streets being already too familiar to him.

As the brothers trudged on in silence, Harker trailing somewhat behind, Stoker noticed that Irving had stopped. He seemed to be talking to a shabby little man with a ratty red face and bedraggled moustache. He was wearing a tatty black jacket and grimy blue waistcoat. As the brothers and Harker drew nearer, Stoker saw just how shabby the man was – not so much sinking into as already sunk in the slough of despond. The man inspired a certain queasiness, as though his whisky-ravaged face were not a mere physical manifestation but a reflection of his very soul.

Drawing still closer, Stoker heard the man speaking – in perfect, Slavic-accented English.

'Please, Mr Irving, like you I was deceived.'

'You're a murderer and a bounder, Ross!' Ross? Could this be the same Ross whom Irving had seen guillotine the girls all those years before? The ratty little man was cowering, holding his fists above his bald pate as if in defence against the actor's verbal pummelling. Stoker and George looked at each other, silently affirming their shared revulsion.

'How did you get into this state?' barked Irving, wheeling around the man as if to pinion him against the wall with his imperious stare.

'I broke with the brotherhood, and with the baron... I had seen too much,' he spluttered. 'Before I knew it, every restaurant and tavern in Danzig was cancelling its orders for my whisky. And then, once a bankrupt before the beak, I lost everything, everything – even my wife!' And now he fell to his knees and began to sob. Neither Stoker nor the others felt any inclination to lay a comforting hand on Ross's shoulder, yet Stoker sensed they all felt unsettled at the sight of the man. Irving, however, continued to look down at him, unmoved. Suddenly, he spoke again.

'Tell me, Ross, do you know a way to enter the baron's castle without being seen?' Stoker started: how could the Guv'nor be so reckless? Ross looked up through his fingers, and then took them away to reveal red, swollen eyes.

'You are not in earnest, surely?' said the little man. 'Why would you want to go there?'

'I have my reasons; just tell me!'

'Like all of you English, you are a fool, Mr Irving!' replied the man.

'I thought you said that you were English – our compatriot!' countered Irving.

'More Scottish than English,' said Ross, now rising and dusting off his torn jodhpurs. 'Just like your Lord Drayfield, who is about to be…,' and here he made a swift slicing movement of his forefinger across his throat.

'Drayfield is from Berwick-upon-Tweed,' snapped Irving, the pedant in him seemingly piqued by his recent humiliation over the painting of Condell, 'so he is English as well! Now, just tell me what I want to know, and I will reward you with forty marks.' Ross's eyes now glistened with the joy of a man anticipating a rare meal or even rarer bottle of Scotch.

'Eighty,' he countered.

'Sixty.' Ross smiled and nodded in agreement.

'Can you really trust him, Mr Irving?' broke in Harker, but Irving simply put a finger to his lip, before removing a large leather pouch from his coat pocket and counting out some coins into Ross's hands.

'That's only thirty,' groaned Ross.

'You'll get the rest when you tell us what we want to we know. Now tell us!'

Ross sighed.

'Well, you'll need to go to the far side of the castle where, about midway along its walls, you will find a deepish furrow – what used to be part of the moat. Jump down and follow the furrow through to its end and you will find a trapdoor, or hatch, directly in front of you… yes, directly in front of you, in the base of the wall. Open the hatch, and you will discover a vault; step inside, and you will be safely inside the castle!'

After Irving had finished talking to Ross, and paid him off, Harker asked him again why he trusted the man.

'I'm not sure that I do,' replied the Guv'nor gruffly. 'But he will only spend all of his money on grog, and so I doubt will be able to inform the baron of our intentions, even if he wanted to. Anyway, let's just hope he has told us the truth about that trapdoor!'

The next morning found all four men riding at a canter, their newly acquired Winchester rifles, along with their pulleys and ropes, astride their horses' behinds – the pulleys and ropes a necessary precaution against not finding Ross's trapdoor, or, indeed, it not even existing. Irving, the Cornishman, led the way, his mastery in the saddle a sure gift from his youth, as Harker brought up the rear, wobbling from side to side on his mount, like a spinning top slowly losing momentum. The sky was a dark granite, reflecting the grim resolve of the party, the mud squelching beneath their horses' hooves. Stoker managed to check his fob watch – not yet eleven o'clock – just as the men pulled into a hamlet.

The scene which met Stoker's eyes appalled him: here were the same pinched peasants that had gasped their last during the great famine back home in Ireland the year that he was born, as his mother had described to him so vividly when a boy.

'The baron's villeins, as I'm sure you've surmised,' pronounced Irving.

This miserable scene was soon repeated further on, this time in a Ruthenian village, presumed Stoker, as the church bore a slanted, not a square, cross atop its dome. Here yet more emaciated peasants emerged from their hovels or laid down their tools to cross themselves at the unexpected sight of the horsemen.

As they rode on, it seemed that the landscape itself was unremittingly bleak and miserable, the leafless trees that dotted the roadside aptly skeletal. Stoker's fear was beginning to be punctuated with disgust.

It was not long before the men caught sight of a dark mass on the horizon, obscured by unmoving clouds that loured over its demesne: the baron's castle. As they drew closer, Stoker was jolted by a spasm of fear as he distinguished more of the forbidding schloss, its towers – and atop these, turrets – projecting from sheer stone walls. Glancing behind him, he saw that his brother and Harker appeared to have undergone a similar sensation. Before the castle lay a crossroads, where stood an empty gibbet. Stoker now looked on in horror as Irving, still out in front, expertly reared his horse and brought the animal to an abrupt halt exactly beside it.

'This must be the spot,' exclaimed George, as he brought his own horse to a more awkward stop next to Irving, instinctively checking that the leather saddlebag, which contained the mallet, stake, crucifix and Bible, was secure.

'Indeed it is,' said Irving, leaping off his horse and tying its rein to the gibbet. 'Before we do anything else, we must make sure the baron is not confined here.' Stoker and the others now secured their own mounts then started surveying the earth for any signs of recent burial.

'No obvious disturbances, by the look of things,' declared Harker. 'Nothing that isn't at least a few months old in any case.'

'Nothing since the baron took some of this earth back with him to London,' added George, dusting off his hands. 'Not pleasant to think of all the suicides buried down there, I must say.'

'Well,' said Irving, 'at least we now know he is not here. He must be in the temple, as I said before. Yes, in the temple – where there is also a crossroads, of sorts! Come, let us discover him!'

Under what seemed an incipient eclipse, so dark was the sky, George retrieved his saddlebag and slung it over his shoulder while the others proceeded to lift the rifles, pulleys and ropes from the horses and divide them up between themselves. Soon all four men were walking silently towards the castle's high, and so it seemed to Stoker, impenetrable walls. Would their pulleys and ropes really be of any use? There were no immediate signs of surveillance, no defensive actions, and yet, as they crept forwards, Stoker expected at any moment to be discovered, and for one of the baron's minions to start taking pot shots at them, as though at grouse in open season.

After about ten minutes, Irving signalled the others to stop. They were beside a block of tufted earth, which provided a sort of shallow defence from which they could marshal their forces for attack. There was no sound of birdsong, only the whine of a thin wind which began to rattle and whistle through the turrets, as though conjured especially for their arrival. On Irving's command, the ropes and pulleys were piled into a heap – so carelessly that Stoker assumed the others must share his doubts of their usefulness. The saddlebag containing the mallet, stake, crucifix and Bible, however, was placed carefully on the ground by George. Stoker looked about him for signs of life but could discern nothing but a copse of stunted birch trees a few hundred yards away – did nothing live in this nightmarish landscape, this waste of desolation?

'Well, Guv'nor,' said Stoker at last. 'What is our plan?' George was already eyeing his outstretched thumb, as though he were a sea captain in search of the Pole star.

'Whereabouts did Ross say this trapdoor or hatch was?' asked Irving.

'At the end of a furrow, about midway along the walls on the far side,' replied Stoker.

'Well, we should not delay.' Irving now snorted, then rammed his top hat onto the crown of his head, as though securing a helmet for battle.

'Let three of us get into the castle and one stay behind on guard,' he continued. 'Tell me, Joseph, are you a good shot?'

'Not bad,' replied Harker eagerly. 'I have won more than a few trophies on the range!'

'Well, it must surely be better than your equestrianism!' returned Irving; slights such as this a habitual method of reminding others of his brilliance. 'You can act as our rear gunner.' He now turned to the two brothers. 'Talking of which, George, you must arm yourself with a Winchester, while you, Bram, must take charge of the saddlebag. As to the pulleys and ropes, they can be left behind without loss, I believe. Let's hope Ross was telling the truth about that trapdoor!'

The men now started to creep around the castle walls, Harker a little way off, at the back. Their silence spoke a hundred presages of doom in Stoker's mind, as the wind began to gust fitfully under the dark sky.

At last, just indeed as Ross had described, they reached a deep furrow and jumped down. Once through the tangle of mud and bracken, they found themselves at the castle wall. But where was the hatch? Irving started shaking his head violently, as George calmly glanced about him then directed the party to what looked like a differently coloured patch of stonework, some twenty yards to their left. Yes, here was the door, secured with a rusty padlock! Suddenly, the gaping jaws and long incisors of the baron welled like a moon in water before Stoker's mind's eye, as though in passing through the door they would be entering the vampire's corpse itself.

'Come, George, on the count of three, shoot the lock!' commanded Irving. 'We'll lift up the hatch and be inside the castle in no time.'

'No,' replied George, shaking his head in defiance. 'Let's make no more noise than we need to.'

With that he removed a file and a long pin from his top pocket and started to pick the lock – a feat he achieved in moments, much to his brother's amazement. From behind the door now came what sounded like the frantic squabbling and squawking of birds, as though trapped inside a tiny, claustrophobic aviary.

'Open the door!' now came the order from Irving.

As Stoker and George lifted the latch, the clamour of birds became louder and deeper until it sounded like the roar of thunder.

Then, out of the dark of the vault, burst what looked at first like a crowd of sans-culottes or communards, overturning George and sending Stoker sprawling onto his back in the mud, his saddlebag flying. The vault door teetered then smashed back down into place. Soon the latch was wiggling again, and the hatch lifted up. Now emerged the emaciated figures of half a dozen desperate peasants, their faces flashing like shards of bone. They were shrieking in their rags as they almost trampled Stoker and George, who cried out in horror as the flock of famished gulls escaped their confines. A shot rang out from behind them: Harker had given volley. Now the peasants uttered yet louder shrieks, as Stoker fixed his eyes silently on the granite sky.

'Are you all right, George?' he breathed at last.

'Yes. No bones broken, I think,' came his brother's panting reply, as he struggled to his feet. Stoker himself now got up, dusted himself off, and picked up the saddlebag. Instinctively, he touched his waistcoat top pocket to make sure his precious fob watch was still secure.

'I think we should perhaps repair and rethink our strategy,' declared George.

'I think we should perhaps take cover!' cried Irving.

'Why?' asked George. Stoker now followed the arc of Irving's arm. Directly above them, leaning over a turret top, was the face of a man, grinning past the bore of a blunderbuss – pointed straight at them!

'Oh my sweet Lord,' cried George. 'Run!' And then a shot rang out. There was a long yelp, followed by a wail and then a thud, as the man crashed in agony into the bracken of the dry moat, right between Stoker and George. The man – who Stoker now saw was sporting the baron's blue and black livery – was wheezing, seemingly suffocating from the horrendous winding he had suffered.

'My bowling is even more accurate than my shooting!' exclaimed Harker, but his companions were too busy pinioning his quarry to respond. As they did so, Stoker noticed that the man had suffered a neat wound to his shoulder, which was now turning the blue of his waistcoat an ominous shade of purple.

'*Ne razbiram!*' gasped the man. '*Molya, molya.*'

'Look, I know you don't understand, but listen, I am a doctor! *Az sum lekar!*' cried George. And then, more quietly, 'Well, well, a Bulgar Gipsy. The baron clearly has to cast his net far and wide to procure his servants these days.' He tore off the man's sleeve to examine the wound and explained to him that the bullet had gone straight through the top of his arm and would not need to be extracted – a scratch, in medical terms.

'Can you get any intelligence out of him?' asked Irving.

'I shall try,' replied the doctor, leaning over the man, who had now recovered his breath. 'But since your friend Ross was not exactly truthful about the position of the vault door and failed to mention the prisoner stampede that would meet us there, there is no guarantee that this man will tell us the truth either.'

'Oh yes there is!' replied Irving, cocking his rifle downwards towards the man's throat.

There now ensued a fraught conversation in which the doctor accosted the Gipsy in broken Bulgarian and became increasingly agitated, ending up slapping the man's face out of sheer frustration. Stoker had kept quiet throughout this exchange, and now looked over to where Harker, still beaming under his bowler from his recent success, was eyeing the turrets above them through his rifle sights.

'Well, Doctor,' demanded Irving, 'what does he say?'

'He says that the baron will destroy us all. That his personal retainers, like himself, remain loyal, and that even the wind and the clouds follow his command, through his familiars.' Stoker looked up at the castle, still covered in its louring, unmoving weather, not doubting for a moment that this was true.

'And where does he say the baron is?' Irving now demanded.

'In his tomb in the temple, just as you said.'

'Indeed! Come here, Joseph,' called the Guv'nor.

'Yes, Guv'nor,' replied Harker, running over. 'Are we off now? Want me to beat the field before you?' he continued excitedly, his ill-timed levity inducing no laughter.

'No, you must wait here and guard this ruffian. If he causes any trouble, don't hesitate to shoot. Bram, George?'

'Yes, Guv'nor?' said the brothers in unison.

'We are set for danger, that is certain. If you wish to stay behind with Harker, please do. But I must stake the baron's vampire heart, to save Ellen – it's her only chance!' He kissed the square and compasses on his ring and gripped his rifle resolutely.

'We're with you, aren't we, Bram?' said George, throwing a cursory glance at his brother, before gathering up his own rifle from the ground.

'Then we three must go – at once!' And with that the men lifted up the trapdoor and stepped into the castle gloom.

CHAPTER XIX

BACK IN THE CASTLE

The three men could barely see a thing, and so George struck a match. Adjusting their eyes to the gloom of the place, and their nostrils to the stench (clearly the peasants had been trapped in the vault some time), the men gasped as they simultaneously discerned the outstretched form of a corpse.

'Don't look! The first rule of the battlefield is to ignore whatever might discompose you and carry on,' cried George. But the warning came too late, as his companions took in the rat-gnawed face of the corpse, its eyeballs sticking out of their sockets like Chinese trinkets. Stoker's stomach churned with revulsion, but before he had time to retch, his brother had extinguished the match and was pushing him and Irving towards another source of light, emanating from a narrow staircase some ten yards in front of them.

'After you,' said George as he gestured towards the stair. Irving took the lead, followed by Stoker, the acting manager's terror mounting at every step as he anticipated some apparition, like the girl he had impaled in the Lyceum, to leap from behind the veils of darkness. Suddenly, Irving stopped for breath, and, in a trice, Stoker was doubling back, terrified the Guv'nor might turn round with a horrifying leer, like Mephistopheles.

'Keep going, frater!' urged George, blocking his descent. 'We must get up the stair before anyone starts coming down.'

Soon they had reached a wooden door, which Irving opened with a hearty shove.

'Now I know where we are,' he declared with seeming relief, as he emerged into a long passageway carpeted with Persian rugs. 'Come, Bram, George, let's ready ourselves for the final Act of our drama.' Irving's natural mastery had clearly returned – Miss Terry's deliverance was in sight!

Soon Irving was leading the men behind a tapestry screen and down some stone steps, at the bottom of which was an elaborately carved wrought-iron door.

'We may have to shoot the lock on this one, George,' said Irving. 'And then, Bram, be sure to act full fleet with that mallet and stake on the baron, while I recite the prayer for the dead, so that, as George tells us, we strike in God's name!'

'No need to use a Winchester,' breathed Stoker. 'Look, the padlock is not secured.' As the door opened, here was Juliet's tomb, or rather, a temple containing an empty sarcophagus. At the foot of the sarcophagus was a pool of water, possibly a font – housed within wood not stone. Beyond the sarcophagus was an altar and, beyond this, standing in front of the wall, what looked like what could be a large cross, judging from its outline, for it had been entirely covered up. To its left were painted demons and their symbols, to its right, the four archangels. On the floor, a crossroads tessellated in brick – just as Irving had described. For a moment all three men stood agog at the temple's beauty. Then suddenly, Irving snapped his fingers.

'I'm afraid, gentlemen, that the baron is not here. We must search elsewhere, before the sun goes down.'

'But *why* isn't he here?' asked Stoker. 'Surely vampires must remain in their tombs by day?'

Before anyone could answer, there was the crash of a door to the left of the covered cross followed by a punishing blast of cold wind. And then, standing before them, his eyes alight like phosphorus, was the becaped figure of Lucarda, snarling and foaming in the dim ochre light. He grinned as he surveyed the three men, confident of his prey.

'I know you have come to stake me,' he screamed, 'but here you will discover your own tombs, not mine!' The three men instinctively huddled together, nervously looking around to see whether the baron's minions would surround them. Irving and George raised their rifles.

'Yes,' continued Lucarda, 'once again I have outwitted you – just like I have ever since I crossed land and sea to torment your mighty London! Yes indeed, it was I who turned Craig's trollop into a vampire down in the cellar while you, Mr Irving, were conducting your rehearsal above. It was I who bit the treacherous Ellen and escaped by turning into a black cat. No, neither you nor your rifles can harm me – nothing can!' Here he laughed demonically, capered like a sailor to a devilish hornpipe, and raised his fists in the air triumphantly. And then he continued.

'And indeed, it was I who killed the housemaid of my cousin, Drayfield, then framed him for my own crime!' And here he laughed once more and recommenced his devilish jig. Suddenly, Stoker remembered the crucifix inside his saddlebag – if he could only get hold of this, it would protect them all... He glanced instinctively at his brother, as if to intimate his plan, only to notice that, for some unknown reason, he had lowered his rifle.

'What's that?' demanded George, pointing at the baron's now-exposed shirt. The baron looked down to where the shirt's cotton revealed a deep patch of red, spreading from his side. He gasped and made to wipe it.

'Vampires don't bleed,' continued George coolly. 'They make others do that.'

Lucarda looked back at him quizzically, then screamed.

'Bertoold, Brennus, come quickly – the wound is open again!'

The three men now watched in horror as blood began to pour liberally from the baron's flank. Like the flickering chimera in a magic lantern, the baron started to waver; and then he started to swoon and collapsed on the floor, all the while muttering, 'I shall have my revenge, I shall have my revenge!'

'Come, Bram,' said George quickly. 'Let's pick him up and place him in his tomb.'

As they laid the baron in the sarcophagus, he opened his eyes and looked up at Stoker, who was propping up his head.

'I cannot die, I cannot die,' he murmured. 'How can I die? I am the Lord Rosy Cross, and I am a vampire – one of the Undead!'

'I am afraid you are neither, Baron,' said George grimly. 'You are, like me, just a common man, who embraced these falsehoods to escape a common death – but to no avail, it would appear.'

Suddenly, a tall Gipsy in the baron's blue and black livery came rushing into the temple, a blunderbuss in his hands. Immediately, George cocked his rifle and threatened him in German, but his adversary merely looked to where the baron was lying in his sarcophagus and snarled in anger. He raised his weapon to take aim at George's head.

'Shoot, George, shoot!' stammered Irving.

'*Brennus, odejść z tobą! Wszystko dobre,*' shouted the baron, struggling to sit up. 'Do not fire, Doctor!' he went on. 'My retainer will leave.' Casting his eyes about him furiously, the tall Gipsy now lowered his blunderbuss and started to back his way out through the door.

All three men looked back at the baron; this last effort at shouting had clearly exhausted him, and he had sunk back down into his tomb.

And then he spoke again, in a low voice. 'I think you are right, Doctor. There is no Lord Rosy Cross here and, I fear, no vampire either.' He fixed his black eyes on the ceiling in seeming despair. 'And it is your theatre, Mr Stoker,' he continued, 'that has dealt me my death blow – as well as the final realisation of my own delusion.' He pointed to his side, which was now gushing with blood.

'What do you mean, Baron?' asked Stoker, his fear resolving into curiosity.

'Sustained the night I jumped from Ellen… Miss Terry's, window. Wounded myself on a drainpipe you really should have got repaired!' Stoker glanced at his brother, who was smiling glibly.

'But I saw you jump from that window that night. And I saw that black cat, which leapt into the back of your carriage.' The baron now laughed weakly, spitting up gobbets of blood as he did so.

'I am as good at deploying props and illusions as you are, Mr Stoker. No, one of my servants arranged for the cat to fool you. Meanwhile, I didn't jump out of the window onto the ground, as you presumed, but onto a concealed ledge. I inched along it, intending to climb down the drainpipe – all Ponsonby's plan, of course, though the fool Scotsman didn't notice the pipe was loose, and jagged, and when I fell…'

'So, you are no vampire, then?'

George was now shaking his head vigorously, much to his brother's bemusement.

'No. I thought that I was, until I wounded myself on that drainpipe… but then I thought I might still be a vampire, and that being back on my estate, in my tomb, would act as a salve, restoring me to the Undead.' And here the baron sighed. 'But now I realise that vampires are as real as the Father Christian Rosenkreutz, and myself as mortal as you, dear Doctor.'

'But why did you go to such extraordinary lengths, Baron?' asked Irving.

'Because I wanted to enjoy a paradise reunited with earth, so that my darling wife and I could live together forever. Then, when my wife died, I wanted her back, and so strove for this all the more keenly – my vanity and desire willing me to believe. But then, when Ellen came, I felt I could find joy in another.' Here Stoker looked at Irving, who appeared most uncomfortable. 'But to no avail. I should have known the English – my own people – are fit only for treachery, and my wife, my one true love.' There was an embarrassed silence as the baron coughed up more gobbets of blood onto his shirt front. The temple now felt like a mausoleum, and Stoker wondered whether they might all be trapped there, like a pharaoh's servants in a pyramid tomb.

'Yes, after years of attempting to invoke the symbols of Dee and Kelly, the philosophies of *The Chymical Wedding* and other texts, I still had not achieved this paradise. And then I thought of a different way – to achieve immortality and my revenge upon you! In February this year I went to London, where I preyed upon my cousin, inculcating him into Rosicrucian rituals and beliefs before framing him for one of my own murders; all so I could get hold of his house and use it later, as my London lair. The murder accomplished, I hurried back to Danzig – before those fools in Scotland Yard could interview me – then immediately went on to Krakow, where I was wilfully infected by a member of the Undead, or so I thought. My hatred of sunlight began to increase, my hair became darker, and I looked – and felt – younger. I believed my transformation to be true, as long as I was drinking blood. It was here that the Yard finally caught up with me, but by then they could see from my youthful appearance that my cousin's testimony was entirely "false" – ha!'

And now the baron started to laugh weakly again, coughing up yet more gobbets of blood, which he proceeded to wipe off with his sleeve.

'And then,' he continued, 'I left Krakow and went to my castle, where I took unhallowed earth from the crossroads so I could rest while I recreated the temple of the Rosy Cross in London, first in Bayswater, where I kept my tomb and provided services for my inner circle, and then in Soho – all mere ploys to enlist the assistance of others, my own belief in the Rosicrucian system by then having completely failed. And then, in September, I began to plague your own theatre, Mr Irving.' And here he almost howled.

'Yes, I could have continued for months, tormenting you with more and more vampires – or seeming vampires – but those wretched Whitechapel murders thwarted my designs!'

'You say it was you who turned the girl in the cellar into a vampire?' asked Stoker. The baron smiled glibly.

'Yes, well, as I know now, belief is everything. I discovered the girl in the props room and took her down to the cellar, where I bit her neck just as she was rousing to consciousness, inducing some loud screams – which I believe you yourself heard, Mr Stoker. I then slipped out of the cellar below while you theatre fools dithered onstage above, my carriage collecting me soon afterwards. The girl had no chance, of course, once the delusion had set in.'

'But how did you get into the cellar in the first place?' demanded Stoker.

'I had my own key, copied some time before from your lights manager's original, when he left it behind in his jacket pocket. Careless, that Irishman.'

'You vile predator!' screamed Irving.

'You blackmailer,' whispered the baron. 'But Ellen... beautiful Ellen... I forgive.'

He now seemed to be slipping away with the final admission of his delusion. Stoker gazed across the tomb at his brother and Irving. Suddenly, the baron roused.

'What am I saying? What am I saying?' he screamed, his eyes bulging insanely out of their sockets, his face newly animated. 'I am the Lord Rosy Cross! I am the Undead and cannot die! I shall wreak vengeance on you all!' Stoker and the others started hurriedly backing away as the baron grabbed the side of the tomb and attempted once more to lift himself up. And then the baron collapsed, for what would be the last time.

Stoker stared at the tomb in shock, as the sweet smell of his own sweat pervaded his nostrils. And then he looked at his brother. George had returned to the sarcophagus and was now raising the baron's wrist.

'No pulse.' He declared. 'The baron is dead.'

'Are you sure?' asked Irving. 'You heard what he said. He is the Undead, he cannot die!'

'His swansong, Mr Irving,' said George. 'The baron teetered continually between belief and unbelief, reality and delusion. Yes, he tried to maintain his belief that he was a vampire, even after his fatal wound, carrying on fooling himself and others, whose credence would only affirm his own. But, as you just heard, he did finally, and completely, acknowledge his own delusion – despite what he might have said in that final outburst. Look,' and here George ran his fingers through the hair at the baron's temples, withdrawing them sticky and covered in something like soot. 'Boot polish!'

'What does this mean?' cried Irving. 'Surely we should still stake his vampire heart?' George laughed.

'Mr Irving, vampires do not exist.'

'What?' cried Stoker. 'You are the one who has been persuading us of their existence all this time!' George smiled.

'As the baron said, frater, belief is everything. When someone believes themselves to have been bitten by a vampire, they effectively have been. I saw this in the Balkans, many times. We London-trained doctors simply could not convince such people that nothing had really happened to them, having to enact bizarre rituals and stake perfectly good corpses so that the credulous could recover.'

'But, Ellen…'

'You made the mistake, Mr Irving, of telling Miss Terry about what happened with the girl in the cellar, when she returned to the theatre – and encountered my brother. Once you had done that, she was easy pickings for the baron.'

'So, Doctor,' said Irving, 'you have gone through with this whole charade, knowing it was just that – a charade?' George shrugged his shoulders.

'There was no other way of saving Miss Terry. Now that the baron is dead, we must simply pretend to her that we have staked his heart. She will be cured of her delusion immediately – I can assure you of that.'

'And the draining of blood, the lengthening of incisors, the photophobia? Surely all that cannot come simply from belief?' Stoker was confounded.

'Yes, it can,' George assured him. 'The mind's tyranny over the body is quite remarkable when belief sets in. I saw canines grow longer and sharper in my Bulgarian patients, and faces become lined, when no physical explanation could be adduced for this. The delusion can be so great that people's conscious acts of deceit can seem to them no more than a necessary part of the greater reality to which they aspire.' And here he touched the baron's blackened temples again.

'Thus the baron boot-polished his hair once he had drunk blood, and then let it return to grey whenever he was in lack; alternately younger, then older, and then younger again – at least he did so, when he believed himself a vampire. Indeed, as the baron himself admitted, he used props and illusions to deceive others, so as to achieve this greater reality.' Here George paused, before adding, pointedly, 'Indeed, is it not true that actors themselves can become convinced of the reality of their roles, melding with the parts that they play while onstage?'

Irving frowned momentarily, before asking, with some urgency, 'But why have you done all of this, for my Ellen? Why for a woman you did not even know?' George smirked and looked down at the baron's face.

'Let's say I have my own reasons.'

'And what might they be?' demanded Irving.

'Well,' George sighed, 'as you know, I was stationed as a surgeon in Danzig when I was but twenty-five years old. When Bram told me the baron was also known as Curdala, I was taken by surprise, but knew immediately that I wanted to exact some sort of revenge.'

'Why?'

'At the time, I was good friends with a young lieutenant in the Prussian light infantry – an exceptional soldier, who was also an exceptional amateur botanist. On one of his excursions to gather rare flowers, he accidentally trespassed onto the baron's estate, the self-same estate we find ourselves today.' Here George stroked his long russet beard, as if for support. 'The baron shot him down like a mad dog, later declaring it was self-defence.'

'And was it?' asked Irving.

'Of course not!' replied George shaking his head. 'No, my friend Georg Mueller wasn't even armed that day, as he was on leave. A more delightful man you could not imagine, and one with a formidable intellect. He was preparing to write a taxonomy of the different plants of West Prussia. His mother insisted I take his notebooks after his death, and I have them to this day.'

'And the police believed the baron?'

'There were no other witnesses, and Curdala was powerful under the old Kaiser.'

'But why didn't you recognise the baron when he raided your surgery?' asked Stoker.

'Because I had never seen him before; nor had I wanted to. I only knew it was him when you told me his name.' And here George sighed. 'Ah well, justice is served.'

As his brother was detailing all this, Stoker noticed the figure of a young woman with long red hair emerge from the gloom. He started – was it Florence? How could she be here? But as the woman drew closer, he saw a less familiar, but no less beautiful, face burst into shapes of anguish. The woman ran over to the sarcophagus and kissed the baron's forehead; and then she flew at George and started pummelling him with her fists.

'*Er ist tot! Er ist tot!*' she wailed as George pinioned her against a wall and tried to pacify her in German.

There was a creak at the wrought-iron door – and then appeared the robust figure of Harker.

'I thought I told you to keep guard,' barked Irving.

'Well, my Gipsy friend was happy to let me keep his blunderbuss, so I was happy to let him go on his way. Didn't want to miss any of the action in any case!'

'*Er ist tot. Wie, wie?*'

'How can he be dead? Simple! *Weil er nur ein Mann war, ein normaler Mann* – because he was only a man, an ordinary man – and had to die, like any ordinary man.' George was still trying to pacify the desperate woman, who was whirling her head and hair hysterically while restrained in his arms.

'Ah… you have then staked the vampire,' said Harker, removing his bowler instinctively.

'Not quite,' said Stoker, 'there was no need.'

'Nothing but bogusry here, Joseph,' added Irving, dusting off his coat sleeves as if trying to relieve himself of the entire experience.

'*Ich kenne diesen Mann!*' The woman was now shouting and pointing violently towards Irving. '*Er ist ein Teuful!*'

'Do you know this woman, Guv'nor?' demanded George, still doing his best to restrain her as she continued to rave. Irving glared at the woman and harrumphed.

'I do declare it may be the daughter of the surly Ruthenian at whose tavern in Danzig myself and Ellen lodged some years ago. Pray tell me, what tommyrot is she spouting?'

'She says that she knows you and has seen you in visions,' replied George as the woman now broke free and rushed towards the pool of water, jabbering all the while in German.

'What is she saying now?' asked Irving.

'Yes, she says that she has seen your image in the water – many times,' replied George. As the woman now knelt down on the footstool before the pool, she seemed to fall into a reverie. A whirring began and a light came through the water; and then appeared familiar scenes of London, the Lyceum, Irving and Miss Terry. The four men crowded around her, and then George laughed. The woman looked up.

'*Können sie auch diese Bilden sehen?*'

'Ja, natürlich! I can see these images,' replied George. He now signalled to his companions to move aside, knelt down, and pulled open a door to the small wooden cabinet which housed the pool. In one swift movement he removed a contraption of glass plates holding photographs, above what appeared to be a crude gas lamp.

'Ingenious,' breathed Stoker.

'Devious,' countered his brother, as he now dragged the woman off her footstool and forced her to examine the device. After a few moments, she looked up with the glimmer of tears in her eyes – the baron had deceived her! And then she suddenly rushed at Stoker and bit him viciously before running out of the temple in a frenzied state.

'Are you all right, Bram?' asked Irving.

'Not really, Guv'nor!' Stoker lifted up his forearm: it was covered in blood.

'I will attend to it once we get out,' said George. 'The wound is not as bad as it looks, and I suppose we should be glad the woman didn't inflict more damage, being desperate to get away.'

'She's not the only one...' muttered Irving. Harker was now looking eagerly around him.

'This is like the temple I used to visit in Soho,' he said, 'but with far superior artwork, I must say. Could I possibly stay and make some sketches, Mr Stoker?'

'Not now, Joseph!' retorted the acting manager. 'We really must go and telegraph Miss Terry's maid as soon as possible.'

'Indeed,' said Irving.

'And get the police to come and witness the body,' added Stoker.

'Are you serious, Bram?' rasped Irving.

'Yes. We now have enough evidence to get Lord Drayfield reprieved. Once the Prussian police confirm that this Lucarda-Curdala was really a much older man, as his lordship claimed, he will surely be granted leave to appeal, and his neck saved.'

'Bram,' said Irving, 'I really think it would be better if we—'

'Let an innocent man hang? Please, no!' The two men looked at each other. 'Don't worry; you are no longer in danger yourself, Sir,' added Stoker scornfully.

George was now standing over the baron's body shaking his head.

'You know, he really was a most extraordinary man,' he said at last. 'As a doctor, if nothing else, I feel I understand, even pity, him.'

'How can you say that, after everything he has done – after everything you have done?' stammered Stoker.

'Because he was a man who went to such great lengths to fool himself, and others; first as a Rosicrucian and then as a vampire – or even both together, as we've just heard him exclaim... all in the hope that in so doing he could make his untruths become truths.'

'And where is the honour in that?' George sighed.

'If you were to understand the finality of death like I do, Bram, you would know why someone might wish to avoid it. He dreamt of eternity, this man, and did all he could to attain it. But, as ever, it evaded him. Remarkable.'

'Come now,' broke in Irving. 'We really must make haste to save Ellen!'

Once outside, making their way back to retrieve their horses, Stoker could not help noticing that the late afternoon sky was now clear and bright, as though the death of Lucarda had heralded the demise of the familiars that had so recently directed the wind and the clouds on his command.

Soon all four men were galloping back to Danzig, the Guv'nor, as ever, leading the field, his coat tails flapping behind him. As Irving's pace finally slowed to a trot, Stoker cantered up beside him.

'So, tell me, Guv'nor, what did the baron mean by "forgiving" Miss Terry?' Irving glanced across at his acting manager and scowled.

'There are some things I would prefer not to answer you, Bram,' he replied. 'For, in truth, Ellen's behaviour at the castle was not as exemplary as I made out; she graced the baron's bed on more than one occasion, in the hope of furthering our desire – to achieve our own theatre.' Stoker practically choked.

'So, she graced the baron's bed, having seen him guillotine those poor girls – or was that whole appalling incident untrue?' Irving bit his lip.

'No, it *was* true, but it happened after a number of nights – after I had upbraided Ellen for her behaviour, and she favoured the baron no more.'

'I see.'

'I believe the whole ghastly ritual was as much a warning to her as a genuine sacred practice.' And now the Guv'nor slowed his horse to a walk and turned to look fixedly at Stoker. 'I'm sure I don't need to ask you not to speak of this to anyone, Bram. I wish to protect Ellen at all costs.'

'I understand,' replied Stoker with a slow nod of his head.

'And please, Bram, please promise never to divulge what you have seen here today; indeed, what you know about this whole Prussian affair.'

'I promise,' replied Stoker; despite everything he now knew about Irving, old loyalties died hard, and he did not, for all their sakes, wish the Guv'nor to be further exposed.

Once amid the gables of Danzig, Stoker rushed to the post office and sent the following telegram to Edith Craig. '*Vampire staked Stop All now well Stop Please tell Miss Terry Stop Bram.*'

Sometime later, back in his bedroom at the Prinz Friedrich, Stoker was roused by a knock on the door. He opened it to see a bellboy with an oblong slip of paper on a tray, angling for a tip. Having given the boy a mark, Stoker took up the telegram to read the following. '*Had excellent meeting at Union today Stop Women's suffrage now very popular Stop Mama much better Stop Edith.*' Stoker ran to Irving's room to tell him the news.

'That's marvellous!' exclaimed the Guv'nor, jumping up from his bed with joy. 'Come, let us all go out at once and celebrate – at Danzig's finest!'

The Spatif was full of light and life, and Irving in his element, as he commanded his party be taken to the best table in the house. Once the men were settled in their seats (Irving having ordered some lavish hors d'oeuvres and wine), Stoker decided to quiz his boss a little further.

'So, tell me, Guv'nor,' he asked, 'why were you so convinced – I assume, still so convinced – that the baron committed the Whitechapel murders? After all, he didn't confess to them.' Irving sighed with apparent irritation at having to go over this ground.

'I told you, Bram – because of the promise he made back in January, to come and terrorise our capital. It all seemed too coincidental, and who else could be capable of such crimes?'

'And what do you think, George? I do myself wonder whether the baron might have been involved. After all, he wasn't really a vampire, which means his victims would suffer normal deaths – like those poor women in Whitechapel did.'

'Judging by what the baron said,' replied George, 'I do not believe he was guilty of these crimes.'

'Ah well,' interposed Irving, 'he might not have confessed to them, but neither did he deny them!'

'Well, no,' continued George. 'He did of course allude to the Whitechapel murders, but only to say that they had "thwarted" him. The spate of murders must have increased surveillance and hampered his movements at the least, I suppose. But in any case, as I say, why should a man who has admitted to so much not also admit to these crimes on his deathbed?'

Irving huffed.

'So, except for Lord Drayfield's maid, the girl in the cellar and Miss Terry,' resumed Stoker, 'he attacked no one while back in London – as far as we know.' And here he shook his head. 'And it was indeed me who ended the girl's life.'

'In self-defence, Bram, in self-defence,' breathed Irving.

'Yes, but she was an actual girl, not a vampire,' added Stoker, looking mournfully at the dainty glass figurines which adorned the centre of their table.

'If she was so lacking in blood as you claim, Bram,' now advanced George, 'then she was about to die anyway, so you have no reason to blame yourself. She may even have been syphilitic, which would have contributed to her derangement. But even if she wasn't, as I said before, belief is everything. If someone believes themselves to have been bitten by a vampire, then their whole body can be overcome by their mind – no matter how rational they consider themselves to be.' At this moment the waiter came up and asked Harker to taste the wine – a deference to the scene painter which annoyed Irving intensely, but which interruption he used as an opportunity to divert the conversation to other matters.

Early the next morning Stoker and George took their information to the Prussian police, who immediately sent an expeditionary party to the baron's castle. Later that day, just as Stoker was packing his Gladstone back at the hotel for that evening's steamer to Stettin, Danzig's very own commissioner of police came to his room to thank him personally for his help, and to inform him that he had telegraphed Scotland Yard with a changed testimony regarding the baron's appearance for the Drayfield case – that he was indeed, as Lord Drayfield had claimed, a much older man. Once the commissioner had left, Stoker slipped out of the hotel and rushed one last time to the post office to telegraph Drayfield's counsel, Johnson, the news. As he made his way, he could not help but notice the young lord's likeness featured on the front pages of a number of the German-language newspapers, as though any final impediment to his sentencing had been removed and the trial was finally about to reach its ultimate denouement. It seemed their intelligence would arrive just in time!

Once back at the hotel, having collected his Gladstone, Stoker knocked on Irving's door. As he was ushered inside, he was met with the distinctive smell of burning: some ashes were smouldering inside a thick glass vase, which was refracting the dying rays of sun.

'Oh,' said Irving, when pressed on this by Stoker, 'it's nothing to worry about, Bram; just an old letter I wrote to the baron some years ago, which I managed to retrieve from his castle.' And then he smiled. 'Now we really are all safe to go home – and sleep sound in our beds!'

It was not long before everything had returned to something like normal back in London. Irving and Miss Terry were rehearsing for the winter season at the Lyceum, while Harker was continuing to job cheerfully around the Lyceum, Princess and Adelphi, his new passion for the sport of rugby alongside his skill at cricket ensuring many admirers. George was once more mollifying society ladies in his surgery and Stoker himself was, as ever, attending to business at the theatre while avoiding such duties at home. The disappearances of young children in the vicinity of the theatre had ceased entirely; indeed, there had been no disappearances since the end of September, leading Stoker to conclude that either the girl in the cellar, or indeed Lucarda – perhaps both – had been behind them. Stoker had the invidious task of telling the careless Irishman, Grafton, that he was dismissed.

On Friday the ninth of November, there was one more Whitechapel murder – the last.

EPILOGUE

THE LYCEUM, 18 MAY 1897

'Dreadful, absolutely dreadful,' came a familiar voice from on high. From one of the boxes, Irving, now somewhat older and greyer, was passing judgement on a ridiculously long play (the play had been in progress for three hours and was still only at the end of Act II), being performed that day, and that day only.

Stoker, his waist now an inch or so fuller, his russet beard beginning to grey, had been busy since early that morning, directing actors – actors with hurriedly prepared playscripts in their hands, no make-up on their faces and barely any costumes to speak of, save for one character in a cape sporting false fangs; apparently a Transylvanian count. The small band of friends and publishers who, along with Irving, made up the audience had been clapping politely as they watched, but were clearly as bored as the players themselves. Only Stoker himself appeared to have any enthusiasm for this reading. Oh, and a handsome aristocrat with thinning reddish-blond hair, who would stand and applaud at each curtain fall; more perhaps in gratitude than appreciation, it appeared.

Stoker sighed and consulted his fob watch: half past three o'clock exactly.

'Mr Loveday, can I ask you to supervise backstage for some time?'

'Of course, Mr Stoker,' came the reply.

'Thank you.'

Stoker now exited the stage and made his way upstairs. He opened the door of his office – or rather, *the* office, Irving having knocked down the wall which separated it from what was Miss Terry's dressing room, making one somewhat austere workspace for himself, his acting manager and Loveday – then sat down at his bureau and began to work his way through his correspondence. As he picked up his pen to write his replies, the office door suddenly opened. Before him stood Irving, trembling with rage. The actor now advanced into the office – slowly (a fall down the stairs at his Mayfair rooms the previous year having left him with a lasting debility).

'Bram, how could you?' he began.

'Sir Henry, what do you mean?' replied Stoker, now standing up.

'You swore you would never reveal what you knew about our adventures in Prussia!' Stoker shook his head.

'I'm sorry, Sir Henry, but I have not.' Irving grunted.

'Yes, you have. The events are similar, the main character similar – indeed, the main character's name is the same!'

'His name is *not* the same,' countered Stoker. 'No one will ever guess.'

'Any Rosicrucian worth his salt will guess that your count's name is an anagram of Curdala's,' protested Irving. 'And think how Ellen will feel!' Stoker ran the palm of his hand anxiously across his mouth.

'I'm sorry, Guv'nor, but were any Rosicrucian ever to guess, he would not make this known, not daring to risk exposure.' Stoker paused, hoping to let Irving's wave of anger subside. 'And I'm afraid I could not let this opportunity pass me by. I need to make money by my writing now, given how poorly the theatre has been doing lately – and you know that this reading of my play adaptation is a

necessary protection for the dramatic rights in my upcoming novel.'
It was an unspoken truth that, despite Irving having been made a
knight of the realm just two years prior, he was past the height of
his powers, and the theatre was losing both money and audiences.

Irving coughed awkwardly, then continued. 'Anyhow, I just
wanted to warn you that Edward is attempting to ply his trade of
New Art at our theatre. I cannot turn him away at the door, as
a courtesy to his mother, but if he approaches you, please, please
decline him. Harker is all we need these days.'

'I will, of course, Sir Henry; leave it to me.' And with that the
great actor turned and limped out of the office, closing the door
quietly behind him.

Edward! The mention of the young scene painter's name suddenly
unsettled Stoker. Edward, the shy, beaky-nosed youth he had
known all those years ago, was now feted in London's Decadent
circles for being even more daring than Beardsley in his painting
of spare elliptical backdrops for the stage. But, for Stoker, Edward's
art was not to be celebrated. For Stoker, it spoke of something so
unhuman, so primitive, that he could not bring himself to grace
the young man's productions with his presence. But while normally
when he thought of Edward, Stoker promptly forgot about him,
today was different: something was amiss – but what?

He sat back down at his bureau and picked up a copy of *The
Police Gazette*. The *Gazette*, usually a dry, unsensational journal,
had recently taken the sensational decision to print photographs
of real crime scenes and victims – even those of long-unsolved
crimes, such as the Whitechapel murders.

Stoker turned to the double-page spread which displayed the
bodies of two of the Whitechapel murder victims, both bearing the
same carved elliptical scars. Suddenly, as if in a flash of negative
enlightenment, it came to him: these lines were almost identical

to the ones he had seen – and been so repelled by – in Edward's sketchbook all those years ago, at Telbin's, around the time of the murders! In an instant he recalled the almost unnatural fears Miss Terry had had about her son, and the fears he himself had briefly entertained regarding Edward, in the cab on his way to the druggist Bartholomew, following the attack on the girl in the cellar. And then there was the matter of the young man's whereabouts, when he should have been in Dublin with Gunn.

Suddenly, there was a rap at the door, and after Stoker had uttered a sharp 'Enter!', there, dressed top to toe in flannels, stood the object of his present thought. Edward had filled out a little in the years since the two men had last met, but he was still the same beaky, bespectacled youth Stoker remembered. Setting the opened *Gazette* face down on the bureau, Stoker stood up and the two men shook hands.

'I was wondering whether you might need some help with canvases for the summer Shakespeare,' began Edward. 'The ones Grieve painted must be very dated by now.'

'I must apologise in advance, young man,' replied Stoker, sitting back down at his bureau, 'but Harker has already prepared some excellent new ones for the *Dream*, and I'm afraid we have no place for anyone else.'

'Well,' said Edward, now seated on a red leather armchair opposite Stoker, 'don't blame me if you continue to have empty circles and stalls. The New Art seems to have quite captured the public's imagination, I'm glad to say.'

The conversation now turned to affairs of a more personal nature: Edith was delighted, declared Edward, with her new 'best friend'; he himself had fathered some four children (as Stoker knew) and so could always do with more work; wasn't it amazing how his mother was able to play Ophelia at her age; Sir Henry was over his nasty fall by now, wasn't he?

After ten or so minutes of this inconsequential chatter, the two men stood up to draw matters to a close. Stoker was about to extend his hand towards Edward's when suddenly he hesitated, then spoke again.

'Edward,' he said, 'I have been meaning to ask you something. It is something that has been troubling me for some time.'

'Yes, Mr Stoker?'

'You remember that some years ago your mother became concerned that you might be responsible for the Whitechapel murders... the man who quickly became known as "the Ripper"?' Edward laughed.

'I do.'

'And I remember feeling reassured that you couldn't be, as you were away from London at that time, at the Gaiety in Dublin, with Gunn.'

'Indeed,' replied Edward, with another laugh.

'Well, when Gunn's telegram arrived announcing your arrival days after you were due at the Gaiety, I was troubled. I later wondered whether you were in Dublin at all, when you were supposed to be.'

'What are you saying?'

'Well, as I say, I was troubled. So, if you could just tell me whether you were actually in Dublin or not...' Edward looked at him, a sunny, boyish smile animating his face, but said nothing.

At this Stoker picked up the opened copy of the *Gazette* and showed it to Edward, who merely laughed again.

'These images clearly do not discompose you, young man,' said Stoker. Edward resumed his boyish smile and chuckled nervously. And then he stopped smiling altogether; the corners of his mouth turned down and his eyes narrowed to reveal a fiendish glare. He snatched the *Gazette* from Stoker and held up the spread where the Ripper's victims were displayed in all their gore, suspending the pages before him like a placard.

'Rather marvellous work, don't you think?' he said. He continued to glare at Stoker as he let this remark settle in the acting manager's bones.

'Good God!' muttered Stoker at last.

'Myself and Mr Telbin did that, and a fair few others with us too – mainly rebellious artists.'

'Why on earth?' spluttered Stoker.

'Because I knew that a New Art was needed… and so did Mr Telbin. Tired of the romanticism of Turner, the sentimentalism of Burne-Jones, and imagined realism of Sickert, I wanted a New Art… a savage, symbolic, *Total Art*, like that of our earliest ancestors – in which the divine and the sublime would be everything, and the human nothing!' And here he threw the *Gazette* back down onto Stoker's bureau. 'But to create such an art, I needed to incite my blood lust and adopt the raw thinking behind the rituals of the pre-Christian world – mere fancy would not be enough!'

'Surely… surely, Edward, you did not have to do such terrible things?' asked Stoker, as he sunk back down into his chair.

'Yes, I did. In the name of art, all is permissible,' and here Edward grinned demonically. 'Mater knows that!' He winked. 'But I did stop short of killing that girl I took back to the Lyceum, as you later discovered to your cost, when she returned – or so Edy told me,' he continued. 'Respect for Irving and my mother, if you like,' he added sardonically. 'God knows who took the trollop down to the cellar and bit her like that, but it wasn't me!'

Stoker buried his head in his hands, as he struggled to compose himself. And then he spoke again.

'And your mother, what did she know of your involvement in the Whitechapel murders?'

'Nothing at first, but then I confessed my involvement to her after the second murder, early on that Saturday – the Saturday of the lights rehearsal; noting, though not of course naming, my accomplices. That was the real reason she packed me off to the ghastly Sedbergh later that evening – anything to protect her precious self and her precious theatre! After that, she thought I would be unable to pursue my calling, once I was away from my company, here in London. But, as you know, I made my return – when I stayed at Mr

Telbin's. That last murder, at least, was not my own work – although my company could by then imitate my particular style quite well.' And then Edward's boyish expression returned, as though the young man had merely acted out this diabolical reverie. 'Goodbye, Mr Stoker. I am sure you will not want to shake my hand.' And with that Edward turned and sauntered out the door.

Stoker remained sunk in his chair for some time, staring blankly ahead as he repeatedly ran a freckled forefinger over his top lip. Finally, his eyes turned to the place on the wall where the painting of the Metal Man had once been, a print of the Blue Mosque now in its stead.

As he thought of the Metal Man, his mind returned to Irving's barber, Kosminski, whom the Guv'nor had tried to frame for the Whitechapel murders. How shocking that the culprit had instead been the son of Irving's leading lady! So, that was why Miss Terry had been so flustered on the evening of the lights rehearsal, as she already knew that Edward was the Whitechapel murderer: 'What am I to do about my son, Mr Stoker?' Yes, those had been her words – he remembered them well. The attack in the lights cellar had merely afforded her the opportunity both to get rid of Edward and divert attention away from Lucarda. Edward himself, however, clearly knew nothing about Lucarda, and Miss Terry had seemingly never confirmed her son's involvement in the Whitechapel murders to Irving, relying on the Guv'nor's infuriation with Edward that Saturday night at the theatre, coupled with his own desire to divert attention away from the baron, to secure his support in sending her son away.

Unable to think any further, or even steady his nerves with a drink, Stoker rose mechanically from his bureau and went down to the wings to relieve Loveday. The reading of the third Act of the play was now under way: this new play – Stoker's own – taken from Stoker's own soon-to-be-published novel – itself taken from Stoker's own horrifying, never-to-be-forgotten experiences from nine years earlier. This new play, this new novel, Stoker's own – *The Un-Dead*, now known, following a last-minute change by his editor, as *Dracula*.

CODA

This novel is, in part, based on real people, events and circumstance, but does not claim to personal or historical accuracy. This acknowledged, it may be helpful for me, the author, to reveal here – in their curtain call – the actual characters and destinies of certain of these people, not least to assuage any concerns of their descendants, who may read what is purely intended to be a work of fiction. As well as these individuals, I also hope to allay any concerns that may have been raised in Rosicrucians, since I trust it is clear that the beliefs and practices described in the novel are informed by the baron's twisted interpretation of the movement's central texts and tenets – and do not necessarily bear relation to those held and conducted by genuine initiates of the order.

And so, back to the individual people.

First, Edward Gordon Craig (also known as Gordon Craig) was not the Whitechapel murderer (the man who became known as 'the Ripper') and, unlike the painter Walter Sickert – who, like Craig, started out as an actor, even touring briefly with Henry Irving's company – has never been suspected of so being. A brilliant, if demanding, man to work with, Edward went on to become one of the most influential stage and set designers of his time, before stopping such work at the age of forty to focus on writing and reviewing for the rest of his life. Edward died, poor but revered, in France in his nineties, the people of Stevenage – the place of his birth – later naming their theatre after him.

Unlike Craig, Aaron Kosminski, the barber, has been suspected of being the Whitechapel murderer; however, any evidence against him is highly contested. What is not contested is that Kosminski did suffer from various mental disorders, dying in an asylum, aged fifty-three.

Like her brother, Edith Craig became well known in the theatre, both onstage and off – as a producer, director and costumier. Living for much of her life with the playwright, Christabel Marshall (also known as Christopher St John), later joined by the painter, Clare 'Tony' Atwood, Edith continued to promote women's suffrage, including through the work of the Pioneer Players – a theatrical society she founded in 1911, of which Ellen Terry was president. Indeed, Edith worked closely with her mother throughout her life, and, on Terry's death, preserved her house at Smallhythe and converted the seventeenth-century barn in its grounds into a theatre, to perpetuate her legacy.

Both Edith and Edward were illegitimate, the offspring of the architect Edward Godwin, with whom Ellen Terry eloped while still married to her first husband, the painter and sculptor, George Frederic Watts. In both cases her children assumed the surname Craig to deflect the stigma of illegitimacy.

Henry Irving (born John Brodribb) spent the remainder of his life in the theatre. Despite being the first actor ever to be honoured with a knighthood (in 1895), Irving's fortunes, and those of the Lyceum, declined, and he eventually lost control of the theatre – though continued to tour. In October 1905, following a performance in Bradford of Tennyson's *Becket* (and just one night after what was to be his final performance as Mathias in *The Bells*), Irving collapsed, dying a short time later in the lobby of the city's Midland Hotel. He was sixty-seven years old. Irving had no connection to the Ripper murders – or, indeed, to any dubious activity in Prussia, his and Terry's adventures there being entirely fictitious. However, it is possible that his portrayal of the devilish but charismatic Mephistopheles in *Faust* did inform Stoker's depiction of Count Dracula.

Ellen Terry's final onstage appearance was not at London's Lyceum Theatre but at the city's Lyric Theatre, Hammersmith, in 1925 – the same year she, like Irving, was honoured for her contribution to the stage, being created a dame. Like Irving, she had no connection to the Ripper murders. Terry died in July 1928, aged eighty-one, at Smallhythe, her ashes later being removed to 'the Actors' church' – St Paul's, in Covent Garden. After Irving's death, Terry admitted, 'we were terribly in love for a while', although when and for how long has never been definitively ascertained.

Edward Dowden continued to write and lecture in Dublin and beyond, and, unlike in the novel, remained firm friends with Stoker throughout the rest of his life. Again, his portrayal is largely fictitious, and there is no evidence to suggest that he was involved in any nefarious activity or associated with occult orders. One of his daughters, Hester Dowden, however, was a noted spiritualist medium.

Joseph Harker went on to become a renowned scene painter, publishing a memoir of his experiences three years before his death, in 1927, in which he acknowledged that Stoker had named one of the main characters in *Dracula*, Jonathan Harker, after him. I do not know whether he was a cricketer or rugby player, but sketches and photographs show a man of athletic build, and so I took some liberties here, while the tone of his memoir is jocular, leading me to characterise him as I did.

William Stead continued his pioneering, campaigning New Journalism until his death, aged sixty-two, in the 1912 sinking of RMS *Titanic*, en route to New York. Civic-minded to the end, Stead was last seen on deck helping women and children to the too few available lifeboats.

George Stoker, unlike the oldest Stoker brother, Thornley, was never knighted for his services to medicine. He retired to relative prosperity in Exeter, dying at the city's Streatham Hall Hospital in his sixties.

Finally, Bram (Abraham) Stoker himself.

Stoker wrote several more novels, as well as an affectionate memoir of Irving, following the publication of *Dracula* by A. Constable & Co. on 26 May 1897 – just eight days after the reading of his play adaptation of the novel at the Lyceum. Like Irving, Stoker suffered as a result of the theatre's declining fortunes and, following a series of debilitating strokes, died a mile downstream from Chelsea, at St George's Square, Pimlico, in April 1912. He was sixty-four years old.

Stoker's wife, Florence, outlived him by twenty-five years. A fierce defender of her husband's literary legacy – most notably, his novel, *Dracula* – Florence took the German makers of the unauthorised 1922 film *Nosferatu* to court for unpaid royalties, eventually winning her case. Despite this close guardianship of her husband's artistic work, Florence always referred to herself as 'Mrs Bram Stoker, widow of the late barrister'.

Stoker himself never glimpsed the huge popularity of his novel.

As for some other notable individuals in this novel – Drayfield, Grafton, Henstridge, Ponsonby, Wladyslawa and, of course, Lucarda – it goes without saying that there is no need to reveal their characters and destinies as they did not really exist; players retired to the wings, perhaps to return to the limelight at some other time for another encounter with Mr Stoker.

ABOUT THE AUTHOR

Matthew Gibson is one of the world's leading scholars on Bram Stoker – the author of *Dracula* – and the Gothic. Born and educated in the UK, he is now Associate Professor of English Literature at the University of Macau. Prior to this he worked at a number of universities in the UK, including at the Universities of Surrey and Hull, as well as at the University of Łódź in Poland and the American University in Bulgaria. Matthew is a former Visiting Fellow at Clare Hall, University of Cambridge.

Currently responsible for curating and annotating material on Stoker for cutting-edge online research resource, Oxford Bibliographies, Matthew is the author of *Dracula and the Eastern Question*, co-editor of *Bram Stoker and the Late Victorian World*, and a contributor to *The Cambridge Companion to Dracula*.

Mr Stoker is his first work of fiction.